GUN RUNNER

GUN RUNNER

LARRY CORREIA
JOHN D. BROWN

BAEN

GUN RUNNER

This is a work of fiction. All the characters and events portrayed in this book are fictional, and any resemblance to real people or incidents is purely coincidental.

Copyright © 2021 by Larry Correia and John D. Brown

A Baen Books Original

Baen Publishing Enterprises
P.O. Box 1403
Riverdale, NY 10471
www.baen.com

ISBN: 978-1-9821-2516-5

Cover art by Dominic Harman
Interior illustration by Joseph Correia

First printing, February 2021

Distributed by Simon & Schuster
1230 Avenue of the Americas
New York, NY 10020

Library of Congress Cataloging-in-Publication Data

Names: Correia, Larry, author. | Brown, John, 1966– author.
Title: Gun runner / Larry Correia and John Brown.
Description: Riverdale, NY : Baen, [2021]
Identifiers: LCCN 2020048132 | ISBN 9781982125165 (hardcover)
Subjects: GSAFD: Science fiction.
Classification: LCC PS3603.O7723 G86 2021 | DDC 813/.6—dc23
LC record available at https://lccn.loc.gov/2020048132

Pages by Joy Freeman (www.pagesbyjoy.com)
Printed in the United States of America
10 9 8 7 6 5 4 3 2 1

GUN RUNNER

PROLOGUE

It was the fall of Gloss.

As Captain Nicholas Holloway flew closer to the port, he could see hundreds of terrified refugees below, desperately fighting for a spot on a dropship that was only meant to seat twenty. They were pushing and shoving their way up the stairs onto the landing pad. Women and children were clawing at the landing gear, and crying mothers were holding up their babies, begging for a place.

More Union ships were coming in fast, trying to get as many people out as they could before the Collectivist forces reached the port, but Holloway was a master of logistics, and could tell there was no way they could get them all out in time. The lucky would catch a ride to one of the civilian freighters waiting in orbit. Those left behind would get executed on the spot or tortured and sent to work in the gulag for the rest of their miserable lives. The Collectivist government held no mercy for those who wouldn't bend the knee. There was no forgiveness for rebels. The Collective were real bastards, which was why Holloway had been happy to run guns to the people who had the guts to stand against them.

His ship, the MSV *Tar Heel*, was one of those freighters waiting in orbit. His involvement in this war had begun by smuggling weapons in. His involvement would end by smuggling rebels out. He had promised the Union that he'd cram in as many bodies as they could get up there, and the *Tar Heel* was one big ship. He would transport those people through the gate and get them to the refugee camp on Amon in the next system. After that, they were on their own. That was a lot of extra mouths to feed for a month. It was an act of charity which would cost him dearly, but the Union had been good customers and he always had a soft spot for the underdog.

Mankind had colonized thirty worlds since the discovery of gate travel fifty years ago. Some of those worlds turned out better than others. A few were paradises. A few were even worse than war-torn Gloss. Hopefully, the decent people who survived today would be able to make a home for themselves on a different rock, but that was out of his hands.

Holloway brought the striker in fast and low over the port facility to avoid attracting AA fire from the Collective forces. The last free people of planet Gloss looked up, briefly hopeful that he might be coming to save them, but then he flew by and left them behind. It sucked. He hated it. But the striker was a small craft, and he had to try and rescue a friend first. After that, he could worry about these strangers.

Ahead of him, the city of Pilling burned.

Captain Holloway had been an honored guest for a celebration at the rebel headquarters in Pilling once. It had been a much happier place then. After nearly a decade of unrelenting war, for the very first time the Union of Free Cities was winning and the Collective was on the ropes. Independence was no longer just a dream. The purpose of that celebration had been for their leadership to make a big show of giving awards for valor to their heroes who had turned the tide, to rally the rest of the rebel troops before their next big offensive. Chief among those heroes had been a mech pilot named Jackson Rook. He was just a kid, but Sergeant Jack, as the propagandists had named him, was already a legend to these people. Holloway had been invited to the party because he had been the one who had smuggled in Rook's mech.

Then everything had gone sideways.

Now Pilling lay in ruins, their headquarters was a smoking crater, and the last of the rebels fought house to house, trying to delay the inevitable.

That party had been only five days ago.

Captain Holloway had really taken a liking to Jackson Rook. It was good to see Union command pinning their highest medal on him. He'd certainly earned it. The feats that boy could wring out of a mech were astounding, stacking Collective bodies from Pilling to Red Valley. Jackson was the most naturally gifted pilot any of them had ever seen, with the bravado to match, but beneath that swagger Holloway could tell he was basically a good kid who'd gotten stuck in a crap situation, doing his best to make things right.

The award ceremony was brief. The people of Gloss were pragmatic that way, another thing Holloway appreciated about them. Get through the speeches quick and get on to the feast. The colonists on this world had tried to seed the local biosphere with Earth animals, but few of the tasty ones had stuck. The giant lizard wasn't bad though. If he used his imagination it could almost be mistaken for beef.

As soon as it was socially appropriate, Jackson escaped the main table with all the generals and politicians and gone out to mingle with the rest of the crowded banquet hall. Of course, as soon as he saw Holloway, he came over to join him. "Captain! You made it."

"Good to see you again, Jackson. Congratulations."

The kid looked down at all the new ribbons on his uniform and grinned. "We both know this is just to give the recruiters some new vids to work with. The important thing is what new toys have you brought us this trip?"

And they proceeded to talk shop for the next hour. The kid had no formal education—hell, he'd grown up in a refugee camp—but Jackson was a genius when it came to mech combat. He was a fighter. The Collective had sent their best after him, over and over, and Jackson had sent them all home in a box. Every few months for the last couple of years, the *Tar Heel* had run the ISF blockade to get more arms to Gloss. Several of those deliveries Holloway had ended up working with Jackson, and each time he'd been impressed. The kid had really grown on him.

To be honest, Jackson kind of reminded Holloway of himself at that age, except that he had been in the prestigious Earth Force Fleet Academy, and he never had tested with the mental acuity or reflexes necessary to pilot a mech that well, nor was he one of the tiny percentage of human beings born with the genes to accept the brain implants necessary to let a pilot fly by thought. Where man and machine became one, and the results were greater than the sum of its parts.

Jackson had the instincts, genes, and Gloss had scraped together the black-market upgrades for his brain. Which meant when he was driving something like the Shockwave that Holloway had smuggled here, Jackson Rook became a lightning-fast, all-seeing, battlefield-dominating god of war.

Someone like that could do really well for himself in Holloway's line of work. "You've got the Collectivists on the run. You might actually win this by winter. Have you given much thought about what you want to do after the war?"

"A little," Jackson admitted. "Why? Are you offering me a job?"

"I am."

"Wow . . ." He seemed a little taken back by that. "Serious? That's quite the honor."

Holloway chuckled. Lifelong groundbounds often had serious delusions about the glamor and excitement of being a spacer, especially a mercenary gun runner. But Holloway had a code he lived by, a good ship, and a better crew, a hundred strong, most of whom were actually worth a damn. So, in the case of the *Tar Heel*, it was actually a pretty good gig.

"Of course, I'm serious, son. Once your term is up obviously. Come with us. Travel. See the other worlds."

"And smuggle munitions to other people like us who aren't supposed to have them?" Jackson asked with a nervous grin.

"Obviously. Most of our business is legit, but that's just to cover for the part I enjoy most. I hate seeing good folks get pushed around, so I get them the means to protect themselves. My contracts are fair. The pay is good. Every man gets a share."

It was obvious Jackson was seriously considering the offer. "I was born here. I've never been through a gate." He sounded a little wistful. Because to someone who'd spent their whole life on one poor colony world, the idea of getting flung across light-years in an instant was rather exciting. Then a look of determination crossed his face. "But I can't. Gloss is my home. As much as I appreciate it, and I truly do, I have to stick around. They need me, and maybe, when this is all over, we can make Gloss into something nice, something to be proud of. They tried to ruin it. It's my responsibility to fix it."

That was a lot of weight for a teenager's narrow shoulders, but Holloway could respect the sentiment. "You're a good man, Jackson Rook. Alright then. Should you change your mind later, my offer stands."

"Thank you." It was obvious the boy was sincere. He stood up to leave. "I'd better go check with my crew chief about how maintenance is going. Tomorrow morning Mech Troop is heading back to the front. We're going to push those shanks into the sea once and for all."

But then Jackson winced and put his fingers to his temple.

"What's wrong?"

"Just a headache." Jackson steadied himself and waved it off. "I've been getting this weird feedback to my implant off and on for the last few days. Diagnostics can't find anything wrong, though."

"I've got a fantastic new technician back on the *Tar Heel*. I'm talking an actual specter-level hacker. She's a miracle worker. Probably way better than anyone in your Union. No offense to your country, but the tech level on this world is downright barbaric. I could have Jane take a look at that for you."

Jackson thought it over. "It's nothing. I'll be fine. Thanks again, Captain. We couldn't have done this without you."

The next day the desperate Collective had activated a technology so vile that its use was considered a war crime by every civilized world.

The attack was like nothing anyone had ever seen before. Even in Captain Holloway's considerable experience, he had never heard of slaveware this aggressive. One minute, the elite Free Union Mech Troops had been crushing their enemy. The next, they turned their guns against their surprised allies. It was a slaughter.

Union Command had gone into a panic. Out of nowhere their best soldiers, armed with their mightiest weapons, had betrayed them. Worse, the mech pilots knew every target vital to the war effort, and went about methodically destroying them, one by one. Units were decapitated. Vital supply dumps obliterated. The rebel army collapsed before the Collective advance.

By the time anyone figured out what had happened to their pilots, it was too late. This was a new kind of weaponized slaveware, far beyond anyone on Gloss' capabilities to make. No one knew where the Collective had got it from, or which offworld maniac had been willing to sell their services. The insidious program had crept in through the mechs' firewalls, invaded the pilots' minds through their implants, and when the opportunity came, the Collective had flipped the override switch.

Every linked-in pilot on Gloss had been turned at once. Their wills overridden as they were forced to murder their friends. All of them were lost.

Including Jackson Rook.

The Union had asked for their help. Holloway had Jane analyze the new slaveware's code. He hadn't been exaggerating when he had proclaimed her a miracle worker, because Jane was from a world so advanced that its technology bordered on magic. But this was something new, even to her, and she had no easy answer to give the Union. From what she could tell, there was no way to stop the slaveware's infection remotely. It would require direct access to the pilots to stop it, and good luck doing that when they were riding around wrapped in twenty-ton killing machines. And the Collective would run their new slaves nonstop until they died of exhaustion. The program itself was so overpowering that Jane said that it would require a miracle of willpower for a pilot to pull himself out from under its spell, even temporarily.

Except then they had intercepted a message from Jackson Rook, begging for someone to kill him.

Holloway deftly flew the striker away from the port, threading it between the crumbling high-rise habitats of Pilling. It was a small craft, fast, and exceedingly maneuverable in atmosphere. Hopefully those traits would be enough to keep him from getting shot down in the next few minutes.

For the Collectivists, to say, write, or even think their ideology was wrong was a capital offense. In their minds, anti-collectivist words led to actions that hurt others. Words could starve people, murder them, oppress them. Words were like flies, carrying disease. Freedom of speech was not allowed. The costs were too high. So a lot of Free Glossians were about to die. And Holloway wanted to be off this planet before the cleansing started.

"Do you have his signal, Jane?"

She was safely high above in the *Tar Heel*, feeding him paths through the city to avoid getting shot out of the sky. *"I do, Cap. Ten klicks north of you. He's reaching out again."*

"Are you sure it's not a fake?"

"It's the Shockwave. The pilot's transmitting his vitals for confirmation. They match what's in Rook's personnel file. I don't think it's a spoof."

He'd come to trust her on tech and comms. If Jane said it was Jackson, it was him.

"But that doesn't mean he's not still mind-controlled and trying to draw more rebels out of hiding to shoot at."

"Maybe." Holloway suspected the boy was in hell. After all, he'd just been forced to murder bunches of his own people. He liked the boy, and so that filled him with a simmering rage. He slowed the striker and hovered a few meters above an abandoned street. "Put him on."

"This is Shockwave One calling for Pilling Defense Battery. I am at grid two-six-niner." It was Jackson all right, and he sounded like death warmed over. Strung out and exhausted. *"Requesting heavy fire on my position."*

"Rook, this is Captain Holloway from the *Tar Heel*. I'm inbound to you so quit asking for artillery to bombard us. They're busy retreating anyway."

"Captain? You're alive?"

"What can I do for you, son?"

"I need this thing out of my mind." Jackson's voice was shaky, raspy. *"I can't unlink from the machine. I can't move my limbs. I tried to fight it, but the voices wouldn't stop. I'm so sorry. It locked me out of every system I could think of to kill myself or disable the mech with. It won't even let me crash it or get it stuck. They missed one system though. When medical came online to keep me awake I pumped myself full of thrillers. It shut down before I could overdose though."*

Thrillers. The powerful stimulants would screw with his brain chemistry and make it harder for the wetware implants to function. It was a plausible story. But it was possibly a lie.

"Why not call one of your mech trooper buddies to shoot you?"

"I think they're all dead... You said your specter was tops. If I shoved the voices to the back of my mind for a minute, I might be able to temporarily power down the Shockwave's firewalls briefly. She could overheat the reactor, or set off some onboard munitions, or something, anything. I've got to stop this."

Holloway was torn. He had flown down here hoping he could get Jackson out, but this could be a trap. He should just fly away, but damn the Collectivists. They didn't deserve the satisfaction. He contacted Jane.

"He's alive, but he's in hell."

"I listened in. If he throws the Shockwave's comms wide open for a few seconds, I can launch a cyberattack and sabotage one of his systems. But it still could be some kind of trick to draw you in."

The Collectivists had surely ransacked all of Rook's contacts. What a splendid show it would be to make an example of the man who had provided the Union with upgraded weaponry, including the mech Sergeant Jack had used to stand up to them. His better judgment told him to forget it. People died in war. That's just how it was. But the boy's damn voice was pulling at him.

"Honest assessment time, Jane. If I got him out, could you save him?"

"He just killed his own people!"

"No. He didn't." It may have been Jackson holding the gun, but he wasn't the one who had pulled the trigger. "Can you save him?"

"I can try."

"Try isn't worth the risk."

"Okay. I have cleared slaveware before."

"This hack? You've repaired this specific kind of attack?"

"An early variation. On rats. And a beetle once."

"A beetle?" he asked in disbelief. He had to remind himself that she wasn't much older than Jackson . . . and that he was too old for this. "Can you do it or not?"

Jane took a deep breath. *"I can do it, Captain."*

Prudence said to leave Rook to his fate. But if Nicholas Holloway had been a prudent man, he wouldn't have ended up a gun runner.

"That'll do. The Shockwave has a pilot ejection system. When Jackson gives you an opening, that's the system I want you to activate. Got it?"

"Yes, sir. Configuring now."

There were warnings flashing on his screen. Collective drones must have sensed the striker and were moving this way to investigate. He switched back to the Shockwave's channel. "Alright, Jackson. Give Jane a window and she'll do the rest. I'm on my way."

"No. Stay back. I'm too dangerous."

"Too late. Get to work, kid." He fired the thrusters and the striker took off like a bullet down the street. The Collective drones were much slower, but they were relentless machines, and once they had a target they'd pursue until he broke atmo.

Holloway was putting a lot of faith in two very young people to come through for him right then. He needed Jackson to fight off the slaveware enough to open a window for Jane, and for Jane to crack the mech's system before Jackson's mind control forced him to blast the striker out of the air.

"*Captain. Rook made a hole. Virus away.*"

"Did it work?"

"*I don't know. The Shockwave's got good defenses. My program will only work if Jackson lets it.*"

Drones behind, killer mech dead ahead. The safest route was up and away... But Jackson Rook didn't strike him as a quitter. Holloway pressed on.

This part of Pilling had been a recreational area once. There had been streams, lakes, and nature trails. Now it was a blasted wasteland of trenches and bomb craters.

Right in the middle was the Shockwave.

It was a sleek mech. Man shaped, but nearly five meters tall, with integrated weapon systems covering every centimeter of the thing, and when it was driven by someone like Jackson, mind linked directly to the machine, it could move with insane speed and grace. Manufactured by Durendal, the Shockwave was one of the nicer mechs Holloway had ever stolen.

In combat on open ground, bipedal mechs usually lost to lower-slung vehicles like tanks. The less you stuck up, the less likely you were to be seen or shot. Mechs were tall, but they really shone in terrain where other vehicles couldn't maneuver, like urban ruins or the steep canyons of Gloss. When you had a pilot who could plug in and become one with the machine, a mech turned from a clumsy walker into something absolutely terrifying. It could low crawl to avoid incoming fire or scale skyscrapers and bound from roof to roof. It could stealthily stalk prey and then run it down like an apex predator.

At that moment though, the mech was on one knee. Massive hands clenched into fists in the mud. And somehow, Holloway could tell that Jackson was doing everything in his power to keep that mech anchored there. It was perfectly still, but the pilot inside was fighting a life-or-death battle against the monsters in his head.

And then the mech exploded.

Or at least that was what it looked like at first. Shrapnel flew and smoke spread, but it had only been from the ejection system. The armored pod the pilot rode in was launched out the

Shockwave's back. It flew ten meters before hitting the ground and sliding through the mud.

Now missing the center of its torso, the massive mech toppled face forward and splashed into a stream. That had been smooth. Jane was an artist.

Holloway aimed the striker right for the pod, full burn. He'd left the drones behind, but they'd be catching up soon. He had a very narrow window. When he was almost on top of the pod, he flared the directional thrusters hard, coming to a dead stop directly above where Jackson had landed.

The pod was about the size of a coffin. Thankfully, the design had several external points set at different angles to fast-hook a grapple to for high-speed extraction by combat search and rescue. Luckily one of them was oriented so that he would be able to grab hold without landing.

Except as Holloway carefully maneuvered the striker into place, he saw people running toward him. They must have been hiding in a ditch. At first, he thought they were Collective soldiers, but then he realized they were waving their arms overhead, trying to get his attention. They were just poor terrified Glossians, desperate to catch a ride before the death squads got here. He checked the scope, and saw the drones were getting uncomfortably close, and would be in gun range in less than a minute.

The grapple attached to the escape pod and the magnets engaged with a *clunk* that he could feel through the soles of his boots. He gave it a bit of power and the striker hoisted the pod out of the muck. Alarms sounded as the Collective drones scanned his craft.

"Captain, you've got bogies incoming," Jane warned. *"You need to dust off now!"*

Instead Holloway turned the Striker's nose in the direction of the civilians and sped toward them. "I've got one more thing to do first, Jane." Wind whistled through the crew compartment as the door slid open. He'd save every one of them he could.

Today might be the day he died, but he'd do it with a clean conscience.

He slewed the striker to a stop, so close to the ground that the directional thruster threw up a mud plume.

"Get in now! Move!" he shouted at the Glossians. "Hurry! Collectives almost here!" They clambered in, and just kept coming, more and more of them, desperate and shaking. The strongest lifted the weak. They filled the seats, filled the cargo area, crammed against him. He moved his seat all the way forward to make more room. They appeared to be women and children mostly, dressed in filthy rags. The striker only had six seats. He had at least twenty people inside by time the drones opened fire.

The refugees outside screamed as bullets ripped through their bodies. The striker shuddered as it took a hit. Holloway could barely hear all the alarms over the sound of children wailing. He lifted off. A Glossian hanging from the landing skid plummeted to his doom. Holloway hit the door override and shouted, "Get your arms and feet out of the way before they get cut off!"

Green tracers flashed past the striker's nose as he flung it hard to the side. His passengers were all crushed against each other or the hull by the force as he launched the striker down a street. He got some ruins between him and the drones, made some distance, and then pointed the craft upward and went to maximum thrust. The new few minutes would surely be the worst ride of these people's lives, but it was better than being massacred.

"Shanks," he muttered when he checked his readouts. Between the bodies and the escape pod, the striker was massively over-weight. "Come on, baby. We've got this."

The striker was so packed with humanity he could barely move his arms enough to steer. It stunk of sweat and fear. Some of his passengers were crying, but most of them were just holding on to whatever they could with white knuckle terror as they were squashed with extra Gs. The engine was getting dangerously hot. One of the drones must have hit a line because they were leaking coolant. If the engine blew they would drop like a rock, but hitting the ground in a fireball would be a far more merciful way to go than ending up in Collective hands.

Other dropships were rising around him, cumbersome Union shuttles and cargo haulers, but Holloway watched, horrified, as one exploded, lanced from the sky by Collective fire. A few seconds later, another was obliterated by a projectile that had been too fast to see. The Collective wasn't supposed to have any railguns, but they did.

Holloway put the striker into an erratic, climbing corkscrew, further tormenting the already damaged engine. "Jane! Do whatever you can to screw with their AA targeting. Scramble everything."

"Already working on it, sir."

"Good girl."

As more ships were swatted out of the air around them, Holloway said a prayer. It wasn't until a couple of the Glossians closest to him said *amen* that he realized that he'd been saying it aloud.

The next few minutes were agony, but they made it past the range of the Collective's guns.

Holloway had ordered the *Tar Heel* to get as close to the planet as she could without endangering her, so that the smaller ships performing the evacuation could make more trips back and forth in the time allotted. His great big beautiful lady was tantalizingly close, straight ahead, camping at the edge of space.

The escape pod slung beneath the striker had been radio silent. All he could do was hope that a bullet hadn't punched Jackson's pod, because that would have been a lot of effort wasted. Holloway looked around to see just how many other transports had made it through but saw none. He scanned back toward the planet, hoping for stragglers. There weren't any.

He, and those he carried on the striker, were the last to escape Gloss.

The *Tar Heel* cargo bay was nearly as chaotic as the port. His overwhelmed crew was herding refugees out of the way as fast as they could. Most of these people had never been in zero G before, so they were flailing and crashing about, endangering each other, while his men were trying to get them tethered for their safety so they could be towed someplace safer.

The striker had been cycled through the *Tar Heel* lock, guided into place with a cargo hauler, and mag-locked to the wall. As soon as the hauler was safely away, he popped the doors. An absurd number of people spilled out of the little striker, as if it was one of those old-Earth clown cars.

The Glossians—at least those who weren't panicking or vomiting due to weightlessness—tried to thank him for saving them, but he hadn't gone down there for them. He'd been trying to save a friend. So he unstrapped from his seat and smoothly floated outside.

Jane was already there, boots locked to the hull, waiting nervously as two of the cargo crew unhooked the escape pod. "I'm so glad you made it," she said when she saw him.

"Me too, kid." Then Holloway looked over at all the suffering wretches and realized that once word spread that their beloved Sergeant Jack had betrayed the Union, and that he was here, among them, alive but helpless, somebody was bound to try and murder the boy. He pinged his security chief and requested a few guards be sent to protect the pod, posthaste. "Let's get him to sick bay."

"There's no time," Jane stated. "I've got a reading on his vitals here. The slaveware's programmed to not let anyone escape. It's killing him. I've got to work on him *now.*"

"Medbay's got better—"

"He's going to crash and die before we get him there."

The captain took a deep breath. "Do it."

The cargo hands popped the locks on the pod and moved the hatch out of her way. The mind-controlled mech pilot lay in the open coffin, hooked to all manner of machines, so still and deathly pale that at first Holloway thought he was dead. It was only the weak and erratic readings on Jane's med display that suggested otherwise.

Jane launched herself from the wall, landed at Jackson's side, and went to work. A few of her little bots flitted around, helping by placing probes on Jackson's skull. A 3D holographic image appeared, floating over the probes. "This is bad. Very bad." Jane turned the image. "He's dying."

The moment struck Holloway. Here she was, barely a woman, frantically trying to save the life of someone who was barely a man. War was a hell of a thing.

"This slaveware infection is far worse than I thought. It's evolved beyond anything I've seen before." She unslung her pack and pulled out her tool kit. "I need to get inside his skull and manually install a block."

"Here?" Holloway asked, but his incredulity was just wasting her time. "Fine. Do what you've got to do." Every member of the crew that had any medical training was already in the cargo bay helping with the many injured evacuees, so Holloway signaled for one of them to grab their kit and come assist Jane.

She hesitated, seemed genuinely terrified, knowing that the life of someone she'd never even met before was in her hands. "I've never done anything like this before, sir."

"Try your best, Jane. It's all any of us can do."

CHAPTER 1

Three Years Later

Jackson Rook was a liberator. Others might use the word "thief," but thief couldn't begin to describe the good work he did. Like how he was about to liberate a Citadel M750 from its rightful owners to sell for an obscene sum to someone else the law said couldn't have one.

The Citadel was a top-of-the-line personal strike platform, a mech suit that stood over five meters tall. It was made by Raycor and had been built to operate in the worst environments imaginable and included a modular chassis which allowed various loadouts. Depending on which package you went with, you could suit it up with tools and bots for a scientific exploration, or to construct an outpost, but the model he was after today was intended for all-out war. The battle suite Citadel carried a full platoon of warbots inside its housing, like a mother scorpion carrying her babies to war. But these babies had a teensy bit more bite.

The Citadel was really a lovely piece of engineering. A very expensive—and highly regulated—piece. Jackson had memorized both the official stats from the company sales literature and the actual end user stats from the defense blogs. Either way the Citadel was an impressive beast. And Jackson couldn't wait to drive her.

The only thing standing in his way was Dwight, one of the morons from the Splendid Ventures corporation.

Jackson adjusted his cap and said, "I'm locking Dwight in my visual now."

"Got him." The response came from a ship which was sitting in the orbital queue. Jane was now watching.

Dwight was on a wide sidewalk in the market district of the Sharmala terraformed zone on the planet Nivaas. The market was a lively place with lots of brightly colored awnings and street vendors hawking everything from custom hats, built on the spot, to the weird red beer the settlers here loved.

Dwight was wearing a white shirt that was open at the collar, a shiny blue suit, and alligator-skin cowboy boots. Real alligator, from Earth. He had dark hair that was raked over to one side and a megawatt smile. He was the supremely satisfied hotshot mech pilot for a bunch of real-estate men who had just landed a big money deal for their investors. Dwight purchased a steaming sausage on a stick from a street bot and took a big bite.

Jane aka Specter aka The Net Goddess of Death spoke via the comm link implanted in Jackson's ear. *"He just closed a billion-rupee deal here, and he's eating a hot dog?"*

Jane fascinated Jackson. On a regular basis he attempted to flirt with her. But Jane was like Medusa—beautiful and deadly. Instead of snakes, she surrounded herself with happy little robots of death. He was never quite sure if hitting on her would lead to tender moments or torture by bot, but the greater the risk, the greater the reward.

"If I'd just landed a billion in cash, I'd be eating one too. You haven't tasted the sausages down here. They're to die for."

"It's a hot dog."

"Yeah, but made out of actual animals, that like graze and walk around and stuff, not vat meat. If you were down here, I'd treat you to one. Call it a dinner date."

"You think stuffed intestine is every girl's romantic dream?"

"It should be."

Dwight took another bite, his white smile flashing in the sun.

Jackson was getting kind of hungry. Maybe he should pick some of those up and bring them back to the ship. Then Jane could see he did in fact have excellent taste.

"What security have you identified?" she asked.

Jackson hitched his backpack a bit higher on his shoulder

as he discreetly made his way through the crowd. "One human. One walker. And it looks like three fliers."

"That's all I see as well."

"I'm going to go for it."

"You're on your own down there. If you want to wait half an hour, I can get some of the crew there to watch your back."

"That's what I've got you for."

"I'm several thousand klicks above you."

"Close enough." This sort of petty crime was how Jackson had spent most of his childhood, and despite the bodyguard, Dwight had the look of an easy mark. "I've got this."

"Okay. The captain trusts your judgment . . . on this sort of thing at least. Prepare for Fifi."

Fifi was one of Jane's many minions. She was a very small bot, about the size of a large pea. Highly mobile and able to snip wiring, cords, and carotid arteries, Fifi was a real gem. Today it would be her job to climb into Dwight's shiny blue suit and cut open the bottom of his inside breast pocket. When that happened, the medallion Dwight had placed there would fall out, and Jackson could pick it up and switch it for a fake. He would then immediately hail Dwight to let him know that he'd dropped something, which was precisely the sort of thing good citizens like Jackson did.

Jackson needed the medallion because Raycor had equipped their Citadel with multifactor user authentication. The end user could set it to require up to ten different factors. Since Splendid Ventures wasn't expecting anybody to try and steal their fancy new Citadel, theirs had the minimal three. In this case, Dwight had set his controller's account to utilize the signal from his personal ID that was implanted in his chest, a passphrase, and a medallion, which was just a fancy security key. The medallion's shell was brass, one side was the imprint of a wolf, and the other had the Raycor logo. Inside was some solid-state hardware.

Jane was ready to spoof Dwight's personal ID. They'd surveilled him with one of her bots and identified the passphrase. And so the medallion was the only thing left. Jane hadn't been able to hack it remotely or find out much about its security protocols, so they had to retrieve it the old-fashioned way.

Dwight offered to buy his security detail a sausage. The man politely told him no thanks, and continued watching the street instead, demonstrating he was serious about his work. That meant he was going to make Jackson's job a bit harder, but not impossible. Dwight shrugged, said something about it being his loss, and stopped at a bot selling the weird red beer that left an aftertaste of apples and licorice.

Jackson tailed them, stepping around a grandmother examining some used replacement parts for farm bots, weaving past a boy with a blue parrot on his shoulder, and then drew close to Dwight as he took another bite of sausage and a swig of the red beer.

Jane's voice was in his ear. *"Are the city's bots still there?"*

Jackson acted like a shopper and looked down to examine a table of flowers one might plant in a garden here. There were blue, pink, and white ones. The tags said they'd been genetically modified for the soil, temperature, and precipitation of this part of the planet. One sported pretty leaves like green lace. While feigning interest in the flowers, Jackson glanced up at the eaves along the street. There had been a mobile security camera at either end. Both were still there, watching. Either could move at any time.

Unfortunately, he also spotted a hornet's nest.

Those were a fairly effective—and intimidating—law enforcement measure. Each one housed a little swarm of mechanical fliers that could chase, search for contraband, and inject chemicals designed to subdue their targets. The cameras patrolled. The hornets detained. Combine those with a couple other types of security bots, and one or two cops could patrol a huge area.

Jackson was close enough to Dwight's security that he couldn't risk answering Jane vocally. It was doubtful a professional bodyguard would assume he was talking to himself. Luckily, the crew of the *Tar Heel* had a system for quiet communication.

He blinked just right to pull up the image of a basic keyboard in his eye implant. Each key was pulsing at a slightly different frequency. All he needed to do was focus on the letter, his brain would automatically mimic that frequency, and that signal would get transmitted to Jane. It took a bit of practice to avoid typos and it was a little slower than just talking, but it made you feel darn near telepathic.

"Got a nest above."

"Your call then."

It was his choice as to whether he wanted to initiate the switch with so many eyes.

"Am I Gray?"

"That's who they'll see."

Every human who set foot on this colony was required to wear some sort of passive ID chip that could be quick scanned by the security bots. Jackson's was embedded by his clavicle, but Jane had set it to transmit a false identity. To the law, Jackson was currently a man by the name of Mufasa Gray, who had arrived on the passenger hauler *Solomon* yesterday. His paperwork was on file with the immigration office and Gray had already applied for a Nivaas work permit. The only truth to any of that was that the *Solomon* was a real ship currently docked. Jane had just added her imaginary passenger to their manifest. It was nice having a specter in the sky who could jigger such things.

Once the Citadel was reported stolen, the cops would search all the security video that Dwight's tag showed up in to figure out how. They'd run Gray's information down eventually, realize he was imaginary, and then try to figure out who he really was using facial recognition. So Jackson was wearing a wide-brimmed hat, a beard, and prosthetic augments for his nose, cheeks, and brow. He wished he could have worn sunglasses, but nobody down here used them. Instead an eye film with loads of built-in tech, including the ability to automatically darken, was popular. To avoid sticking out, Jackson had done the same. Half the people on the street were wearing them. They looked like bugs.

Jackson considered all the security but figured he was unlikely to find any place in Sharmala that was any better. The market was loud, busy, and crowded. Plus the clock was ticking. The Citadel was at the freight yard and would be moved sometime in the next forty hours. Their only shot would be to intercept it before the transfer.

"It's a go."

Fifi was cupped in his hand and locked onto her target, and so Jackson simply walked past Dwight. As he did so, Fifi jumped like a flea from his hand to Dwight's shiny blue slacks. She immediately sprang up and under his suitcoat.

Dwight didn't seem to notice.

Jackson walked a bit farther down the sidewalk and stopped to look at an aquarium with blue and green fish in it. The sign said these had been modified and tested to thrive in the waters of Nivaas and provide the finest combination of protein, fat, and a whole list of other nutrients.

"The lady's in place," Jane said, the lady being Fifi.

The woman hawking the blue and green fish stepped over toward Jackson. She was far taller than Jackson, who was shorter than the average unaugmented human height, but she had that tall, lean look of someone who had grown up here. Nivaas gravity was lighter than standard. "Hello, young sir. Do you have a pond?"

"Not yet. Just arrived. I'm trying to decide between birds and fish."

"You'll want both. The quality of the fish meat is excellent, and you could survive nicely on that alone. But you have to think about more than food. What about the shang fly? It loves to bury itself in human flesh. Bots can help find the devils, but they're so clunky. Why not set a flock of birds on them? I have some blue swallows that are a beauty to behold. A dozen of them will keep ten acres clean. And their eggs are delicious."

Dwight and his companion passed behind Jackson, and he pretended not to notice. Instead, he asked the woman, "They're layers then?"

"Not like chickens, but frequently enough."

He nodded. Swallow eggs. What where they—the size of thumbnails?

Jackson pretended to ponder over the idea of swallows designed to lust after shang flies.

And then Jane said, *"She's almost done."*

Jackson smiled at the tall woman. "Birds and fish sound good. But I need to talk to the other settlers I'm working with first. I'll likely be back." And then he excused himself and walked after his target.

Dwight had been drawn to three local yokels who had taken up a commanding position on an artsy sculpture made of blocks. They were making a lot of noise. The yokels were urging a gathering of small-claim owners to unite into some kind of co-op to compete with the ultrapowerful Splendid Ventures Corporation. Sadly, they didn't know the fix was already in.

SVC's advertising proclaimed that it was a company dedicated to the "responsible development of habitable real estate on many worlds." Those ads usually featured smiling families in outfits directed at targeted ethnic groups. A recent one had featured sombreros.

But what SVC really did was vacuum up tracts of good land for rich investors, usually by bribing local governments after the expensive and risky terraforming and settling parts of the process were complete. Very frequently that meant using vast amounts of capital to stomp on the little guys in court. In this particular case, they were stomping a lot of little guys who owned various claims in an eleven-thousand-square-kilometer tract surrounding the settlement of Sharmala. The tract had originally been seen as almost worthless and gone for cheap to settlers who couldn't afford anything better...until they'd discovered rare mineral deposits under it. Instead of the colonial equivalent to winning the lottery, they were getting eminent-domained by their government, paid a pittance, traded for other undeveloped plots, or evicted. SVC could move in and get the ore, the politicians would get massive kickbacks, and everybody wins. Except for the poor dumb settlers who had broken their backs to tame an unforgiving desert world obviously, but you could always get more of those from Earth.

To celebrate the deal, the SVC executives had just hosted an event with a few of their wealthiest investors and their corrupt local officials. Part of the activities had included taking their new Citadel for a spin and blowing apart some of the more aggressive fauna in a stretch of wilderness in the noncataloged areas. Everybody knew the real purpose of that little expedition was a show of force in case any of the settlers being forcibly relocated decided to get uppity.

SVC had done this sort of thing many times. The colonists might be willing to fight for their land, but will didn't mean squat if they were pitted against heavy-duty, top-of-the-line, high-tech weapon systems.

Dwight stood there chewing his sausage and drinking his red beer, his obnoxious suit sparkling in the sun. He was smiling, enjoying the rabble-rouser's speech. He seemed to find the exhortations the locals were making to the crowd the height of entertainment. Passion is great. Massive money transfers to morally flexible politicians were better.

Jackson slowly browsed his way over until he stood only a pace behind Dwight.

Dwight turned to his security man. "Who is the one on the right?"

The bodyguard must have had an eye implant too, because he looked like he was reading. "He's a nobody."

"I want a report on him when we get up in orbit."

"Yes, sir."

Dwight turned and began to walk away. Jackson paused a few seconds, then followed.

"*Ready?*" Jane asked.

"Ready," Jackson transmitted quietly.

A moment later the wolf's head medallion dropped out of Dwight's suitcoat. Fifi was clinging to one side, riding it down. The medallion clanged on the ground.

Jackson immediately reached down, grabbed and pocketed it, then held up the fake. "Excuse me." He held the fake aloft.

Dwight's security man turned. He had a camera hooked over his ear, a gun and some kind of bafflement spray—stuff to put a man to sleep—on his belt. He scowled.

"I think you dropped this."

Dwight turned and saw the medallion. A look of confusion crossed his face. He patted his breast pocket and felt that it was empty. Then pulled open his suit jacket to look and make sure.

"Thanks," Dwight said and took the medallion, his confusion deepening.

Dwight's security man narrowed his eyes and scrutinized Jackson. No doubt right now he was receiving a report on Mufasa Gray, a technician who specialized in sewer and waste. SVC's data people wouldn't be as good as Jane, but they wouldn't be chumps either. They'd be hacking the fake records from the *Solomon* in no time, but those fake files were boring as could be.

"Have a good day," Jackson said in a helpful citizen fashion and began casually walking away.

"*Dwight's watching you, talking to his man,*" Jane said.

Jackson moseyed on, prepared to run, but playing it cool.

"*They're moving on.*"

Fantastic. Jackson just kept on walking away with everything they needed to unlock and drive the Citadel.

Then a male voice came on the line. "*That was well done, Mr. Rook.*"

"Easy as pie, Captain. How are things up there?"

"*Gloriously boring, son, just how I like it.*" Captain Holloway was old school, former Earth Bloc Navy, with that peculiar accent that came from the southeastern half of its United States. "*The Splendid Ventures morons are sending the goods back up to their ship soon. It's all neatly packaged in a container waiting in line at the taco bar. No ETA on its launch time yet so we've got at least a day. Come back up here. Tui and his boys will be ready to grab the container as soon as it breaks atmo, and then you can park a shiny new Citadel in my cargo bay.*"

He'd been enjoying the feel of real natural gravity and hadn't been in a hurry to go home. "Swapping crates in low orbit should be a milk run. Even if you needed to just steal it out of the container, you know you've got two or three other crew aboard qualified to fly a mech, right?"

"*I do? So that's why I sign all these paychecks. But we both know there's a big old difference between just driving a mech and being an actual mech pilot. You're the least likely one to scratch the paint on my fancy new mech. Now get a move on in case something goes sideways, Pilot.*"

"Roger that, Captain." Truth be told, he really wanted to fly that Citadel anyway. It was light-years ahead of the mechs he'd grown up on.

"Tar Heel *out.*"

Back to the port then to catch a hopper back to the ship. Except on the way Jackson saw another of the little bots selling sausages and caught that delightful aroma. *Why not?* No guts, no glory, no luscious Jane lips. He walked over to the bot and purchased two of them. One for him. One for her. Jackson was a mech jock, smooth-talking smuggler, and once upon a time on a world very far away . . . a war hero. He wasn't used to being rejected by women. Surely this magic sausage would be able to pave the way where so many other ploys had failed before. As he got the food sealed in a to-go bag, he noticed some shady types walking around the corner.

You live a life of crime, you get really good at recognizing other criminals, especially when they weren't trying to hide the look. The ones giving him that vibe were only a few meters away, three men and a dog. One was a big brute, the other was smaller, but equally nasty. Only it was the one in the lead with the dog on a leash that really caused his instincts to twitch.

Jackson suddenly got a bad feeling because there was something familiar about that one. The leader was surveying the street.

He was shorter than Jackson but double the mass, bald, with a close-cropped white beard. The dog next to him was a fat pit bull. A dog that needed less eating and more running. A dog that had a cyborg eye.

"Ah, hell," Jackson said, lowering his head and trying not to be noticed, though he was afraid it was too late. He started walking away. "Come in, *Tar Heel*."

"*What's wrong?*" Jane asked.

"Prunkard's here with his mangy pooch."

"*Who?*"

Jackson kept his head down and pushed through the crowd. "You remember the gig where we stole that Orion about two years ago? The one with the goats?"

"*The livestock ship? Ugh. How could I ever forget?*"

That job had been one of the first Jackson had pulled after joining his current crew, and one of their favorites. A client had wanted an Orion-class freighter. Grandma had found one for them to boost, but it had been filled with goats. They could have jettisoned the animals into space, but the captain had said they were too valuable to waste. And even though the goats were tranquilized and stacked, they still pissed. And shat. Endlessly. And the bearded-polygamist billy goats stank like nobody's business. The crew had spent days attaching and reattaching the waste vacuums that were supposed to catch the goat pee and turds but constantly broke down instead. That had been loads of fun in zero G.

"That ship was part of Jeet Prunkard's fleet."

"*Uh-oh.*" Their captain had a very specific moral code. Part of that code was that they tried to only steal from scumbags who really deserved it. Prunkard had *really* deserved it.

"*What's he doing here?*"

"Why wouldn't he be here?"

"*Space is really big, Jackson!*"

Prunkard had made his fortune as a claim stripper—the type of pirates who loved going to planets that were still relatively untamed and stealing everything that wasn't nailed down. Colonies were a great source of heavy machinery and specialized equipment, which was easy to resell, no questions asked. On Nivaas there wasn't much law away from the main settlements, and very few people around to protect their valuables. Claim strippers were a notoriously brutal lot. Fighting each other and killing anybody who got in their way. Even among that vile bunch, Prunkard had a rep. He murdered anybody who crossed him. Stealing his livestock hauler was one hell of a cross!

Jeet Prunkard knew Jackson well enough that this weak disguise wouldn't fool him. It was designed to defeat facial recognition algorithms, not someone you'd once looked in the eye as you lied and cheated them.

Jackson saw an alley and made a beeline for it. Just before he turned the corner, he glanced back.

Unfortunately, Jeet was also really good at noticing other criminals. The pirate was pointing right at him.

"Shanks," Jackson cursed, slipped his other arm through his backpack strap and ran. If Prunkard's crew caught him, he was dead.

Back out on the street, the fat pit bull woofed.

CHAPTER 2

Jackson sprinted down the alley. Then turned into another, and another, trying to shake his pursuers. On the bright side, in this gravity he could run all day and feel like an Olympian. On the downside, when he looked back, it appeared so could the goons who were chasing him.

"Bad news," Jane told him. "Prunkard's guys are right behind you. Their chasing you looked suspicious enough it triggered the security algorithms. Cops have been asked to check it out."

That was the problem with these law-and-order towns.

Above him on one wall, a group of maintenance spider bots clung to the side of a building, cleaning and repairing a patch where some weird Nivaasian fungus had grown. The bots were pale and about a foot across. He ran underneath them, hoping they weren't connected to Sharmala's security system.

None jumped, and he sighed a bit in relief, having dodged at least that bullet. And then one flung itself off the wall, sailed smoothly over his head, and landed a number of paces in front of him. It reared up on its hind legs and spoke.

"Mufasa Gray, halt and wait for the authorities." Its voice was surprisingly tinny. "I have been authorized to interdict you."

He looked back just as Prunkard's goons entered the alley. They saw him.

Next to Jackson was a little four-wheeled bot snugged up against the side of the alley. It held the supplies the maintenance bots used to do their work. It probably weighed twenty kilos. Jackson picked

27

it up and hurled it at the spider bot, which easily leapt out of the way and up onto the wall of the building. The supply bot crashed to the pavement and splashed water and cleaning agents all over.

"Mufasa Gray," the spider bot said. "Destruction of property will not be tolerated."

"Jane," Jackson said. "They've pegged my ID. I need to go dark." If he didn't, everything tied to the city's security grid would be looking for him.

"Working on it, Jackson."

"Mufasa Gray!" the spider said.

Jackson kicked it out of the way.

The other spiders didn't like that, because they all increased their volume and began blinking lights. "Mufasa Gray! Halt!"

Jackson did not halt.

A spider bot leapt at him.

There's nothing quite like having a large metal spider fly right at your face. Jackson was wearing gloves. Nice gloves that could pack an extra punch. He activated the iron fist feature, hardening the outside, and struck the bot in midflight.

He was rewarded with a satisfying crunch, but the spider wrapped its legs around his fist and gripped his forearm, refusing to let go. He could hear the footfalls of Prunkard's goons, but Jackson stopped long enough to punch the spider into the wall of the building. It crunched. He punched it again. The bot sprayed out a stream of green fluid that splashed Jackson up the side of his face. Jackson punched it a third time. This time the spider bot cracked right down the middle and fell to the ground.

"Mufasa Gray!" the broken thing said. "Halt."

"You're dead, thief!" shouted the bigger goon. They had nearly caught up. Jackson took off. When the remaining cleaning spiders told Prunkard's men to stop and wait for the authorities, there were gunshots. He didn't dare look back as the pirates blasted the maintenance bots.

Every sensor in the city would pick up the gunfire. Now the cops would be *really* interested.

"Jane," he said urgently as he ran down the alley, dodging trash piles and scaring stray cats.

"You are about to become Father Patrick Mullane. An Irish-Catholic priest who is known for his love of butterflies. The picture I have has him surrounded by a cloud of blue ones."

Where did she come up with these stolen IDs? But it didn't matter—priest, pope, or mullah, as long as he wasn't Mufasa Gray. "Just tell me when you're switching." He reached the end of the alley and glanced behind to see the goons freeing themselves from the meddling bots.

"Hold still one sec."

But the short goon was pointing a handgun at him. There was a crack. The projectile made a loud *slap* as it hit the bricks next to him. Bullet or tranq, he couldn't tell, but either was bad. Jackson dashed out into the street to avoid getting shot. It was nearly as crowded as the market, and it must have had cameras too, because as soon as he was in the open an alarm sounded.

"Anytime now," he said to Jane.

"You need to get to a blind spot. If I switch your ID in the open it won't fool the AI."

"Where do I go?"

"Turn right. Hurry."

He ran past a tall man smoking some kind of pipe, past four women with bright headscarves sitting at a table, past a rack of three public scooters. He briefly thought about taking one, but then discarded the idea because with the alarms, they'd be shut down. All along the street people were obediently moving to the sides of the streets to make way for the police.

"Uh-oh. Bad news, Jackson. Prunkard's got his own specter. Nivaas security just received a flag that Mufasa Gray is an alias for a wanted criminal. I should have thought of that."

"Can you do anything?"

"Working on it."

A cop appeared at the far end of the street riding on a defender, a small mech that was capable of detaining people, other bots, and vehicles. It had a little platform that hung down from its backside, just big enough for two humans to stand abreast like a modern-day chariot. A defender usually housed more bots that could be used for everything from forensics to tracking by smell. So much for that direction.

At least the goons hadn't followed him out of the alley. They must have heard the sirens. Even Prunkard's crew weren't cocky enough to get into a shoot-out with the police.

He looked up to see another hornet's nest, its activation light blinking.

Hornets had a few modes. Sometimes they followed a target silently, acting as quiet little surveillance eyes in the sky. Other times they shot after their prey with a shrieking buzz, loaded for bear. The sound was on purpose, designed to inspire fear, designed to convince you to stop and raise your hands before the screaming hordes of hell descended upon you with their vicious stingers.

The coverings popped open, and dozens of robotic hornets— each as big as his pinky—spilled out.

"Shanks."

The first hornet shot out of the nest. It circled up high above the street. Another one followed.

"Mufasa Gray," numerous speakers broadcast up and down the street. "Halt and lie facedown on the ground."

Jackson stopped. This was a lot of firepower for one destruction of cleaning bot charge. What had Prunkard told them? That he kidnapped and ate children? Whatever it was, Jackson didn't have much time. A few more seconds and he would be boxed in.

The people of Sharmala were getting out of the way, happy that they weren't the ones being screamed at. Law enforcement had a reputation for being heavy handed in this settlement and they didn't want to get caught in the cross fire.

"Jane!"

"You'll have to make your own blind spot. Are you ready?"

"I was ready yesterday." He spotted the front door to a restaurant and decided that would be it. But he didn't run for the door. Instead, he ran for the service bot standing like a statue on the sidewalk, holding a pitcher of ice-cold lemonade. He reached into the pocket of his cargo pants and pulled out a canister of Shine. "Say when."

"Prepare to be sedated," the speakers declared. Then the first hornet began to shriek and then a swarm exploded out of the nest. The noise was deafening, aggressive, and downright terrifying. The psyops of this security system really was top-notch. It was enough to scare the soup out of anyone.

Many of the people on the street shouted in alarm and ducked for cover. The worker bot with the pitcher of lemonade in its hand held perfectly still in the middle of the road. At least it didn't try to tackle him.

Above Jackson, the hell swarm dived.

"Now!"

Jackson pressed the button on the canister, tossed it high into the air, and darkened his eye film to max as he looked away.

The canister detonated in a searing cloud of light. The spreading cloud of tiny particles reflected and amplified the sun, emitting thousands of lumens. The fog of light temporarily blinded every eye on the street, but it also emitted a pulse of jamming radio waves on all but Jane's selected frequency. The effect should have been enough to mask his signature from all but the most powerful top-of-the-line sensors.

"You are void," Jane said as she cut the transmission of his personal ID chip. For the security systems, one moment they'd have Mufasa Gray in their sights, then a burst of static, and then Mufasa Gray had vanished.

Shrouded in blinding, celestial light, Jackson pivoted away from the lemonade bot and sprinted for the restaurant door. Because the hornets were built to use GPS coordinates, calculate speed and direction, and adjust their flight accordingly, they streaked through the blinding cloud to clang off the plastic body of innocent Mr. Lemonade.

Jackson reached the restaurant door. Even with his eyes shaded enough to safely use a welder, the brilliance of the Shine off the glass made it nearly impossible to see. They'd gotten this batch of Shine from a Triad mafia group who had promised high quality, and it appeared they'd delivered. These were not your ordinary unicorn sparkles.

As he grabbed the door handle, Jackson heard the wicked, unmistakable buzzing shriek of a lone hornet. It came out of the light, a black bullet, streaking fast and low to strike him in the leg. It seared him with a hot, thin stab, as its stinger injected a burning cocktail of drugs.

CHAPTER 3

Jackson grunted in pain and struck at the hornet, but the device had sent the hooked tips of its six legs through his pants and latched onto his skin.

Hornets were made smooth as silk to resist removal. Jackson clutched at the thing, but it slipped between his fingers. All the while it was burrowing its legs into his flesh and injecting whatever chemicals this security system used. A circle around the spot where it had struck was burning and rapidly moving outward. It really *hurt.* And then ground zero of the hornet sting went totally numb.

That was bad.

As long as the hornet was attached, it would continue to poison him, and they'd be able to track it, but he couldn't grab its exoskeleton, which was as slick as wet, soapy glass. He engaged the magnetics on his gloves, but the hornet's shell must have been made out of some kind of composite.

Luckily Jane was on it. Fifi dropped out of Jackson's pocket and landed on the hornet. There was a buzz and shake. And suddenly the hornet released its hold on his skin, fell to the ground, and lay there like a dead animal.

Fifi sprang back up to Jackson's shirt and climbed onto his shoulder.

"Keep moving," Jane said.

"I think I have a crush on Fifi," Jackson said as he yanked

33

the door open. Inside, the diners were shielding their eyes against the light and trying to figure out what was happening on the street. He shuffled toward the back, the burning and numbness in his leg spreading at an alarming rate. It was now halfway up his thigh.

There was an emergency anti-tox pad in his pocket, about half the size of a deck of cards with a mounding lump in the middle where all the chems and counteragents were stored. Jackson pulled it out, removed the covering on the adhesive side, then reached down his pants and slapped the pad onto his leg just above the burn. It immediately latched onto his skin, sampled his blood, and started analyzing how to respond.

The diners continued to shield their eyes and peer out at the street. He took another step, and his calf suddenly stopped working. He fell over a table, spilling a few plates and disturbing someone's lunch. The street behind him was still sparkling and blinding. Inside the patrons were murmuring and making small cries of dismay. But the Shine wouldn't last forever. He limped for the back of the room and what he assumed was the kitchen. There was a farmer's hat woven from grass on a table. He stole it, hobbled a few paces farther, and stole a tall drink in a bright pink, disposable cup.

The expanding burning circle in his leg and the numbness that followed it continued to spread. And suddenly his leg stopped working entirely, and he stumbled against the wall.

"My leg is nonresponsive."

"*Keep going,*" Jane urged. "*There's an alley behind the restaurant.*"

Easy for her to say. He grabbed an empty chair and schlepped along using it as a crutch. He pushed open the swinging half doors at the back of the dining area and found the kitchen. The light from the street cast weird shadows here, but the staff hadn't been blinded. He saw cooking machines, an operator, and a waiter, along with plates, utensils, and food preparation knives. It smelled very strongly of curry.

"What's that racket?" the operator was dressed in a white chef's shirt.

"The street's a madhouse," Jackson said.

"You can't come back here!"

"I twisted my ankle trying to get away from whatever that is!" He tried to sound afraid, which wasn't a stretch at all. "I'm going out that emergency exit or I'm gonna sue!"

It wasn't much of a story, but the cook was more concerned about what was going on out front than weird customers blundering through his kitchen. The Shine cloud was beginning to disperse, and Jackson needed to make himself scarce before it did.

He hopped to the back door, traded his hat for the freshly stolen one, and stepped into a service alley that ran behind all the shops on this street. This was where deliveries were accepted and garbage picked up. Before the door closed behind him, he snagged one of the server's aprons from a peg on the wall.

On his head, Jackson wore the grass hat. In his hand he still held the tall, pink cup. People frequently saw what they wanted to see. And no kind of fugitive Jackson knew paraded around with an apron and a pink cup. But just in case it wasn't enough, he changed his shirt color to white, removed his nose augment, and pulled another bigger type of moustache out of his pocket and slapped it on his face. A moustache might be simple, but the truth was that moustaches worked. At least when dealing with those who didn't know you.

The burning in his leg had stopped climbing, but it was still moving down. Right now, his foot was on fire, and he knew very soon it would be numb.

"ID?" he asked Jane.

"Bless me, Father Patrick, for I have sinned."

"That sounds interesting. You can tell me all about it when I get back." He was now Father Patrick Mullane, who liked butterflies. Other facts about the father scrolled up his display. He pushed aside the bio and pulled up a map of the town. Jane had marked each security asset searching for him with an x. There were a bunch of them.

"Okay. Captain's here too. He wants to know if you can make it to the taco bar?" That was their code word for the accelerator where the Citadel was waiting to be launched into space.

"This leg is not going to get me to the bar."

"Did you apply your tox patch?"

"Yes. It's not doing much yet. Can I get a ride out of here?"

"Maybe you should pray for one, Father."

"You can be sure I'll be offering sacrifices to Fifi if I get out of this. Please tell me you've got somebody nearby who can pick me up. Where's Tui and his skull crackers?"

"I haven't been able to reach him yet. They might be on a

shuttle back up here so they could be ready to snag the package in transit."

Jackson swore under his breath. Of course. Their mission had been to gain access to the accelerator and rig his ride while he'd been tailing Dwight.

"You're on your own, Jackson, sorry."

"Okay," Jackson said. And then he hobbled down the back alley toward a cross street. Above the buildings, hornets and sirens sounded. Here and there wisps of shining brightness rose into the sky.

"Warning. Bogey approaching." And there was indeed an x heading this way on the map. Jackson looked around. There wasn't any place to hide. Not one he could get to with his leg in its current state, anyway. So he hopped to the side and took a seat on a loading dock, looking in the direction of the commotion. Like he worked here, was taking his break, and trying to figure out what was going on.

A moment later the big defender appeared at the end of the alley, with a cop riding the chariot platform. Jackson pretended not to know they were there. He just sat with the big grass hat on his head and the big pink cup in his hand and stretched out a leg. He took a sip on the straw, found out that he'd stolen a salty vegetable drink of some type, then glanced casually down the alley like he'd just noticed the cop. He scooted back as a good citizen should, making room, trying his best to hide that fact that his leg was lame and his toes felt as if they were on fire.

Thankfully over the course of his life Jackson had gotten a lot of practice at looking nonchalant even while breaking the law. The cop waited just long enough for the defender's facial scan to say he was someone other than Mufasa Gray before he clomped past. Luckily he didn't bother to look at the record it pulled up long enough to wonder why a priest was hanging out on a loading dock, but like the captain said, too much automation made people sloppy in their critical thinking... a weakness he loved to exploit.

A security bot appeared in the sky above the buildings at one end of this alley. It paused a moment, lights flashing on its underbelly. Jackson knew he had to get moving. It was only a matter of time before one of them saw through his disguise.

But there was no way he was going to make it to the accelerator with his leg. "Jane, you've got to get me a ride."

"I'm working on it."

Another security bot flew over the roofs. Jackson knew the next one was going to fly down the street and come get a good look at him. And that would not do. Once their quick search failed to find Mufasa Gray, they'd go old-school police, check the images and do a BOLO for every Caucasian male, early twenties. The AI would know he was approximately 172 centimeters tall and weighed in at 70 kilograms.

On Gloss where he'd grown up, a little gunfire in the streets wasn't even noteworthy. You pretty much needed an orbital bombardment for anyone to care enough to call the cops...not that they had cops anymore. But Nivaas was an orderly place—in the cities at least—where all the crime was done politely between politicians and megacorps who could afford war mechs. They didn't have any patience for thuggish shenanigans here. On the bright side, hopefully that meant they'd already arrested Jeet Prunkard.

There was a whine as a smaller drone zipped down the alley. This flier was small, dark, and didn't look at all like the local government ones he'd seen so far. The privately owned drone paused, hovering a few feet above him.

"Buzz off," he muttered.

But instead it suddenly dropped to about waist level, so it could get a picture of his face. Jackson looked away, but then it flew off.

"Jane, you said Prunkard's crew had a specter too?"

"Yeah. And he's surprisingly good. Not as good as me, obviously. But he's got skills."

So like Jane, Prunkard would probably have a lot of extra eyes flying around, and would know all the usual bag of tricks of how runners avoided them. "I just got sniffed by someone." Jackson looked around and spotted a faded sign on a wall with the icon for a public restroom and an arrow pointing that way. "I'm going to a place that's a little quieter."

He found that shorter strides made it easier to schlep his leg, so he quick-schlepped it in that direction. Once they found the hornet Fifi had killed, they'd see that it had stung someone, and he couldn't let any of the drones see him limping suspiciously. Luckily his destination was just around the corner.

Nivaas had the sort of orderly society that allowed for things like shared public restrooms. There were three sinks and five stalls and it was remarkably clean. Probably because of the same little city worker spiders like the one he'd broken earlier. Nobody else was inside. He selected the stall at the very end, then locked himself in. Thankfully they were western-style toilets, so he'd at least have a place to sit while the tox pack did its job. If the cops or Prunkard's men came in here, he'd be cornered like an idiot rabbit. He gave an exasperated sigh as he pulled his legs up so they couldn't be seen beneath the stall if anybody wandered in.

"*I've got to warn you,*" Jane said in his ear. "*Grandma is really mad at you right now. She was just yelling about how your 'antics' are going to cost us this job. You might be safer down there with Prunkard.*"

"Ride?" Jackson prompted.

"*Ooh, yes. I think that will do nicely.*" But it sounded like Jane was talking to someone else.

"What have you got?" He figured it would be something innocuous. Maybe a little cart for invalids. A scooter maybe. But sometimes Jane surprised. It could be a car.

"*Expect—going dark.*"

And then she was gone.

"Jane?"

But Jane was offline. Probably someone was getting close to tracking their signal. So Jackson waited. A minute went by. Then two. The burning began to fade, but his leg was still mostly numb. The tox pack was working, but depending on the strength of the concoction, it could take time to counteract the agent.

Another few seconds ticked by, and then the bathroom door opened and someone walked in. The footsteps were loud. Large. A man, Jackson thought.

Jackson slowly pulled the tiny illegal throwaway pistol from his belt. If it was the cops, he'd have to hope the gun and the stolen medallion were small enough to flush. Then he'd surrender, plead his innocence, and hope the penalty for resisting arrest, fake identities, and punching spider bots wasn't too insane. If it was Prunkard's crew, he'd gladly shoot those guys dead. Except there was no way he was going to be able to hide a body or bodies on one leg in the middle of a city. What was the Nivaasian sentence for murder? Probably something like a hundred years hard labor in their mines. He'd rather not find out.

The individual walked slowly down the line of stalls, but rather than picking one, he hesitated, listening.

Bang. Jackson flinched as the first door was kicked open.

Cops would have announced themselves before searching the place . . . Probably.

There was a moment's hesitation. Then the stranger kicked in the second door. *Bang.*

It was definitely a man. Jackson could see boots underneath the door now. They were big and sturdy with thick, mag-lockable soles. Spacer's boots.

Third door. *Bang.* Fourth. *Bang.*

Jackson said nothing, just trained his gun for where he figured the pirate's center of mass would be and got ready to shoot. But the door kicker paused. Someone else was talking. Apparently, he had a partner who had been left to block the entrance.

"Sorry," the man at the entrance said. "You can't come in here. We're doing a little maintenance."

Except the potential witness to Prunkard's maintenance work wasn't turned away that easy. Jackson couldn't really hear them, but Prunkard's goon replied, "Well too bad, pal, the restroom's closed. So beat—ooof."

Jackson couldn't see, but from the noise it sounded like somebody had just gotten kicked in the chest and launched across the restroom hard enough to bounce off a sink.

The boots in front of Jackson's stall turned to face the new threat, and he didn't have to wait long, because a heartbeat later the newcomer closed on him. Now two pairs of big spacers' boots were crashing back and forth. The room shook as Prunkard's man was slammed into the wall, followed by the distinctive cry of someone who'd just gotten an arm put into a joint lock. Then Jackson's door flew open.

There stood a giant Samoan, holding a pirate whose face had just been used as a battering ram. The pirate didn't look so good. The giant, on the other hand, looked like he'd just been served up a big dish of ice cream.

"Hey, Jackson," he said as he twisted the bad guy into a pretzel. "Hope I didn't interrupt any business."

"About time, Tui."

Tuitama Abinadi Fuamatu was one big Samoan, and chief of *Tar Heel* security team—which was usually more of a raiding party. His hair was braided in small, tight cornrows. He had a pe'a—warrior's tattoo—from his waist to knees. When exposed, it looked like a pair of permanent crazy pants. One half of his torso was tattooed as well, from pec to powerful shoulder to wrist. A full sleeve plus some. The tats were supposedly loaded with symbolic meanings, protections, and blessings.

He effortlessly flipped Prunkard's goon over one hip to smash him against the tile wall. The move knocked the wind and the sense right out of the poor fool.

"Bro," Tui said with a grin. "You're all squashed up like a rat. Come out of there."

"A hornet stung my leg."

"Can you walk?"

"Sorta."

Tui held out a hand to help him up. Jackson took the hand and tried to resist Tui's crushing grip. He was no wimp, but Tui had cybernetic augments and military gene mods, so that was basically impossible. Tui liked to joke that the army doctors had unlocked the old dormant chimp genes, but whatever upgrades Earth Block had really given him, he was freakishly strong.

From the two handguns Tui had just stuffed in his waistband, he'd managed to disarm both goons in the three seconds the fight had taken. It was a good thing Tui was so damned friendly, because otherwise he'd be terrifying.

The pirate who had manned the door was lying on the floor, struggling to breathe. Neither one of them was Prunkard, which meant that piece of nasty work was still out there somewhere.

"Nice," Jackson said as he stashed his gun away. "But I could have taken them."

"Sure you would have, Junior," Tui said as he helped Jackson toward the door. "Now let's see about getting out of here without getting arrested...Jane, I've recovered Jackson."

"*Great. Do you still have the medallion?*"

"I do," Jackson said, patting his pocket to make sure. "Maybe Tui should hold onto it in case I get rolled up. Worst-case scenario I can try to talk my way out of some lesser charges while Tui gets it back to the ship. The cops are looking for someone half his size and half his age—"

"Hey now. I'm not that old."

"*Well, that's gonna be a problem.*" The voice in his ear was no longer the dulcet tone of Jane, but rather Captain Holloway's drawl. "*Change of plans, boys. We just got word. This security alert made Splendid Ventures nervous. Since it was so close, they probably thought it was the evicted settlers taking a shot at their pilot, because they just sent a priority request to the taco bar to bump them up. They want their Citadel back on their company ship, ASAP."*

That was not good. The plan had been to wait for the shipping container carrying the Citadel to be accelerated along the thousand-kilometer launch track and shot toward heaven. Once in orbit, Jane would create a blind spot, and the good folks of the *Tar Heel* would make a quiet swap away from the many eyes in space. By the time SVC realized they'd been robbed, the *Tar Heel* would be through the gate. But for all that to work, the security medallion needed to be there, three feet away from the Citadel, to override its security. Otherwise, that fine piece of engineering would set off all sorts of alarms when it deviated from its course.

"How much did they move the schedule up by?"

"They're going to launch within the hour. Turns out there's some perks to being a giant megacorporation."

Tui and Jackson shared a glance. There was absolutely no way they could get to the port, catch a shuttle, and get the medallion into orbit in time to make any kind of swap. And once the Citadel was aboard the SVC ship, they could kiss that prize goodbye forever.

"So have Jane stall them."

"She's trying, but it's not looking good."

"That's a whole lot of money to just let float away."

"Well, that's exactly what I was thinking, son. But all is not lost. There's one surefire way to make sure that medallion is in the right place at the right time."

Jackson thought it over for a second . . . He checked the map in his eye display. The Citadel's container was only a short drive away . . . parked at the launch track's hub. They were close enough to get there before the container was accelerated to escape velocity and hurled into space.

"You can't be serious."

"That depends on how badly you still want to get paid, Mr. Rook."

CHAPTER 4

"Bro," Tui said as he drove them out of town. "Stowing away is a bad idea."

"It's only bad if we get caught. Or I fall off and die. Or the launch kills me. Or a piece of cargo shifts and crushes me. Or there's another layer of security on the Citadel we don't know about, I can't unlock it, so I run out of air and Splendid Ventures finds my frozen corpse when they finally get around to doing inventory...I think I'm gonna stop now. Making this list really isn't helping."

"I think it's clarifying," Tui said.

Jackson was lying on the floor of the backseat, out of sight. Tui was up front driving this rental manually because the vehicle's self-driving system would never allow something this illegal and dangerous. Jane had easily cracked the system and overridden all the security protocols and recording devices, so the car wasn't putting up any fuss. Furthermore, they could speak freely without the cops having a record to listen to later.

"Hey, Jane, I just thought of something," Jackson said.

"Yeah?"

"My blood is on that hornet. They'll get my DNA and be able to match it to my military records from Gloss."

"Don't worry. I had Fifi punch its battery. It was on fire by the time you limped out the back."

"You're so thoughtful."

"It was nothing."

"I just really want you to know how much I appreciate everything you do for this team."

"Oh, thank you. That's sweet."

"Focus, Jackson," Tui warned. "We can do the employee of the month thing later. We'll be on the access road in a few minutes. You know how the accelerator companies always say no cargo liquid, fragile, perishable, or living things allowed for? They say that for a reason! You got your Raj?"

Jackson patted his backpack. "I don't leave home without it."

"We're past all the cops if you want to suit up then."

So Jackson dug into the main compartment of his backpack and removed Raj, his space suit. In addition to providing pressure, oxygen, and a way to control temperature, a suit needed to protect its wearer from solar radiation and micrometeorites, tiny bits of who knows what flying through the ether at enormous speeds. A speck of ice hitting you at thirty thousand klicks per hour could really ruin your day. The fact that his suit could accomplish that, while being this light and compact, was a miracle of modern technology . . . And probably one of the only things worth a damn that had ever been invented on Gloss.

The Mirage 360LR was made of composite layers of thin materials that allowed a wide and flexible range of movement while providing a good amount of protection from the surprises Mother Space liked to hurl at you. There were some suits that were even thinner now, but this had been the same suit he'd been wearing when he had escaped his home planet. Raj had carried him through many a dicey spot. Sure, there were more advanced suits available now, but Raj had a funky smell that Jackson welcomed. That funky smell meant luck.

He stripped out of his regular clothes and got into the suit. It was briefly warm, the heat of his body radiating back at him, and then the cooling system kicked in and Jackson settled into his old friend, the material feeling like cool, worn cotton. He checked his mask but didn't put it on yet. The rebreather canister didn't last that long, and if he couldn't get into the Citadel and its supplies, he'd need every bit of air inside it to survive until the *Tar Heel* could pick him up.

All his regular clothing went into the pack, which still had a bunch of useful tools in it, and he put that on his back. He felt something crawling across his neck, and he almost reflexively swatted at what he thought was a bug, but then he realized that was just Fifi, tagging along to help.

Jane contacted them again. *"I think SVC and their cronies are really trying to ruin our day."*

"What do you mean?" Jackson asked.

"They just advanced the container's launch time. It's on the move. It's on the accelerator."

"They don't really take off until they get away from population centers," Tui said as he jammed the pedal to the floor. "We can still catch it."

"That's the hub up there," Jackson pointed out the front window. "Looks like it's got a lot of security."

"Good thing we're not going in that way," Tui said as he turned onto the access road. "You about ready?"

"Almost." Normally he'd be doing this in weightlessness, not bouncing along in the back of a rental vehicle. But with practiced efficiency, Jackson kitted up. He attached the grapple to his wrist mount and checked that it was charged. He tapped his thumb against his palm to activate the adhesive, confirmed it was working, then killed it. Then did the same for his feet. They'd only provide a fraction of the grip here that they would in space, but every bit helped. He checked, and then double-checked that he still had the medallion. Good to go. "This will be just like grabbing it out of orbit."

"Pretty much. Only if you miss this time you'll probably fall under the train. Or I'll drive over you. Try not to fall this way. I'd feel bad if I killed you. That would really stress me out."

"Yeah, I'd sure hate to do that."

Out the side window, Jackson could see a big, rectangular, container starting down the maglev track. It was going relatively slowly. That wouldn't last. They would be parallel for only a short window.

There was a security gate ahead of them, with a big sign saying that this area was off-limits except for accelerator maintenance crews. "Jane, the gate's still closed," Tui said, but they didn't slow down. It was a pretty sturdy-looking gate, and their rental was a lightweight polymer electric commuter vehicle. Hitting it this fast would probably kill them. "Jane? Please?"

The gate started sliding open, but it was moving at ultra-slow speed.

"I don't think we're going to make it," Jackson said.

"We'll make it," Tui replied.

The gate inched its way open like some two-hundred-year-old grandpa was pulling it.

"Tui," Jackson said and put his hand on the ceiling to brace for impact.

And then they shot through the opening, the gate scraping the mirrors of the rental completely off. There was a screech as the gate scraped alongside the car, and then they were through. Jackson glanced back and saw the mirrors tumbling along the road.

"They're going to take your deposit for that," Jackson said.

"*Sorry,*" Jane said. "*I was busy killing alarms and spoofing cameras. The security on this launch track is tight. Tui, the second Jackson's aboard you need to flip around and get out of there if you don't want to get caught.*"

"If it was easy, more people would hijack containers this way," Tui said.

"What are you talking about?" Jackson asked. "This ain't hard. All you need is a super hacker, a giant cargo ship waiting in orbit, and an idiot willing to kamikaze leap from a moving car onto a moving train to ride it into space."

"When you put it that way…"

Outside the Sharmala terraformed zone, Nivaas was a desert of purple-tinged sand and jagged rocks, but thankfully the maintenance road was paved and in good repair, so they could keep this smooth.

They had a good view of the container. It was a big rectangle with a disposable nose cone on the front, and a reusable rocket on the back. It proudly wore the orange and white Splendid Ventures logo, but Jackson still visually confirmed the ID numbers painted on the side, because it was one thing to risk your life to hijack a mech worth millions, rather than a container full of toilet paper or something. Their target had been doing a leisurely 100 kph until it got out of town, but it was already starting to accelerate.

"Pulling alongside," Tui said.

Jackson rolled down his window. "I think I liked plan A better."

"Plan A was the dream. And now you woke up. Go!"

It seemed stupidly dangerous, climbing out the window and onto the roof of a speeding car, but truthfully, he'd done a lot worse. He used Raj's gloves to stick himself to the polymer body of the vehicle, and then pulled himself up and onto the top. He immediately regretted not closing his mask, because some purple sand grit of this planet got him right in the eye. That had been stupid. Luckily, the shaded eye film gave him enough protection that it didn't blind him, but he unstuck one hand to pull up his hood and visor before an insect hit him like a bullet.

Jackson crouched and held on tight as Tui maneuvered them as close as possible. The captain had come up with this last-minute desperation plan by looking at the aerial view and seeing that the access road ran relatively parallel and close to the accelerator track... Except that what looked easy from a few thousand klicks in the sky was a whole lot different on the ground.

The road was *kind* of close, off and on. Except there were enough small veers from side to side that Tui had to keep compensating. So they were swaying from side to side. While the container was on a path of unerring straightness... And going faster and faster.

"Your window is closing, Jackson," Jane warned.

A basic psychological feature of the people chosen to be pilots was that they didn't get too riled up under pressure. Jackson scanned the road ahead and picked what he thought was the best spot. Then he checked the container—which was now pulling past, even though Tui was giving it all they had—and picked his landing zone near the rockets. It wouldn't do any good to stick himself to the container if he wasn't anywhere near an access hatch.

He aimed and launched the grapple. It hit the flat surface of the container and locked on. Monofilament cord reeled out, so thin but strong, it was the galaxy's best fishing line.

Tui veered away, then curved back. They had to be going 150, the container faster. They were closing again. Nearing the best spot. There was a quick, instinctive calculation of speeds and vectors...

The car closed in.

Now was the moment. And Jackson leapt.

The impact was hard. He slapped at the container wall, but Raj didn't stick well. He skidded, then dropped toward the maglev tracks.

Tui hit the brakes and instantly fell behind. He hadn't been kidding about not wanting to run over him.

Jackson dropped another meter, and then the grapple line snapped tight and kept him from falling. It would have ripped his arm from the socket, but Raj's pressure compensator spread out the impact. That sudden cessation of movement enabled him to get one palm stuck down tight. He followed that by getting a toehold.

Jackson looked down, saw that his other foot was dangling centimeters from the maglev track flashing by beneath, and carefully lifted it away. He began to climb, like a fly on a wall. He'd been wrong. This was a *lot* harder in gravity. Space was unforgiving, but it had a few perks.

"Did you make it? Are you alive?"

"Working on it." Though it was nice how Jane sounded genuinely concerned for his safety.

The rear access hatch was locked, obviously. Plus it was an old-fashioned mechanical, so Jane couldn't unlock it for him remotely. It took him a few seconds to get his multitool from the pouch on the outside of his pack, but then he used the plasma cutter to burn the latch. Jane couldn't open this for him, but she could at least jam the alarms his rough methods surely set off.

"I'm in."

CHAPTER 5

Inside the container, all was complete darkness.

Jackson turned on his visor light. It illuminated the interior of the car, casting odd shadows. Down the middle of the car lay the Citadel M750, strapped down tight. About it were stacked Splendid Ventures cargo boxes that had also been tightly secured. It looked like a giant warrior in some tomb on his way to Valhalla, surrounded by mounds of loot. But even with all the loot, there was still enough room for Jackson to move, and more importantly, room for him to move the Citadel.

Jackson was something of a connoisseur of mechs, but there was no time to admire this beauty. Shortly, they'd be in space. Nivaas was a little smaller than Earth. So instead of having to accelerate to twenty-nine thousand kph to get to near-planet orbit, you only needed a little above twenty-five. The accelerator would provide a good portion of that speed. The last chunk would be provided by the rocket. And while the track was about eleven hundred klicks long, at a constant acceleration, it wasn't going to take long to get to the end. The ride now was smooth as glass, though the rocket portion might get bumpy, and he didn't want to be bouncing around in this can.

All he had to do now was free the Citadel, break into it, and figure out how to drive it well enough that he could escape with it during the three-minute window between when the rocket burn ended and the spaceport gremlins hooked up to guide the container to the Splendid Ventures ship. Going too soon most likely meant a fiery death. Exiting too late and working too slow meant capture by the port authorities.

Right now, the constant acceleration was causing just over two Gs. It was real pressure, but below that of most roller coasters, nothing Raj couldn't compensate for. They'd start climbing soon—Nivaas had some truly epic mountain ranges—and it would get worse. Being at the bottom of the car was a precarious place. If any of the cargo busted loose, he'd be bludgeoned or squashed.

"How are we doing, Jane?"

"*I stomped on the alarms. Nobody saw you. Tui is on his way to the port.*"

"Good. I'm going to try and unlock the Citadel. Change my ID again, please."

"*Congratulations. You are now Dwight Oaks, mech pilot at Splendid Ventures. Like most fighter jocks you are extremely well compensated for your talents, but you secretly suffer crippling self-doubt, which you hide behind a veneer of cockiness.*"

"Poor Dwight. I kind of like being the priest with the butterflies more."

"*What makes you think I was talking about Dwight?*"

Jackson laughed as he climbed up the sleeping mech. "Danger close, Jane."

It was truly impressive up close. It was the first time he'd ever seen a fifth-generation mech in person. This was by far the nicest machine he'd ever seen, let alone stolen.

When turned on, the Citadel was programmed to hook up to the nearest communications link and send its owners its coordinates and a notification that it was in use. Hopefully Jane would be able to block that until he could get it manually shut off. Otherwise this would be a really short trip. Jackson climbed up the sleeping giant until he was next to the cockpit, which took up a big chunk of the chest cavity. He took the medallion out and held it up to where the access reader was embedded. A light on the cockpit flashed. The Citadel pinged his personal embedded ID chip. He waited. And waited.

"Come on."

And then the Citadel said, "Passphrase."

Jackson smiled. "My monkey's uncle." Thank you very much, Dwight.

"Access granted." The canopy opened. A puff of pressurized air escaped.

Okay, so he knew he could get in, he just couldn't do it yet. He still needed to cut the Citadel free. It was so powerful, it could probably easily rip itself free of its tethers, and then punch its way through the walls. But if he damaged the container at all, SVC would see that immediately. Ideally, the more time it took them to realize they'd been robbed, the more time the *Tar Heel* had to make its escape.

"Jackson, you're three minutes from rocket burn."

He felt the car rise vertically. The Gs increased slightly. He checked once more to make sure everything on him was secure, then set the timer in his display to three minutes. This was going to get really uncomfortable, really fast.

The Citadel was secured with six straps that locked to the brackets in the floor. Using the plasma cutter on his multitool, he sliced the first strap holding the legs. Then the second. He worked methodically, but the problem with a compact tool with that much power was a lack of juice, and he'd already used a bunch cutting the lock. And so when the blue arc died partway through the second strap, he extended the diamond saw blade and started working on the strap the old-fashioned way. He finished cutting through the third strap and moved to the fourth.

And not a centimeter in, the blade snapped in half. He held up the now useless tool in his hand and looked at it.

Unbelievable.

The seconds ticked down. There was no time for dismay. He got his regular folding knife from out of his pack, and began to saw, but the straps were made of tough material. He put as much pressure into it as possible, but the straps defied the normal steel blade. The timer dropped below two minutes.

"Fifi," he said and pointed to where he'd been sawing with little effect. "I need you to slice through this. Pronto."

Fifi crawled out of Raj, sprang to the strap, and began her work.

"Follow the scoring of my knife," Jackson said, then moved to the next strap and began sawing again. This was unbelievable. The seconds counted down. Fifi finished her strap.

"Here, Fifi. Cut here!" Jackson said and pointed at the fifth strap. Fifi jumped and worked. Jackson moved to the last strap.

He was getting dizzy and realized the container had climbed enough that he wasn't getting adequate air, so Jackson pulled on his mask and clicked it to his hood.

They reached one-minute-forty, then thirty, then twenty-five. He directed Fifi to the next strap and hoped that the religious members of the crew were praying for him.

The clock ticked to sixty seconds and then rolled to fifty-nine. Fifi finished cutting through the last strap. "Good girl, Fifi. Get back!"

Fifi sprang back to the pack.

The Gs increased again. Moving was getting really hard, even with Raj squeezing the blood from his extremities and back to his brain. Then there was a low pop at the end of the launch tube as the rocket motor started its initiation sequence.

He looked at the Citadel. It was time to drive.

Jackson pulled the canopy wide. Inside the controls glowed, blue and green. It was a fairly standard setup—seat, controls, pedals, displays, levers, switches. Though there were a few icons and buttons he didn't know, he recognized enough of them. He slid into the chair and buckled himself in. It still had that new-mech smell.

A trembling anticipation ran through him. There were two ways to drive a mech. One was with manual controls, stick and voice. That's how the vast majority of people did it. With enough practice, one could become very smooth. Or at least as smooth as anyone who learned to drive complex, heavy equipment.

But the second way to drive a mech—the *real* way—was to connect it directly to your brain and make it a part of you. That's when the mech sang. And the pilot sang with it.

The difference in effectiveness between the two methods was astounding. One made for a lumbering, clumsy, walking tank... which was still pretty darned effective. But the other made it into a supernaturally responsive, quick-handling death machine. The problem was only a tiny handful of humanity had the natural gifts to do so.

But there would be no merge for him today. Or ever. Jackson was never going to jack anything into his brain again, wired or wireless. He didn't dare.

"Close canopy."

The canopy began to close.

"Full power."

The Citadel powered up.

Memories of first soaring in an old Thunderbolt, the mech he'd wielded in the war on Gloss, his home planet, rose in his mind. Along with it came an echo of the artificial joy he'd been flooded with during those days. The craving ran along Jackson's bones. A part of him still yearned for that mad euphoria, and always would. He ignored that part and locked the skeleton frame around his arms and legs.

The sensors would read his nerve impulses and muscle twitches, then translate those into mechanical movements. It was sort of like driving if you were driving four cars simultaneously. He scanned the status of the Citadel's systems. They were all a go.

Jackson worked the controls, engaged the skeleton, and rose. Or at least his tiny movements against the skeleton mimicked rising in a truncated way, and the Citadel's computer extrapolated the rest. His wishes were transformed into mechanical exertion, and the Citadel rose like a wrathful demi-god.

"Whoa." This thing was *smooth*.

The timer was counting down. The rocket was about to go off. Since the Citadel was unstrapped, he needed to brace himself and hold on. Mechs were sort of man-shaped, two arms, two legs, because it turned out when you hooked your brain directly into a machine, that was intuitive. By stick, however, it still took some getting used to, and since Jackson exerted a bit too much pressure, the Citadel's fist smashed a crate flat. On the bright side, whatever was stored in there turned out not to be explosive. Jackson crouched and pushed the mech's palms against both sides of the container. Carefully. Because Jackson didn't want to knock a big obvious hole in the side. He clicked the skeleton to lock it in that position, perfectly still.

The rocket ignited with a mighty roar. The force crushed Jackson back into the seat, but Raj kept him conscious. For this part all he could do was hold on.

The container blasted through the atmosphere. Jackson passed that time using his eyes to flip through the Citadel's menus until he could figure out how to shut off the signal beacons and go dark.

This thing was impressive. It had active camo skin over a layer of non-Newtonian fluid armor that could take hits from a tank's main gun. Jackson pulled up the power plant, and grinned when he saw that it was a thorium reactor putting out numbers sufficient to light a small city. He kept flipping tabs. The computer was powerful—but not an actual AI, because mankind had learned the hard way about sticking those in combat machines. The sensor suite was the best he'd ever seen. And the weapons...so many weapons...Most of those were unloaded for safe shipping, but Jackson knew they had most of these munitions available on the *Tar Heel,* because the captain prided himself in being the one-stop shop in illegal gun running.

This was a nice mech. It wasn't just the big things, but also the little touches. Everything in front of him turned into a display. This thing had no blind spots. The Citadel's cockpit was so insulated that even though he was riding in an unaerodynamic brick on the end of a massive solid-fuel rocket, it was quiet. The liquid armor layer made such an effective shock absorber that the only reason he knew the container was shaking so violently was because the sensors told him so.

The rocket blast and thrumming vibration of the car suddenly stopped. The pressure lessened, and all was silent. That was his signal. They'd reached space. Jackson closed the Citadel's status tabs and started a new three-minute timer on his display.

That was how long containers usually coasted between their rockets stopping before the robotic gremlins that controlled orbital traffic took over to steer them to their final destination. Nivaas commerce ran on a very tight schedule.

Jackson unlocked the Citadel's limbs, and very gently moved toward the main door. Since Jane had squashed the alarms, he pulled up the manual override. The instructions for accessing it were in his visual. He brought up the access screen and punched in the maintenance codes Jane had found. The wall in front of him flashed "You are now on override" while a male voice repeated the message.

"I'm ready to move, Jane. How are we doing on blind spots?" If someone was looking in their direction, there really was no such thing as stealth in space.

"*There's Taco Control, the SVC Profit, and two gremlins with eyes on the container now. I'll do what I can to confuse and divert. There's a lot of cargo moving fast right now, so I'm going to send you a very specific trajectory navigation worked up to minimize exposure. Stay between the cars. Hopefully nobody will get a good look at you and just think your heat signature was just debris.*"

"Debris from what?"

"*The explosion. But don't worry about that. The captain's just had to adjust plans again.*"

Jackson sighed. There was a human-sized locking lever on the door. It looked tiny beneath one of the Citadel's fingers, but Jackson managed to turn it without snapping it off. The doors made a satisfying snick, indicating they had unlocked, and then they began to open. There was a sudden whistle and whoosh as the remaining air inside the car blasted into space. Small bits of grit flew out with it into the starry blackness. That pressure change was enough to move the Splendid Ventures car off course. And the port watchers would note it.

Jackson grabbed the lip of the cargo bay with the Citadel's hands and felt it through the pressure of the skeleton. He wasn't totally in synch with this machine, but it was close enough, and he clambered out of the cargo car and squatted just forward of the bay doors.

The clock was down to twenty-nine seconds when he got the path from Jane. He opened the door. Below was Nivaas. Half of it gleamed in the sunlight, purple and green. The other half lay in shadow. In the opposite direction the spaceport shone no bigger than a star. He was now down to twenty-three seconds.

There was a lot of traffic up here, but none of what was nearby was manned. Most of it was accelerator containers awaiting their pickups. He floated away from the car, gently reclosed the door, engaged the small thrusters in the legs and arms to orient the Citadel, then hit the main thruster to shoot away, back toward Nivaas, back toward the next car that had been launched from the accelerator. It was close and coming fast, shining in the sun.

If their navigator was right, the container he'd just bailed out of would block the SVC ship's view, and the new container would conceal him from accelerator command.

A bipedal tank wasn't exactly aerodynamic, but in this environment, that was irrelevant. The clock ticked down. Twenty-one seconds. Twenty. Nineteen. The gremlins would have eyes on him soon. Jackson juiced his thrusters, zoomed toward the car, and then blinked at the display.

A warning light began to flash. "Collision imminent," the Citadel said.

Dwight must have liked to play it safe, but then again, he

wasn't the one writing the checks. Jackson pulled up the settings menu with his eye and cut the danger radius by ninety percent. "Drive it like you stole it," he muttered. Advice to live by.

Still, he juiced the thrusters just enough to move out of the way. Suddenly the oncoming container's rocket engine did an emergency burst and it began to veer off course. At first, Jackson wondered if this was some treachery, but then realized the car must have sensed the collision as well, but because Jackson was jamming the Citadel, the two vehicles weren't able to communicate.

Holy hell! He was going to hit it!

Instead of secretly transferring the goods, Jackson was going to crash them. He opened up all his thrusters at ninety degrees to his current direction. They flashed, shooting out long tails of propellant.

The container was still emergency firing, this time in an opposite direction, but Jackson didn't know if his response would be enough. Jackson flattened himself, causing the Citadel to squeeze its arms tight against its body. It probably looked something like a really big skydiver going for speed. The container flashed past, with hardly any distance between them.

Relief washed through him. And then worry. He'd just created a lot of heat. Were they going to pick that up?

But that turned out to be nothing compared to the massive explosion that ripped the Splendid Venture's container apart. Warnings lit up all over his screens as the rocket went up. Nothing was left of the Citadel's container but an expanding cloud of gas and shrapnel.

Jane must have remotely caused some major system to fail and had just created one heck of a mess for the gremlins and port control.

He also saw he was well past his window. Seven seconds, eight, nine, and counting. With luck, those gremlins' cameras were really distracted right now. It wasn't too unusual for a rocket to pop, and then their biggest priority became steering the big bits back into the gravity well in a way that they'd burn up entirely, or on a trajectory that would put them into the ocean, then policing up all the garbage they could before it damaged any other containers, ships, or satellites.

After that suspicious explosion, Jane had gone radio silent. The *Tar Heel* couldn't risk sending any transmission out this way without drawing attention to themselves.

Jackson's only hope was to stick to the path given him. At least she'd let him get out of the blast radius first. He kept flying, ping-ponging his way between the ascending and waiting containers. Originally, Grandma had pulled some strings so one of their cargo containers was supposed to have been the car in line behind the one for Splendid Ventures, but that was before the Citadel had been bumped up in the queue. He got a sinking feeling in his stomach. Had the police on-planet stopped it?

He needed some options and quick. He could just turn around and fly into port. Maybe wave hello as he zoomed past the authorities. They would surely love that.

Or he could change his vector, and float farther out into space and hope the *Tar Heel* picked him up, but regulations required the citizens of Nivaas to keep their orbital lanes clean of debris. They had deployed a huge fleet of garbage collecting bots to do so. One of them would certainly spot him long before the crew came to his rescue.

He could go back to Nivaas. The Citadel was drop capable and would have no problem surviving re-entry, but air traffic control would track him and quickly find out he'd stolen the machine. There would be tons of security waiting for him when he landed.

"Come on, Jane. Give me a sign..." But he didn't dare actually transmit that, because then port control would for sure know he wasn't debris. He cursed.

Then something winked in the sunlight between him and the planet. He zoomed in and confirmed it was another cargo car. This one was white, with a fat, red diagonal stripe running down the side.

"Ha!" That was one of theirs. Somehow—either Jane's technical skills or Grandma's bribery—they'd gotten it bumped up in the launch queue too. Now he just had to hope that the port jockeys were distracted and that his little dance with the previous car had gone unnoticed. Each time he was hidden by a car, he reversed thrust to slow his approach.

As he approached the *Tar Heel* container, the Citadel understood his subtle motions and effortlessly grappled on. Nice and easy. No sudden snap. Jackson was super impressed. This was one nice mech.

Twenty seconds after that he was right above the car, matching speed. He reeled in the grapple until he could latch on. Even though they were going orders of magnitude faster, it was far easier than the first time he'd hopped a train today. He hugged the Citadel close to the body, and hoped that even as big as it was, it wouldn't change the car's radar signature that much.

"Activate camo." It took a few seconds to adjust the tones, but the Citadel gradually turned white and red. At least visually it would look like a bulbous growth on the outside of the cargo container until the camera got really close.

He looked toward the port and could actually make out ships waiting there. This was way too close.

He was so exposed. So far outside his window. He sent a contact signal through the skin of the Citadel ordering the doors to open. For a moment, nothing happened, and he began to worry something was wrong, but then the doors slowly unsealed. There was no burst of air to cause a change in course. Captain Holloway was way too smart for that. He waited, waited, couldn't wait another second and then crawled the Citadel into its new tomb a bit too fast. Its rounded head hit the roof hard enough to dent it. The car shuddered. The Citadel barely bounced.

He sent the remote signal for the doors to close and lock behind him, and then laid the Citadel to rest on the floor of the empty container. He engaged the magnetics to stick it in place.

Now came the nervous part where he could do nothing but wait for everyone else to do their jobs.

It would be chaos out there right now. Accelerator failures were rare, but they happened. People would be angry. SVC leadership would freak out when they discovered their very expensive mech had just been obliterated. There were surely a bunch of cops, insurance agents, and accident investigators getting emergency calls right now.

That was fine. Provided Jane was right, and nobody had seen him fly out, he'd be clear. All he had to do was sit here until the port started moving containers again. Nivaas was a thriving settlement with massive amounts of trade, so they'd want to clear the lanes fast. There were dozens of freighters big or bigger than the *Tar Heel* waiting their turn, and time was money. He just needed to kill time. It could take hours. It could take days.

Jackson checked the Citadel's air tanks and discovered that the emergency scrubber system for resisting nuclear, biological, or chemical attacks, which could recycle a single tank for days, was working ... Except it hadn't been outfitted with any extra air tanks for extended use out of atmosphere at all.

Wow ... Better hope for hours rather than days then.

Jackson shut down Raj's air supply so he could save it for later. Then he told the Citadel to turn its supply to the absolute minimum for human survival and set an alarm for when its supply was running low ... Just in case he fell asleep.

That habit had stuck from his military service. Sleep when you can because you don't know what's going to happen next. Mech pilots had to have ice water in their veins or they didn't survive. So it didn't take Jackson long to come down off the adrenaline rush, and about a half an hour after that for the after shakes to stop. Then he took a nap.

He was woken up, not by the air alarm, but by the sensor warning him that the container was being moved. The cargo gremlins must have grabbed them.

The air alarm wasn't due to go off for ... Jackson glanced over ... Three more minutes. Yay. He'd have to switch to Raj and hope for the best. Come to think of it, if the captain ever used this type of scam again, instead of an empty container they should fill it with air tanks, beer, and snacks.

But they were moving, which was good. Gremlins were bots designed to latch onto containers and take them in an orderly fashion to the various ships waiting in their lanes around the spaceport.

There were two ways this could go for him. They were delivering him to the *Tar Heel* or they were delivering him to the cops ... Well, three possibilities actually, as he tapped Raj's air gauge and saw he had about an hour to live.

Well, probably a bit longer. The Citadel's scrubbers would keep recycling smaller and smaller amounts of useable air. He already had it turned down to where he was dull-witted and sleepy. He could probably go all the way to coma and stretch it out even longer. The next nap he took he might not wake up from. Not seeing much choice, he lowered the oxygen supply into the orange zone. If he lived, hopefully he wouldn't have too much brain damage.

A minute ticked by and then two. His fingers were tingling. The gremlins altered the speed and direction of the container again. He flipped to the port channel and heard the normal radio traffic. Of course, if the port police were bringing him in, they might be using some other encrypted communication line. He didn't risk an active scan of the surroundings to figure out where he was, because someone might detect that.

He waited, sleepy, as the container decelerated. There were a series of thumps as the gremlins detached. There was some bumping, more movement, and then the car came to rest.

Jackson must have faded back out, because when he came to, someone was knocking on the Citadel's canopy.

CHAPTER 6

Jackson popped the Citadel's hatch. The people floating around the container weren't wearing helmets, so Jackson removed the front of his mask. Breathable air rushed in. He took a few quick lungfuls, happy to see familiar faces. He was home.

The *Tar Heel*'s cargomaster, Garrick Hilker, knitted his brows as he checked the air gauge and said, "What were you doing on the way up? Aerobics?"

Jackson shook his head. Things were still a bit blurry. "How long was I out there?"

"You've been parked in this box about four hours."

"Well, at least we know this thing has one really good oxygen scrubber." Jackson patted the Citadel's control panel affectionately. It was funny, nothing made you more fond of a machine than having it save your life. Too bad the captain wouldn't let him keep it. "Are we in the clear?"

"You know the drill." Like the majority of the crew's long-timers, Hilker was another Earther. The first people the captain had hired had all been from his home country. Their no-nonsense cargomaster was originally from one of their farming provinces... Iowa or something. "We're never clear until the package is delivered, we have our cash, and we're out of that system. But so far there's been nothing from port security. It looks like they're treating it as an accident."

Good. That meant the cargo-jumping acrobatics had worked.

As far as Nivaas was concerned, the *Tar Heel* was just one more unremarkable freighter among a legion of unremarkable freighters. He was feeling better already, but his hands were too clumsy to unbuckle the harness. "Give me a hand here?"

Hilker did, probably not because he gave a damn about Jackson, but because he couldn't stash and secure his precious cargo with a human being still in it. "However, you've got trouble topside."

Jackson thought about the captain, about Jane, and then knew who was mad at him. "Grandma."

"You'll especially have trouble if you call Shade that to her face. She's pissed about, let's see, how did she put it? 'Your profligate ways.'"

"Profligate?"

"It means wasteful, I think."

"I know." Free from the harness, Jackson extricated himself from the cockpit and floated out into the container. Through the open door he could see they were attached to the *Tar Heel*'s massive interior cargo bay. With bots and lifters the bay boys immediately began to secure the mech. Even as big as it was, they'd quickly get it moved and hidden amongst their legitimate merchandise. Hilker was an artist when it came to hiding contraband.

"Now get to decon before you kill us all."

Hilker wasn't trying to be rude. That was just ship policy. Different planets had different breeds of bacteria, virus, fugus, and parasites. Nivaas was supposed to be pretty clean, but if you could avoid an outbreak of some strange bug onboard your ship that was always a nice thing. They were already spraying down the Citadel and one of Jane's little bots was zipping around scanning for fleas, not the literal bugs, but the smaller cousins to Fifi, bots that could be used for spying, sabotage, or even assassination. Normal ship's decons didn't look for such things, but this crew wasn't normal, and they certainly didn't run in normal crowds. Jane's bot darted back and forth, checking him out.

When he was cleared, he pushed away from the flea zapper, and went to the portable decon box. He shucked Raj and underclothing and put them in the containment bag Hilker provided. That would all get scanned and irradiated. Then he pulled himself into the vacuum shower. There was a blower tube at one end. In the middle was a flexible hose with a gentle, disease-murdering spray. At the other end was a grate and a vacuum tube. It was basically a wet wind tunnel. No matter how many hundreds of times he'd done it, Jackson still found showering in zero G weird, with the vacuum sucking in the myriad floating and bouncing balls of water, large and small. When he finished, he wiped down, turned it off, and pulled himself out of the tube. He was spaceman Jack again. Spic and span.

Hilker handed him a clean jumpsuit and the customary pill everyone took after being planetside, which Jackson suspected didn't do much, but he swallowed it anyway. None of his embedded medical sensors had caught anything, but the drug would supposedly help his sensors trace burgeoning foreign bodies.

Jackson shoved off and out into the main bay. Up above he saw a familiar face. From the look of things, Tui had just got out of decon himself.

"Glad to see you're still alive, bro."

"Glad to see you didn't get arrested."

"Just barely got here." Then Tui shouted so Hilker could hear him. "Hurry up and lock that thing down. Captain's waiting."

"Working on it, Chief," the cargomaster answered.

Jackson took his time getting across the bay because he was still feeling dizzy and kind of out of it. Not that he liked to admit such things, but that had been cutting it way too close.

"You're looking rough," Tui said when he got close. "Bad flight?"

"The Citadel didn't have any extra oxygen stowed."

Tui grimaced. "Ouch."

As soon as Hilker's men finished securing the Citadel, they raced each other back across the bay, pushing off or pulling along whatever handrail or storage racking they could find, trying to win. Rodrick Su, the smallest of the crew, suddenly caught up with one of the bigger ones, climbed along his back, planted his feet on his shoulders, and shoved. Su went zooming ahead, stealing some of the big man's acceleration.

But zero G didn't mean zero mass. Su glanced back to gloat and struck a post, which caused him to careen away in a wild spin.

"Jackasses," Hilker muttered.

Su cartwheeled through the air. He was going to strike his head against one of the storage struts, and wasn't wearing a safety helmet. Jackson sprang to help him, already knowing he was too far away.

But Tui shot down like a bird of prey snagging another bird

in flight. He grabbed Su's arm. The man's velocity pulled Tui off course. A lesser spacer might have tumbled out of control and hit the wall, but Tui, with his abnormal strength, caught himself on a perpendicular stack of shipping crates, swung Su around in a decelerating arc, and released him on a corrected and straight line for the exit.

Su floated past Jackson at a safe speed, giving him a salute as his passed by.

"One more like that," Tui called after Su, "and I'm going to let you select yourself out of the gene pool."

"Thanks, Chief!" Su called back.

Tui sprang back to where Jackson was, caught a handrail and steadied himself.

"One of these days," Jackson said, "I'm getting me a set of your monkey mods."

"It's going to take more than that to compete with me, bro. My power comes from good, clean living."

Which was probably true. All Tui did for fun was exercise, and he didn't have any bad habits that anyone on the crew knew of. "Yeah, yeah. Are we done?"

Tui looked to Hilker, who gave a thumbs-up. "We're good. Time to move."

The *Tar Heel* was a Multipurpose Supply Vehicle, which was an old Earth War designation for a really big transport. It was in the standard configuration, with the propulsion system in the stern, the habitat ring fore, and everything else dedicated to cargo. The long central cargo space they were in now felt like a monstrous warehouse. Containers could be attached all over the exterior as well, but those were exposed to micrometeorite hits and depressurization. For some things that was acceptable, but everything else went inside where it was climate controlled and *relatively* safe. Sometimes the cargo was alive. Shade had, on occasion, brokered transportation of rare and illegal fauna from various worlds. But it wasn't just the living stuff that needed protection. Their bread and butter was smuggling munitions, and nobody wanted an XG missile or a container of bombs getting hit by a fast-flying projectile.

Jackson and Tui jump-zoomed their way to the hatch and entered the tube exchange, which was a section of the ship that could spin independently of the habitat ring. The exchange allowed you to go from spin to stationary and vice versa. Currently the ring was stationary, so they floated right down the corridor to the hub. From there they could enter any of the five spokes of the habitat ring.

When they reached the hub, they entered the spoke that led up to the main living area, stepped onto the lift, and stuck on. Once they were set, they activated the lift and accelerated along the spoke, which was a little over one hundred meters long. The diameter of the whole habitat ring was double that, about two hundred and twenty-five meters, which meant the circumference of the outer ring was just over half a klick wide.

These old Earth War transports had stuffed the ring with long barracks for transporting troops. Only, the captain had served his time and never wanted to be in the business of driving a bus for large numbers of people ever again. There were now only about a hundred crew members total, living in a ship that had been originally designed to hold thousands. Some of the barracks had been converted to more comfortable living space, some to special cargo space that needed a semblance of gravity.

The lift accelerated, cruised for a bit, then began to decelerate. It brought them to a stop at the ring. The smell of food was in the air.

"Sweet. It's almost chow time," Tui said.

"We're not in the clear yet," Jackson warned.

"Yeah, but even if the captain calls battle stations and we make a run for it, it isn't like my guys have anything to do until we get boarded or the place catches on fire. So until then, food. Bummer you have to go report first."

"And explain how I almost blew the entire op because I ran into a dirtbag with a good memory and his dog? Fun. Save me some, would you?"

"I'll do my best."

And so they split, Tui going one way, Jackson push-floating away in the other direction.

"Captain?" he pinged.

"On the bridge," Captain Holloway replied.

The corridor wrapped around the whole ring, an unending walk. It was three meters wide. Large enough to allow quick movement of lots of people. Little ports dotted the wall of the eternal corridor, allowing you to look out at the stars or switch to one of the many stationary camera views.

Jackson went to one of the portals and clicked for an area image. It appeared they were traveling at a leisurely speed away from the port. Ships couldn't use their main drives this close to a planet, something about the gravity well. The actual math was way over his head, but Jackson guessed they had another five or ten minutes at this speed before they could kick it into high gear. He switched to an image of the port. The gigantic Splendid Ventures ship, *Profit,* was still docked, but there weren't any flashing lights there. Or really anywhere around the port.

He pushed on and floated down the corridor. It was punctuated every ten meters by extra-wide doors. In case of an emergency, the doors would automatically shut to seal that section off, for things like depressurization or fire, although in the three years he'd spent on the *Tar Heel* he'd only ever seen them activated to contain living things. Like one trip when someone had screwed up the sedative for a Kodiak bear they were hauling. It woke up angry and hungry, smelled food of the human variety, and blundered into the ring. Or the time some moronic Caliman terrorists had tried to hijack them. Good times.

The bridge door was open, and Jackson swung in. The displays were monitoring traffic between the port and the SVC ship. The crew manning the consoles looked a little tense. From the looks some of them gave him, Jackson knew the mood was his fault.

The commander's station was typical of an old Earth ship, plastic and stainless steel, however, Captain Holloway had spruced it up with a small red, white, blue, and gold flag of North Carolina on one wall. Below the flag was a plaque with the phrase "c."

The captain had activated the mag lock on his boots, and he was standing there, hands clasped behind his back, watching the camera feeds carefully. He was unaugmented Earth standard fifties, bald, with a scruffy beard. He glanced over when Jackson floated in.

"How was the ride, Mr. Rook?"

"The Citadel is awesome," Jackson said. "Are you sure we can't keep it?"

"You miss it much?"

He was referring to the full connection, the plug into the skull, the thing that had turned Jackson into a monster, the thing he'd been saved from. "No, sir. Not in the least."

The captain nodded. He knew what Jackson had been, because he had been the one to go into that hell, get Jackson, and take him to Jane, so she could save his soul. "And to think you almost didn't get to make that test drive."

"Sometimes you have to improvise."

"Did you have to stir up the whole planet in the process?" a woman said from behind him.

Jackson glanced over to see that their broker had entered the bridge after him. "No, Shade, I didn't. That was Jeet Prunkard's doing. Not mine."

The name on her passport was Julie Thomas—whether that was her real name, none of them knew—but Shade had stuck, and she liked it that way. Nobody called her Ms. Thomas, or Julie. She wasn't nearly approachable enough for that level of familiarity. Some of the crew referred to her as Grandma, but only behind her back. Not because she looked like any kind of grandma. In fact, just the opposite. She had dark eyes, smooth skin, and currently had a suicide blonde thing going on, her hair pale, and standing up on end in the weightless environment. The codename Grandma came from the fact that she was probably the oldest person on the crew. But she'd had so many genetic mods and upgrades that nobody knew for sure if she was fifty, sixty, or pushing eighty.

Those kinds of therapies were expensive, so she must have been money once, or come from one of the worlds rich enough that sort of thing wasn't a big deal. Which planet? None of the crew knew that either. From her condescending attitude they assumed it had to be one of the wealthier of the thirty worlds. Nor did they know much of anything about her except that she had contacts on seemingly every colony and station, arranged their deals, and was one of the only people who could actually sway the captain's opinion on anything.

Shade asked, "Do you think you can do one op where something doesn't go to pieces?"

Jackson held out his hands apologetically. "How was I supposed to know Prunkard was going to be there? And you're the reason Prunkard even knew who I was to begin with."

"He's got a point," the captain said.

"You should have just slipped away."

"Easy for you to say. You ever try to outrun a hornet's nest?"

"Yes—I have in fact." Shade gave him a very patronizing grin. "Only I wouldn't have needed to because they never would have seen me to begin with. Sadly, I subcontracted you lot to do it for me. My mistake. My clients hire this ship to supply them because they require discretion. You know who that Citadel is for. He can't afford that kind of attention."

"Well, that sucks for him."

"I like you, Jack, but you're too damn expensive."

Which meant she would hang Jackson out to dry.

"Listen, Shade, my job is to fly the mechs we liberate. I'm not a spy or whatever it is you used to be in your old glory days. I did the pickpocket job because the captain ordered me to. I'm assuming he figured I'd be good at it."

"He's pretty decent at that whole sleight-of-hand thing," the captain admitted.

"That's because of where I grew up," Jackson said. "Kids either learned how to steal or starve."

The captain snorted. "And this whole time I just figured you were practicing for a lucrative career as a stage magician."

Jackson turned back to Shade. "I didn't ask to go down there and get chased by a mobster you decided to steal from in the first place. I got away. We adapted. We overcame. I was the one out there risking my ass while you were up here safe, yet somehow you get a bigger share than I do."

"The only reason there are shares at all is because of the deals I cut," Shade snapped. "Get it through your head, Jackson, you're hired help."

The captain gave Jackson a sideways glance and shook his head.

He didn't want to let it go, but he did, out of respect for his boss, mentor, and friend. "We got the goods. We're good."

"Not quite yet." The captain nodded at the display. "There's a Nivaas security cutter shadowing us still. Hopefully, he's just giving us the eyeball. Any activity from the SVC ship yet, Ms. Alligood?"

"Nothing, Cap." Their electronic warfare tech was hunched over a console, watching for any sign of trouble. "They still think they've got the right container as far as I can tell. No alarms. No chatter. Gate control has us marked as a regular law-abiding trader."

Jackson blew out a breath, then looked at the wall display

showing the area around the *Tar Heel*. The spaceport was marked with green. Smaller dots were the gremlins and transport cars coming up from the surface. There were also red triangles representing security ships. There were several of them nearby.

Nivaas was still a relatively new settlement, but everyone made enemies. Potential hostiles could still lob projectiles from millions of klicks away. If the target was mobile and could detect such things, there was time to evade. If you were stationary, or traveling in a consistent orbit, you could be in big trouble. So the security for a planet and its orbitals usually extended a few hundred thousand klicks into space. A prosperous planet would have an array of thousands of sentinels in a grid to track ships and relay information. Nivaas only had a few dozen, but their defensive measures were integrated with a couple of beefy installations on Nivaas' moon and some of the larger asteroids.

Which meant that there was no way in hell their old, lumbering beast of a ship could make a run for it successfully.

"You think they're onto us?" Shade asked.

"I don't know. Jane covered our tracks. Even if they do figure out they got robbed, there's a hundred and eighty other ships in range that could have snagged it." Captain Holloway walked back to his chair and retrieved his thermos of coffee, his magnetic boots clanking as he went. "We'll find out if they're suspicious of us in particular when they light up their railguns and send a line of steel cutters to shave the thrusters off our hind end."

"I really wish you hadn't used that mafia Shine," Shade muttered.

"Hm. Shine or get caught? Such a hard decision. Were you wanting me to get caught?"

She glared at him. Him getting caught was better than all of them getting caught, but that went unsaid.

"Ditching you might have saved us some money on the books, but, no, I didn't want you to get caught. Because if you did, their forensic techs would discover that they were dealing with well-supplied professionals, instead of some common street gang."

"I'm overwhelmed with your concern for my safety."

Jackson had a strong urge to bring up his recording and review the facts of the situation with her, but knew now wasn't the time. Later, they'd rerun the video and see. He was confident there had been nothing else he could have done. "What about Prunkard alerting them?"

"The rest of us should be fine. I don't think he ever found out who you were working for when you robbed him. You, however, I'd advise you not to plan any vacations on Nivaas anytime soon." The captain sounded genuinely amused by that. "Regardless, Jeet's a little occupied right now, what with Jane sending over a fake warrant saying that he's wanted on Earth for terrorism and whatnot."

"Couldn't happen to a nicer guy. Well, despite a few wrinkles, the good news is that you now have this." Jackson pulled out the Citadel's medallion and held it out to Shade. She took it and nodded.

"Don't count on Prunkard being out, though," the captain said. "He's got money and lawyers. He'll get it sorted, and if you thought he hated you before, now he's really going to hate you. Speaking of which, Alligood, put up that shot we got of Prunkard's ship."

Another freighter appeared on their display. The CSS *Downward Spiral* was from the same class as the *Tar Heel*, but a lot newer, and flying under the Caliman flag, which meant basically nothing because anybody who could afford the bribe could register with them. From the nominal readings on the display, it was hanging back, far outside Nivaas security's jurisdiction. Prunkard must have taken a smaller vessel down to the surface.

"Q ship?" Jackson asked.

"Total sleeper. I'd bet my life on it."

"Well, you do know a thing or two about making a mean ship look harmless."

"I wrote the book on it." And the captain wasn't joking. He literally had authored the manual Earth Block Navy used on the subject. "I've got no idea what that pirate is doing here, but I'm sure it's something nefarious. If we didn't have a delivery to make, I'd try to find out what he's here to steal, so I could steal it first."

Alligood interrupted their captain's musings about their potential nemesis slash business competitor. "Port Control is signaling us."

"What now?" He sighed. "Put them through."

"*MSV* Tar Heel. *You have been picked for random inspection. Please reduce speed and prepare for boarding.*"

He looked at Shade and spread his hands apologetically. As a privately registered trader, not flying under anyone's flag, there was no legal way to turn them down.

"Tar Heel," the port controller repeated. "*Do you copy?*"

The captain responded, "Roger that, Port. *Tar Heel* is halting progress." He punched a few buttons to kill the feed. "Random, my ass." Then he turned on the ship's intercom. "Prepare for jackdaw. This is not a drill. Prepare for jackdaw."

There was no way they could escape. Their ship was far more capable than it looked, but there was no way they could engage a planetary defense force in battle and survive. Score lots of hits maybe, but then die horribly. So they couldn't win a fight, but at the same time, it was much harder to convict you if you didn't have any stolen goods in your possession. Jackdaw meant jettisoning their containers, including those with the most damning contraband. Shoot them out like rockets. Send them hurtling toward the planet's atmosphere where hopefully the really illegal stuff burned up before it could be retrieved as evidence. It was the high-tech version of a junkie tossing their stash out the window when their car got pulled over by the police. There was a fine for jettisoning cargo close to a port, but better to pay a fine than go to prison.

"Damn it," Jackson muttered. He'd got shot at, hornet stung, and nearly asphyxiated for nothing. No Citadel and no munitions meant no big payoff. The crew wouldn't just lose out on their shares of the smuggling, but worse, they couldn't just dump the illicit stuff and keep the legal cargo. That would be too suspicious. Jackdaw meant dumping the whole bay, and then blaming it on an industrial accident.

"That's a lot of valuable tonnage," Shade said.

"Sorry, Shade. This ship is my life savings, and its crew are my responsibility."

"This is Hilker. Cargo bay standing by. Say the word, Cap and the good people of Nivaas will have quite the meteor shower."

"The client is going to be very upset if we burn that Citadel," Shade warned.

"He can leave me a bad review," the captain said. "I'm too pretty for jail."

"Do you know how long I worked to set this deal up?"

"Time to call in your favors then."

"I work deals, not miracles." But she brought up her assistant and began speaking to it in hushed tones, obviously trying to send a message to whoever it was Shade had inside the provincial government.

Jackson closed his eyes. So much for this operation. He wondered what Nivaasian prisons were like. On the display, the port was sending them new trajectory information, herding them out of the regular traffic lanes. A cutter was inbound. ETA, two minutes.

"Shade?" the captain asked.

Shade held up a finger for him to be quiet. Then everyone on the bridge got to hear her half of the conversation.

"Simon, it's me. What's going on?" There was a pause. "I don't care about some container explosion, I've got a schedule to keep." Another pause. "If this ship is boarded then I'd have no choice but to release the records of every transaction we've conducted over the years to the ISF auditors, and believe me, Simon, I keep meticulous records."

A beat passed.

"I'll give you fifty thousand," Shade said. "Not an anna more."

Another pause. Jackson looked nervously toward the display. The cutter—the NSS *Kolkata*—was getting awfully close.

"I'm waiting," she said.

A moment later, the port controller contacted them. *"Never mind,* Tar Heel. *That random inspection is cancelled. You are clear to proceed."*

"Roger that," the captain replied. "We will resume departure."

Jackson held his breath because that "clear to proceed" business could simply be a ruse to keep them complacent while the *Kolkata* maneuvered in to get a clean shot on their bay doors. If those were disabled then they wouldn't be able to pull a jackdaw, and they'd be caught red-handed. Jackson was a damned good mech pilot. Nothing phased him while driving, no matter how hairy it got, but he sure hated being a passenger. Remarkably enough, even though his livelihood and potentially his freedom were at stake, the captain wasn't so much as sweating. The man was cool enough under pressure to impress a pilot.

"Nivaa's cutter's breaking away, Captain," said Alligood. "We're clear."

"That was a bribe well spent, Shade."

"It should come out of Jackson's share," she said.

"Hell no, it's not. I'll be damned if—"

"Good thing that decision isn't for either of you to make." The captain shut that argument right down, even though afterwards their broker was still staring daggers at Jackson.

As they engaged the secondary thrusters again, the ship began to move forward, slowly leaving the *Kolkata* behind. The minutes ticked by. Once *Tar Heel* reached the border of the port's control area the captain initiated the command to turn the ship so its thrusters were pointed toward the dead zone, away from all the other traffic.

"Engaging main engines and heading for the gate."

"Safe travels, *Tar Heel*," the port controller told them.

"Thank you," Captain Holloway said. "Have yourself a wonderful day."

And then the ship began to accelerate.

"Stand down, Mr. Hilker. We are good to go. There's no need for you to vent my retirement savings into space."

The cargo master's voice came over the intercom. *"Cancelling jackdaw protocol."* And the entire ship breathed a sigh of relief.

Jackson looked at Shade, who was floating there with a superior look on her face, and wondered once again how a fixer for one smuggling ship managed to have that much clout.

Shade said, "Call me if Nivaasian Security decides to change its mind." And then she ghosted off the bridge.

The captain slowly ran both of his hands up and back over his bald head. "I think I might be getting too old for this."

CHAPTER 7

Once they were underway, the captain told Jackson to join him. His office was just off the bridge.

"Have a seat." He clapped Jackson on the shoulder as he clomped past in his magnetic boots. "I think Shade was about ready to sell you off to the highest bidder."

"And you weren't going to stop her?"

"Nope."

"Thanks for all the love."

"Lots of love." He chuckled. "This is a big ship full of love."

"Did Shade put something in your drink?"

"She didn't need to." He touched a display on his desk. A woodland image appeared. "You see that?"

"Trees and a pond."

"I own those trees. I own that pond. That's actual, old-fashioned real estate."

"On Earth," Jackson said.

"Of course, Earth. There are deer on that property. Raccoons. There are fish in that pond. There are women in that town who are looking for a husband like me. Lot of lonely widows on Earth. When this job is done, I'm going home."

"You've decided for sure this time?"

"I got the property. I got the permits. And once we sell that Citadel, I'll have enough money to never have to work again. Hell, I might even get some treatments and set this body's clock back a few decades."

"Got to look good for all those widows."

The captain sank into his chair and pulled out two small globes of amber liquid from a drawer on his desk. "Have a beer, Jackson." He floated one over.

Jackson caught it. "You'll miss the fun."

"No," the captain said and looked at his little spread. "I don't believe I will."

Jackson didn't blame him. The captain had got his start fighting a war on behalf of his home planet, and a bunch more for hire since, commanding everything from barges to gunships to cruisers. He had fought the good fight. But it made Jackson a bit melancholy thinking about him leaving. The captain had been like a father, the kind who goes into hell to save a son.

"So Hilker told me about the sorry state of your air when he picked up that crate you were riding in...Except you never broke radio silence to call for help."

"They would have been watching closely by that point, and I didn't want to endanger the whole crew if I got picked up."

"But if the cops had found you, they'd at least have oxygen."

Jackson shrugged. "I had plenty of time."

"Sure...Sure, you did." The captain grinned, shook his head, then took a drink. "You know, of the many characters flaws you may possess, a lack of loyalty is not among them."

Jackson cracked open his beer and changed the subject. "You'll get bored with that pond and all of those widows. I give you six weeks, and then you'll be sending an interstellar, wanting to get back in the game."

"Not on your life."

"If you don't call, then I'll suspect it's because the law finally caught up with you."

"Nah, that's what the money's for."

The two of them sat there and drank their beers in silence for a time, because it had been a really stressful day.

"I tell you, Jackson, what we do is necessary...we both know that. But I'm getting worn out."

Understandable. It was tiring, having to stay one step ahead of the authorities and to do business with people you could never really trust. The things the captain had seen had given him a peculiar code, which he stuck to like the most devout stuck to their religion. He'd bought this ship to practice that religion.

"You've been like a modern-day Robin Hood. Stealing from the rich to give to the poor."

"Only I steal weapons for embargoed worlds, and I don't exactly give them away."

"Okay, I'll admit the analogy needs work. But if my people had had a mech like that Citadel back on Gloss, things might have turned out a whole lot different for us," Jackson mused.

"Exactly. The powers that be said you weren't allowed, no military grade hardware for the proles. That kind of dangerous firepower only belongs in the hands of the state. Monopoly of force, blah, blah, blah. Except when the law is two systems away and doesn't give a crap about protecting you, the little guy gets stomped. Every. Single. Time."

"Gloss sure did..."

The captain nodded.

"To running guns," Jackson said and raised his beer in salute. "You've done the Lord's work, Cap."

He snorted. "When's the last time you cared about what the Almighty wants?"

"Eh," Jackson shrugged. He'd been raised in a faithful community, but his faith had died along with most of his people. "Just phrasing it like you or Tui would, I suppose. The universe, God, karma, whatever you believe in, some things just aren't right."

"Meaning it's unfair for regular people to be disarmed just because some sheltered bureaucrat said they ought to be. I've armed the defenseless and helped the helpless." The captain laughed. "And gotten well paid doing it."

Jackson knew that the mercenary schtick only went so far. Most of the crew was in it for the money, but the captain himself had a code. Once he could no longer abide seeing people get pushed around, he'd broken the law, and started supplying those people with the tools needed to push back. Jackson had a code too, though his was a little more pragmatic. Growing up in a refugee camp would do that to you.

"Serious talk time though, Jackson. You've been a valuable part of this crew for a few years now, but you need to think about your future. You've got valuable skills. You're a smart guy, you could go far. Maybe even get your own ship someday or pick a colony and settle down. Right now, you need to think hard about what you're going to do when I'm gone."

"That depends. Are you selling the *Tar Heel* to Shade? And if so, is she going to make Javi captain?"

Javier Castillo was their XO. He was a very competent spacer, but also a stern, deadpan, nearly antisocial man with the emotionally stunted personality of a synth. He and Jackson weren't exactly besties. The XO had some real problems with things Jackson had done in the past. Things which the captain understood and overlooked, but which Castillo made no secret he would not. A few times he had referred to Jackson as the captain's "rehab project."

"I know you've got issues with Castillo, but he'd take good care of this crew. Shade's Shade. She's got the capital and her business needs experienced runners."

"She's already made you an offer, hasn't she?"

The captain took a sip of his beer. "Yep. I'm considering it."

"There's no way you would've let Shade hand me over to the cops."

"Yeah, you keep telling yourself that, son."

"Six weeks," Jackson said, "and you'll start feeling your old age and decide retirement's overrated."

"Well, I ain't there yet. So why don't you get back to work and let me continue my slow descent into decrepitude and senility in peace."

"I was heading down to the tech dungeon anyway to thank Jane for saving my bacon." Jackson got up and headed for the door.

"There's an old Earth saying, Jackson, that you shouldn't fish off the company dock. Although I don't think you can call it fishing if there's a zero percent chance the fish will take the bait."

"It's not like that. Jane's just one of the few people who appreciate the sacrifices I make for this crew of ingrates."

"Uh-huh."

"It's purely platonic."

"Well, good. Here I was thinking there's something like ninety billion women out there, but you had to be sweet on my chief specter, who you also just happen to have insurmountable baggage with."

By that he meant that Jane had seen him at his worst, since she'd literally poked around inside his brain and then put him back together again. But that couldn't be *that* insurmountable. "Is this the part where you get out the employee handbook and lecture me on the dangers of crew fraternization?"

The captain gestured around his office. "Does this look like the sort of outfit that has a *handbook?* Carry on, Mr. Rook."

Some time ago someone on the crew had spray-painted *Specter's Domain* and a stencil of a cutesy cartoon skull and crossbones on the wall next to the door to the tech department. Jackson pulled himself through the open door. Jane was there working, a schematic on one wall display, with the guts of a robot in her hands. Stowed neatly against one wall were about half-a-dozen other bots of various sizes. They were Fifi's companions. There was Dora, Squeak, Waterboy, Sam, Chachi, and a number of others.

All of them killers in their own right, capable of autonomous actions. But when they were linked to Jane, they became a coordinated cloud of death-dealing monstrosities. Which made it unnerving that she'd designed them all to be *cute.*

"Hey, how's our demigoddess doing?"

Jane turned to look at him. "Jacky!" She was the only person on the ship who routinely called him that. And she got away with it because Jackson thought she was hot. Today her hair was in pigtails, which were turned up in the zero G. She had blue lipstick, blue eyes, and a little blue heart on her cheek.

Though she had joined the crew a year before he had, she was about his age, or maybe a year or two older. Not that Jackson knew that for sure, since Jane's background was as mysterious as Shade's. The captain seemed to enjoy collecting people who liked to pretend their pasts never happened. Like they were one big crew of blank slates with bad memories. Jane never said where she was from, nor dropped any hints, but it was obvious that it had been one of the more advanced worlds and she'd been the recipient of a top-tier technical education there.

She smiled at him, her teeth a luscious row of white.

"How's your leg? Still bothering you from that hornet?"

"Nah," he lied. Those nasty things hurt. But Jane probably knew that. She knew more about bot-related tech than anyone he'd ever met.

She nodded. "And how's my little girl?"

Jackson fished in his pocket and brought out Fifi. "Spectacular." He held his palm up, allowing Fifi to spring over to Jane.

"You're a good girl, aren't you?" she said in a cuddly voice.

Fifi said nothing.

Jackson said, "I got something for you on the surface."

"Oh?" Her brows knit in question.

He lifted the bag of sausage.

"What is that?"

"A bit of Nivaasian heaven."

He unwrapped it, but, to his disappointment, all his derring-do had mushed it. The top half suddenly broke off and fell out of the wrapping. He caught it before it floated away.

"So that's heaven, huh?"

"Don't let the sad appearance fool you. Warm it up, and you'll thank me. It got irradiated in decon, but that's not supposed to change the flavor."

She took it and sniffed, then crinkled her nose. "This doesn't smell like the others."

"What others?"

"Tui picked up a case of these at the port. He's throwing a party in the mess tonight."

Jackson sighed as he looked at his cold, mushed sausage. It had been a good plan. A tremendous idea. *Damn you, Jeet Prunkard.*

She sniffed again. "It smells a bit like Raj."

He took the sausage back and smelled it. And it had indeed picked up some of the funk-smell of his space suit. "I guess I should have wrapped it better."

"It's the thought that counts."

"And I was thinking of the death goddess in the sky."

"That's sweet." And Jane was the kind of person that when she said that it wasn't in the least bit patronizing. "You know who would still want that? Shoe Guy."

That was one of the crew assigned to her tech team. He had reddish hair, a hobo beard, and ate constantly. "I'll put it in his dog bowl," Jane said.

"You do that, I'm going to finish fixing Ron." Who was an adorable little robot teddy bear that could assassinate you with his chain-saw paws. She turned back to her workbench and he got the impression she was blowing him off.

"Well, I just wanted to say thanks for the help down on the surface."

"All part of the job."

He never could get her. Jane was always nice, and often seemed as interested in flirting with him as he was with her, but then just when things were going well, it was like a switch got flipped and she'd get awkward. He was never quite sure if it was something he'd said just then, or something from the past that he had no control over. It was a little exasperating at times.

"Okay then." That woman had to have a crack in that armor somewhere. "Well, goodbye, Fifi."

"What do you say, girl?" Jane asked.

Fifi suddenly sprang from her shoulder onto Jackson's neck. There was a pinch, and he startled. That's what you did when a little flying razor blade hit the spot with all the arteries. Then Fifi leapt right back.

"What was that?"

"A thank-you kiss."

Jane was looking at him, watching his reaction. As were all the other robots in the room. And he had to admit that weirded him out. He gave her a two-fingered wave and said, "Headed for the mess." And then he pushed off and floated out into the corridor.

Jane smiled after Jackson left. She really did like the guy. He was like a gooey chocolate dessert. So tempting, but indulging would only lead to regret. Of course, what could one nibble hurt?

No, she stopped herself.

No, she reaffirmed.

The block she'd installed wasn't a perfect solution. It could fail. It didn't matter if it had been years. And he should know that.

If it failed, his old military command could take him over again. Or something worse on the net. And then the bloodlust would come upon him and Jackson would become their tool, just by flipping a switch.

Should that occur, it was Jane's job to execute the protocol that would end it. She held the key to shut him down if necessary.

So she couldn't get entangled with Jackson emotionally, no matter how enticing that path looked. Because if she gave into her feelings, it could cause her to hesitate when that dark moment arrived. And that could mean many other deaths. And a betrayal of her promise to Jackson.

No, she thought. That piece of pie is not on your menu.

And so Jane put it out of her mind and turned back to Ron the teddy bear to finish servicing his saw blades. And maybe give one of his ears a little pink flair.

✧　　✧　　✧

Jackson put the riddle of Jane out of his mind. What he needed was food, and if Tui was giving out real, made-from-actual-animals Nivaasian sausage, he was going to enjoy one for a job well done...even if Shade refused to recognize it had actually been done well at all.

He grabbed a catch rail and pushed off toward the mess hall. A few moments later, the captain's voice came over the corridor intercom. "Starting spin."

Jackson oriented himself to what would soon be the floor. In front of him the corridor had a slight curve that gently rose until it disappeared upward in the distance. He engaged the magnetics in his shoes and started to walk. Soon enough the ring would be traveling a little over a hundred and sixty kilometers an hour. At that time, he could turn the magnets off. Until then, they would allow him to move and accelerate with the spin. By the time he made it to the mess hall he was feeling about half a G.

Since the crew's work schedule was broken into three eight-hour blocks, a third were at their posts, a third were asleep, and the rest were here for dinner. They were an eclectic bunch. When the captain had first bought this ship out of surplus a decade ago, he'd hired nothing but Earth Block Navy, like he had been. Over time many of those had moved on, quit, or gotten killed somehow, and their gradual replacements had come from wherever the *Tar Heel* had been working at the time. And since they ranged back and forth across most of known space, the captain had picked up crew from basically everywhere.

But they were all loyal and good at their jobs. Considering they were all—by definition—criminals, the captain ran a tight ship, and the crew got along remarkably well. They weren't pirates. They were smugglers. It was the same thing to the various governments they disobeyed, but to the moral makeup of the crew, it made all the difference in the world.

A whole bunch of people called out his name as he entered. Because regardless of whether he was friends with each of them individually or not, his last-minute escapades today had made it so they were all going to get paid well at their next stop. It was kind of nice being the hero.

"Just in time," said Tui. "Get yourself one of these Sharmalans. The yellow sauce is to die for."

"I did nearly die for one earlier." Then he took one of the

sausages and wrapped it in some of the local bread, which was sort of like a fluffy tortilla. He took a bite and enjoyed the savory explosion of juices in his mouth. Some taste engineer really earned his chops on this one. He added some sauerkraut and took another bite. And then Katze Yeager, one of Tui's security team, pointed at Jackson's neck.

"What happened there?" she asked.

Everyone turned and looked.

"Looks like a hickie," Katze said.

Jackson reached up and felt his neck, then looked in the reflective surface on the wall to see what they were talking about. There was a nice little bruise where Fifi had given him her goodbye bite.

"That's definitely a hickie," Katze said.

Jackson had to agree. That's exactly what it looked like. Had Jane sent Fifi to give him a little love peck? Was the Maiden of Death weakening?

"That's just a bump I got during that shoot-out down at the surface."

"Of course, you did," another one of the crew said.

The others all laughed. And Jackson wondered—maybe Jane was giving him some kind of come-hither in her weird robot language.

The banter moved on. Jackson enjoyed his sausage, some chocolate-covered mango strips, and a few glasses of the crew brew, then bid the others farewell and headed back into the corridor for his room. The spin was up to a full G, and so he simply strolled along the corridor that led eternally up, music wafting from some room up the hall.

He proceeded to his room. Because of the *Tar Heel*'s size compared to its crew complement, everyone had the perk of private quarters, a remarkably rare thing to have as a spacer. Even so it was a small spot that was just big enough to include a sleep station, a place to stow his personal gear, a foldout desk, and a magnetic stool. The room recognized his presence, and the wall lit up, displaying the picture of a fantastic lagoon where the crew had vacationed a year or so ago while waiting for Shade to arrange some work.

He looked at the room, thinking about the captain's woods and fishpond, and the cubby seemed very poor in comparison. But it was enough, he told himself. The captain had told him to think of his future, but he'd already been working on that. The plan was to keep making runner money for a few more years. Big money. Then get himself his own ship. And this cubby allowed him to funnel every spare dime into starting his own business.

If not on this ship, then he'd hire onto another. Even without plugging in, he was still a top-tier pilot. Somebody would be hiring. Though the odds of finding another captain this good to work for, and another crew this solid, were slim.

He shucked his clothes and crawled into his sleep station, a bag in a partially enclosed area, tethered so that he wouldn't float off and get injured during periods of weightlessness. The surface of the bag was soft and cool and felt good against his skin.

Out his port, Jackson could see a couple of the radiators extending, the long sections of honeycombed material that shunted the heat generated by the ship out into space. Planetside the air did that for you. Out here, unless you were sitting on a hunk of frozen asteroid, there was nothing. It was radiate it or shunt it all into a heat sink and jettison that into space. That was the fun part about life on a ship, you were always only one equipment malfunction away from roasting or freezing to death. But it made for an incredible view.

As he stretched and lay there, his thoughts turned back to the old days, and the war for independence on the planet Gloss. He told himself it must have been because of those few minutes he'd spent driving the Citadel.

Jackson had only been a boy when the rebellion had started. The hab he'd grown up in had been bombed. His parents had spoken against the Collectivist takeover, been branded as dissidents, and then executed. He'd been forced to watch them swing before being loaded onto a train to spend the next few years surviving in a tent city hell. When the rebels had become desperate enough to start drafting child soldiers, he'd jumped at the opportunity. Anything was better than fighting for scraps in a refugee camp.

Most of his peers were sent to the infantry, to be fed right into the meat grinder, but Jackson's reaction times and mental acuity had tested astonishingly well, so he had been trained to drive one of their few remaining mechs. But by that point in the war, they'd needed more than just drivers. They needed warriors who could become one with the machine.

Embargoed by all the civilized worlds, most of the rebels' equipment was secondhand trash, picked up from arms dealers so unscrupulous they made Captain Holloway look like a saint in comparison. They only had a handful of weapon systems that could go toe-to-toe with the enemy, and Jackson was one of the few who possessed the raw neural processing power to fully link with such a device. They were so desperate for pilots that his brain surgery had been done in a tent, using black-market equipment, by a medic who had been in veterinary school when the war began. Of the three prospective pilots given implants that day, Jackson alone survived the process. He'd been fourteen years old.

With a bootleg mech and less than a week of training, Jackson had been sent to war.

Piloting a Thunderbolt 5 that was practically an antique, he'd somehow survived. Driven by stick, a T-bolt was about as responsive as a tractor but connected directly to his brain, twenty tons of armor had felt like a seamless extension of his body. For the first time in his life he was able to hit back at the cowards who had ruined his whole world, and he had plenty of hate to give. He'd spent the next few years stomping Collectivists like the roaches they were. Outnumbered, outgunned, it didn't matter, because the rebels had justice and God on their side.

Jackson had been a good pilot. Really good.

The tide even turned for a bit. The rebels actually gained ground. Briefly, the people of Gloss had even started thinking they might have a real shot at freedom again, and Jackson was one of the handful who had saved that dream.

Only it had all turned into a nightmare when the desperate Collective had transitioned to net war and sent a worm to invade the linked pilots' brains. Their antique firewalls never stood a chance. It was like being possessed by demons. Even now all he could remember about those dark days was the demons whisper-ing in his mind while Gloss burned before him.

The captain had saved him from that fate, which was why Jackson would be loyal to this crew until the day he died. He'd failed his people...but he had survived, so he owed it to those who hadn't to make something of himself.

After he'd escaped the hooks that had been sunk into his brain, Jackson had made a vow. Never again would he connect his mind with a mech. The last time he'd done so, he'd lost his freedom, and his friends had lost their lives. The risk was just too great.

Jackson drifted off to sleep thinking about a future with money and independence. Maybe a house at that lagoon. Maybe a huge tract of land on one of the new worlds. But as he fell into sleep his brain, like the addict that it was, turned to the old days, and dreamed about the wetware flooding him with intelligence and desire. It took him back to when he operated like a god of flesh and metal on the field of blood, the battle joy singing in his veins. Back to the time before the monsters found him.

Shade sat alone in her quarters, with a receiver set against her left temple. She couldn't trust that the captain's pet specter, Jane, wasn't watching and listening, and so this was the only way to send a private message. The tiny implant the company had put in her brain translated and encoded it.

"We have it," Shade said.

Even though the coded message was traveling at the speed of light via tight beam, her handler was currently about ninety million kilometers away. So she had to wait about ten minutes to get a response. Five minutes to get there, a few seconds to compose an answer, then five minutes back.

Norman Johnson's response was deciphered by the implant in her brain, *"You need to get a different host. This crew you're working with almost botched the operation."*

"My host is fine."

Another ten minutes.

"Your captain is a cowboy," Johnson said.

He was, but this idiot was still wasting her time. "Who is my contact at the gate?"

A delay.

"We are working on it."

Shade's alarm rose. If gate security found the mech, there would be serious repercussions. "You don't have that locked down yet?"

A delay.

"Our mule was hit by a wrench. She's out. We will find another in time. Proceed as planned."

The mech was the lynchpin in their new strategy on Swindle. A risky one. And Shade was not going to take the fall for someone else's mistake.

"We can wait."

A delay.

"This is too high-level an op. We have other assets. Proceed."

Did they really expect her to believe their asset inside gate security had suffered an accident with a wrench?

"Is it the Syndicate? If it is, they will scuttle the whole thing, and the big man will be hanging in the wind."

A delay.

"It was an accident. They happen. Proceed."

Shade didn't like it, but as usual she'd get the mission done, no matter what.

Jane saw each of Grandma's short messages leave. Shade used a very clever program that enabled her to temporarily highjack and aim the ship's tight beam. As Jane had done before, she piggybacked the messages. And as before, the packets shed her pig, which was maddening.

And worrying.

The captain had entrusted her with the information security of this ship. And Shade was the one dark box she'd not been able to open. It posed a risk to the captain and crew.

It posed a risk to Jane.

For years she had thought she'd been watching all communications to and from the *Tar Heel*, but then she'd discovered Shade's secret comms that had been sneaking out right under her nose. Nobody else had noticed because the *Tar Heel* used its tight beams constantly, flickering them in a random search pattern searching for potential impact dangers, and Shade only borrowed the array for a fraction of a second each time she sent a message. The responses she got looked like sensor static to the rest of the crew, but not to Jane. She was good at picking the secret patterns from the chaos.

Jane received an alert whenever Shade activated her program now. She'd intercepted several of the messages hidden in the beams, except they were in a code even she couldn't crack. Of course, the captain hadn't ordered Jane to do this. She was watching Shade because her instincts told her not to trust the broker.

Jane adjusted the piggy's slant and this time the message did not shed. Ten minutes later, Jane found where Shade's message had been sent, an unlicensed installation way out in the Nivaasian system. Immediately after Shade's conversation, that installation sent a regular message packet to be relayed through the gate.

Jane may not be able to hack Shade's messages yet, but she might be able to finally discover who she was talking to. So she piggybacked that signal too. Maybe she'd get lucky and be able to track the message to its final destination on the other side of the gate.

Ride 'em, piggy. Ride.

A few minutes after Jane went back to work, the icon of a red flower appeared on her visual. It was a particular red flower, with blue spots on its petals. The kind that in all her travels Jane had only seen grow in one place—a small town on the coast, back on Savat.

She felt a tingle of alarm, as she always did when reminded of home.

The icon meant that one of her sisters was trying to contact her. Of course, Jane never talked directly to any of them. That was far too dangerous for all of them. Instead they communicated using a method they'd devised years ago to hide their messages from the scientists who had made them. There had been thirty of them then. Thirty genetically engineered sisters in the sibling cohort of Mary 231.78. Now there were only four of them left.

Jane selected the flower, and in the corner of her visual a video played. It showed an outdoor café on a street in a city on another planet that Jane knew would take two gate hops to reach. In front of the café were a number of tables. There was a lime-green napkin on one of them. A few tables away was a set of dishes some diners had left for pickup. At another table was a man and woman and a child. There were bottles and plants and a hundred other items, including the positioning of a number of chairs, and Jane read them all in the blink of an eye.

It was all about how those seemingly incongruous items had been arranged. Everything in that video meant something. It was a language known to only four people in the whole universe.

It was a message from their 22nd sister. It was a warning. The geometric folds in the napkin said there was a new hunter snooping around. Possibly part of an Iyer Affiliate. The color indicated the emotion of wrath. The tablecloth, fear. The bend of the leaves and number of plates and even the shape and position of the crumbs told her that 22 was still upset with Jane accidentally drawing attention to them, and a hundred other subtle things.

Jane read the message again to be sure.

She sighed.

So Savat had not given up on finding the daughters of Mary 231.78.

Jane closed the message. She would have to tread carefully.

CHAPTER 8

For Jackson, the next few days were occupied with maintenance on the ship and some friendly games of longball in the corridor. He was outside helping repair a spot on one side of the cargo area that had taken a micrometeorite hit, when the captain announced they were only a few hours away from the first gate security check and that all the crew were to prepare themselves in case the authorities wanted to board and inspect the ship and its cargo.

Checkpoint security was not something you wanted to mess with. At least not openly. And so Jackson finished his work quickly and returned to the ship.

Gates were some of the most valuable things in space. The more a government could control, the more powerful it became. The ISF owned this one, as well as about two dozen others across seven systems. Just as with planets, their security system extended for hundreds of thousands of kilometers around them. Nobody wanted to build something that cost a significant percentage of a planet's GDP only to have it threatened by malcontents.

Gates were always located a good distance from a system's star and a few degrees off the orbital plane of any planets or smaller objects. The math that explained why was far over his head, and he was no slouch in the brains department. He might be rough around the edges academically, but as much real-world work on mechs and ships as he'd done, he figured that was as good as any engineering degree from a planetside university. Especially since out here failing an exam meant dying painfully. However, even halfway comprehending the crazy physics behind gate travel caused nosebleeds in geniuses. It was all frankly way beyond Jackson's grasp.

There were two gates in this system. One was dedicated to traffic between Nivaas and Earth. The second could be adjusted to transit to a few other systems. That was where they were heading.

There was always a specific route you had to use to approach a gate. Any ship or object outside of that approved route was deemed hostile and targeted for elimination. Three years back, at one of the seven Earth system gates, some poor ship strayed into a forbidden zone. There were many conflicting stories about how and why it had strayed, but what everyone agreed on was that the ship had been lit up by the gate defenses. Ten thousand people had been on board, and ten thousand dreams of a home on some new colony world had been instantly snuffed out. Of all the stories, Jackson figured the story claiming it had been a hijacking and ransom gone bad was probably the most accurate.

So, if you wanted to stay alive, you followed the approved route to the gate. And along that route were various security checks.

The first checkpoint was usually millions of kilometers away from the actual gate. This one was an asteroid that was maybe twenty-four kilometers in diameter. Part of it was being mined, while the other half housed the security forces. Five other ships were already lined up at the checkpoint ahead of them, waiting for processing.

As it approached, the *Tar Heel* called in and was given parking coordinates. They took up position. And waited.

And waited.

The next day, ten gate cops, a dog, and a horde of sniffer bots boarded the ship. Eight of them spread out on a quest for contraband. The others interviewed crew members and took DNA samples.

Nerves were high, but the crew played it cool. Nivaas was an independent colony, but they paid for ISF protection and to use the ISF gate system. If Splendid Ventures had decided their Citadel had been stolen, rather than accidentally destroyed, surely Nivaas would have asked the ISF to be on the lookout for it. But the cops seemed bored as usual, and Chief Hilker was an artist when it came to hiding whatever they were smuggling. There were places on this ship that Jackson didn't even know about, and he spent most of his duty hours repairing her.

Six hours later, after reconciling the manifest with the cargo and everyone on board, the gate patrol cleared the *Tar Heel* to proceed to the next checkpoint a few million kilometers away.

Jackson didn't know who Shade was connected with, whether it was some organized crime group, or old wartime network, or someone she personally had on the inside, but the gate cops rarely found anything amiss. When they did, it was usually over minor things that were handled with an under-the-table fee.

Before leaving this checkpoint, an official escort pod was attached to the hull of the ship. Its job was to continually report the position of the *Tar Heel*, monitor conversations and communications, and take control of the ship's propulsion system if it was deemed a threat. The problem was that sometimes the pod system and the ship system conflicted, and that was never a good thing. Ships had been damaged from it. But what could you do? You use the ISF's gates, you played the ISF's game.

As they were accelerating toward the next station, they received a news report about the destruction of a container in Nivaas orbit. Sabotage was suspected. There was an ongoing investigation, but no suspects at this time. Normally the crew would have loved to gloat about that, but with the ISF pod attached to the hull, they said nothing.

Instead, they enjoyed another few days of maintenance, carefully generalized banter, and zero conversation about the client, until the *Tar Heel* arrived at the next security point without fanfare.

There were more ships waiting for their turn at the gate. Back in the Earth system, many of the vessels traversing the gate would be huge migrant freighters full of people trying to make a new life in the stars. There were no migrant freighters here, just cargo ships that had transported out-system goods in and now were transporting Nivaas goods out. The *Tar Heel* was nothing special. They were just another hauler making the rounds in the vast and interconnected system that was galactic trade.

This check wasn't as invasive or as intensive as the first. There were so many tons of freight moving between worlds that it would take an army of gate cops to check it all. So they did the cursory, mandatory minimum percentage of container checks, looking for things like slaves, endangered species, or stolen mechs, and once nothing super obvious jumped out to bite them, they signed off on the transfer.

Jackson was never sure how Chief Hilker managed to hide so much of the good stuff so well, but the man had a gift for creative stacking. What could be disguised was disguised, what could be broken down into parts was broken down, so on and so forth. It helped that the *Tar Heel* was so massive. It would take weeks to search everything, and nobody ever took that long because time was money.

Then the cops checked their escort pod to see if it had found anything suspicious from the ship's logs, but of course, it only saw what Jane wanted it to see. So they took their toy, filed their paperwork, and the *Tar Heel* went on its merry way.

They arrived at the gate a few days later. This one was about eighty kilometers in diameter, huge white rings floating in the black. Each ring was connected to a facility called the gatehouse, which held the control center and power source, which in this case was a massive solar farm.

It was a busy day. About thirty ships were there, waiting their turn. There was a supply depot nearby, as well as a repair yard. The service rates would be astronomical there, but you really didn't want to have a major system go down during transit. A horde of garbage trucks flew constant patterns around the gates in an effort to keep the area clean. If a gate took an impact sufficient to alter its orientation even the slightest bit during a transit, that ship would end up who knew where. Every spacer had heard horror stories about that happening, with the vessel never being seen again.

There were legends of lost colonies, created by ships filled with settlers who had been accidentally sent to unknown destinations. Based upon the vastness of space, Jackson knew those stories were wishful thinking created by relatives of the missing, and somewhere out in all the big empty were dead ships filled with frozen corpses.

The queue for the Earth gate moved a lot faster than theirs, because that was a constant stream of traffic toward the same location. The secondary gate took hours of adjustment between each transit. The targeting calculations factored in the movement of the gate's orbit, the orbit of the Nivaas system, the movement of the target system, the size of the ship, its magnetic resonance, and five hundred other complicated factors. Since your life was literally in their hands, nobody ever rushed the gatehouse's calculations.

The *Tar Heel*'s turn finally came. Gate control gave them a precise position, angle of entry, and time. And then the *Tar Heel* slowly moved out of the line to its launch spot.

Jackson went up to the bridge because he enjoyed watching this part. The captain halted the spin of the habitat ring. Gate control checked and double-checked all their settings. Then the gate lights turned from blue to red. Blue meant inactive, you could fly right through and nothing would happen. Red meant they had begun to stack space and generate the pathway.

The stars that were visible through the gate winked out one by one, and then the path began to form. It looked like a ripple at first, then grew into a massive funnel that had the appearance of swirling clouds. Every once in a while they'd see a soft flash of violet light deep inside, like distant lightning...Funny thing was, nobody had ever conclusively proven what caused that effect.

"Countdown in tee minus five," the captain said over the speakers. "Four, three, two, one." Then he flashed the thrusters and their ship began to move forward.

A gate transit was an act of faith. You had to trust the gatehouse had gotten their numbers right. You had to trust your ship's engines would work throughout, or that there wouldn't be a power glitch, or that they weren't about to smack you into an unexpected object as soon as you exited.

The farther a gate sent you, the less precision it had. Nivaas system to the Swindle system was only 8.4 light-years, which promised their placement somewhere within an area approximately three hundred thousand kilometers in diameter. If you put that on paper and compared it to the distance traveled, it was incredibly accurate. But when thinking about it from the point of view of the ship, it was a shot in the dark. It was a blindfolded leap.

And you'd really better hope that the government didn't think you were enough of a troublemaker to get rid of you, because it would be super easy to make a "slight miscalculation" and hurl you out into some empty part of the universe with no way of ever getting back. Gates worked one way. If you wanted to transit back, you needed to build another gate at the other end. The means to do so were way beyond the resources of most nations, let alone a lone cargo ship.

"Your line to Swindle looks good, Tar Heel," gate control told them.

"Roger that," the captain said.

The swirling vortex was getting bigger on the screen.

"Isn't that the planet where the air catches on fire and every-thing on the surface is huge and wants to eat you? I don't know why anybody would want to live there."

"Beats me, Gatehouse. I'm just the delivery boy with their groceries."

"Safe travels."

"Thank you."

Then they slowly entered the dark path.

Nivaas to Swindle was a sixteen-hour ride through the dark-ness of transit space, lit only by that occasional soft glow the scientists still couldn't explain.

They couldn't really explain the god moment either.

It didn't always happen during a transit. But when it did, it was always at the midpoint, and it was a rush. In the god moment, people heard things. Saw things. Thought things. Your mind expanded. Some had tremendous insights. Jackson had taken mind-altering drugs before. He'd been linked up and melded with machines. The god moment was nothing like either of those. It was inexplicable. And when it ended, many people collapsed.

There were some religious groups and spiritualists who paid the gate fee just so they could experience what they thought was a hack into God's mind. Jackson didn't know what it was. Nobody did. But he did hope to enjoy this one with a hamburger and coleslaw. Jackson was in the galley, eating his lunch at the right time, but the midpoint came and went without anything to note. Just a brief chill, and then it was gone.

Eight hours later they reached the end of their dark funnel. And as the MSV *Tar Heel* emerged from the path into a new system, a billion stars suddenly winked into existence.

Right about now the ship's sensors would be scanning in every direction and matching stars to charts. This was the part where they found out if they'd reached their destination, or if they were in that not statistically insignificant number of transits that got tossed into an uncharted part of the universe, never to be seen again.

The captain came over the speakers. *"We've arrived in the Swindle system."*

There were cheers all up and down the corridor. No matter how many times you did this, that part was always a relief.

"All systems are green. Now let's clean house. Setting course for Big Town."

And with that the crew went into action removing all the bugs and other devices the ISF gate cops had planted. There was excitement in the air. It was time to get paid.

The storm blew in like an angry caliban, turning the sky purple and gold. With it came a wind that howled and thrashed the trees, and acid rain that fell in sheets.

Wulf wiped the water off his helmet's visor, in a vain attempt to see better. Ten paces in front of him was his father. Ten behind was the tech named Pridgeon. Each of them was wearing a basic exoskeleton frame that enabled them to lope along the trail with augmented speed and strength. The Originals' exos were old and battered and had been repaired dozens of times, but they still did their job. Mostly.

"This rotted helmet does nothing but fog up," Pridgeon said over the commlink. "I can't see worth a kacke. Climate control's been on the fritz since we left."

"Put on your mouthpiece," Wulf's father replied over the comm.

Pridgeon cursed, but he lifted his visor, temporarily opening his helmet to the caustic air. Even brief exposure to Swindle's atmosphere was irritating. A few minutes would scar your lungs. A few hours and you were dead. But Pridgeon got his breathing apparatus on in practiced seconds and closed his lid.

"Better?"

"Better."

"Then shut up and keep walking."

They'd been out on a service patrol to conduct preventative maintenance on three of their sentinels when the alert had come through. Just as the ping had appeared on their heads-up displays, there'd been a series of lightning strikes, and the signal had gone dead. It could be nothing. It might be something. They had to find out.

All three of them carried rifles. You had to when dealing with the nasty creatures that lived on this planet. Wulf had a 6mm HyperV. It would be good for the regular wildlife, but if one of the big predators caught their scent he was out of luck. Anything short of a cannon bounced off them. When you found one of the big ones, your only hope of survival was running and hiding. The original settlers had a lot of practice at running and hiding.

Wulf enlarged the rifle's targeting display on his heads-up, then scanned the woods on the left and right, flicking through visible spectrum, UV, and IR, just as father had taught him. The site cam connected wirelessly to his helmet's visor for quick aim and ballistic calculations, He saw no clear signatures in the woods around him. If the alarm had been from a caliban, surely the infrared would have picked up such a large beast, but it could only see so far through the vine-choked underbrush. It was thick here, but it was thick everywhere. As a rule of thumb, if there was a game trail on Swindle, it was made by an animal that could hardly be called *game*. If there was a clearing, it was because something large had flattened it. Everywhere else you could see three or four meters if you were lucky.

They marched for a time as the rain and wind grew worse. Swindle was the only place Wulf had ever known so he was used to the suck, but this was shaping up to be a bad one.

"Forget the alarm, I say we go back," Pridgeon said.

"It's thirteen kilometers to base," Father replied. He meant actual traveling distance, it wasn't nearly that far in a straight line, but nothing moved in a straight line through this rugged terrain. "Even maxing our exos that's going to take a while. There's a spider hole less than ten minutes away. We can ride the storm out there."

"If something's got our scent that spider hole won't—"

Wulf waited for the rest of Pridgeon's sentence, but it never came. He glanced back to find the trail behind him empty.

A bolt of fear shot through Wulf. "Pridgeon?"

There was no response.

"Father!" Wulf gripped his rifle tight and scanned, ready to shoot. "He's gone."

But how could Pridgeon just be gone?

And then Wulf thought about the canopy and fear seized his guts, for there were a number of ambush predators on Swindle that hunted from the trees. He looked up and found only the lofty branches thrashing in the wind.

His father froze in place. His older—but more powerful—rifle only had a low-tech glass scope, good for magnification but not much else. "What do you see?"

There were the footprints of Pridgeon's exo in the mud. He could see where they stopped, but Pridgeon and his heavy backpack full of parts and tools were gone. Vanished. No heat trail. Nothing but the pouring rain.

"*Nichts.*"

"Pridgeon, come in," Wulf's father demanded over the comm-link. "Ryan, can you hear me?"

Wulf swallowed and listened, but all he could hear was the rain banging on his helmet.

"Maybe there's a hole?" his father said. "See if he stepped in a kinsella burrow."

Only then there was a flash in the corner of Wulf's eye. He jerked his rifle that way, but before he could fire, the shadow sped out of the woods and slammed into his father.

Father grunted at the blow, then growled as he struggled. As they fell to the ground Wulf realized the figure wasn't an animal, but a man. His active-camo was automatically adjusting to match its background, but it flickered as they rolled through the mud. Their attacker was in a combat exo, a frame which would give him four or five times his normal strength, far more than the antiques Wulf or his father wore.

Except Father somehow bunched up his legs between them and shoved. Servos whined in protest, but the kick sent their attacker flying back into the trunk of a tree. The impact knocked his helmet off. The man fell to the ground, rolled, and came up in a crouch, the rain wetting his dark hair.

Wulf aimed, but before he could pull the trigger—

"Peder?" Wulf blinked, hesitating... because the face in his targeting display belonged to his brother.

"Shoot him!" Father roared as he rolled to the side and scrambled to his feet. His rifle had landed somewhere in the mud, but he scooped up a large stick, to swing like a club.

"It's Peder!" Wulf shouted.

His older brother snarled and sprang at father.

Father dodged to the side, but his exo wasn't nearly as responsive as the one Peder wore. Father was thrown violently down. He struggled, but Peder pinned him and raised a knife in one hand. Father managed to grab Peder's wrist on the way down.

Wulf used to tell himself that Peder would escape Warlord's prison and come back to them. Come back clean. And things would be like they had been before. And he and Peder would play wicket. And Peder would tell his dumb jokes. And things would be like they'd been before... Only a year had passed since his brother had been captured and Wulf had slowly accepted that he was dead.

This was worse than dead.

Knife hand trapped, Peder pounded Father's faceplate with his other fist, shattering the visor and slamming Father's head into the ground.

Peder wasn't Peder anymore. Wulf had a clear shot. His finger was on the trigger. The display was shaking all over the place. But maybe they could heal him? Warlord had sent other captives against the Originals before. Doctors could fix slaveware, right? Pick it out of his brain and turn him back to himself?

"Wulf!" Father shouted. His exo groaned and whined as he fought to stop Peder's slow stab.

"But it's *Peder*!" Wulf screamed. But a voice inside his head told the truth. *Not anymore.*

"Shoot him!"

Peder let out a bloodcurdling cry, and the sound struck Wulf like a fist. That animal howl confirmed it. As Peder pushed his long-bladed knife toward Father's face, the metallic groaning from the old exo got louder. It was about to seize, and then Father would die.

"Wulf!" Father begged.

Wulf took aim, tears welling in his eyes, his hope snuffed out because he knew there was no way they'd ever get his brother back. He tagged the spot on Peder he wanted to hit then fired. The rifle kicked. The bullet struck Peder in the back.

But the armor was quality, and the bullet fragmented off.

Peder didn't even glance back. He simply growled and kept pushing the knife closer toward Father's eye. The old exo was weakening. Father was now using both hands to keep the knife back but was still losing the struggle.

Damn the Warlord! Wulf thought. Damn them all!

Wulf took a step to the side and fired again. The gun flashed in the rain. The shot cracked like thunder.

It took Peder in the neck. Blood flew out the side.

Peder didn't immediately crumple but put an arm down to steady himself.

Father threw Peder to the side, then ripped the knife from his hand.

Father was too close, and Wulf needed a clear shot. "Move!"

But Peder didn't rise. Instead, his arm spasmed, his chest fell and rose, and then he lay still.

The rain fell all about them, a loud hiss.

Father crept over and cradled Peder's head in one hand, then wiped the hair back from his face with the other. "Oh, son." His voice was full of grief. "My bright boy."

Wulf walked over in a daze and sank to his knees in the mud beside Father. Peder's neck wound was much larger than it had at first seemed. Wulf looked at the ragged hole, then at his brother's face.

"Peder..." He was numb with shock.

"You did what you had to do. What Peder would have wanted."

Peder the Magnificent. His brother. And there was his blood, thinning in the rain. And his ravaged neck.

While Father hurried and got his emergency breathing apparatus on, thoughts tumbled through Wulf's head. Maybe if he had hit Peder in the head with the butt stock, maybe he could have knocked him out instead of killing him. Maybe he and Father could have wrestled Peder together and somehow subdued him. They could have carried him back and held him until the doctors had figured out how to save him.

But he'd shot him instead.

"I should have—"

"No!" Father said. "He was beyond repair. You gave him the best thing a brother could. You gave him a quick death."

Grief boiled up in Wulf. He'd just had to kill his own brother. This was Warlord's doing. He'd taken their land, taken their lives. How many had he sent back this way? And how many more corrupted would come? Wulf's sadness turned to rage.

"I'm gonna kill him," Wulf growled. "That greasy whoreson. I'm gonna kill the Warlord."

"Someday, son..." And then Father held up a transmitter from Peder's suit. "Verdammich! Help me find them."

The suit was sending data back to the monsters who'd enslaved him.

"Destroy them! Quickly."

The man everyone on Swindle knew only as Warlord stood in front of the displays and smiled to himself as he watched the last signal go to static. The fight between son and father and son had been rather satisfying. It would remind those wretched Originals who they were dealing with.

"That howler didn't accomplish much," Fain said in disgust. Big Town's security chief held a container with three kava in it. They were long, multilegged creatures from the planet's surface with mandibles that could slice a finger off, but despite that they were rather delicious. Fain skewered one with a long fork right behind the head. The kava wriggled and writhed. Fain brought the kava up, held it out to his employer, but Warlord was full, so he waved it off.

"He got a good reading of their perimeter."

"But only one kill. We'll never exterminate all the surface rats at this rate." Fain took hold of the body of the kava, twisted and yanked, separating the head, and then he brought the decapitated body up and sucked out a chunk of meat.

"It's not about the numbers," Warlord told his subordinate. Fain was extremely dangerous, but in a direct sort of way. He hadn't hired the man for big-picture thinking. "We send in a few more uncles and mothers and fathers down there, a few of them explode for good effect. That's incredibly demoralizing."

"Implanting slaveware isn't cheap."

"I'm aware."

"Not to mention it's a war crime."

They both chuckled at that. Out this far the law was whatever Warlord said it was. "Oh no, not more sanctions from the ISF. Whatever will I do?" Warlord snorted. "Regardless, this amuses me. And Howlers keep the surface rats distracted while we prepare the final solution, Fain. The next arms shipment should be here soon. If the runners deliver half of what they've assured me they can get, I'll finally have the resources to root out the Originals once and for all."

"I'll believe that when I see it."

He knew the mercenary meant no disrespect. Fain had fought

in the crag mountains of Gloss and the glass-steel cave cities of Motonari, both terrible places indeed, but as far as the planets human beings had actually managed to settle and eke out existence, there wasn't anywhere less forgiving than the caustic, monster-infested, nightmare hellscape they were currently orbiting. The air slowly corroded their flyers. Satellites couldn't see through the thick canopy. The ground was too rugged for most vehicles. The plants so aggressive that if they burned a road, within days it was re-covered, and that was if the work crew didn't get torn apart by the wildlife in the process. Sending more men down only made it more likely they'd attract a kaiju. Those circumstances combined made it frustratingly easy for the guerillas to sabotage his operations and then vanish.

Warlord would have loved to drag a giant asteroid over and drop it into this wretched planet's gravity well, but he needed Swindle's vicious, yet extremely valuable, ecosystem alive. It was of no value to anyone dead. The original settlers who had stubbornly refused to fall into line, on the other hand...

"There's a weapons shipment coming. And once it arrives, we'll wipe them out—every man, woman, and child. We'll exterminate the rats. All the rats in all their filthy little ratholes."

CHAPTER 9

Gates were funny things. Sometimes you really couldn't get there from here. Though humanity had built hundreds of gates now, there were only five that had the proper angles to transit into the Swindle system. To avoid interference between those, each of the five arrival areas had a separate entry zone, which was a sphere as many thousands of kilometers in diameter as needed to accommodate the exit variance. All the zones were well outside the planetary plane.

Of course, all of them were watched.

There was no way to hide the sudden heat signature that appeared at the end of a transit. In the cold of space, a radiating ship was practically a glowing beacon. The only real way to hide a ship was in plain sight, which was the *Tar Heel*'s forte.

There were five paths into the Swindle system, but only one gate out. The place just hadn't been worth the investment until recently. The exit zone from the Nivaas system followed Swindle closely in its orbit. At normal speeds, it would take *Tar Heel* about five days to catch up to the planet. They were going to make it in three, because the captain was really eager to get this transaction over with. The crew was happy to push it, because every one of them was set to make a killing on their portion of the sale. After this, Jackson would have enough saved up to buy himself a modest little barge if he wanted to. Not that he'd decided to make the jump to owner-operator just yet, because he still wasn't convinced the captain was actually going to go through with his retirement plans.

Jackson was into kilometer two of his daily run around the eternal corridor with Tui and a few of the crew when the intercom told him to report to Shade's office.

With his shirt stained with sweat he wasn't exactly presentable, but she'd just have to deal with it. The captain and Shade were already there waiting for him. Though she didn't really have an official place in the ship's hierarchy, Shade had the second biggest cabin on the *Tar Heel*. It was part business office, and also her living quarters, along with her two bearded dragons. They were huge things, two and a half feet long at least. One was white, the other a deep red. They were sitting on a desk that folded out of the wall, tails draping off the side.

"You sent for me, Captain?"

"I did." He gestured at the chair next to him. "Have a seat."

Shade pulled a live cricket out of a little tub and held it out by its leg. The red lizard reached up and nipped it out of her hand, crunched it, and swallowed. That one's name was Ares. There was a little storage room dedicated to Shade's bugs. One time her hornworms had gotten out and disappeared who knows where. A few months later, moths had begun to fly about the habitat ring. It was amazing how much nonsense the captain would put up with, provided you made him enough money.

"We were just discussing how we're going to go about meeting with the buyer. I'm going to send the *Tar Heel* to the League port at Raste."

The little station above the dead planet Raste belonged to the League of Merchants. The league was supposedly independent, but ultimately answered to the ISF, the International Space Federation, the eight-hundred-pound gorilla that managed the exploration of stars and allotment of land claims for this section of the galaxy.

The ISF made laws and had its own courts, law enforcement, and military, all of which their client brazenly defied.

"Are you sure that's wise?" Jackson asked.

"We're sure," Shade said. "Our client might take it as an insult docking at Raste instead of Big Town, but it's insurance."

"You think he might try to rip us off?"

The captain shrugged. "I think the only reason he's not done that before is because we were more valuable to him still alive and making deliveries."

"The Warlord is a very intelligent man," Shade said. "He does nothing without a cost/benefit analysis."

"I was gonna say he knows not to kill the goose who lays the golden egg."

Shade's eyes narrowed suspiciously. "I'm not familiar with that saying, Captain. You tend to lose me with your bits of folksy Earth wisdom, but I can gather the context. Yes, in the past it benefited the Warlord for us to continue doing business. However, this is the most valuable shipment we've ever brought him. He may conclude it's easier to just seize it rather than pay for it."

Jackson nodded. "Makes sense. So you arrange your deal, get paid, and then we transfer the goods. You want me to fly the *Tar Heel* to Raste?"

"Naw, that's why I called you in here. Castillo will be in charge of the ship. I want you to come with us to meet the client."

"To meet the Warlord?" Jackson laughed. "Aw, come on, Cap. You know I'm not good with people."

"Yep," Captain Holloway said. "Believe me, I know."

Shade held out another cricket to her dragons. This time the white dragon took it and gave it a munch, the cricket's legs kicking a bit before it disappeared. That one's name was Zeus. "Previously, we simply dropped the containers with their requested items into orbit, and they wired us the funds. It has been an acceptable arrangement with minimum exposure for both parties. This shipment, however, will require a face-to-face negotiation. You know more about ground combat hardware than anyone else aboard. The Warlord likes his toys. You two can talk shop."

"I can talk mechs," Jackson grudgingly agreed with her. He'd spent a lot of time over the last few days inspecting their new prize, and it had confirmed his initial impression, that the Citadel was the finest mech he'd ever seen. If they'd had a few of those on Gloss, it would be a free planet today instead of a third-class suck pit.

"We want you to solidify the relationship," she said. "Talk up the finer points of the Citadel. Compare it to the other models we've delivered him."

Jackson had never been to the surface of Swindle, but he'd heard legends about how bad it was. The workers down there needed mechs to protect them from the giant wildlife, only the ISF—in their infinite bureaucratic wisdom—had declared military tech off-limits to these people. Luckily for the workers of Swindle, the captain didn't much care for those sorts of rules.

Since the beginning of their business relationship the Warlord had become something of a collector. He'd accumulated five mechs from them, but the Citadel was something new. Something far more responsive and flexible than anything he'd probably seen before.

"You want me to butter him up."

"We want you to make him drool," the captain said.

Jackson nodded. "If he knows anything about mechs, this thing sells itself."

"He does," Shade said. "He's a mech pilot too."

"Really? Manual control?"

"Linked."

Jackson whistled. "Impressive." That was a pretty elite fraternity. It took a special kind of brain to seamlessly perceive a walking tank as your own body, and only a small percentage of those could accept the implants.

"See? You're practically a brother from another mother. Talk shop, and help seal the deal," the captain said. "So you'll go with us in the striker to Big Town while the *Tar Heel* continues on to Raste. The striker holds six, so we'll take Tui and two of his men. More than enough for a friendly meeting with a longtime customer. If he's in a good mood, we should be able to move everything we've got. And I mean everything."

They had procured a whole lot of controlled items and illegal goodies on this run. The Citadel was just the really expensive cherry on top.

"That's a big payday," Jackson said.

"Huge."

"I like huge," said Shade.

"On the other hand," the captain continued, "if he thinks we're working for one of the factions who want to muscle in on his operation, we'll be taking a short trip out of an airlock."

"Airlocks are too dull for the Warlord," Shade said. "His justice usually involves a trip to the surface with cameras and betting to see just how long the idiot who got caught survives."

"What's the record?" Jackson asked.

Shade shrugged. She didn't have time for blood sports. There was business to conduct.

"We shouldn't have any problems," the captain said. "He knows what we traffic in, so he'll assume the *Tar Heel* is better armed than it looks. If he gets to feeling treacherous, it's not like he's in some hardened facility a thousand feet below ground. He's in an orbital. A big fat whale, floating on a predictable course. So it's in everyone's interest to play nice."

"There's no way in hell you'd ever give the order to open fire on an orbital with hundreds of thousands of innocent people living on it."

"Of course not," the captain said. "But the client doesn't know that."

Shade waved off the conversation about obliterating the orbital. "There are many ways to use nukes. That's not what I'm worried about. I'm worried about flyboy here." She looked directly at Jackson and narrowed her eyes. "Don't screw this up like you did on Nivaas."

Irritation rose in Jackson, but there was nothing to be gained by fighting with her now, so Jackson held his tongue.

"I don't trust the guy. Hell, his people literally only call him *Warlord* for goodness' sake, so he ain't exactly cuddly. However, he's kept his people alive in a godforsaken place, and he's done it all while thumbing his nose at the ISF, which I can respect. We get in, we close this deal. It's my last hurrah. With a nice fat parting bonus for the whole crew if everything goes right."

Jackson didn't know exactly what all was in inventory, but he'd helped steal enough of it to have a pretty good idea. The share payout on all of it was going to be big, add a bonus on top of that, and it put the dream of being an independent operator within reach, and not just of some crappy rock hopper, but an actual decent ship. Two months from now he could be Captain Jackson.

Jane was hacking into the security system of the league station above Raste when a red flower icon appeared on her visual.

She selected the flower and watched a video of a beach with an older couple on it. The sun was setting, the tide going out, the waves crashing on the rocks. There were trails of footprints walking along the edge of the surf line. The whole place was strewn with the detritus from a storm. In the distance, garbage bots were cleaning and grooming the sand.

The image was from her homeworld. A land of order and unmatched technological knowledge, which kept itself purposefully separated from the lesser branches of humanity.

Jane never talked about where she was from to the other members of the crew. It was safer for them that way. Only this was no mere postcard to remind her of her childhood. It was another coded message from her sister. Jane deciphered its hidden meaning within seconds.

The new threat hunting them wasn't from the Iyer, or the Boroughs. This was something new, yet familiar. And her sister had nearly been hacked. Nobody ever got close to hacking the girls of Mary 231.78, especially not their 22nd sister, who was smart and careful and always covered her tracks. She was the one who had initially devised their secret language. Hacking her would be like trying to hack the wind.

It had been several years since any of Savat's hounds had gotten this close to catching one of them. Since there were only a handful of people in the universe who could do what she did, as well as she could, she would have to be extra careful not to leave any trace. If the hunters got closer, she would have to disappear again and start over with a new identity somewhere else. She didn't want to do that. This ship was her home now. For the first time in her life Jane had made real human friends. Normally she had to build them.

The next day they boarded the striker—one of the two smaller ships the *Tar Heel* carried—and strapped themselves in. When everything was a go, they engaged the electric pushers that nudged them away from the hull. When there was enough separation, the captain turned the striker so the wash wouldn't blast the other ship, then engaged the thrusters. Though half of them aboard were certified to fly a striker, the captain had claimed the stick, probably for the fun of it.

While the little striker accelerated toward Big Town, the *Tar Heel* continued on without them. She was kind of pretty, in a big, awkward, lumbering sort of way.

"That's one majestic lady," the captain said wistfully as his ship grew tiny in the distance. Jackson exchanged a look with

Tui, but neither of them said anything. Only a handful of the crew knew about their captain's planned retirement, but all of those had already started a betting pool on how long his self-exile back to Earth would last.

"Alright ladies and gentlemen, Big Town, ETA three hours." Once the *Tar Heel* was just one of a million dots in the sky, the captain turned his chair around to face the compartment where the rest of them were strapped in. "You all know the basics, but Shade, would you make sure everyone knows enough about the political niceties of this deal so they can avoid screwing it up?"

She looked over at Tui and his handpicked goons, Katze and Bushey, and then finally at Jackson. "I don't know if I have the time or the crayons sufficient to do so."

"She means you," Tui fake whispered loud enough so everyone would hear anyway. "I'm educated."

"Yeah, but you got a degree in *philosophy*," Jackson muttered back.

"Gotta love correspondence courses." Then Tui turned back to their broker. "Don't worry. The captain asked me to pick only the sharpest and most diplomatic members of my security force for this mission."

"Thanks, Chief," said Katze.

"But since I didn't have anyone sharp or diplomatic available, I chose these two. Shade, this is Katze Yeager," he nodded toward the female goon. "And Mike Bushey," the male. "Trust me, despite appearances, they'll do."

Jackson had enjoyed working with both of them. Katze Yeager was younger and relatively new to the crew, Mike Bushey was older and been with them for a few years, but they were both vets, and like Tui, they'd both been gene-modded and cybernetically augmented by the militaries they'd served with. Katze had been an Amonite marine, and Bushey, a sergeant in the Earth Force Infantry. Though the crew of the *Tar Heel* mostly tried to avoid outright conflict, the captain liked having a few dedicated trigger pullers on the payroll. Tui had twelve people on his security team, most of whom never had anything to do with Grandma if they could help it.

"Thank you, Chief Fuamatu," said the captain. "Now get on with it, Shade."

"Very well. Our buyer is this man." Shade activated the holo projector on her wrist. The image was obviously a propaganda shot, showing a very handsome black man, lean, bearded, with way too many medals on his uniform. "This is Warlord."

Katze spoke up. "Warlord? No the? No title? Just Warlord?"

"That's all anyone calls him," Shade said.

"He actually doesn't have a name?" Katze asked.

"That is his name. Nobody knows what he was called before. All we know is the story he painted of himself when he seized control of Swindle. He was drafted to be a child soldier on Earth but worked his way up the ranks and survived the Ghana Wars. Afterwards he emigrated here in search of a better life. Came with his sister. Because of the implants he'd gotten from the Africa Pact, he got a job protecting harvesters down on the surface. When the corrupt territorial government fell to pieces, and his sister was killed during the food riots, he rose up and defeated the lawless gangs who had turned everything to chaos."

As Shade spoke, the pictures flipped through a slide show, but every image of Warlord was either a stylized piece of artwork, a propaganda shot, or an election poster. It was apparent that he maintained a very well-cultivated image.

"Warlord brought peace, order, and prosperity to Big Town, saving hundreds of thousands from death in the process. He's the hero of the orbital, and he's run this place with an iron fist ever since."

"Huh," Katze said, not satisfied.

"Yeah, one of those types." Bushey had seen plenty of dictators. "I'm sure he bleeds like the rest of us."

"Maybe," Tui said. "You never know what kinds of mods he's got."

"This is a friendly visit," the captain said. "You'll need to smile, Bushey."

Bushey smiled. It was a slightly hideous thing.

"Tremendous," the captain said. "We'll make sure to put you out front when the shooting starts."

The others chuckled. Except for Shade, who just kind of scowled, and then continued her briefing.

"That's the official version of events. In reality, I can confirm almost nothing about him. The faction he fought for collapsed, and their record keeping was spotty even before that. His personal infosec is top tier. Not even Jane could crack it. Compared to the gangs who fought over Big Town after the territorial government collapsed, he's probably an improvement. From all available intel his rule is strict, but the people are decently cared for. He keeps getting reelected ... by an inevitable landslide, with a hundred and ten percent voter turnout."

"He sounds like a real peach," said Katze.

"Actually, he's rather charming in person. However, this is where it gets interesting." The image changed to an extremely complicated looking chemical compound. "This is CX. I won't confuse Jackson by trying to pronounce its actual name. What you need to know is that it's very costly to synthesize, but is required in large quantities for gate operation, which makes it an exceedingly valuable commodity. The precursor agents are only found in a handful of places in known space. Swindle is one of them."

"But it's not like the others." said the captain. "Swindle's has the highest quality."

Shade changed the holo to a map of the sector. There were a lot of different color border lines clashing here. "After the territorial government was deposed, the ISF, the Syndicate, and the Pact all made claims on this system."

Their broker waited for that to sink in, because those were the three most powerful alliances in human history. As mankind had spread across the stars, most new worlds had remained independent, but a few had united to form powerful defensive coalitions. When superpowers butted heads, things could get very ugly.

"It's currently listed as a disputed territory on the registry of planets and Big Town isn't recognized as a legitimate government by anyone respectable. Hence the arms embargo. However, should one of the major powers attempt to take Swindle by force, the others would have no choice but to send fleets in response. If the flow of Swindlen CX is interrupted, it could have dire economic ramifications, so they each only keep a token presence here."

"Let me guess," said Bushey. "As long as the Warlord keeps CX production up, selling to all of them, the superpowers are happy to keep it to a cold war, and they leave him alone to run his little kingdom."

"Very good," said Shade. "And if Warlord were to openly side with any of them, the other two competitors would be forced to act. So he plays all three ... You're smarter than I originally assumed, Mr. Bushey."

"Eh, you do enough merc contracts for dictators, you learn their games."

Tui said, "No offense, Captain, but I gotta ask. Why'd you decide to start doing business with this guy? I thought the policy was to support each individual's *right to protect themselves and their property, governments be damned*. Ruthless dictators aren't our normal customers."

That was the code. And the captain did more than give lip service to that ideal—he'd risked life and limb to make sure others had the tools they needed to defend themselves.

"Show them the thing, Shade."

She flipped the holo. From the way the viewpoint was bobbing along, and the labored breathing, this clip was obviously from a helmet cam, and whoever was wearing it was running for their life. The view flashed across rough terrain, craggy rocks, and roots so gigantic they had to be climbed over. When the camera panned up, it showed a thick canopy of supermassive branches, densely covered in colorful leaves.

"This is from the surface of Swindle. You can find raw CX on other worlds, but it is exceedingly rare, and always lower quality. But on Swindle, it's comparatively common and pure, the result of a complicated biological process by an organism that lives on the bark of those trees. A process that nobody has been able to replicate anywhere else. Thus, teams of harvesters drop down to the surface to collect the CX, and then get out of there as fast as they can, because of—"

Then there was an earsplitting screech from the holo, so primal and angry it made Jackson instinctively flinch.

"Those," Shade finished.

The camera jerked up as something incomprehensibly large leapt between the trees. Despite being so vast, it was lightning quick. Jackson had seen elephants and mammoths grown from the original Earth DNA in person. This thing appeared to be far bigger than that but ran and jumped like a monkey. There was a flash of what had to be meter-long mandibles, as the camera was scooped up, the harvester thrashing through the air, and dropped, screaming, into what looked like a circular pit of quivering knives. Shade paused it there.

"That's a *mouth*," Katze said incredulously. "Those are *teeth*."

"Yes. And you can be thankful I stopped before the mastication process started. It's rather... grisly."

"Dear lord," said Tui.

"I doubt your god dwells on the surface of Swindle, Mr. Fuamatu," said Shade. "It's a rather unpleasant place."

The captain laughed. "That right there should accentuate why I decided to start running weapons to these folks. Believe it or not, I'm told that one's medium-sized. They also come in large, extra-large, and jumbo. Workers were going down to pick flowers in hell no matter what. Their casualty rate was insane, but since the pay's good there are always more hungry immigrants from Earth showing up to replace them. The only thing the ISF had allowed these people for protection down there were some old, worn out, T7 Jackals."

Jackson just shook his head. Those were light scout mechs from the Africa Pact. They were relatively fast, but their armament was negligible, and they were fragile enough that whatever that thing was in the video, it would pop them like a grape. Something as tough as the Citadel on the other hand... As fast as that creature appeared to be, you'd want to jack in—fly-by-mind—to be able to chase that thing, bounding from tree to tree, total commitment, fire and fury. It would be a challenge, a real hunt to remember... But then he dismissed that tempting thought, because those days were behind him. He was never going to risk plugging in again.

"Shade introduced us a few years back. Warlord made his case. Screw the ISF and their silly rules. So I started selling them stuff, though nothing nearly as advanced as what we've scored this trip. With proper kit, fewer workers get eaten, and we get paid. It's been a good arrangement. And now Warlord's got himself quite the shopping list, most of which we can check off with this shipment."

They accelerated toward Swindle until they were doing close to a hundred and thirty-two thousand kilometers per hour. The planet was easy to pick out from this distance. It was a much larger dot than all the surrounding dots. It also had a slight green tinge. Sensing their curiosity, the captain enlarged the view of the planet on the main display. It was covered with swirls of white and green clouds with red-and-brown-flecked land peeking up from below. The oceans were so blue they were nearly purple.

"So it is as nasty as they say," Katze muttered.

"A literal nightmare world," Shade answered, "with a caustic, poisonous atmosphere, extreme temperature swings, violent storms, and best of all, incredibly deadly wildlife."

"That doesn't sound too bad."

"Sounds like a party," the captain said. "Time for lunch."

They broke out the bags. Tui added some of his favorite snacks, little squares of chocolate with a sweet ant paste inside that was supposed to be a delicacy in the Xindalu system. They tossed the bag around in the weightless environment, enjoying the ant creams. Everyone except Shade partook. She was too busy reviewing the inventory they'd procured. She kept running her hands through her short pale hair, probably trying to decide how much she could get away with overcharging Warlord.

While he ate, Jackson got curious, pulled up the guidebook entry on Swindle, and started reading.

The planet's official name was Lush, or at least that was the name the exploration company who had discovered it had registered it as. They'd sent back glowing reports. Pictures of waterfalls three hundred meters high. Stunning woodlands, plains, lakes, and rivers. Sunsets on magnificent beaches. Huge parts of the planet, the official report claimed, were a veritable Eden.

The citizens of the poor, overpopulated, and crowded countries of Earth had rejoiced, as they did every time a habitable planet was found.

Exploration companies got paid in shares of whatever they discovered. They sold the tracts they'd been granted and made a huge profit. The rest of the planet was ceded to various countries by the rules of the International Space Federation. The countries then distributed their claims or sold them off according to their individual laws. Soon millions of people had been buying, selling, and trading tracts of land on a planet that only about a dozen explorers had actually seen with their own eyes.

Eventually three settlement companies formed to fund the construction of colony ships to Lush. One was big enough to hold a hundred thousand people. Many spent their life savings to buy a claim, supplies, and pay for the journey. The broke and desperate bonded themselves out. They made their epic journey through the five gates, eager to claim their slice of paradise.

Except when they arrived, they found that the reports were a fraud.

Oh, it was as beautiful as the photos made it out to be. The exploration company had merely omitted some inconvenient facts, like how the atmosphere was *breathable* in only the most tortured sense of the word, and how everything that lived there wanted to kill you.

"Wow, these people got screwed." Jackson closed the page, then asked Shade, "Did they ever find the executives of the exploration company?"

"No," Shade answered, annoyed at having her paperwork interrupted. "They rolled up a number of the peons, but the ones behind it all took their money and disappeared."

Katze had been reading too. "Imagine coming all this way, with no way to get home. A hundred thousand people stuck in a ship above this crapsack world because of a con, those poor suckers."

"Maybe the first ones that died off, before they found CX." Bushey snorted. "As for the rest, I'm crying big old tears for them and the gold mine they got down there. I don't care if it does come with a few kaiju."

"I think that's Warlord's take on it too," the captain said. "Maybe you and he will get along after all."

A couple hours later they began their approach toward the port of entry into Swindle's sovereign space. The port was simply a spinning habitat ring with an array of cannons that moved in an orbit that kept it in a fixed position relative to Big Town.

The port control radioed the captain, who identified himself. They sent out a gremlin to verify they were just a little striker. They got a cursory scan, and that was it. It was nothing like the layers of complex security around Nivaas. Big Town simply didn't have those kind of resources.

Not much later, the captain turned the ship a hundred and eighty degrees and began to decelerate. The force shoved Jackson into the back of his seat. Big Town's "navy" consisted of a few civilian ships they'd welded railguns onto, but they'd still smoke anything that came toward the orbital too fast.

Katze pointed at a conglomeration of objects orbiting Swindle. "Is that it?"

"That's Big Town and its outlying facilities," the captain answered. "In all of its hideous, crowded awfulness. Since I've been here, I guess I can play tour guide."

The central part of Warlord's domain was the shape of a closed-off tube, almost a kilometer in diameter and over eleven kilometers long, rotating to provide the close to two hundred thousand inhabitants something akin to gravity. That part had been the original colony ship, but Jackson only knew that from reading the guidebook. It was impossible to recognize as having once been a ship now.

"When the colonists couldn't go down, and most of them couldn't afford to return to Earth, or didn't have anything to go back to, they turned their bus into a space station. They started adding modules onto it and have never really stopped."

"It sure doesn't look planned," said Tui.

"Only if the architect was a crazy cat lady with hoarding issues. I don't think the builders were big on zoning regulations."

Big Town was ugly from the outside. There were huge solar arrays, and radiators, and various other appendages sticking out of it. Some were straight, some crooked, some short, some long. It looked like a crazy tentacle monster. On this end of the orbital, a long, stationary port arm stuck out, extending for about a half a klick. With all its branches, it looked like it could accommodate several transports at a time. On the far end the inhabitants had attached a huge asteroid that was in the shape of a human ear, the lobe sticking out into space.

"The mountain there is full of ice. They recycle their water supply, of course, but they always need more to send down with the harvesters who brave the surface, and they lose even more during the CX processing. When this one's mined out, they'll tow over a new one from their belt. You see that big lump there?" The captain highlighted a section on their display. "That's the CX processing plant they built for their gold rush. Lots of security there."

And indeed, that lump bristled with bots. Warlord's sad little fleet was mostly positioned to protect it, because that was their moneymaker.

"And the large asteroid trailing Big Town?" Katze's military service had been spent performing boarding actions, so of course she was the one to notice such things. "Gun platform, I assume?"

"Cheap, but effective. He's got a number of them covering the place. The other two long orbitals in visual range are their farms. Warlord took me to one once. Think big greenhouses with high levels of carbon dioxide to help the plants grow. They're actually kind of amazing. There's one other big station in orbit, built out of one of the smaller colony ships, but it's always on the opposite side of the planet. It's run by some guy named Riku Kalteri, and they claim to be their own country."

"They rivals?" asked Tui.

"Oh yeah. He hates Warlord, and Warlord hates him. They would have blasted each other out of the sky a long time ago, but that would force the ISF to step in, and neither of these little tinpot dictators want that to happen. I don't supply him, and I don't rightly know who does, but I'm sure he's got a similar arrangement going. Kalteri has his piece of Swindle. And there are a half-a-dozen corporations jockeying to get pieces as well."

"A lot of complications," Katze said mused.

"It's a powder keg," the captain said.

"It's money," Shade said. "Lots and lots of money."

Big Town control sent the captain his docking destination. They flew past three cleaning ships, collecting garbage. They flew past gremlins. They flew past a dropship on its way to the surface, probably carrying a crew of harvesters. And then they were approaching their designated bay. They moved in gently. Their approach was textbook. Once they were close, mechanical arms reached out, attached, and dragged them the rest of the way. A moment later there was a thump as they locked on.

"See, Jackson? I've still got it." Then the captain turned his chair around. "Okay, team. Game time."

They all unbuckled from their seats. The light above the port door turned to green, indicating it was clear to open.

"Please wait," Control said over the open channel.

They waited.

"You may now disembark."

Tui flipped open a cover and swung the lever to release the door. There was a brief whoosh and whistle as air flowed in from the corridor, indicating the port had a bit more air pressure than the striker. There were two security guards waiting there with carbines slung. One was male, one female. They wore dark blue body armor with snappy orange accents. On their heads were black helmets with faceplates and heads-up display. They were accompanied by a couple of hovering bots with menacing ports, which were probably also guns.

"You will need to leave all weapons on your ship. We're here to make sure you comply," the female guard said. "Welcome to Big Town."

CHAPTER 10

"No guns?" The captain seemed genuinely surprised. "Is that a new policy?"

The female security guard said, "Big Town is a gun-free zone now. It helps keep the peace. You'll also want to leave behind anything that could be used as an explosive. You will be thoroughly scanned."

"Can we keep sharp, pokey objects?" Jackson asked.

"Jackson." The captain shook his head, warning him to behave. "We'll do as the lady requested." His tone indicated he knew this was nonsense, but they needed to get paid.

The rest of them glanced at each other, then began to shed weapons.

"Seems funny," said Tui as he took a short-barreled autocannon from beneath his coat. "Somebody who needs us to run guns for him because he's not allowed to have any, banning the people below him from having guns."

"We're guests here," Shade admonished him.

"Wasn't arguing, just amused by the irony is all."

Jackson wasn't going to go in naked. He'd dealt with police like this before and knew he could count on Fifi and a couple of other accessories, so he shrugged, then removed the holster that was clipped to his belt, and went to stow it.

The captain looked at the one gun, and gave Jackson a pointed look, "Didn't you have two?"

"You're right," Jackson said in mock surprise. "I plumb forgot."

119

And he removed the tiny holdout piece and set it next to its companion.

"All of them," the captain said to the crew.

Tui, Katze, and Bushey complied, and soon a bunch of weapons had been crammed into the storage compartment. A nice big display of firepower.

During all this Shade had simply watched. It appeared she was a step or two ahead. Or maybe she had something else that wasn't technically a gun or explosive. Maybe Jane had given her a Fifi as well.

The captain turned back to the security guards. "I think that does it."

"Thank you. As you exit your ship, please engage your shoe magnetics and stand here to be scanned. When you're cleared, you will step down the corridor to where Frans will wait for you."

The crew moved into the corridor. The place had that rough, uneven look of a facility that had been slapped together from whatever modules they could get their hands on. The construction was metal grating—probably made from local meteorite ore—and exposed tubing. The air had a faint whiff of burning plastic.

As the guard turned, Jackson noticed a white strip at the top of her chest. The name Lotte was printed there. Frans had a similar strip on his uniform with his name.

"You Dutchies?" Jackson asked, because he'd once known a soldier with that last name from the Dutch colony back on Gloss.

"*Ja hoor*," she said. "There were several thousand of us among the first arrivals here."

The captain stepped out of their striker, went to the spot the guard designated, and held his hands crossed over his head. Three of the hovering bots surrounded him and then moved from head to toe in a choreographed pattern. When they finished, one said, "State your name, the name of your ship, and your business."

"Captain Nicholas Holloway. MSV *Tar Heel*. Here to negotiate some trade with the Warlord."

The scanner asked for him to open his hands. He did that. The second scanner hovered over each momentarily, taking a detailed image of his hand and fingerprints. The first scanner asked him to turn his hand over. The captain complied again. The third scanner reached out with a probe. A thin filament appeared. It slipped into and back out of the skin of the captain's hand, taking a speck of blood with it.

"You know your crew took my biometrics last time," the captain said to Lotte.

"We do this with every arrival now."

"Something happen to make Warlord more paranoid than usual?"

"Nothing of the sort. Records can be misplaced or changed. It's good to refresh them once in a while." And then she locked a thin orange bracelet around one of his wrists. "This is an identifier. It's read throughout Big Town. The governor has given you credit to use at restaurants and places of entertainment. Just have them ping the identity on the bracelet. Please do not remove it during your stay. However, should something happen, and the lock opens, it will alert us. And we'll come fix it for you."

That was a nice way of putting it, Jackson thought.

The scanner blinked green.

"Please proceed down to Frans," she said.

Frans had taken up a position farther down the corridor. The lights made a reflection on his faceplate that obscured his eyes. The dude was standing so perfectly still Jackson wondered briefly if Frans was a synth but decided against it.

Shade went next, then it was Jackson's turn. He tensed just a little as the scanners passed over where Fifi was hiding in his pocket, but the scanners didn't seem to recognize her or care, and he was given a bracelet and cleared to go stand with Frans. The others went through the same process. Tui was last, and when he finished, he closed the door on the striker and sent a signal to the *Tar Heel*. The door locked with a loud series of snicks.

They walked in single file along the corridor toward the main tube that led to the orbital, Lotte in front, the crew in the middle, and Frans and his bot brigade in back. It was pretty tight security, Jackson thought. The bracelet did more than provide their identity, it was probably transmitting video and audio. It seemed Governor Warlord wanted to keep tabs on his visitors. Jackson understood the need for security in orbitals—even a small bomb in the right place could wreak havoc—but he still didn't like the intrusion. When Jackson retired—should he live that long—it certainly wouldn't be to an orbital hab.

At least their escort seemed to relax a bit after they'd passed their scans, because they lifted the face shields on their helmets. Both of them were younger than expected, and also exceedingly pale. That was probably more from living beneath artificial lights than being Dutch.

The main port tube acted as the trunk of a tree. It was stationary and therefore provided a weightless environment. It was also spacious—wide enough for three or four cargo tows to use at the same time on their way to and from the ships.

At the mouth of the corridor a cart waited. It was long and narrow, nothing more than eight two-person benches placed one in front of the other. There was a place up front for Lotte. Another at the back for Frans. The rest of them selected a bench and strapped in. And then Lotte gave the word, and the cart flew them down the long tube toward the orbital.

They passed corridors leading to other landing bays above them, below them, and to the right and left. They passed other bench carts with people going the other way. One in particular was very long, made up of multiple segments, and must have seated at least seventy-five. They passed maintenance crews dressed in yellow. There were large wall displays in the spacious tube delivering news. One report was about a sighting of some huge creature they called Moby Dick down on the surface. Another was about a fire on an outpost in Swindle's solar system. A third was the announcement of a new park being built somewhere in Big Town.

They proceeded to the end of the port tube which ended in a huge wall, the other side of which had to be Big Town. Right in the middle of the massive wall was a circular door twenty meters wide. It was closed now, but Jackson suspected it opened straight into the center axis of Big Town. There was a large mechanical ring around the door and placed at equal intervals around it were three wide bays.

Their bench cart flew into one of the bays and parked. Lotte asked them to engage their shoe magnetics and exit to the left. There were windows here, so Jackson walked over and got his first view of Big Town's interior, which was spinning like a huge Ferris wheel.

"Please grab a handhold and brace yourself," Lotte warned.

They did. And the ring which held the bays began to move, slowly accelerating to match the spin of Big Town. It took a few slightly nauseating minutes for the ring to accelerate until they were moving at the same rate. From the window, it now appeared that Big Town was stationary, and the port tube was spinning.

Lotte said, "I suggest using the handrails until you get used to our gravity." Then a double door slid open. "Please follow me."

Jackson followed Lotte out and took in the amazing view. Take a regular city, and then roll it into a tube. The landing they came out on was near the center. Buildings covered the whole interior, running from where they were to the far end, eleven klicks in the distance. They were below, to the sides, and above, their roofs pointing toward the center, because that was basically *up*. A few of the structures looked to be a few hundred meters high and stuck out past the rest, but most were only three or four stories tall.

From here they had one heck of a view. Some parts of the city appeared tidy, but most of it was ramshackle chaos. Living pods stacked on living pods, with bridges between them, and pop outs, and crazy alleys. On a street above his head a group of people in white shirts walked along a street. They looked small at this distance. Tiny people walking on the ceiling. To Jackson's left, three women stood on the roof of a building, drinking something next to a small tree. Both the women and the tree stood almost perpendicular to him.

"Is that supposed to be your sun?" Katze asked. She was pointing to a cluster of bright globes in the distance, hovering in the center of the tube. They were bright enough that Jackson had to shield his eyes.

"Yes," Lotte said. "They move from one end to the other, simulating sunrise and sunset."

"Good for the circadians," Katze said.

"Indeed. Rhythm is necessary for public health and one of the first things our people added when Big Town was founded." Lotte pointed. "You can see the governor's mansion there. That's our destination."

Jackson followed her finger, but the place wasn't hard to spot. It was more like a palace than a mansion. It had wide grounds and trees and a couple of soaring towers. It was especially notable because there weren't that many other open areas in the tube. There were trees on roofs here and there, but it appeared most of the plant life in Big Town ran up the sides of the buildings in the form of moss and vines.

Bushey asked, "Is that an actual beach? Just down from Warlord's place?"

"That is our public pool. Four meters at the deepest spot. Warlord wants his people to be happy, reduce stress. There are a limited number of passes given out each day to access it."

Bushey held up his orange wrist band. "And this can get me in?"

"It can," Lotte said.

"There will be no time for swimming on this trip," the captain said.

"Captain!" Bushey said.

Their superior shook his head.

"You're disappointing a lot of women," Bushey said.

"I'm sure they'll recover."

Bushey sighed and gave the beach a wistful glance. "There are some real negatives to living on a spaceship."

"If you'll follow me," Lotte said, "we'll take a ride down to the street level. There is a car waiting."

They entered a lift and went down. Spin gravity worked in many ways like planetary gravity, but in other ways it didn't. For example, up on the observation platform the gravity was almost nonexistent. However, as they descended in the lift, the gravity increased until it felt like one G at the bottom. Maybe a little more. That was one of the reasons why the buildings weren't super tall here. Living in low G took a toll on a body. Still, some of the buildings seemed too tall, and he wondered what living up there would be like. Planetside people paid extra for a penthouse with a view. Here it would probably be miserable.

They walked out of the lift area into a lobby and through some automatic doors *outside*. A sort of junction converged on this lift. At street level the buildings looked even more haphazard. There were some structures that were obviously parts of the colony ship but stacked onto them were all manner of construction. There were rooms made of converted shipping containers. Others were habitat modules, probably from the original supplies meant for the surface. Then there were many more built out of every material imaginable, like cinder blocks that were probably a by-product of the asteroid mining, or an odd-looking sort of lumber that must have come from the surface. In every direction Jackson looked, all of the streets running away from this junction had some building or house popping out into the airspace above them.

Two shiny black cars were waiting for them. They weren't large vehicles by any means, just carts, made of composites and plastics to keep them superlight and energy efficient. But they were enclosed with tinted windows. On their sides was painted an official-looking flag of green, yellow, and black. On top was a cartop billboard. It was playing a video of a handsome, dark-skinned man in a military uniform smiling and waving, while people threw white roses at his feet. The picture changed to a closeup of the Warlord's rugged face. Then he brought up his other hand and raised two fingers wide.

"Rabbit ears?" Katze asked.

"It's a V," the captain said.

"For victory," Bushey explained to his associate. "Old Earth thing."

"Oh. I thought for sure he was giving us the bunny," Jackson said. "That's a really bad insult where I'm from."

The doors on the cars opened. Lotte ushered the captain, Shade, and Tui into one. When Tui got in the whole vehicle tilted toward his side. It was the mods. Denser muscles and bones made him weigh a ton. Lotte climbed in behind them, and only slightly corrected the tilt.

Frans directed Jackson, Katze, and Bushey into the other, and rode with them. When the doors closed, Jackson noticed the slightest hint of a woman's perfume. He couldn't tell if it was left over from the previous occupant, or if the car just normally smelled that way. It was kind of nice. Then he realized it was coming from Frans.

The electric cars pulled out of the junction and into one of the joining lanes. Jackson saw their car had two little flags on the end of the hood to whip in the wind.

"How far is the mansion?" Bushey asked.

"Just a few minutes," Frans snapped.

"You know that's a measure of time, not distance, right? How many klicks?"

"Not far." Frans wasn't near as talkative as his partner.

Bushey glanced over at Jackson with a look that said he'd assessed Frans and determined he was a dick.

They passed shops and houses, soft music playing over the car's speakers. They passed people eating. Other people walking. One man was riding an old-fashioned pedal bike. There was a boy with a dog. A woman carrying a sack of oranges, which Jackson figured had to be scarce in these parts. But then he saw a bunch of them growing on the wall of a building and reconsidered.

Their little convoy rolled through a rough part of town. The houses here were smaller. Shanties all snarled together and stacked high. Outside one shack sat a haggard man wearing a respirator and carrying an oxygen tank. A few doors down, there was a woman sitting on a porch stoop. Big patches of her hair had fallen out, giving her the appearance of some kind of witch. There was a man up against a wall being busted by two police.

Then they were out of the poor section and flashing lights caught Jackson's attention. A hovercar was flying above the buildings to their right. The car looked like it was slowly spiraling, but it was flying straight, and it was the city that rotating around it.

And then the buildings abruptly ended. Ahead was a tall rail fence and a gate. Jackson noticed a number of cameras, bots, and even a hornets' nest. Beyond the fence was actual grass and trees. In a place this crowded, it was a pretty ostentatious show. In the middle of the green space rose the palace.

Guards dressed in blue and orange armor manning the gate waved the two cars through. About thirty seconds later Jackson and the others stopped in front of the entrance. The palace had porticos and arches and pillars. It looked like it was made of marble, but Jackson assumed it was some composite made to look that way, and whatever was underneath had gotten dug out of an asteroid.

The car doors opened. A voice from some hidden speaker said, "Welcome to the governor's house."

They all got out and looked around. It was an impressive piece of real estate with a nice view of Big Town curling up around it. There were more guards patrolling the grounds, a sniper team on the roof, and Jackson thought he picked up the faint buzz of an aerial drone as they were ushered toward the front walkway. Before they reached it, the doors of the mansion opened, and a few more guards walked out, followed by a man who seemed very familiar, probably because they'd seen his face on a several dozen posters on the short drive here.

The infamous Warlord had dispensed with the chest full of medals and was dressed in plain olive fatigues and combat boots. He opened his arms wide. "Friends," he said with a big smile. In person, he was of above average height, with a strong, angular build, as if someone had used oak in his construction. "Welcome, Captain Holloway, Ms. Thomas, and associates. You've traveled so far. Please, please, come in."

Jackson looked at the guards here on the walkway, those above, those back down by the car, and followed the captain into the Warlord's lair.

CHAPTER 11

Inside the wide entry area were more cameras and another guard. Warlord led them down a hallway with a gorgeous real-stone floor. Or was it a composite so cunningly made it was impossible to spot as a fake? The hall opened into a large room with a ceiling three stories up and tall windows. The windows were mirrored so those inside could see out, but nobody outside could see in, and Jackson assumed they were massively bulletproof. Still, they were too large for his security tastes.

In the middle of the great room were couches arranged around a low table. On the floor was a rug made of the skin of some animal that was almost twenty feet long. The skin had a jagged stripe pattern to it. On one wall was a large display showing various video feeds of Big Town along with graphs and other metrics. On another were feeds and displays of Swindle's solar system. The third wall was a collection of claws, teeth, and a few taxidermized heads of strange animals.

"Come. Sit down." Warlord gestured toward the couches.

The captain and Shade walked over and sat. Jackson, Tui, and the others decided to stay alert and standing. The Warlord and one of his lieutenants sat down. The lieutenant was a big man, hardened by battle, scarred, and clearly a mod job. He watched the crew with a predator's eyes. Six guards stood in various places around the room and down the hall.

Warlord saw that most of the crew had remained alert and

frowned. "Please, do not insult my hospitality. I understand your line of works requires a cautious mindset, but we are all friends here. Your associates should sit."

The captain nodded at Tui, so they did.

They were all imbedded with Jane's short-range wireless, which allowed them to text by brain wave. Jane had originally wanted to embed it in their brains. But there was no way Jackson was going to give anything direct access to his brain again, so she had relented and planted his subdermally. That way, if he wanted it out, he could cut it out with a knife. Up to this point, they'd kept the chatter quiet, but the captain sent a message.

"Play cool but be ready."

"Would you like a drink?" Warlord asked. "A bite to eat?"

"We're fine," the captain said. "Maybe later."

"It's always straight to business with you, isn't it? You must forgive my need for conversation. Swindle is so far off the beaten path that I rarely have visitors." Their host looked to Shade. "How is your father?"

Father? Jackson thought. He didn't know Shade had a father. Not a living one, at least.

"He's doing very well, thank you."

"And you," he said to the captain. "How is your leg? Last time you had complaints."

"It's better. Doctors actually regrew the knee."

"And here I thought you didn't believe in mods."

"It's a regrow, not a mod," the captain said pointedly.

"A valid distinction. I don't entirely trust bio mods myself, but sometimes you have to have them. Isn't that right, Fain?"

The lieutenant shrugged.

"Fain is a big believer in mods."

"I'm a believer in getting the job done," Fain said.

"Indeed. He has accumulated so many mods. It's amazing he still looks human at all."

Jackson noted that Fain was studying the *Tar Heel* security force. He seemed almost dismissive, until his eyes lingered on Tui. The big, tattooed fellow just smiled, affable as could be, but Fain clearly recognized someone who was as extraordinary as he was and gave a small nod of acknowledgment. Tui returned it. Soldier to soldier.

"My apologies, this is Fain. Think of him as my right-hand man."

"This is my Chief of Security, Tui Fuamatu, his men Katze and Bushey, and Jackson Rook is one of my pilots."

"It is a pleasure to meet you all...I am happy to hear about your knee. They regrew my foot a year ago. Can you believe that? One of the most complex structures of the body, yet science allows us to make a new one."

"What happened?" Shade asked. It was unlikely she cared, but she was polite.

"A small caliban bit it off down on the surface." He flexed his foot. "But it feels fine. Splendid even. They're ambush predators. The bugger was waiting for me."

"That sounds like a story," the captain said.

"We were out on a patrol looking for something larger. There was a small ravine off the side of the trail. An eight-footer burst out and knocked me over. By the time I blew its brains out—although they're not really brains like we have—it had chomped through my exo and taken the foot. Swallowed it whole." He snapped his fingers. "That fast."

The captain shook his head in wonder. "That sure is something."

"I got the better end of the deal." Warlord pointed at one of the mounted heads and grinned. The hideous thing looked like it came off an ant crossed with a crocodile. "My foot wound up in his belly, but his skull ended up on my wall."

Jackson was kind of starting to like this Warlord. But then he noticed there were two human skulls decorating an end table, one slightly larger than the other, and he wondered who those had belonged to.

"And how is Big Town?" Shade asked.

"We're surviving. But not all. Those ISF bastards are slowly killing us with these sanctions. The ISF presents itself as a garden of peace, but its flowerbeds are full of vipers."

Jackson found himself nodding in agreement. The ISF had backed the rise of a brutal and illegitimate government on Gloss. They'd supplied the scum who had murdered his family and friends. Jackson was more than happy to help anyone the ISF was against, to defend what was theirs on general principle.

"I can afford a new foot, but how many of my people can? They work like dogs down on the surface. They bleed. They die. Some come out worse with ruined lungs. Ruined eyes. Missing limbs. We could help them, but the ISF hampers me. They set quotas on our exports. I could triple exports, easily, but they shut down my traffic through the gate."

"They're a meddling bunch. It's not right," the captain said.

"No, it's not. It was our people who were stranded here. Our people who died. It's our people who risk their lives on the surface. Our people who built this orbital and keep it safe. And those jackals in the ISF want to take it from us. Did you know they are strip claiming us now?"

"The ISF?" Shade seemed a bit surprised.

"Not directly. Their robbers go in and out through Kalteri. And the ISF just looks the other way. They allow it. There's no way they don't know what's happening. They rob us, sabotage our operations. But it's going to end."

"I brought you some goodies, but if you want me to bring you something sufficient to take on the ISF, I'm gonna need a bigger boat."

"A direct confrontation against the ISF would be futile," said Shade.

Warlord smiled. "Let's keep them thinking that, shall we? So, show me what you've brought. You did source all of my order, right?"

"And more." The captain unrolled the clear tube he'd brought with him on the table, activated the display, then tapped an app. The picture was of leaves. The warlord and his lieutenant moved a bit closer and looked at it.

"A plant?"

"Your people are going to love you for this," the captain said to the Warlord.

"What is it?"

"Mangoes."

"The fruit?"

"They're delicious. These are engineered to grow like vines on the outsides of your houses. These are everbearing, so you'll have a continuous crop. And they've been designed to produce a load of nutrients. It's the latest from Earth."

Warlord shrugged.

Shade looked a little disappointed with his reaction. She'd probably been hoping the mangoes would make more of an impact, but that was before she'd seen on the drive here that somebody else had already sold them genetically modified oranges. "We've brought seeds in three flavors. Your people will appreciate the variety."

Warlord nodded. "Very good. What else?"

The captain showed him the formulas for some new medicines they could replicate for various ailments. He showed him a high-yield meat-growing vat, complete with an edible packaging they could make here on the orbital. He showed him the crate of a new quantum computer chips that could process at massively parallel speeds. There were the plans and tech for better water filtration. Tech for mining and reducing ore. There were dozens of things.

When the captain finished, Warlord sat back. "You are making me very happy. You have all of this in that ship you have docked above Raste?"

The captain glanced at Shade.

"You thought I wouldn't know?" He cocked his head toward the surprisingly advanced display of the Swindle system. There was a real-time marker for everything bigger than a garbage truck. Including one for the *Tar Heel*, which was sitting next to the fourth planet. "We picked you up way out there. You know, I could still take that ship if I wanted."

The captain just smiled. "Except you're too smart to ruin such a long-term mutually beneficial business arrangement for a temporary gain."

"The golden goose eggs," added Shade, who had apparently decided she was now an expert on Earth sayings.

"You should have just flown straight here and saved yourself the fuel. Do you not trust me?"

"It's not you, Warlord," Shade said. "It's standard operating procedure. Not everyone is as trustworthy as you are. And we simply can't be lax."

Warlord gave her a patronizing smile. "I'm not insulted. If I were you, I wouldn't bring my ship here either. Of course, what's to prevent me from simply taking you hostage, until they deliver everything you've showed me for free?"

Jackson noticed all the guards in the house were standing ready. Tui, Bushey, and Katze had already picked their targets.

But their captain was too cool for that. "Well, you wouldn't want to do that, because the moment any of my crew is threatened, a message will get sent to the ISF and the Americans, detailing the *full* inventory of every delivery we've ever made here. If they knew how bad their embargo's been working, they'd have no choice but to beef up their presence. That would put you in a bit of a pickle, now wouldn't it?"

Warlord seemed to be enjoying this. He motioned at his lieutenant. "Fain here told me I should kill you because you know too much. But I like you. I've always liked you, Holloway. You have to choose your friends wisely, I tell him."

"Yes, you do."

Despite the casual death threats, Jackson knew he had been witnessing a dance of negotiation. But still, that last bit was a reminder. Maybe even a threat.

"So, what else have you brought me?" Warlord rubbed his palms together greedily. "Let us get to the *good* stuff."

"Jackson, why don't you tell our client about the Citadel?"

Warlord turned to him curiously. Jackson had done his best to stay quiet and unnoticed so far. "This one was a pilot, you said?"

"Of ships, passable. Of mechs . . . a virtuoso. Jackson here fought in the civil war on Gloss. On the people's side, of course."

Now that had gotten Warlord's attention. "By hand?" He tapped the side of his temple with two fingers. "Or by head?"

"Fully integrated," Jackson said.

"The only way to fly! Not a mere operator, we have a real warrior in our midst." Warlord was impressed. "And a freedom fighter to boot."

Jackson shrugged.

"You're a hero."

"I was just another guy who didn't like having a boot on my neck."

"That's how all heroes feel. Believe me. That's why I'm here. Nothing good will ever flourish without men who are willing to get a little blood on them. Civilization needs men like you and me. Without us, it all descends into chaos."

"He's just a kid," Fain said, scowling at Jackson. "What are you, fifteen?"

He was twenty-two standard, but Fain was just being insulting. "I got a real early start."

Warlord nodded, because apparently so had he. "I too was a child soldier. You wouldn't understand, Fain. When it comes to flesh and blood, you're as good as it gets, but when a soldier's mind is fully integrated with a mech, together they become an unstoppable force. The information comes upon you like a flood. You see all, know all, react faster than thought, and move like the lightning strike. You feel through plastic skin, walk on titanium bones, and dispense death with a whim. You become a god of the battlefield."

Jackson nodded. If anything, Warlord was understating the feeling. "Yeah, pretty much that. Only Citadel is the latest in mech tech. It's a step above anything I've seen."

The Warlord's eyebrows raised a bit, and he leaned forward on the couch. "Tell me more, brother."

Shade seemed pleased at that honorific. On a personal level she obviously didn't like Jackson much, but she did like closing deals.

Jackson reached down and slid the display to a video from Raycor of Citadels in action. As it played, a grin broke out on Warlord's face. "Beautiful. Simply beautiful." It was a series of quick cuts of the sleek machine, running, leaping, climbing sheer cliffs, diving through buildings, while stats like power to weight ratio, reactor efficiency, and armor density scrolled by, that sort of thing.

"Point zero *zero* six reaction lag? Incredible. That's an order of magnitude faster than my first mech!"

If the available intel was to be believed... "Jackal, correct?"

"Yes," the Warlord answered. "The factory advertised them as swift and deadly. They did not tell us the swift was for how soon before they broke down, and the deadly meant for the pilots." He laughed. "And what did you fly in your war, Jackson?"

"A cobbled together Thunderbolt 5, until it got shot out from under me. Then I was assigned the lone Shockwave on Gloss."

"Ah, both classics. Was yours made by Alphex or Durendal?"

This guy did know his stuff. "The Durendal. The captain here smuggled it in for us. That's how we first met."

"So tell me, Jackson, have you flown this Citadel yet?"

"Yes. Briefly."

"And?"

"Supple. Very smooth. No lag. No jerk. No truncates. It's like wearing a set of summer clothes. It's shockingly quiet, but with power to spare."

"Did you link in? How was the interface?"

"I did not." He wouldn't do that ever again, but Jackson didn't feel the need to spill his whole life story to some random dictator, so he lied instead. "Didn't have the chance. But according to the stats though, it should blow your mind. Gen seventeen neural uplink speeds are off the charts."

"Oh." Warlord groaned in anticipation. "And it's up there above Raste with those League fools."

"It's in good hands," the captain assured him. "It's not going anywhere until we bring it here."

"You sure? The Swindle system has no shortage of pirates." Not that Warlord had any relation with those unsavory types, of course.

"My very capable XO is in command of the *Tar Heel*, and my infosec is in the hands of someone who regularly bests tier-one AIs."

He was, of course, talking about Jane, who was basically a wizard.

"Woe be unto the fool who tries to heist that ship," said Shade.

Warlord nodded. "Yes, indeed."

And Jackson figured he probably had his own people up there on Raste. Heck, he might have paid off the League.

Warlord turned to the captain. "I could talk mechs all day, and perhaps later Jackson and I shall, but I must be concerned for my people first. What other cargo do you have for me aboard this magnificent treasure ship?"

"Everything that you requested," Shade said. "Chemicals, assemblers, raw materials, plans. Designs for new centrifuges."

"I need weapons."

"How about plans for a laser cannon that will extend the range of your grid? But more importantly, a design for mirrors that won't degrade as fast when the laser hits them."

Shade pulled up the details of everything they'd brought on the weapons side of things. It was a gold mine. Truly. And Jackson realized he hadn't known the half of it. It surprised him how well the captain and Shade had kept the full extent of the inventory hidden. If they sealed this deal, Jackson wouldn't be stuck looking at low-end, mechanic's-special freighters. He would be able to buy a *nice* ship.

Only then a worrisome thought came to him. Warlord's arsenal was larger and more sophisticated than Jackson had first thought. Much larger. Too large, too much for strictly defense. He was planning some kind of strike. He had to be. And then another thought came right on the heels of that realization. If word got out, it could undermine the Warlord's plans. How could he trust the crew of the *Tar Heel* to keep it quiet?

Maybe Warlord hadn't been making threats before. Maybe he'd been revealing his intentions. A sinking feeling formed in Jackson's gut. He glanced over at Tui, who was looking as jovial as usual...except for his eyes.

"You have working models of each of these?" their host asked.

"Of course," Shade said. "They're currently dismantled so we could slip them past the inspectors, but how else could you know plans were worth anything without the actual goods to test?"

The Warlord nodded, pleased. "You *are* a fat goose. Very fat. And I want it. I want it all. What are you asking?"

That confirmed it to Jackson. This wasn't just another delivery. This was a life-and-death gamble. And Jackson suddenly saw just how precarious the team's security situation was. It would be so easy to attach some explosives to their ship while they were offloading. Or kill them quietly here, load their corpses on the *Tar Heel*, and send it out into interstellar space, never to be heard of again.

The captain said, "I had to hit six systems to cross everything off your shopping list. It cost us a pretty penny to get through that many gates. Plus we got searched twice, and that was just in the Nivaas system. Did you know that? They're tightening things down."

"The sanctions," Warlord said. "I told you."

The captain continued, "I think this is a fair price." And he touched his display.

Warlord looked at it and smiled. "My friends, that is far too high."

"It's the agreed-upon price for the items you ordered," Shade said. "Plus a good value for the others."

"We are not a prosperous world. Big Town is but one poor orbital, and I have many hungry mouths to feed. I can go seventy percent on the munitions, but I will pay you only fifty percent of the price you list for the other items. Surely mangoes don't cost that much. We have spectacular oranges, you know."

"Same food, day in and day out, gets old," Shade said. "The goodwill of your people does not."

And so the negotiations began. They haggled for a bit, but

finally got close to a price that was less than what the captain and Shade had asked for, but much higher than Warlord had originally offered. They seemed stuck on the price of the Citadel. It was hard to read the man. He seemed confident, open, even friendly, and it appeared that he was almost happy at this price, but that didn't mean the Warlord still might not decide to kill them anyway.

"Ah, enough squabbling over money. Let us take a break before I make my final decision." Warlord suddenly stood up, then pointed at Jackson. "I have something to show you. Come with me."

CHAPTER 12

The change was so sudden, every one of the crew went on alert.

"I thought we were the goose," Jackson said over Jane's network.

Jane's silent network was rather clever. It only took a fraction of a second for their brain to match the frequency of the letters that only the user could see, and it was downright brilliant at personalized predictive text, so communicating was quick and effortless after a bit of practice. Every member of the crew had the same system installed.

"He'll be more than happy to sacrifice us for a bigger prize," the captain replied.

"He's got a bigger prize?" Jackson asked.

"Maybe."

"Of course, he has a bigger prize," Shade cut in.

"Come on then!" Warlord looked at them and smiled with delight, then motioned them toward a hallway.

They followed their host out of the main room and down a long corridor. Fain and some of the guards came too. Bushey and Katze casually spread out, while Tui assigned everyone a target should things go south. Jackson sent a little thought to Fifi and awakened her.

"Hello, Fifi. Prepare to attack that guard's eye."

There was an almost gleeful chime in his ear of confirmation.

"Can he hear us?" Bushey asked.

Shade's face betrayed no expression but from her response it was obvious she thought Bushey was stupid. *"Jane's custom*

OS. Jane's language. They would have had to hack Jane." It was very doubtful there was anyone on this world—or very many others—who could do that.

At some point the hall turned into a tunnel. They took a lift down beneath the grounds and into the hull of the original colony ship. The air started to smell like oil. There was a doorway up ahead, and Jackson figured that was where Warlord's men would make their move, but they filed through without incident into a gigantic hangar.

And then Jackson saw what Warlord kept here and smiled. There were nine different mechs and exos lined up in a row, all of them polished and shining beneath the lights. Jackson immediately recognized the ones that had been delivered here by the *Tar Heel* and was surprised by the others.

"This is my collection... Not all of them of course, just the ones that are currently off the harvesting rotation."

They walked across the gleaming floor to the well-lit mechs. There were more guards posted here, as well as a few security bots, and a crew of mechanics servicing some of the machines. Jackson marveled at the collection. There was a vintage suit—Russian from the look of it—that was really nothing more than a souped-up exo. A couple of high-end scouts, one of which was definitely of serious military grade. And there was a third-gen giant. Standing up, it would probably be ten meters tall. There had been a brief period of experimentation with monster mechs, but they had proven too unwieldy. Mechs excelled because you could use them in the most unforgiving terrain. If you were going with something that heavy you might as well use a tank. But the Warlord had one anyway.

Jackson whistled. "I've never actually seen a Spider in person before."

"Beautiful, isn't she?"

This one in particular was an oddity. Most mechs were bipeds, because that was the most natural thing for a linked human brain to function with—though Panhard had some success with their four-legged Centaurs, except they were really more of a walking gun platform than a proper mech—but the Baihu Spider was legendary. With eight segmented legs, it was obvious why the sleek black mech had gotten its name.

"Scary looking," Tui said.

"The Spider is supposed to be the highest mobility mech ever fielded," Jackson said.

"It is," Warlord said with quite some pride. "Especially in zero G. It takes some getting used to, having the freedom to move in such unexpected ways. To reach its potential, you must become it, and think outside of the constraints of the traditional form. If time allows, I'll let you take it out for a spin around the exterior of the orbital."

As tempting as that was, there was no way. Driving this thing manually would be so complicated that it would verge on the impossible. It would require plugging in again, and that option was forever off the table for him. "Thanks. We'll have to see."

"Well, huh," mused the captain as he looked at a beastly mech at the end of the line. It was fifth-gen tech, like the Citadel. "That's new."

Shade frowned. "And where did you get it from?"

That was a good question. Just looking at it, from the wear patterns on the joints, Jackson could tell it was almost brand new. It hadn't been here for very long at all.

"Ah, Ms. Thomas. I am terribly sorry, but I am afraid you are not the only broker whose services I use. You have some competitors."

"I have no competitors, only imitators."

"Regardless, the *Tar Heel* is not the only ship willing to cross the ISF anymore. When there is competition in a niche market, it requires the suppliers to adjust their prices accordingly. I've been asking for a fifth gen for quite some time, and as you can see, I recently received one. Two would be a bit ostentatious."

"Eighty percent of our original asking price for the Citadel," Shade sniffed.

"Seventy percent. I doubt any of your other clients could afford better."

"Seventy-eight. Less than that is robbery, and I'd be inclined to ask the captain to launch the Citadel's container into your star rather than sustain such an insult, just on principle."

"Correct me if I am wrong, but robbery is how you obtained it to begin with. Seventy-three."

The captain held up one hand to interrupt them. "I'm amenable to that figure, provided you also tell me what ship delivered this thing to you."

Warlord laughed. "Seventy-five then."

"A couple percent is a good price for information."

"It is, but it's not for sale," Warlord said.

The captain nodded. "Seventy-five it is then." And stuck out his hand.

Warlord took it, and the two men shook hands, sealing the deal.

Jackson glanced over at Shade and saw she was actually smiling. *"Somebody take a picture of Shade's apparent good mood. We need to document it for the ship's log."*

Shade gave him a look, but she was still smiling.

Warlord called for his accountant. The money was put in escrow with Djinn, a black-market organization both had agreed on for this transaction. They would get part now, another upon inspection, and the final big payment upon delivery. At each step Djinn would transfer the money to Shade.

While the decisionmakers and number crunchers hammered out the details, Jackson wandered over to look at the mechs.

In the far corner was a Thunderbolt 4, a mech very similar to the one he had fought with years ago. He walked over to it and ran his finger across the red hull. The memory of the surge of sensory data suddenly being fed to into his brain rose like a ghost. He remembered feeling with the suit's arms and fingers, smelling with its acute olfactory senses, seeing with its piercing, multispectrum enabled gaze. When connected, the senses came alive to things a mere human couldn't experience. And then there was the joy. A suit was designed to work with the brain's natural processes, stimulating the production of chemicals to make you alert, quick-minded, and confident. To fill you with a rush that couldn't be approximated by any drug.

A voice came from behind him. "There is nothing quite as exhilarating as suiting up for war." Warlord had left his people to sort out the paperwork.

"I don't miss it." Which was mostly true.

"Ah, but you do," Warlord said and smiled. "You were indeed a warrior. I can see it in your eyes."

"That was a long time ago." Jackson wasn't old enough to have anything be considered a *long time*, but Warlord understood well enough.

"This one is an antique, but still a fine mech. As smooth and rich as butter. And a killer. I had it enhanced with a Sabador sighting system, twenty-millimeter cannon, plasma grenade launcher, and javelins."

"Javelins? Where in the world does it store a missile that big?"

"Not missiles. Literal javelins. For quiet work." He mimicked a throwing motion.

"You mean like a spear?"

Warlord walked over to the Thunderbolt, unlocked a housing in one arm to reveal a whole magazine of four-foot javelins. He pulled one out. "Sometimes you need to kill quietly. Once you learn how it's done, you can throw these four hundred meters with ease."

"Wouldn't a six-inch pneumatic bolt be better?"

"Maybe when you're killing humans. Not when you're hunting something like a caliban."

"Interesting," Jackson said.

Tui, Katze, and Bushey walked over to join them, because weapons systems made for far more interesting conversations than escrow accounts.

Warlord seemed to enjoy the audience. He pointed at three slots at the back end of the javelin. "Once this pierces their skin, a ring of blades explodes out in an arcing slash, capable of cutting through bone. Fins extend here so it can guide itself to the marked target."

He tossed the javelin to Katze, who caught it, and tested the weight. "That's going to hit with a wallop."

"The caliban and a few other Swindle species usually hunt in packs. They're smart buggers. If you reveal yourself with gun or rocket fire, they'll surround you. Even worse, the bangs draw the attention of other creatures. Larger ones. And so you must stay silent as long as possible."

"You can't suppress the fire?"

"A bit. They still hear it, if not the shot itself, the impact. And if they don't, there are other creatures who call to the caliban. It's some symbiotic thing. They're like crows leading the wolves to the kill. Sometimes they call others who come to kill us just for spite."

"Or territory," Tui suggested.

"It's spite," Warlord insisted.

"Huh," Bushey said. "Sounds like some people I know back on Earth."

Katze handed the javelin around to everyone to heft. It was heavy. Probably close to fifteen kilos. Definitely something that could only be thrown with some kind of exo technology. Jackson handed the javelin back to Warlord, who returned it to the magazine and closed it.

"Speaking of Earth, that's where this mech was built," Tui

said. "I remember there was one of these mounted above the entrance to Fort Benning."

Jackson just shook his head sadly. Something that was a museum decoration on Earth had been his planet's best line of defense.

"I remember they were designed to go underwater," Bushey said. "Imagine a squad of these appearing in the surf and walking up your beach..." And then he seemed to get an idea. "By the way, you got javelins, but what about harpoons? You know, to go fishing."

The Warlord smiled ruefully. "We don't go into the deep waters. Not on Swindle. That's where the big ones live. And that's where we'd prefer them to stay."

They waited for an explanation, but Warlord moved on and began to detail more of the mech's features. When he finished, he said, "How would you like to see the surface? We could go now."

Jackson got that uneasy feeling again. Wasn't a one-way trip to the surface precisely what Shade had warned about?

Luckily, the captain had rejoined them, and gave them a way out. "Business before pleasure. Let's finish the transfer. Then we can talk about my crew going on an excursion."

"Work, work, work," the Warlord said. "You've got to live a little, Captain Holloway."

"Oh, I intend to live for quite some time."

Warlord shook his head, then he looked pointedly at Jackson. "But you want to go down, don't you? You want to see what's down there."

Jackson shrugged.

"I want to see," Katze said excitedly.

"A tigress," Warlord said.

"More like a mad cow," Bushey muttered.

"I heard that."

Warlord seemed to enjoy being a good host. "She wants to go down. But you, I hear you would prefer swimming."

"Hopefully with a lot of women," Bushey said.

The Warlord shook his head. "A hunt then, without the swimmer. I'll plan it for tomorrow."

"Let's see how it goes," the captain said.

"It's an experience not to be missed. It's *primal*. It takes you back to our roots. To what it meant to be human back on Earth all those years ago."

"Tomorrow," the captain said.

CHAPTER 13

Warlord put them up in a very nice hotel not far from the governor's palace. A fine establishment with so much surveillance Jackson figured they had bugged the toilets. So as not to disappoint, Bushey gave them a fine symphony, flushed, and then they went down to the dining room, where they were served a tasty, Swindle version of cricket curry finished with a saffron rice pudding. It had to be expensive. Jackson doubted they grew much rice on their platforms.

After the millionaire pudding, Jackson convinced Katze to join him on a walk to see the city. When you live on a ship, you never pass up a chance to get out. Except since the drinks at the hotel bar were free to them, Bushey elected to stay. Only the captain didn't think it was a good idea.

When Jackson asked why, he said, "We're in a foreign country that's made of the dregs of thirty different cultures—most of whom you're totally unfamiliar with—who are all crammed into a metal tube together. You don't know their problems. You don't know their tensions. And you two are guests of their boss."

"I got this, Cap. Consider it a fact-finding mission," Jackson said. "And besides, if there's trouble, I've got Katze."

She grinned at the compliment. Katze didn't seem that dangerous—she looked like an athlete, but more of a runner than a power lifter—but the Amonite Marines had wrapped her bones in carbon fiber weave and given her gene mods so potent they were still crazy illegal on Earth. She was smaller than Jackson but could curl him like a dumbbell.

"For some odd reason that don't make me feel better. This ain't a boarding action, Katze, and these people aren't pirates... Well, half of them probably. So play nice."

"I'll go with them, Cap," Tui said. "I'm curious to see what this place is like myself."

The captain scowled as he thought it over. Tui was the most levelheaded and mature one of the bunch. "Let me guess, Chief. You want to see how this place has changed in the years since the last time we were here?"

"Maybe." But then Tui used Jane's net to send a message the bugs couldn't pick up. *"I'm curious to see what kind of man we've been running guns to."*

"You sure you want to find out? It's too late now."

Tui shrugged.

"Alright. Have fun. Don't let the youngsters do anything stupid."

Outside the hotel, the sun globes had moved and dimmed a bit, so the trio strolled along in the orbital evening. The neighborhood around the hotel was straight and tidy, the walls of the buildings covered in all sorts of plants. Everything here was stacked, businesses at the bottom, homes on top. There were archways and exterior stairs. A few blocks later, they moved into a slightly poorer part of town that was more crowded and haphazard. They passed a group of people watching a woman who was dressed up like a cat doing some tribal dance. Farther on, they passed some little food-vendor bots, selling noodles or vat meat on sticks.

They turned a corner into a neighborhood with a different feel, and a writing none of them recognized on the windows. There were a lot of dark and narrow alleyways. They saw two men who didn't have any legs. One was walking in a shabby, broken-down exo with one stride that was longer than the other. He was pulling the other no-legged man in a cart. Jackson saw a woman up in a window. She looked at them, sneered, and then drew back behind a curtain. They passed a string of adults who suddenly crossed over the street and refused to look their way.

"Not the best vibe here," Tui said. "I wonder if they have a bar."

"The piss and vinegar kind?" Jackson asked.

"Yeah."

But there weren't any bars.

They turned another corner, saw a sign that suggested drink, but found it was simply a food machine that offered a variety of shaggy balls of some kind of dough. The odd thing about walking around an orbital, no matter what, it always felt like you were going uphill.

Tui asked, "Where are all the kids?"

Jackson shrugged.

"Maybe there's a quarter in town for families," Katze suggested.

A low voice said, "Only a fool keeps a family in Big Town."

Jackson startled and turned. There was a man they hadn't noticed sitting in the shadows of a porch. He had a tattoo covering his neck.

"What did you say?" Tui asked.

But the man just rose and walked into his flat.

The three of them continued on. Jackson transmitted through Jane's net, *"It's as if they've been warned to avoid us."*

Tui never let his perpetual smile slip as he sent back. *"Us in particular? Or all strangers? I think Warlord is hiding all sorts of things."*

Katze responded. *"Maybe Swindle isn't the happy place it's made out to be."*

"Do you think he's telling the truth about our trip tomorrow?" Jackson asked. *"Or do you think he's going to try to eliminate us after the trade?"*

"Because we're going to tell the worlds he has mangoes?" Katze chuckled.

"More like he's stockpiling sophisticated weapons, and not just what he's got from us, but somebody else has been supplying him too."

Katze didn't seem convinced. *"I'm sure the superpowers already have spies and informants here. They must know all about it. In fact, I bet he leads them to believe he has more than he actually has. Just to keep the ISF piranhas cautious."*

"Whatever the game is, we keep our eyes open," Tui said aloud. "Stay alert."

Both Katze and Jackson agreed to that.

There was a church sandwiched in between two bigger buildings. All over the front of the church were plastered little crosses and stars and other religious symbols. Tui walked over and looked more closely at them. "They're names."

Names of the dead. Jackson didn't know that, but he was pretty sure that's what they were.

Big Town got uglier the farther they got from the hotel. They finally came to a neighborhood that was practically a shanty town. It was so far around the orbital from the hotel that the Warlord's palace was visible in the distance, except sideways.

"Should we turn around?" Jackson asked.

"No, look," Katze said, pointing down a street. There was a commotion a few streets ahead and locals were flocking in that direction. There was music. Flashing lights.

"Maybe this is where the nightlife is." Katze sounded curious. "A little concert in the park."

They joined others walking that way. A fairly large group was gathering. An unfamiliar song was blaring as they reached the back of the crowd. This wasn't a park. They'd taken over an intersection. Furthermore, the people already here weren't happy. Their faces were somber.

Someone was projecting an image onto the side of a building. It was a picture of a boy, maybe nine or ten, with bruises all over his face. The video cut to another clip of a cluster of tall trees. They looked like palm trees, but these were thinner and taller than any palm tree Jackson had ever seen. Thinner with feathery leaves. In the clip, there was a small cluster of people at the base of the trees, shouting up at two kids close to the top, and waving for them to come down. A large creature suddenly flashed into the picture from the side. It leapt halfway up the tree trunk, grabbed hold, and began to scuttle up toward the children.

The people below the trees started shouting. Two women began firing guns up at the creature. All of this was playing on the wall of an apartment building, large as life. Someone had brought portable speakers. The cries of dismay from the people in the video sounded like it was happening right there in the street.

And then a woman in the picture screamed and fled from the trees. Others followed. One of the women with the guns turned to face a new threat. Another creature flashed into the picture, charging the woman. It knocked her over and bit into her neck. A third creature took the other woman down.

Up above, in the tree, the first beast bit into a boy's leg and ripped him from his perch. The boy flailed and screamed, and then the creature changed its grip and bit into his neck. The other boy in the tree suddenly fell.

Jackson watched in horror. The tree had to be sixty, seventy feet high. The boy turned in the air, then struck the ground. Some of the people in the crowd gasped in dismay.

The boy lay stunned for a second, then tried to raise an arm. But his body was broken, and his arm looked like something out of a horror show.

Back up in the tree, the beast was feasting on the first boy's head. The image froze. The sound cut.

The crowd was silent, their faces full of anger.

"That was number fifty-four and fifty-five," a man said over the sound system. "Out in the red zone. Out where he promised us no children would work. Fifty-five lost this *month*!"

"How do we know it's not another fake?" someone shouted. "Kalteri is always trying to stir things up."

"Because I was there," a man said and stepped forward. He had a fresh, livid scar running right down his bald head.

"And me," another man said and joined the first. He was tall and built like a mountain.

"And me," a woman said. Her face was stitched from a recent gash. "I'm the one there at the bottom. And this is what's left of my son." She held up part of an arm and a hand.

The crowd took a collective gasp.

"Oh damn," exclaimed Katze.

"Could be a stage prop," Tui sent over the link.

But Jackson wasn't thinking of stage props. He was thinking that surely Warlord's security forces wouldn't be happy with this gathering. He glanced around the rooftops and poles, but there were no stationary cameras visible. There was a hornet's nest, but one side was missing. It was clearly defunct. But that didn't mean this happy party wasn't being watched by a drone.

"Come and see it," the woman declared. "Satisfy yourselves. It's his, right down to the birthmark. How many more have to die? He lied to us. He's importing children. Children you don't know and sending them out. We can prove it!"

Most of these people had to be harvesters, the poor bastards who went down to the surface, and it didn't look like they were going to give the Warlord's operations a ten on job satisfaction. Jackson could feel the current of anger growing stronger.

Tui said, "So I think this is where we turn around."

"Yep, time to backstroke," Jackson agreed. Only that meant shoving their way through what seemed to be an ever-increasing number of bodies.

There was a commotion at the far edge of the crowd. A number of people began shouting and banging on something.

"Please disperse." The voice was loud, like it was coming out of a loudspeaker. *"Return to your homes."*

Jackson turned. A small security car had pulled up. The vehicle was like the ones that had driven them to the mansion, made of superlight composites and running on magnetics, only instead of sleek black, this one was painted blue with white and orange accents, like the colors Lotte and Frans had worn. Inside the car were two cops.

The warning was repeated in Spanish, and the crowd around the car started booing and throwing trash. Someone bashed a brick against the car's window, but the plastic was far too strong.

The thump must have made the cops panic because the driver threw the vehicle in reverse. Unfortunately, some people had moved behind the car. Two of them got knocked down. Luckily, instead of running them over, the car got stuck on something. The cop gunned it anyway. A man screamed in pain. Someone else shouted, and then the mob surrounded the car and started rocking it back and forth. They got it up on two wheels and...it turned out the thing they had been stuck on was a person. His friends dragged the man they'd tried to run over clear. Three others tossed a large hunk of stone or composite under the car to keep it wedged, and then the mob really started to vent their rage on the vehicle.

The loudspeaker on the car activated again: *"Step away from the car!"* The driver gunned the engine again, but they were high-centered on the hunk of composite, and so the car simply zipped around in a tight circle. However, that was enough to hurl people aside. And then the car broke free, only to slam into a security pole.

A number of harvesters charged the side of the car. One of them was wearing an exo. The men lifted. The car rose onto two wheels again, this time a bit higher. The men continued to lift, exposing the undercarriage. The wheels were spinning, and the cop might have broken free, but even an old exo could deadlift a ton. The car went onto its side, and then crashed onto its roof.

Tui put one big hand on Jackson's shoulder and shoved. "There's about to be riot or a murder. I don't want to stick around for either."

Someone tossed a clear bag of liquid that burst when it hit the car. Someone else followed the bag with a burning bit of cloth. There was a whoosh, and then a surge of orange flames leapt into the sky.

"This way." Katze slipped into a jagged slit in the crowd. Jackson and Tui followed, weaving through people whose faces were set with hard determination.

A bloodcurdling cheer rose from the crowd behind them, and Katze picked up her pace.

And then the street sirens around the area began to sound.

"Lovely," Tui said.

A few steps and shoves later they broke free from the press of bodies. The sky above them began to buzz. Jackson looked up, expecting hornets, but saw a swarm of fliers. There was a soft pop, and something struck one of the drones. It flipped, careened down into the side of a building, and fell to the ground. More soft pops followed.

People in the crowd were shooting at them.

"Pick up the pace," Tui said, and moved into an all-out sprint. But Katze had already beat him to it, and the three of them ran down the middle of the street in a jagged line.

Jackson dodged a man with an eyepatch, then ran around a woman who was pulling a pistol from underneath her shirt.

Two cops in exos rounded the bend ahead of them. They were carrying shotguns, heavy drum-fed models. Jackson had seen those used on angry mobs before. They basically turned protestors into hamburger.

"Take cover." Tui turned off the road and dashed for a clump of waist-high shrubs growing in front of a building. Katze was faster than either of them and got there first, sliding in and squatting behind the plants. Tui and Jackson crowded in behind.

"They're not here for us," Tui said. "Stay down and we'll just wait here until they pass by. This isn't our problem."

"It's a regular peace and daisy festival," Jackson said.

"Yeah, and you forgot to get me a flower," Tui retorted.

The little clump was barely big enough for the three of them to hide, but a man was suddenly shoving Jackson from behind, also trying to take cover with them. He was so grimy his odor just about knocked Jackson out.

"Back off, scrub," Jackson warned.

"What's going on?" Tui asked the stranger.

"Fah no pay callum," the man said. "You dem blind?"

Or something like that. Some Bigtowner dialect or language that Jane's codes didn't have translations for.

"We aren't from here," Katze said.

"You be lucky dan," the man said. He had odd eyes.

Jackson wondered if they were mechanical and peered closer, but the man rose, extended some kind of gun, and shot one of the cops.

"Shanks!" Jackson hadn't seen that coming.

The gun didn't make a huge bang. He wasn't throwing lead. It was something else. But the cop that Stink Man had hit grasped his neck and stumbled.

"For con hala," Stink Man said, then pointed his gun at the other cop who was targeting two men down the street. But the cop saw the danger, and sprang up, a huge leap that took him at least a story high.

The gun popped again. But this time whatever he was shooting bounced off the cop's body armor. This was not good. Jackson and the others had picked that spot because it was a good place to hide. The bum had picked it because it was a good ambush point. And they were now going to draw fire.

With superhuman speed, Tui grabbed Jackson by the arm and pulled him up. "Run!"

Stink Man kept shooting. A moment later, a flier buzzed from over the building. There was a *tat, tat, tat.*

"Hobo down!" Katze said as they ran for their lives.

The guy might have still been alive. Drone guns were usually small caliber to save weight. But then the exo cop opened up on the bush with his automatic shotgun and shredded everything. Jackson didn't dare look back. It took everything he had to keep up with the two augmented former soldiers ahead of him.

They made it half a block before Tui suddenly looked back. "Get down!"

They took cover behind a pile of trash and old crates. Jackson was squatting there, trying to catch his breath, when he heard heavy footsteps walking down the street in their direction.

The mech wasn't a huge one. It couldn't be if you wanted

to navigate these streets. It was maybe a nine-footer. More of a glorified, armored exo than a proper mech, but a nine-footer could still pack a punch. Still moving, the mech lifted a rotary cannon and banged out three rounds that arced down the street, trailing smoke. He lobbed them right into the mob, an easy shot for anything with a targeting computer. A moment later, there were three bangs, and gas began to pour out.

Jackson caught movement out of the side of his eye up on top of one of the buildings. Another small mech was up there, jumping from roof to roof, running with huge, powered strides. Three hovercars with flashing lights flew overhead. One opened up bay doors. And that's when the hornets finally came flying out. A huge black cloud of them.

The mob was about to get dispersed, whether they liked it or not.

Jackson waited nervously, hoping nobody had spotted the three Tar Heelers behind the trash. But the mech that had launched the gas canisters stomped past to engage the crowd.

"Wait," Tui whispered.

They waited long enough to hear a series of screams and gunshots.

"Now we go," Tui said.

Sam Fain straddled his motorcycle at the end of the street, watching the police engage the rioters. What a mess. What a waste. It was time for a purging. Long past time. He'd told Warlord this was coming. He predicted the dissidents would grow and act out if he wasn't given a free rein to take necessary action. Malcontents were like weeds, and weeds were controlled best by removal, early and often.

"This is Fain. Have you identified the instigators yet?"

"Facial recognition caught Mion and Eberle," one of his security team transmitted back. *"There's a third man with them we can't match."*

Somebody smuggled in by the Originals, then.

"He's a big man. They're on the run."

"Visual," Fain said.

An overhead view of this part of the city appeared in front of Fain's eyes. It wasn't a projected image because Fain, just this last year, had been fitted with a next-gen mod that fed directly into his optic nerves. It was much better than depending on some external display that could be broken or knocked away. The targets popped up on his display. They'd been tagged. He watched them for a second, saw where the trio was running.

"They're armed and dangerous," Fain's security man transmitted *"They just gunned down a squad from the fourth precinct."*

"Continue to track them," Fain said. "But don't interdict. Leave that to me."

"Yes sir."

Fain's computer plotted his route and he was just about to give his cycle some throttle when he spotted some familiar faces among those trying to get away from the chaos.

Fain blinked. His mind processed what he was seeing. It was three of the gun runners who had been meeting with the governor earlier. The trio ran along the front of a building, then turned down a narrow alley and sprinted away.

Fain watched them go and wondered. You couldn't have an uprising without weapons. And if that prick Graf had pulled back his support from the Warlord, then Kalteri would want to accelerate whatever plans he had and send over ordnance for the dissidents here. Who better to deliver arms than an arms dealer? Especially one that had Warlord's trust.

Fain called the tech back. "Have you been tracking the crew of the *Tar Heel?*"

"Yes, sir."

"There are three near my current position. Put a flier on them."

There was a momentary pause.

"Yes sir, we have them. We will track them."

"Good. Make sure they go directly back to their hotel." Fain twisted the throttle and his motorcycle leapt forward. Fain leaned into it. It was a security vehicle, so unlike most of the transportation allowed inside Big Town, the electric motorcycle didn't have a governor to limit the speed. Furthermore, he had access to the traffic protocols. A signal was sent ahead, alerting all pedestrians and traffic to clear the way, and if they didn't? Too bad. He took the next right, leaning low into the corner. He straightened and opened it up to full speed for the next three blocks, not worrying about traffic because the eyes in the sky would alert him if anything was in the way. Fain raced down the road, silent as death.

Even as quick as he was moving, he knew his grendel would keep up. Greyhound thin, but twice as fast, it would be shadowing him, leaping from rooftop to rooftop.

Fain reached his destination, parked his bike, and was waiting when the criminal ringleaders appeared, out of breath, and thinking that they'd gotten away. He knew them all from their files. J.D. Mion was a thin man who worked on the gas lines at the CX plant. Aus Eberle was a blond with a scar on his face who'd fought as a sniper in the orbital's gang war. Like most of the gangsters, he'd had to get a real job and was in the engineering detail now. The final man, the unknown, was at least a head taller than either of them. A head taller than Fain himself. With a broad chest and thick-muscled arms.

Fain aimed and shot three times. He hit each one in the neck with a small dart.

The men yanked them out. They'd been planning on starting a riot. They'd probably juiced for that in anticipation.

Eberle tossed his dart to the ground and sneered. "You're going to have to do better than a little sleep juice, pig."

Fain could have just killed them all, but he needed someone alive to interrogate.

Mion tossed something at him, then went for a gun.

Regular humans seemed to move in slow motion to him now. Fain leapt away from what he assumed was a grenade, grabbed hold of a second-floor balcony, and clung there. Below him, the thing Mion had thrown exploded in a cloud of purple numb gas.

The three ringleaders smiled, then the gas began to disperse, and they realized he wasn't there. They looked around, confused.

"Slow, slow, slow," Fain said. "You guys have got to keep up."

The big man saw him and shouted. Mion raised his pistol.

Fain dropped and rolled behind a garbage container.

Mion's gun rang out. Several bullets pierced the wall above Fain.

Fain smiled. He could do this all night. But it was time to end this foolishness. He only needed one for torture. He sent a mental command. The targeting system on his motorcycle activated and relayed a visual to Fain's brain. He put the sights on Mion's head.

Mion pulled another canister out of his coat and prepared to toss it back behind the garbage can. The man was a regular arsenal, but it was clear he hadn't done his homework on Fain.

Fain sent the command. The bike's guns cracked. Mion went down in a spray of blood.

Eberle snatched up the canister Mion had meant to throw and hurled it at the motorcycle. This one turned out to be a grenade, because the resulting explosion took out his ride.

The wave of heat washed over him, and Fain smiled. He flipped the selector on his sidearm from less-lethal darts to fragmentation rounds, rolled out from behind the garbage container, and fired at Eberle's thigh.

Eberle cried out and went down.

"Come on, Aus, they're not so bad," Fain said and moved back behind cover.

Eberle and the stranger fired back, but the bullets struck the garbage container. And the ones that made it through were slowed down enough they just bounced off his armored skin.

"Got to do better than that, Aus. This is just damn sloppy of you. You didn't even come with full armor." Fain had known that because in the first second he'd seen the trio, he'd done a full target scan, IR and magnetic, and noted that Eberle had ceramic armor hidden beneath his coat. But he had nothing covering his legs. And so Fain had shot him there. And a leg shot was perfectly acceptable because you didn't need both legs for an interrogation. In fact, you didn't need any legs at all. The medics could amputate all his limbs and Fain would just question what was left. So Fain leaned out, saw Eberle trying to stand to get a good angle, and shot him in the other leg too. And then Fain drew back behind cover. The whole thing had taken less than half a second.

There was a thump as Eberle fell to the pavement, and then another set of rounds struck the garbage container. Fain had to admire the tenacity of the man, firing away with all the blood and pain.

And then a shadow fell over Fain. He spun around, raising his gun, but the third man, the big one, smacked it away. He too was moving with superhuman speed.

Good. A real challenge.

Fain pulled his other gun, but the big man kicked him down, then stomped on his hand. It would have crushed normal bones if he'd still had any. However, Fain still had pain receptors, and Fain grunted. Then the big man reached down, grabbed Fain by the throat, and lifted him off his feet.

"*Aqui você morre cachorro,*" he snarled.

Fain's assist immediately translated it. *Here you die, dog.*

No, not today, Fain thought, and grinned.

At that moment, a shadow dropped from the top of the building onto the big man, bearing him to the ground.

The dissident tried to rise, but the grendel locked its mandibles around his throat and twisted. The man screamed and thrashed as it bit and clawed. Say what you will about Swindle, but the beasts that had evolved there were incredibly efficient killers. The grendel was one of the few that could be tamed... Not domesticated, mind you. But tamed. *Briefly.*

Even though the big man must have had some strength and speed mods, he wasn't quick enough. The terrifying surface creature wrenched, and the big man went limp. And then it savaged the man's throat, blood splashing its muzzle.

"Took you long enough," Fain said to his companion, fingering his own throat where the rebel had tried to crush it. The grendel didn't care. It had no pity or love. It just did what it was told.

Warlord came on Fain's commlink. *"Did you get the instigators?"*

Fain walked over and looked down at Mion in his pool of blood. His eyes were flat, dead. He was useless. He looked back at his grendel savaging the big man's face. That one was soon going to be dead as well. Eberle was still alive, though barely conscious. And yet he was still trying to reload his gun with blood-slick fingers, but Fain went over and stepped on his hand.

The frag rounds had turned his legs to hamburger, and a cursory scan showed Eberle's blood pressure was dropping rapidly. Fain's scan warned that the medics would need to tourniquet him in the next two minutes if he was going to have anything to question.

"I've got one we can interrogate," Fain said. "Give me a second." He sent an expedited request for an ambulance. When the request was confirmed, he said, "The gun runners were here."

"Holloway's men? From the Tar Heel?"

"Three of them at least. I'll send you the recording. We can check the bracelets to see where they've been, and where the others were."

"They might have just been innocent bystanders."

"If I were a betting man, I'd bet on a double-cross." Gun runners were so untrustworthy.

Warlord sighed. *"Well, you'll find out, won't you?"*

"I always do."

Jackson followed Tui and Katze as they sprinted down a narrow road, through a tunnel, and then along a back alley that brought them out by the church with the names papering the front wall. Tui slowed to a walk and looked back the way they came. Jackson and Katze caught up to him and stopped as well.

Jackson was breathing hard. The other two were fine. "So much for a relaxing evening walk."

"You okay, Jackson?" Katze asked. "You don't look that good."

Of course, she was fine. Amon was a high-gravity world, Katze could probably run a marathon around this orbital and not break a sweat.

"Give the kid a break, he's still getting by on factory specs."

"Except my brain, Tui." Jackson took a deep breath. "Everything except my brain."

A tiny van sped past in the direction of the riot with at least six cops in it.

"If Grandma hears we were there, she's going to kill us," Katze said.

"Who says she has to know?" Jackson asked.

Tui held up his orange wrist band. "She's going to find out."

"Maybe," Jackson said.

"Regardless, the quicker we get back to the hotel, the better."

Jackson agreed to that, and the trio walked at a brisk pace back to the hotel. It turned out sound really carried inside Big Town, because they could still hear the sirens and occasional gunshots for quite a while. The other neighborhoods were quiet though. It appeared the locals had retreated inside and were keeping their heads down. Nothing seemed amiss at the hotel, and they took the lift back to their floor. When they entered, the captain, Shade, and Bushey were there with inventory records up on a display.

"You're back early." The captain looked up from his reports, sized them up, and immediately knew something was wrong. There was no lying to this man. "How was your night on the town?"

Jackson tried anyway. "It was okay."

"Saw a church," Katze said.

Shade was looking out the window at the flashing lights in the distance. "What about all those sirens?"

"Chief?" the captain asked. "Report."

Tui sighed. "There was an altercation between the indigs. We observed but did not participate. Then exfiltrated the area in a most expedient manner."

You knew it was bad when Tui went all official.

"Aw, hell. Out with it."

"Nothing much," said Jackson. "Just security exos and mechs. Fires. Guns. Cops getting shot. Police cars getting flipped. You know. Normal stuff."

Shade looked up at the ceiling. "Jackson, I swear—"

"We were not involved," Tui insisted, and then he gave a very succinct report.

Shade was still pissed. "He's going to know you were there. He's going to bring up the footage and see you three idiots right in the middle of it. Let's hope you didn't just scuttle our deal."

"More like scuttle our ship," the captain said grimly.

"You think he'll still let me swim?" Bushey asked.

CHAPTER 14·

Early the next morning they ate an aromatic breakfast loaf made out of cricket flour. The menu said it was loaded with fiber, which Bushey thought was splendid. He launched into a sermon about the value of being regular... until the captain ordered him to stop talking. They were also given small, sweet plums grown on one of Swindle's farm platforms. It was a decent breakfast, and as soon as they finished, Frans and Lotte appeared to escort them back to the governor's mansion.

The sun globes were at the other end of the orbital, acting like early morning. There was a lot more security visible today. A couple of policemen on individual hoverbikes flew overhead. There were more cops down the street.

Lotte motioned at two cars waiting for them. Jackson, Katze, and Bushey got in one car with Lotte. Frans and the rest got into the other car.

"I hope you all slept well," Lotte said.

"Like a baby." In actuality, Jackson had spent the night agitated and restless, because it took a while to come off the adrenaline rush of being in a riot. He didn't know these people or their situation that well, but the stuff in that video from the surface had been messed up.

The captain told them over their secure net, *"Jane called to say the* Tar Heel *will be here shortly and we can start unloading."*

"So he didn't cancel the deal?" Tui asked.

"Apparently not."

"And did you sleep well?" Jackson asked Lotte.

"It was a very late night," she said.

Jackson imagined it must have been very late indeed, with a whole neighborhood rioting. Every cop on this station had probably put in some mandatory overtime last night.

Shade began giving instructions. *"We're going to broach the subject of your evening walk first thing. Diffuse the tension. If the client asks you questions about the experience, just answer him straight up."*

"Will do," Jackson muttered.

"What did you say?" Lotte asked.

Jackson realized he'd spoken out loud and recovered himself. "A late night will do anyone in."

"Yes, it will."

They rode in silence the rest of the drive to the mansion.

Warlord was standing in the main room, watching a display of a ship at one of the docking stations. From the distinct shape, it was easy to pick out the *Tar Heel*. As agreed upon during yesterday's negotiation, one of Big Town's vessels had gone out to meet it for an initial inspection of the goods.

"Friends!" He gave them that same politician smile. "I was just informed things are looking very good."

There were four guards in the room with carbines slung, muzzle down. They appeared to be relaxed. Of course, that could change any second.

"We only bring the best," the captain said.

"That you do. That you do...I heard you had some excitement last night?"

"So much for us broaching the subject first," Katze's brain texted.

"I'm afraid so. Three of my crew went on an evening stroll, thought they'd found a street party, and landed in the middle of a riot."

"A most unfortunate breakdown of order caused by the worst sort of anarchists. It's odd how your men blundered into this event though." It was remarkable how the Warlord managed to convey both suspicion and menace, without ever changing his friendly tone. "You'd have to take just the right twists and turns to get there from your hotel."

"We were looking for beer," Jackson said.

"Was there not beer at the hotel?"

"They wanted to see Big Town," the captain said. "Can you blame them?"

The Warlord nodded and smiled. "Show me James Overturf."

The wall suddenly switched to the face. Clean-shaven and bathed, Jackson almost didn't recognize the man who had taken cover behind the bushes with the team last night. The one who had spoken a bunch of gibberish, and then attacked the cops. On the massive display his head was two meters tall.

"That's the guy who almost got us killed last night," Jackson said.

"And that was just his smell," Tui said.

Bushey cracked a smile, but nobody else did.

"Do you know who this is?" Warlord asked.

"Never seen him before last night, before he practically used me as a human shield and started shooting at your men."

"Mister Overturf is part of the Originals. A gang. Their actions have resulted in over eight hundred deaths this year. They agitate the citizens of Big Town and claim to represent the pioneering settlers..." For the first time Warlord allowed a little anger into his voice. "But in truth they're working for Kalteri. Or possibly the Tri-Planet Alliance. Or the ISF. Trying to destabilize us. You know, I give good jobs to people wanting to escape terrible circumstances. I ship them here at my cost. I make sure they have housing. If they don't like the work, they don't have to renew their contracts. They can hop the next cargo ship that comes along. But the Originals don't want good jobs. They want it all and will burn down anything they can't have."

Shade asked, "Are you sure they're not agents of Redcor? Destabilization and then capitalizing on the chaos is their trademark strategy."

Jackson knew Redcor was a megacorporation run by a trillionaire tech baron named Graf, but he'd not known they were in the conquering business.

Warlord gave their broker a curious look. "So you are familiar with that vile organization. I guess it makes sense, considering your family's business. As for Redcor meddling, it's possible. Every year we have thousands immigrate here. And all you need are one or two to saboteurs to slip in. Last year someone tried to poison one of our farm platforms."

"I hope you caught him," the captain said.

"There were three of them. We caught two. A man and a woman. We gave them a standing ovation execution."

"And the third?"

The Warlord shrugged. "Still at large."

That would be a little unnerving, Jackson thought. An orbital was no place for a terrorist.

"Such things keep me up at night. The safety of a quarter million lives is in my hands... Which is why I must know, what you were doing associating with a wanted criminal?"

As the Warlord said that, Jackson noticed that the guards seemed more alert. Their fingers were off the triggers, but they looked ready to move. Even though there had been three Tar Heelers at the party, Warlord focused on Jackson. Maybe he was appealing to Jackson's sense of honor, since they both came from an elite brotherhood of mech pilots... but more than likely, it was because he thought the youngest member of the crew would be the easiest to intimidate.

"I told you, we didn't know who he was. We took cover because we were trying not to get shot, gassed, or stung to death by that hornet swarm your men turned lose on that crowd."

"You're lucky. Twelve people died last night, including our good friend Overturf." He nodded toward the big display. "We've been hunting him for a long time. It's curious that he just happened to join you there. A crew from outside."

"I bet you got video of the whole thing," Jackson said.

"Some," Warlord admitted. "Unfortunately, the ruffians in that district like to vandalize our cameras."

"Then I'm sure whatever you do have confirms what I'm saying. We were just trying to keep our heads down. I thought your terrorist was a homeless guy talking gibberish, until he started shooting people."

Warlord was quiet for a really long time. One of the four guard's finger moved onto the trigger of his carbine.

Tui sent a message. *"From right to left. Katze, one. Bushey two. Jackson three. Captain, four. I've got Warlord."*

The captain sighed. "Hold on, now. Are you insinuating that my crew are in contact with these Originals?"

"Are you?"

"No. Nor any of their agents. Or anyone involved with them.

This is the first I've ever heard of them. It was coincidence. And here's how you know that to be true. If my people were wanting some clandestine meeting, would they go with their tracking devices on? And don't insult me by pretending they're not trackers. You have a visual and audio record of them all the way from the hotel and back again. If they were going to meet some crazy guy in the bushes, I guaran-damn-tee that my crew wouldn't be sloppy enough to get caught doing it."

"A valid point, Captain Holloway. A crew which makes its living through subtle deceit would never be so clumsy . . . Yet I must be very careful. A great many people depend upon my vigilance."

"*Stay ready.*" Tui looked at guard number four and smiled.

"When you find the troublemakers, I hope you make good use of the airlock."

"Puff and fry," Bushey said. "Sometimes that's the only way."

"That is our traditional method for dealing with criminals here. Yes, that is an apt description. The body expands. An incredibly painful process. The air rushes from your lungs. Bubbles form in your blood. In the agonizing minutes before death, the unfiltered rays of the sun burn beyond all comprehension." Warlord motioned at Bushey. "The swimmer's right. Sometimes it is the only way."

The threat hung in the air.

Jackson looked Warlord square in the eyes and stated, "I did not know that asshole."

He stared back for a long moment, judging, and then smiled. "I believe you."

The guards visibly relaxed. So did Jackson, because he'd been ready to hurl Fifi at the third guy from the right and then follow her in.

"I am glad we got that matter cleared up. The vast majority who come here are good, hardworking people searching for a better life. It's the meddling governments and their agents who cause the problems."

"Amen," the captain said.

Another guard entered the room. "Sir, the inspection team says the inventory matches, and passes all their quality checks. We're green."

"Splendid! I will let Djinn know. Holloway, if you would kindly contact your ship . . . docking permission is granted."

"I will do so." The captain still sounded polite, but Jackson could tell he was angry about having his integrity questioned. They were a gang of thieves, but honest ones. Relatively.

"And I will authorize the release of your payment. Another satisfying transaction! I think we should celebrate. Let us drink to freedom from the outside."

"I'm down," said Bushey.

"I don't pay my folks for partying," the captain said. "They get to do that on their off time."

"Work," Warlord said. "Always the work."

"Work on staying alive," the captain warned them silently.

"He's going to take offense," Shade said.

"Tough."

"Some peach brandy. It is delicious and distilled locally. I am rather proud of it."

"If he's going to poison us, there are a hundred other ways to accomplish it. Just take the drink." Even via text, Shade managed to convey her annoyance.

"Sounds great." The captain relented, most likely because he knew if the Warlord murdered them all and tried to commandeer the ship, he'd still have to deal with Jane. Good luck with that.

"Franco," Warlord summoned one of his guards. "Peach brandy with ice."

Franco prepared the glasses, then handed them out.

The Warlord raised his glass for a toast. "To freedom."

"To freedom," they repeated, then drank. Jackson had to admit that it was pretty damned good.

They watched the *Tar Heel* maneuver into position on the displays. As soon as they received word from Jane that Djinn had released the funds, the captain gave them the go-ahead to dock and begin unloading.

"Wonderful," Warlord said as he sipped his drink and watched his new treasures arrive. He turned to Katze. "Is the tigress still raring to go to the surface? You don't want to come all the way to Swindle and miss the surface."

She looked to the captain.

"Say yes," said Shade.

"I don't know," the captain said. "It sounds dangerous."

"This is important. Do it."

Jackson was never quite clear exactly how the relationship worked between their captain and their broker. Shade wasn't really part of the crew, and the vast majority of the time it was clearly the captain calling the shots, but in matters of business, he often deferred to her wisdom.

"Thank you for the invite," the captain said, "but I'll need to supervise the unloading. If some of my crew want to take a little hunting trip for their R&R, I'll allow it. Who wants to go?"

There was no way Jackson was going to leave Katze alone with these people. "I'm in."

"I've heard the fauna is spectacular," Tui said. "I have to see to believe."

Warlord looked at the others. "Ms. Thomas? Mr. Bushey?"

"I'll relax up here," Shade said.

"I'm by the pool," Bushey said. "You know how long it's been since I've been swimming?"

"It looks suspicious if it's the same three who got in trouble last night," Shade sent.

"But on second thought, I'd kick myself if I came all this way and didn't check out the surface." Bushey tried not to let his disappointment show. "I'd love to go . . . down to the nightmare hellscape filled with giant terrifying murder animals." Then added silently, *"I better be getting a bonus."*

"Fantastic, my friends. Let us go to the docks, because I am eager to see my new treasures. Then you can gather your things, and we will take a dropship to the surface."

"Behave yourselves."

"Like angels, Captain," said Katze.

"If they get killed down there, Shade, it's on your head."

Shade took a delicate sip of her brandy. *"Keep the Warlord in a good mood. We want him loose and happy when we take his order for the next deal."*

Shade put the receiver to her temple. The connection here, for obvious reasons, was much quicker. There were so many secret assets in this system it was ridiculous. Everyone wanted a piece of Swindle.

"The deal is finalized," Shade said.

There was the obligatory delay.

"Well done," Norman Johnson said. "You will be recognized."

"I don't want recognition," Shade said. "I want what we discussed."

"We're working on that," Johnson said. "Don't get uppity."

Stiff me, Shade thought, *and you'll have more to worry about than an uppity agent.*

But to Johnson she said, "Please give the old man my regards."

Jane sent another batch of piggies on their way. But she wondered if something wasn't happening at the destination because none of her first piggies had reported back.

Who do you really work for, Grandma?

CHAPTER 15

The team accompanied their host and his security detail to the cargo holding area in the arm of the port where all the containers they'd sold him were being offloaded. While the captain went to check on his ship, Shade to count their money, and Tui to grab their kit, Warlord perused the goods and started opening random crates. He picked up a warhead, put it down, went over and looked at the mango seeds. The man in charge of the Big Town docks reported that the inventory matched the order so far, and everything looked as good as promised.

Warlord then walked over to the container that housed the Citadel, eager as a kid on Christmas. He opened the container, activated the skid, and slid it out. When he pulled off the wrap, his eyes lit up with delight. Jackson recognized that look. He'd worn it himself many times. Soon Warlord would link his mind directly with this badass piece of hardware to become an unstoppable god of war. Jackson had to bite back the sudden feeling of jealousy.

"We need to set up administrative rights. I'm assuming that's you?"

"Yes," Warlord answered. "I test every mech and determine if we can fabricate more here, or just keep it for my own personal use."

"Okay. The scanner is right here. Let's get your credentials set up."

He then brought up the display to show what weapons and warbots the Citadel was currently outfitted with. The loadouts were modular and swappable, but Splendid Ventures had made some odd choices.

Warlord gestured at one little cookbot and said, "That one's going to die down on the surface. What did you include it for?"

"Troops got to eat." Bushey had followed them over to the Citadel. "That little guy will swallow Swindle and crap crème brûlée."

"Crème brûlée?" Warlord asked.

"I swear I read it in a brochure somewhere," Bushey said.

"Do you ever go on multiple-day missions down there?" Jackson asked.

"Sometimes. Usually we drop, harvest, and exfil, usually no more than twelve hours tops, because much longer than that the atmosphere starts eating through our seals. Though multiday scouting expeditions are sometimes necessary to find new groves."

"Well, for those days, that bot is a lot lighter than all the food and water you'd otherwise have to carry. It can purify water, and be taught to forage or scavenge for food, and then make it safe, if not palatable. Some things on Swindle are edible to humans, right?"

"Our fundamental building blocks are not so different, though Swindle proceeded on a much different, and more aggressive evolutionary path. A handful of the animals are digestible to humans. It is a most unfair arrangement, since everything down there seems to find us a nice addition to their diet."

"Well, since the loadouts are modular, you can always swap out the space to carry more ammo."

"Crème brûlée or grenades," Warlord mused. "I don't know how I'll ever make the decision."

"There's training on how to integrate the Citadel into whatever system you have. Here in the orbital..." Jackson trailed off as he thought back to last night's riot.

"It could help with internal security."

"Well, it's more a main battle implement than a peacekeeper—"

"Ah, but Jackson, we both know the difference between the two is mere semantics. I suppose it could help our future guests avoid meeting confirmed killers in the bushes."

"Bush meetings," Bushey said. "They're just not civilized."

Warlord glanced over at him. "The funny man, eh."

"That's what he thinks," Jackson said, trying to draw his attention back to the goods. All of the Warlord's biometrics had been scanned, and Jackson had set up a temp user account for him. "You'll need to change the password the first time you drive it." Jackson held out the Raycor medallion he'd stolen back on Nivaas. "And you'll need to have this in your possession too. The Citadel is now at your command."

Warlord took the token. "Citadel, arise."

The powerful mech engaged its magnetics, rose silently, and stood on the floor, towering over them.

Every worker on the docks turned to gawk at it, because it was truly an impressive sight, over five meters tall, sleek and gray. Like most mechs, it was bipedal, but only vaguely man-shaped. Each powerful limb was a bit too long, the body of the thing a bit too thin for its height, and there were bulbous weapons lockers mounted all over it. It looked like a skinny soldier weighed down with armor plates and pouches.

Warlord used the tablet that came with it and swiped through the Citadel's various battle configurations. He stopped on one. "Deploy security formation one."

A door popped open on the mech's right leg. Three small scout bots flew out to take a position above Warlord's head. They paused for a few moments as the Citadel made readings and calculated the dimensions of the space they were in. Then one of the sentinels went one way down the dock. The second went the other. The third remained where it was. Machine-gun barrels popped up out of the Citadel's shoulders and rotated toward the crew.

"They are all known friendlies," Warlord said, "except that one."

The guns swiveled and pointed at Bushey.

"So much for my standup routine," he muttered.

The tension stretched a little long, and then Warlord said, "This next joke had better be a good one."

Bushey swallowed hard. "What did they find in the toilet of the spaceship?"

Jackson groaned inside. *He's dead.*

Big Town's dictator waited for the punch line.

"The captain's log."

Warlord blinked, then grunted, then barked a laugh.

"They clearly don't get out much here," Bushey said over Jane's net.

"He's cleared," Warlord said.

The Citadel's guns swiveled away.

"Most impressive, Jackson." Warlord swiped again. "Deploy security three."

Another door opened, and two larger bots flew out. Each one was basically a flying gun, housed in a body the size of a shoebox. Since the Citadel's scouts had already scanned the entirety of the docks, the gunbots raced down the corridors to take up the best defensive position. In the distance, a crew of cargo workers in a hover cart approached, and one of the gunbots tailed them.

Warlord smiled. "This one is going to be great fun."

"Do you want to take it down to the surface when we go?"

"Oh, I've got special plans for this one. A lot of people are going to be in for a surprise." He turned to the Citadel. "Shut down and stow."

The five sentinels came rushing back, landing themselves in the storage racks inside the Citadel's legs. Then the housing doors closed, the shoulder guns retracted, and the Citadel squatted down and sat, its knees up, its butt on the floor, all nice and compact. However, even in this position, the top of its head was still two and a half meters high.

Warlord motioned to one of his men as he unlocked the mech's magnetics so they could move it. "Take it straight to my garage."

"Yes, sir."

Katze and Tui were approaching and were each carrying a spare go bag of clothing and supplies for Jackson and Bushey.

"A new day is coming. A new day," Warlord said as he watched his latest acquisition being picked up by a hauler. He cocked his head as if receiving a message. "And it looks like we timed it perfectly. Our transport to the surface is ready." He offered Katze his arm. "Would you do me the honor, my lady?"

"Better take it," Tui warned silently. *"Shade doesn't want us to offend him."*

Katze smiled and slid her hand around his arm. *"Ooh, he is surprisingly well-muscled,"* she sent back.

"Splendid. You're all going to love this." Warlord led her to the front seat of a waiting hover cart. The crew took the next rows. The security detail came behind.

"*Why does she get all the attention?*" Bushey asked.

"*She is the pretty one.*" Tui managed to sound sarcastic, even while typing with his retinas. "*But I'm feeling a little left out. Hold me, Jacky, I think I might swoon.*"

Jackson just shook his head, because he was getting a bad feeling about this.

Thirty minutes later, Jackson and the others were on a cramped and claustrophobic dropship heading for the surface.

Swindle was up on the displays. Most of the planet was covered in green and white clouds. Here and there gaps showed the oceans and landmasses below.

"It's beautiful," Katze said.

"Yet unforgiving," Warlord warned. "The air is breathable but caustic, you have about forty-five minutes before your lungs begin to bleed. Death comes soon after."

"A harsh mistress then."

"Indeed. It seems right up your alley."

Katze smiled mischievously.

She was good, Jackson thought. Very good. Captain had hired her because of her face-shooting, door-kicking résumé, but it appeared she could play the honeypot when she put her mind to it.

Warlord truly seemed to be enjoying her company, as he began to tell her the sad yet ultimately triumphant history of Swindle. It was as if he had rehearsed telling the story, the fraud the exploration company had perpetrated on them, the thug war, and now how much CX they harvested each year. It was a lot like the briefing Shade had given them on the way here, only with more dramatic flair, and of course, Warlord was the hero of the tale.

That really set Jackson's teeth on edge. He'd had myth grow up around him once, only he'd not done a thing to perpetuate it himself. It was more that people in dire circumstances really needed someone to believe in, and if no one was good enough, they'd exaggerate someone until they were.

The hard part was when you inevitably let them all down.

The dropship reached the deflection point and decelerated, entering the atmosphere smoothly. Wings deployed, and they were soon gliding, passing through the green and white clouds. A gap offered a brief view of the land below before closing again. They dropped lower and lower.

"Why no engines?" Tui asked.

"The sound riles up the big ones. I have teams of rangers down there checking on groves and hunting for new ones. I don't want to cause them any trouble."

And so they glided in at a very high speed. The display showed a ridge of bare, rocky peaks rising far above a dark forest. The pilot began to communicate with someone on the ground, as Jackson noticed something on the display—a landing strip in a tiny saddle between two high peaks.

"That's the base?" Jackson asked.

"That's the landing zone this week. It's a challenge to actually keep anything in one piece here long enough to call it an actual base, but this one has lasted far longer than most. At nearly three thousand meters above sea level, it's high enough altitude nothing too big climbs up here. Every once in a while, we'll gets some screechers or other flying predators, but they're easy enough to shoot out of the sky."

The shuttle juddered in a crosswind, but then they dropped below the ridges, and the turbulence lessened. Normally a dropship would just flare the engines hard and land vertically, but instead they descended to the runway, landed smoothly, and rolled for a few hundred meters. An electric pusher moved them into a hangar that had been partially dug into the side of the mountain. A boarding bridge extended from the side of the hangar and locked onto their craft.

"Don your helmets. Make sure you're covered."

Jackson had been issued a black full-body suit with boots, gloves, and all, but just in case, he'd worn Raj beneath. Not that he didn't trust the loaner equipment, but as the captain liked to say, two is one, one is none. He pulled on a mask that enclosed the front of his face, and the heads-up display immediately showed the temperature and a number of other things, including a little green bar that signaled the air in here was good to breathe.

"Respirator check." Warlord went to each of his guests, making sure everything was on right. While he checked them, his bodyguards checked each other. "I used to do this with my teams in the old days. You won't know you have a bad seal until it is too late, and you are either paying to vat-grow new lungs or suffering with the scar tissue for the rest of your brief and miserable life."

"Fantastic," Jackson muttered as Warlord gave him a thumbs-up after confirming his helmet was on right. When their host wasn't looking, Jackson checked it again himself because he didn't trust the guy.

Satisfied their equipment was working, Warlord gave the signal for the pilot to proceed. There was a small hiss of pressurized air as the door opened. Most of the security detail exited the shuttle first. When they were satisfied all was clear, they signaled for the rest to proceed.

The temperature here was cooler than in the dropship. Jackson's air quality meter dipped a bit but was still green.

Katze observed how the bodyguards fanned out and formed a perimeter. "You still have security issues down here?"

"We're in the CX business. We have security issues everywhere. Everybody wants some."

It was taking Jackson a moment to find his feet. The gravity here was lighter than Earth standard, but the air pressure was much higher. Maybe that was the reason megafauna flourished on this planet? He didn't know. There hadn't been a real strong science curriculum at Tent City High School for Orphans and Refugees.

They walked down a little corridor deeper into the mountain. Warlord patted one of the walls as he walked. "The stone gives great protection against the extreme weather and all of the hyperterritorial things that live here."

"*And protection from prying eyes in space,*" Tui said over Jane's net.

"We have a few stations like this. At any given time, there are only a couple thousand of us on the surface. Mostly rangers, who stage from here to scout for groves, and the techs who support them. They rotate in and out, a week at a time. We tried building lower down, in the arboreal areas where the CX is harvested, but the kaiju would simply swarm them. We lost a lot of people those first years. Up here, we are mostly safe from the big ones, but down in the valleys below is where the money's made."

They reached an elevator that two of Warlord's men were holding open. It was a gigantic thing. Large enough for fifty people. The doors closed and they descended for a very long time.

"The rangers use exos for speed and concealment. They find groves and mark the targets when they are ready. Unfortunately harvesting is noisy and draws the planet's ire. So we drop the harvesters in, along with a mech to protect them, gather as much

CX as we can before the predators swarm, and then get it back to Big Town."

Jackson's air meter was still showing safe. "Everything's filtered in here. Why did we need to mask up?"

"Because you are my guests, and I would not lose you to an accident. When a seal corrodes, and they inevitably do, the results can be rather sudden. Sometimes burrowers will dig their way in. Swindle destroys everything eventually. This planet is manifest entropy. You may see some of the workers inside the mountain without their masks on, but believe me, they still keep them close at hand."

Then the elevator stopped, and the doors opened onto a large, well-lit commons. There were people in various uniforms there, all of them a little frayed or stained, talking to each other or walking to some other destination. The place had that rough, decaying feel of a frontier outpost. The furniture and fixtures were industrial prefabs or 3D prints. Jackson got the feeling these people worked hard for a living.

When they saw Warlord emerge from the elevator, they all stopped and came to attention. He gave a casual nod of greeting as he walked through them. From the body language Jackson guessed the workers' reactions ranged from awe to nervous fear. Either way, it was obvious Warlord wasn't the sort of boss who went out for a beer after work with his employees.

The group entered a guarded hallway and left the commons behind. They came to a room with a full bank of windows that looked out over the landscape. It gave them a fine view of the forested hills and valleys far below.

Tui whistled. "Majestic."

There were mists that prevented Jackson from seeing more than a few kilometers out, but he was able to see a flock of white bird-looking things flying in the distance. They had very long tails.

"From here you can see the area we have cleared. It's not much. Plus the plants grow so quickly that we have to flamethrow the perimeter daily. I've been hesitant to try genetically targeted defoliant because it may endanger the CX production. There is much we do not understand about the biology of Swindle." He pointed at a bunker near the summit. "Those are protective gun batteries up on the side of the mountain, although the mists sometimes limit their range."

"I thought you didn't want to attract attention," Katze said.

"That's for the rangers out in the unsecured zones. If something starts climbing up here, we kill it."

"Even one of those big ones you were talking about?" Jackson asked.

"Short of using nuclear weapons, those are exceedingly difficult to kill. Luckily for us, they do not seem to like the altitude." Then Warlord pointed toward the mist-shrouded valleys. "Those are the manaloa groves. That's where we harvest our CX, and where we will be doing our hunting."

"I like the sound of that," Katze said.

"Yeah," Bushey sent over the net, "it's perfect if he wants us to have a hunting accident."

"If he wanted us dead he would've just poisoned these respirators," Tui sent back. "That would be a lot less work."

"I don't know, Chief. He seems like the kind of psycho who likes the personal touch. If he goes all Most Dangerous Game on us I'm gonna say I told you so."

"Come, my friends. Let's get you all suited up."

Sam Fain received a call from his boss down on the surface. "What did you find?"

"None of the cameras caught what went on behind those bushes. It's a blind spot. I find that curious." They'd had enough time to exchange a message with James Overturf though, and even though the bracelets hadn't caught anything, it was still nagging at Fain. It was obvious that this crew had some method of silent comms going on that his hackers couldn't crack, so it still could have been a coordinated meet.

"You did your research?"

"Lots of fake IDs and dead ends. Just as we found before."

"Which is expected for people in their line of business."

Fain wasn't so sure about that. He'd spent enough years first working for the Russians and then freelancing that he'd seen a lot of clandestine ops. This felt like a government cover. Nicholas Holloway's jacket was too good. The Americans should have promoted him to admiral, not run him off because of a scandal. Julie Thomas' family was too rich and connected for her to end up slumming it across the outer edge of space with a bunch of smugglers. His gut was telling him this was some kind of setup.

"I pulled the military records for the big islander and the woman from Amon. Nothing too unexpected there, provided they're not totally fabricated, but the kid's from Gloss. That was one nasty civil war. The place is a real mess now. Hard to get any concrete data out of it at all."

"He is what he says he is."

Fain figured the boss would know. "You want me to just poke around what's left of Gloss' net and ask about their mech pilots?"

"There were not many. He will be known."

"I still don't trust these people."

"Tell me when you actually find something." Warlord ended the call.

Fain leaned back in the seat and began to go over his reports again. These *Tar Heel* morons were going to slip up. Everyone did. And when they did, the puzzle pieces would fall into place.

Jackson walked out of the hugely reinforced door at the base of the mountain wearing an exo. The entire hunting party was suited up in exos that had been borrowed from the Big Town rangers. Jackson's suit smelled like its regular user smoked cigarettes, an archaic habit that was still popular among some cultures that saw it as a tough-guy habit. To spacers used to living in recycled oxygen environments it was seen as a foolish affectation. Jackson's peers drank or chewed their bad habits.

He stepped out onto a rough road, the gravel crunching beneath the big metal soles of his feet.

Exos worked on the same basic premise as a mech, but like most pilots, Jackson recognized they were inferior in every way... well, except for cost. There was no armor, not even a shell or a cab even, just a mechanized frame that moved with you, providing far more strength than was possible for even an augmented human. These were older units, refurbed dockworker rigs, but they were quiet, and they had pretty good battery life.

He was carrying a Wakal pneumatic bolt rifle, which was powered by an air compressor and fed by a large magazine mounted on his back. The bolts themselves were huge, 25 centimeters long, and were launched out of a nearly meter-long barrel. Jackson was impressed. Wakals were not cheap guns. Tui and Bushey were outfitted the same way. Katze had picked out a 20mm rifle that even she wouldn't have been able to lift without the exo.

Warlord carried a huge crossbow that must have had a three- or four-hundred-pound pull, a quiver of javelins, and two sidearms. He was the only one whose exo wasn't borrowed, but rather he had a personal one staged for his use here. It was newer, nicer, smoother, and had been painted in some sort of white dot tribal warpaint style Jackson wasn't familiar with. Apparently, he went on these hunting trips rather often, sometimes even going out solo.

But today he was accompanied by two members of his security detail, also in exos, and carrying jet-suppressed rifles. And just in case of emergency, they were being tailed by a mech. It was an older model Mirage, just a little three-meter-tall unit, but even then, it still packed more firepower and a far better sensor suite than the rest of their party put together.

"Alright everyone, check your HUDs. Make sure this location is tagged on your map should we become separated."

Jackson looked at the Heads-Up Display. It was a balmy twenty-five degrees... That would be seventy-seven on the *Tar Heel,* since the captain still thought of temperature in American. High humidity. The air meter was red. *Very red.*

"We will follow this road down to the hunting grounds. That should give each of you a chance to get used to moving in these exos in this gravity."

They took an accelerated stroll toward the manaloa groves. Warlord suggested they jog, and so they did. The combination of the light gravity and the exos meant they could take monstrous strides.

Despite their battered appearance, the exos were well maintained. The hunting party didn't make much more noise than they would have just on foot. The key was to let the frame do all the work to conserve your energy. The former soldiers, Tui and Bushey, seemed comfortable in their rigs. Katze not as much, because most of her military experience had been ship-to-ship boarding parties and fighting in tight corridors where exos were often too big to be of use.

For Jackson, he felt like a racing driver playing with bumper cars. He had to admit he was a little jealous of the guard driving the Mirage, and often found himself glancing back over his shoulder to see how that guy was doing... He was a clumsy amateur, and obviously driving by stick, not plugged in directly. The difference between the two was night and day. Jackson hadn't asked, but he was starting to suspect Warlord was the only man in his operation with the necessary implants to fly-by-mind.

As they got closer to the mist, Jackson saw that the trees were exceedingly tall, a hundred meters at least. They had tall narrow trunks with short branches that feathered out. Along those boughs, instead of leaves, they grew needles, but they weren't pine needles. Instead, they were segmented and soft.

"*These are the same trees those children were climbing in that video that started the riot,*" Tui sent silently.

"*We still don't know if that was real or propaganda,*" Katze answered. "*Either way, it's not our fight.*"

Up until now all the brush had been cleared away, leaving nothing but gray stone and yellow dirt. There were small bots moving along the perimeter, occasionally blasting out streams of burning napalm to burn back the plant life. Like everything on Swindle, even the foliage was aggressive. They crossed the ashen DMZ into the thick undergrowth.

"Tread carefully, my friends. Many of these bushes have a sting to them. If it doesn't have thorns, it probably has a nest of swarming insect living in it," Warlord warned. "I will take point. Follow my path. Remain alert."

There was a breeze, and, here and there, thin clumps of mist the size of houses ghosted by. The group scared up a flock of blue butterfly-looking creatures, each as big as Jackson's hand. One landed on Jackson's gun barrel and then sprang away again, and he saw it had a tiny snout and tusks. Farther on, they passed a scattering of what looked like birds, except they were covered in long thin hairs instead of feathers. These too had snouts.

A few minutes after that, the hunting party came to the overgrown ruins of what had once been a ten-meter-tall fence, with crumbling guard towers that now served as nests for the snout birds.

"This is from before my time, when they tried to build a fortress so the harvesters could work in safety. They were fools. Swindle cannot be tamed, only temporarily bested."

They continued the easy jog. At one point, Warlord drew a javelin from his quiver, then ran forward, stopped, and stabbed down. A huge snakelike thing thrashed in the grass, then lay still. When it was good and dead, he called them over. It had two eyes on each side of its head. He used the top of the javelin to hold its head, then forced open its mouth with the tip of his exo's boot.

"See those teeth? Not only are they razor sharp, they are coated in venom."

There were no fangs, just multiple rows of very sharp teeth.

Jackson hadn't even seen the snake-analog lying in wait. "That was pretty well camouflaged."

"Indeed." Warlord nodded upward. "Sometimes they like to camp in the branches, so they can dive onto their prey."

"This planet sucks," Bushey sent.

"What happens if we see one of those big kaiju types?" Tui asked.

"As soon as one of those is spotted, an alert is sent out. Harvesters return to their dropships and take off. Rangers, or in our case, hunters, go to ground, hide, and wait them out. Do not worry. We know where all the caves and burrows are to shelter in."

"There were women at that pool," Bushey sent again. *"I could have been swimming."*

They continued on, but now Jackson kept a close eye on the trees and the ground. They had to slow their exos a bit because of the terrain. The silky leaves were so thick that visibility was minimal. The ground was broken and uneven, and they often had to bound over massive root bundles. This was why Warlord needed mechs. Tanks were far cheaper, better armored, and could have just as much firepower, but no tank could traverse this sort of terrain.

Meanwhile, the Mirage was effortlessly keeping up, even with its clown of a pilot. Jackson could have leapt and sprinted through this tangle, even by stick. Mind, would be no problem at all...

He sighed. Even though a connect was no longer an option for him, sometimes, like right now, he kind of missed it.

Tui startled some animal that screeched and went crashing away through the brush. From the noise and the thermal signature, it had to have weighed a hundred kilos. And they'd never even seen it. Warlord just chuckled at how they'd all flinched and continued marching.

Jackson had set foot on many different worlds since he'd signed onto the *Tar Heel* crew, but there was something about Swindle that was truly alien. His home world was cold and bleak and life struggled to find purchase there. Truthfully, this place didn't look that different than the images he'd seen of Earth, just stretched out more... but there was a strange feeling to it. Something primordial. Like a vague sense of dread, as if the entire planet was subtly warning them mankind didn't belong here.

They continued on through the thick, alien wood. A few klicks later, the Warlord said, "We're almost there."

"I'm getting excited," Katze said.

"Oh, you just wait. Our hunting grounds are in the next valley."

"What's in there?"

"Surprises," Warlord answered. "This way."

"I hate surprises," Tui said over the net, but they followed Warlord anyway.

They traveled another klick up a hill, then followed what appeared to be a game trail into a different sort of forest. Some of these had the odd, piney needles, but some were flatter. There were vines and undergrowth and red saw grass. And a lot more of that strange, low-hanging mist. It was a heck of a walk, and Jackson sure would have hated to do it without the exo. Another twenty minutes of hiking and they came to the edge of a wide clearing covered with gravel and stones.

"Check out the guards," Bushey said.

Jackson glanced over and saw that their escorts were falling back a bit, and since the ground had flattened out, it wasn't because they couldn't keep up... The locals were getting nervous.

Warlord, on the other hand, was either fearless or possibly insane, because he didn't seem worried in the least. Suddenly he held one fist up, signaling for them to stop. "We're here."

"It's a rockpile," Tui said.

"It's a kinsella nest."

"A what?" Katze asked.

"They're named after the scientist who cataloged the species. Michael Kinsella. He was a biologist among the first settlers and attempted to study them. He lasted three hours before they ate him. Fascinating creatures. We have to thin out their population, because when a nest gets too populated, they split off and make new burrows. Often right under my harvesters' feet."

Katze unslung her gigantic rifle. "I don't see any nest."

"There's a fat hole right in the center of this field."

Jackson spotted it. A dark burrow.

"There are a few other holes around. Over on that edge. And there's one down there. Let me show you." Warlord picked up a big stone with the exo's hydraulic grabber that extended past his real hand. Then he hurled it out into the center of the field. A moment later something earth-colored rose just a little out of one of the holes.

Tui flipped on his bolt gun. Jackson followed suit.

"They know we're here now." Warlord was obviously having a fine time. "Let's see if we can't stir them up a bit."

He landed another rock in the middle. A moment later, a nightmare scuttled up out of the central hole.

It was two meters long, thin with a scaly hide and had more legs than Jackson could quickly count. It was a dull, earthy color, with a red head and a nasty looking black pincer mouth. It pounced on the still rolling rock, mandibles flashing.

Warlord pulled the spanner lever back on his crossbow. A bolt from a magazine automatically fed into the groove. He sighted on the creature. It moved. He adjusted his aim. *Thwump.*

The bolt streaked across the clearing and struck the kinsella.

The thing jerked, rose up, and let out a harsh whistle. Warlord spanned his crossbow again. Another bolt automatically fed into place. He aimed and let it fly, this time taking the creature in its midsection. The kinsella fell onto its back and writhed.

"That thing was nasty!" Katze exclaimed. "Good shooting."

"Oh, we are just getting started, my friends."

And as if waiting for their cue, all around the field, whistles and pops began to sound.

"Now the fun begins," Warlord said as he reloaded.

There was a whistle behind them. Jackson spun around and caught sight of something rushing along a branch above.

"Incoming!" Jackson shouted.

And then dozens of kinsella attacked.

CHAPTER 16

Jackson raised his Wakal and fired. There was a fast *thump, thump, thump* as three of the bolts streaked out the barrel. He'd rushed. The first two missed. The third one hit the creature in midflight and blasted right through it.

Katze turned and opened up with her 20mm. The exo took the massive recoil and the suppressor kept it remarkably quiet. Huge bullets shredded one kinsella's neck. Its head landed at Katze's feet, the pincers still grasping. She kicked it away and searched for more targets.

"More movement in the trees," Bushey warned.

Jackson spotted another kinsella moving in the branches, he took aim, led the quick-moving creature, and fired a bolt that struck clean and pinned the kinsella to the tree. The rest of the crew were knocking kinsella out of the trees.

Warlord sounded a little amused as he said, "One of you might want to help me with the clearing."

Jackson turned. Kinsella were pouring out of holes. Long and multilegged. All the clacking mandibles and scuffling legs made a clicking, buzzing wave.

"Lord," Tui said.

Warlord spanned his crossbow, aimed, and shot, spanned, shot, spanned again. He was smooth and calm, like they were all out on a picnic.

Tui automatically fell into command mode as he realized just

183

how many of the things were coming at them. "Katze, watch our backs. Jackson, Bushey, zap the clearing."

"Got it, Chief!" Katze said.

Talk about a target-rich environment. Jackson sighted on one, shot, sighted on another, shot again. Shot yet again, and again, and again. The sound of the kinsella turned from a buzzing wave to a furious hiss. And the Warlord began to laugh. This wasn't hunting, this was slaughter, and he was loving it. He spanned, aimed, and released. Spanned, aimed, and released again.

The muffled noise of Katze's rifle continued as she fired at kinsella in the trees behind them. And then there was a human scream as a creature dropped from a branch and latched onto the faceplate of one of the security guards. The exo flopped over, powerful arms flailing uncontrollably, as the man fed the exo's limbs far too much stimulus.

Katze shifted a bit, and suddenly hot 20mm shell casings were bouncing off Jackson's exo. He turned, shot a kinsella that was three feet away. Shot another. Shot another that was winding at such a rapid rate it took him three tries to hit it.

The kinsella were writhing and whistling and slithering all over the field. The chittering and had grown in tempo so that it was almost a high RPM engine wail, a near banshee sound.

"I hate this friggin' planet!" Bushey shouted as he stomped on one that was trying to run up Tui's leg.

And then the ground shook. A mound of dirt rose in the center, bulging as something huge pushed from beneath. Insectoid legs pierced through the mud.

"There she is!" Warlord cried. "There she is!"

"There who is?" Tui bellowed.

"The queen!"

The biggest, scariest, nastiest thing Jackson had ever seen tore itself free of the ground. This kinsella was pale, the color of grubs, but was at least triple the size of the others and wide as a horse.

Right then Jackson really wished he was the guy in the mech. He risked a quick glance back, but the old T-Bolt was busy trying to pull the kinsella off his buddy's helmet.

Warlord let a bolt fly. It struck the queen's thick carapace and glanced off. His next shot hit it square on, but that bolt simply bounced away.

Jackson shot a smaller kinsella that was almost on him, cursed, then shot two more. Tui killed one in a tree and another far out into the field. Jackson scanned his zone, saw one more kinsella, shot it, but he knew the monster that had just arisen was the one they needed to take out. Jackson emptied the rest of the Wakal's magazine at the queen. Some of the bolts bounced off. Some seemed to penetrate, but not deep enough.

"Call in your mech to blast her!" Jackson shouted.

"That would hardly be sporting," Warlord replied.

The monster kinsella let out a terrible roar, slammed down to the ground, and charged.

Warlord grabbed one of his javelins and ran to meet it. "Cover me."

"You're nuts," Tui said. Jackson couldn't believe his eyes. Did the man actually think his javelin was going to pierce that armor? But he was already on the way, so they'd better do as he asked! Jackson saw a smaller kinsella streaking toward the Warlord and shot it. Tui dropped another. And then they watched in horror as their host closed on the queen.

The white monster rose up and opened its pincers.

Warlord leapt, javelin in hand.

The exo-powered lunge took him high. The monster's head tracked upward, following his arc, but on the way down Warlord hurled the javelin straight into the creature's maw. It sank deep, and then the javelin shuddered as the powered blades released. There was a grinding noise as they sliced through bone and chiton.

The queen let out an earsplitting cry of anger and pain. It thrashed to the side, trying to dislodge the weapon.

Warlord landed in a crouch, exo limbs taking the impact. He pulled another javelin from his quiver, and waited just a moment, looking for his opportunity to close on the thrashing beast. Then he surged toward the kinsella's head, driving the javelin through one of its four eyes.

The kinsella shuddered, whistled. The javelin's blades sprang open inside the creature's skull. The queen whipped her head to one side. The Warlord leapt away, rolled, and rose with another javelin in his hand.

The smaller creatures out on the field stopped and turned to look. They paused as if confused. Some lifted their heads up in the air as if smelling something.

And then the mother kinsella dropped to the ground with a thud.

Warlord casually walked up to it, picked another eye, and sunk his javelin deep.

The queen shuddered, then lay still.

The remaining kinsella dropped to their bellies and scurried away from the clearing as fast as possible. They vanished nearly as quickly as they'd revealed themselves. The sudden retreat made Jackson think of roaches scurrying away.

Warlord retrieved his blood-soaked javelins and walked back toward the crew. He was grinning.

"He's crazy," Katze sent over their net.

"Or trying to send a message," Jackson responded.

"Or just full of toa," Tui said aloud, with some respect.

Old habits die hard, and Jackson found himself reloading the Wakal by reflex. His hands were shaking. There hadn't been time to be afraid when those things had swarmed, but it had been terrifying. Then he looked down at all the dismembered bodies, some of which were still kicking, pinned to the ground by pneumatic bolts.

A moment later, Warlord joined them again. "Did I not promise you a hunt? A primal experience?"

"Oh, you promised," Katze said, obviously trying not to sound freaked out.

"Such a thing cleanses all, does it not?"

"Maybe the bowels," Bushey transmitted.

Warlord smiled with a hungry bliss. "Do you wish to try the javelin next time, my dear?"

"I think I like my twenty." She patted her rifle.

Their host turned to Jackson. "How do you feel?"

"Alive," Jackson said, figuring that's what Warlord would want to hear.

"Alive," he nodded. "It's different, isn't it? Being outside the protective shell of a mech. It is good for men like us to remind ourselves what it feels like to be mortal."

"One of your men is dead." Tui nodded toward where the guards were standing around the bloody exo lying in the mud. "His face is bitten in half."

Warlord looked over, then shrugged. "Leave him."

"We're not taking his body back?" Katze asked.

"The kinsella should have their due."

Bushey, Tui, and Katze glanced at each other. They all came

from cultures were soldiers simply didn't do that kind of thing. *Leave no man behind.* But life was cheap here.

"Don't worry. We will strip his gear. We need every exo we can get." Warlord eyed Katze, who was so spattered with kinsella blood that was so dark it was almost purple. He wiped a glob of kinsella off the side of her faceplate and flung it away. "Sometimes there are two or three queens. It's too bad we just had the one. You would have enjoyed the fight, I think. But this was a good one. Worth a token. Why don't you take one of your kills' heads? They clean out and mount nicely on the wall."

"Good idea," Bushey said, then bent to the largest one in the area. He pulled out his knife and began to cut through a soft part at the base of its neck.

"Are you serious?" Katze sent over the net.

"We can put it up in the exercise room," Bushey said.

"Would you like one?" Warlord asked Katze.

"That one's plenty. Not a lot of head room on the ship as it is."

"Very well. Now I am afraid we must hurry, my friends. The noise will have attracted predators and scavengers. Swindle rarely allows one time to relax."

Bushey finished sawing and picked up the head. The security detail started walking back the way they'd come in. Jackson followed, passing by the body of the fallen man. They'd already stripped him of his exo and weapons, so he was just lying there, in a tattered suit, missing most of his face.

Jackson couldn't believe they were just leaving him. Even on Gloss, they'd have at least tried to give the guy a burial. "Does he have any family?" he asked. "A companion?"

Warlord turned to one of his other men. "Did Norris have any family?"

"No," the man answered. "A girlfriend maybe."

Warlord said, "There you go. We were his family."

Jackson looked at the stitched identity tag. There was a splatter of blood across the name Joshua. He figured whatever kinsella were left would soon devour him, and Jackson wondered if Joshua had known that would be part of his job.

They started onto a different trail. When Tui asked why, one of the men said, "Standard protocol. You don't want your routes to be predictable."

"Ambush predators?"

"Them and other things that live in these woods."

And so they trekked along a trail that took them in a slightly different direction. The crew were on full alert now, constantly scanning the woods about them. Whatever they'd been expecting down here, this hadn't been it.

They traveled for quite some time, and then Warlord told them they were getting close to the road. Jackson began to relax, but then a warning signal began to flash in the heads-up display. They were all sent a prerecorded message.

"Attention, Rangers, return to your nearest shelter and await orders."

Shelter? Wasn't that the protocol for when one of the really big monsters was sighted in the area? The kinsella had been bad enough. He really didn't want to see a kaiju up close.

"So which way is the shelter?" Katze asked nervously, clearly thinking the same thing Jackson was.

Warlord held up a finger for her to wait for a moment as if he were listening to someone on the radio, and then turned to his men. "The bastard Originals are assaulting two crews. Let's go get them."

"Sir," one of the security men said. "Perhaps we should wait for backup to arrive."

A hardness came into Warlord's eyes. "No, by then it will be too late." He looked at the crew. "It's time to do some real hunting now."

CHAPTER 17

Warlord led the way, running swiftly through the woods. The security men fanned out, the one in the mech motioned for the crew to move. "Come with us for your safety," but then he ran off before they could ask for details.

"What the heck is happening?" Jackson sent.

"Sounds like they're under attack," Tui sent back.

Not seeing much choice, the crew followed.

About five minutes later, the woods ended and opened up onto a long strip running through the hilly woods that had been recently burned clear of all trees and brush. The strip was about half a klick across. Warlord paused at the edge of the clearing and started giving orders to his men. "Achebe, dismount. I'm taking the mech."

"Yes, sir." The T-bolt slid to a stop in the grass, knelt, and locked its joints as the operator popped the hatch.

"What's going on?" Tui demanded.

"The whoreson Originals are massacring my harvesters," Warlord snapped as he began unbuckling himself from his exo.

"I thought that was a gang up in Big Town."

One of the guards said, "A bunch of them live down here. They claim we stole their lands, so they sabotage our groves and ambush our crews."

"Only they're not getting away this time." Warlord's persona had changed almost as if a switch had been flipped. While hunting the kinsella, he had been having a grand time. Now, he was seething with murderous anger. "We'll hit them from the rear while they're focused on the harvesters and slaughter every single one of them. Let no one escape."

Tui held up one hand. "Hold on. My people signed up for a hunting trip, not a war."

Warlord really didn't like that, probably because he wasn't used to people on this planet not immediately doing what he told them to. "I have given you my hospitality, but if you do not wish to help defend my home, then so be it. Hang back and stay out of my way. I will return you to your ship once this problem has been dealt with."

The guard had made a clumsy exit from the mech, practically falling out the front, but Warlord vaulted into the cockpit with the practiced efficiency of someone who had done it hundreds of times. As the hatch closed, Jackson saw Warlord plug a spike into the base of his brain. Then the Thunderbolt took off like a shot, tons of metal zipping through the trees with the grace of a running deer. The difference between fly-by-mind and manual was staggering.

The security team ran after their boss, except for the one named Achebe, who was trying to get into Warlord's abandoned exo.

Bushey muttered, "I really don't want to try and find our way back without our guides."

"No," said the guard as he buckled the straps around his legs. "You guys really don't want to do that. There's safety in numbers, especially since all the predators in the area will hear the gunfire and get curious." They couldn't see the guard's face through his breather, but he sounded sincere. "Would you give me a hand with the arms?"

Jackson moved to help the mech driver. "Any chance you could guide us?"

"You *have* met my boss, right?"

"The kind, forgiving one?"

"Yeah, that one. Look, you've got two real options. You follow us at a distance and act as a snack out on the perimeter for the caliban or pinkers or whatever shows up. Which could slow them down for the rest of us. Or you stay close. And if you stay close, you fight."

Jackson locked in the guard's arm on this side. Katze locked in the other. The guard moved his arms and twisted a bit, making sure everything was tight. "Perfect," he said. "Thanks and good luck." And then he sprang over a huge root and ran after the others.

"Well, crap," Tui said. "Bushey?"

"I don't mind shooting terrorists, Chief."

"Assuming they're actually terrorists. Katze?"

"Shade said to make the client happy..."

"Jackson?"

The Warlord's team was getting farther away, so it was decide fast, or the decision would be made for them. "I say we follow, observe, and make a call when we see it."

Tui sighed. "Let's go."

They sprinted after the security team, which had already been left behind by the swiftly moving mech. Jackson had to admit he was impressed by Warlord's piloting skills. The 4 wasn't the smoothest runner, but he was rapidly outpacing them.

It still took some muscle power to drive an exo, and a whole lot of movement, which meant a whole lot of heat. They were sprinting now, so Jackson was sweating down the inside of his face shield. He was in excellent shape, but this was brutal. They ran up a hill with huge strides, ran along the crown for a bit, then sprinted down the other side, motors whirring. Strange animals were startled from their path. Bushey swore as he blundered into a bush that was filled with some sort of stinging wasp-analogs. The mech was now out of sight, but the tracks were easy to follow. They climbed one more hill.

And heard gunfire.

Down below were a pair of dropships, each far bigger than the one they'd used to get here. Jackson guessed that each one could easily carry twenty or more workers, and they had massive external tanks for the harvested CX. Except one of the dropships was lying at an awkward angle, its landing skids broken, and it was smoking as if it were about to catch on fire.

Around the ships was a chaos. The harvesters were in orange suits and work exos. They were running, hidden, or lying there bleeding. A little T7 Jackal had been pulling security for the crew, but Jackson could tell that it had taken a hit from an AP round, and the pilot had limped it behind the wounded dropship for cover. It was sparking and bleeding hydraulic fluid, but the pilot was still leaning around the tail, firing bursts from an autocannon.

The enemy were in exos camouflaged with rags and Swindle plants stuck all over them. It looked as if they'd come out of the forest to the north and opened fire on the harvesters. They were armed with a wide variety of weapons, most of them regular old civilian hunting guns.

The Big Town harvesters were a tough bunch, because Jackson noticed a few of the camouflaged attackers were down, and not from the mech's guns, but by small arms, and one had a pickaxe stuck through his helmet.

Jackson took all that in during the brief seconds before Warlord rained hell down on the Originals.

The Thunderbolt 4 came flying out of the trees, powered by an insane leap. One massive steel foot drove an exo to the ground and crushed the life out of the human inside of it. Before the other attackers could react, Warlord had turned into them, firing cannons, machine guns, and grenades as he ran. Men died.

Some of the attackers started trying to engage Warlord, but Jackson could already see how that was going to go. The analysis, processing, and engagement time of fly-by-mind had to be experienced to be understood, but by the time the first gun was pointed his way, the man holding it was getting blown to pieces, and Warlord had already moved on to the next.

When bipedal mechs were first used in battle, they were vulnerable because they stood so tall. As a rule of thumb, the lower to the ground the better. The higher, the more things could see you. They were only used in terrain that tanks couldn't easily traverse. But that had all changed when mankind had figured out how to truly plug in. With the right mind in control, a mech no longer moved like a vehicle, but a giant, superpowered athlete doing parkour.

The antique Thunderbolt bounded between the trees, dodging fire, sliding prone, crawling, and firing accurately every time a target popped up. Then he was up and running, flinging a line of grenades across the treetops to kill the snipers that Jackson's regular human eyes hadn't even seen. Bodies fell from above. A giant armor-piercing rifle was fired but missed. Warlord dove and rolled tons of steel across its shoulder and one arm. He landed behind a massive log.

A rifleman took aim at Warlord and let loose a series of

rounds. It was powerful enough to punch through the thick wood to send splinters flying. But Warlord just swung one arm around the corner of the log and fired a 75mm explosive round into the general vicinity of the rifleman. It detonated, and the shrapnel tore him to bits.

"He's good, isn't he?" Tui asked.

"Professionally speaking... Yeah, really good."

And then they hurried off the hilltop, because they didn't want to silhouette themselves and draw any fire. The security team was descending as well, firing at the Originals, or anything that looked suspicious.

"What's that sound?" Katze asked.

Jackson realized he'd been hearing an eerie bugling, punctuated by chuffs.

One of the security guards looked at the woods, eyes wide with fear. "Goat-shagging Originals."

"They've put out a caliban caller!" another one of the guards shouted.

"A *what?*" Bushey said.

But the guard had got on his radio. "Sir, they've put out callers. We've only got minutes before a big one arrives!"

"Then you'd better help me kill all these whoresons before they get here," Warlord responded.

The obviously terrified security team kept moving down the hill, but Tui signaled for the crew to take cover.

"Isn't a caliban what bit the Warlord's foot off?" Katze asked. "Why would someone be calling one of those?"

"It's like dropping artillery on your own position. They lost and they know it," Tui said. "I don't want to take sides in someone else's war, but we aren't getting eaten by monsters. Get down by the transports and take up a defensive position until we can catch a ride out of here. Got it?" He waited for everyone to acknowledge that, then jerked this thumb toward the bottom. "Move!"

The four of them ran down the hill with augmented strides. There were a bunch of smaller vehicles, lightweight cargo lifters and tankers, which had ridden down on the dropships. Tui gestured at one, and they took cover behind a little tractor.

Down on the battlefield things had gone nuts. A harvester was beating a fallen raider over the head with a big wrench, but then someone blew a massive hole in his chest and the worker went down. Another harvester was trying to detach a gun from the exo arm of a fallen Original. The dirt around the man danced as bullets hit. He looked up, gave the approaching raiders the finger, tried to bring the stolen gun around, but got shot instead.

A hundred meters away, a camouflaged figure broke from the woods and ran for one of the supply vehicles. From the size of him, he was only a boy, but he climbed into the driver's seat, got it started, then stomped on the accelerator and began driving away. The transport bounced over the uneven terrain and roots.

"Little dude isn't going to make it very far," Katze said.

"They're trying to steal provisions!" Bushey shouted to be heard over the gunfire.

Jackson could already see how this was going to go down. He'd been that kid, swiping food and medical supplies from the army. The young raider was never going to make it. "Bail out!" Jackson shouted in vain.

Bullets pinged up the side of the transport, then struck the boy, who slumped over. The transport continued in a slow arc then slammed into a boulder, jolted to a sudden stop, and rolled onto its side.

Jackson reflexively stood up and started that way, but Tui grabbed his exo by the pack. "Stay down!"

The security detail reached the transports and began to shoot at the Originals in the trees. Bullets came flying back. One punched a hole in Katze's exo, just missing her arm. "Screw this, Chief! I'm jumping in."

Katze got on her radio. "We've got an overlook position. What's the priority target?"

A guard responded. "Five o'clock! Five o'clock!"

They all turned to look, just as something enormous shook the trees at the woods' edge. The ground vibrated beneath them, and both sides stopped shooting.

And then it came out into the open.

"Good lord," Tui said.

It was a huge beast, standing on four powerful legs. It was easily four meters at the shoulder and twelve meters long, covered with mottled ridges and spikes. Its face had a long muzzle full of teeth, and like many of the animals here, there were two eyes on each side of its head. As it moved into the open, they saw that it had a whip tail that ended in a club.

The harvesters began screaming, *"Caliban!"* and even the ones who had been fighting a moment before ran for their lives. Warlord's men started shooting at the caliban as the raiders fled into the forest.

The giant was *fast*. Like Jackson-couldn't-believe-his-eyes fast.

Muzzles flashed. Tracers flew, some hit, but some the caliban dodged, lighting quick, springing to an outcropping of stone. It immediately leapt to another spot, a huge distance, then again right onto the wounded Jackal mech. With its front claw, it grabbed one arm and ripped it completely off.

Even as bullets and shells were hitting it, the caliban bit the head of the mech suit, wrenched, wrenched again and succeeded in pulling half the pilot out the hole.

"Open fire!" Tui bellowed at his crew.

Jackson had already been pulling the trigger. Bullets tore off chunks of spikes. Bolts were embedded in the thick skin. The caliban was engulfed in a chain of small explosions.

It turned toward the crew and growled.

"I hate this planet!" Bushey shouted as he reloaded his gun. "I really hate it."

The caliban crouched, giant muscles gathering power, and then it leapt at them.

Warlord hit it in midair.

The 75mm round caught it in the leg, and the explosion and flinch were enough to send it off course. The caliban hit the dirt and slid, plowing through a tanker.

The force of the collision was so violent, the side of the tanker ruptured, and orange, gooey CX spilled everywhere.

Meanwhile the caliban thrashed, a huge gaping wound in its front leg, then struggled up onto the other three.

"Get the harvesters on the remaining dropship and dust off," Warlord said over the radio as he reloaded his cannon.

"Door's jammed, sir. We're working on it."

"Get it open, or I will personally feed you to a sabolar. Do you hear me?"

"Yes, sir!"

If Jackson had been thinking more clearly, he would have realized that a power-hungry narcissist wouldn't be going out of his way to order an evacuation if the only threat was the monster that had just been terribly wounded...But then again, Jackson was running on just regular old eyes and ears, rather than a mech's sensor suite, so he'd not realized just how screwed they were about to be.

A second caliban sprang into the clearing, cleanly biting one harvester in half. The exo soldiers turned to shoot at it, but it lashed them with its tail, sending two of them flying.

"Holy mother," Katze said and raised her twenty.

"Nine o'clock!" Tui shouted. "Nine o'clock!"

Jackson turned. Racing through the forest toward their overlook was a third caliban. It wasn't as big as the others but seemed to be moving twice as fast. And it was heading right at them.

"Katze, light it up! Jackson, me and you wait until it's closer so these damn pneumatics can have maximum effect."

Katze brought up the huge rifle. She didn't waste her ammo in a wild spray, but began firing rapid, aimed shots.

The little caliban began darting side to side, impossibly fast for something the size of an elephant. Katze tried to adjust for the jerking back and forth. The caliban took the hits and kept coming. Bits of horned skin flew into the air. A purple splotch of blood appeared. Jackson was waiting for it to be within a hundred meters before emptying the Wakal into it, but suddenly the caliban snarled and sprang into a gully.

"How the neuken does something that big friggin' disappear?" Bushey screamed.

Jackson turned to make sure something wasn't charging from another direction, when he felt the earth tremble.

"Did you feel that?"

The earth trembled again.

"The rebels are using bombs," Katze said.

Except the rebels were busy escaping. Warlord was firing on one of the other caliban and his men were concentrating on the crippled one. A cold ball of dread formed in Jackson's stomach. The vibration had a pattern to it. "Those are footsteps."

Trees cracked and fell in the distance. That sound was followed by a low thumping rumble that penetrated right to Jackson's core. A vibration that made him tremble.

A vocalization, he realized.

"Something's out there. Something big!"

The first caliban was down, probably dead. The second was wounded and running away. But the Big Town troops were worse off. The bodies of exo soldiers lay strewn and bloody around the site of the battle. As for the harvesters, they were piling into the remaining dropship.

The rumble beat through Jackson again. "The caliban aren't running from us. They're running from *that.*"

"We've got to move," Tui said.

One of the security men said over the line. "*Gorgon. Three klicks out and closing fast.*"

"*Cover me!*" Warlord ordered as the mech ran into the forest in the direction the Originals had retreated.

"*But sir, he's got our smell!*"

"*I said cover me. I want information.*"

It was obvious the man was terrified, but he managed to stammer, "*Yes, sir.*"

Warlord flung a javelin as he moved into the brush. It took a running man in the back, who fell. Two other rebels, a woman and a girl, tried to help him up, but the mech charged them. They saw it and ran, but they never had a chance.

A few guns fired from the forest's edge, but the security detail let loose with a buzzing barrage that sawed through the brush, cutting down the last of the Originals' stragglers.

Warlord caught up to the two rebels. The closest was the woman. She raised a rifle, but he knocked her down with a fist the size of her torso. It was a gentle blow by mech standards, so he probably didn't kill her. "*Fall back, three hundred meters north of the vehicles,*" Warlord said as he slung both prisoners over his shoulder and ran back toward his men.

Another thump made the ground tremble.

"*Fall back,*" the security man repeated.

"There's a third caliban out there somewhere to your ten o'clock," Katze warned over the radio.

"We'll go in rotation," Tui said. "Katze, you first. Go!"

Katze ran a quick fifty meters down the hill in her exo, then took up a covering position with her fifty.

"Go!" Tui said to Jackson.

Jackson turned and sprinted for Katze's position. He was there in five strides.

"Next!" Katze said.

Bushey turned and ran.

The smaller caliban that had been coming for them suddenly

rose out of the gully to their left. It narrowed its four eyes and growled at them.

Katze opened up with her rifle, but the caliban ducked back down, and the rounds only kicked up dust.

"Run!" Jackson yelled at Tui.

Tui stretched his strides, exo humming. But the caliban suddenly sprang out of the gully farther down to cut him off.

Jackson opened up with his Wakal. It made a steady *thump, thump, thump,* as he planted a stream of bolts into the creature. Most of them glanced off the caliban's thick skin, but a few sunk into its belly.

The caliban sprang at Tui, trying to slash him with its massive claws.

Tui sprang back. Dodged. But the thing had a wicked, reflexive speed and jumped in front of him. Tui tried to reverse, but the massive force Tui sent through the exo's foot simply plowed a groove in the earth instead.

Jackson fired at the thing's belly. It lunged at Tui, but then the bolts hit, making the beast wince, giving Tui just enough room to duck beneath its slashing claws, get his footing, and sprint back toward the crew.

Katze's next round hit the side of its horn-skinned muzzle, and she walked the following bullets up its head, bloodying its face up past its eyes. The caliban sprang away, then thwacked the ground with its tail, sending dirt and a barrage of stones the size of dog's heads at them.

Bushey dove to the ground. Jackson wasn't as quick, and a huge stone whistled past his face. Other smaller rocks and chunks of earth pelted him. One stone hit his hand, smashing the bones.

Tui sent a burst of bolts at it, then ran to join the others.

The caliban leapt at him.

Desperate, Tui dodged left.

The caliban landed where he'd been, not a pace behind.

"Run, Chief!" Bushey shouted and fired from the ground.

Two of the Warlord's security force opened fire on the thing.

Jackson discovered he couldn't pull the trigger with his index finger, so he used the middle one. More bolts struck the creature. 20mm rounds clobbered its face. Tui reached them and yanked Bushey to his feet as he passed.

The caliban roared and whipped its tail around, whipcrack

fast, the club portion of the tail struck Warlord's security men and sent them flying into the brush.

Jackson kept hosing the monster. The bolts pin-cushioned its neck, and now they were so close they were sinking deep. He walked his projectiles up its head and into its mouth, then back a bit. His last bolt sank deep into one of its eyes.

The caliban screamed and whipped its long tail around again. *SNAP!*

It was like getting hit by a truck. Jackson flew forty meters at least. The exo took most of the impact, Raj cushioned more, but then he hit the dirt, bounced, flailing over the lip of the gulley. An awful second later he slammed painfully into the far side, then tumbled down to the bottom.

He landed hard.

Head swimming, Jackson slowly realized he was still alive. He groaned.

Above him shots were fired.

He had to get up, although he couldn't quite remember why. He tried to rise, but was too dazed, and his legs didn't seem to work.

A voice came over his radio. It was Warlord. *"Get my guests to the dropship. Quickly!"*

Jackson tried to rise again, but the sky began to slide, so he lay on his back in a dizzy heap.

"The last guy's not here," one of the security men said.

"I'm down here," Jackson croaked.

There was another tremble of the ground. Another one of those deep rumblings that made Jackson's heart flutter in his chest.

"I can't see him," another security man said. *"There's no time!"*

Jackson rolled over. The sky was spinning, and Jackson closed his eyes, hoping it would stop. Hoping he could get his bearings.

"We have to launch, now!"

Jackson heard the security men call to each other. Heard the buzzing of bullets. Heard the high-pitched whine of a dropship engine. Then it was all consumed by a thunderous roar.

"Tui," Jackson said. Or at least he thought he said it. "Tui," he repeated again.

But there was no response, and then Jackson's world sank in and out of blackness.

That thunder became louder, closer. He opened his eyes.

There were little pieces of gravel next to his face. Each time the thunder sounded, the pebbles shook.

Suddenly he was covered in falling rocks and a cloud of dust, as a vast shape clambered down the slope. There was a crocodilian face, bigger than his entire body, with three eyes, because the fourth had a Wakal bolt stuck into it. Terror seized his body as Jackson tried, feebly, to get away from the caliban.

It spotted him. Angry, it stalked toward him.

Jackson couldn't move. He thought he was paralyzed. Had the fall broken his neck? But then he realized he was straining futility against the broken and depowered exo. He tried to get his thumb around the quick-release buckle, but it was stuck.

The caliban opened its mouth. The toothy, gaping maw filled his entire visor.

But then the thunder was right on top of them.

A mountain moved in front of the spinning sky.

The caliban looked up as it was engulfed in shadow and let out a pathetic squeak.

The mountain suddenly bent over and snatched up the wounded caliban with a webbed appendage the size of a house. Claws as big as constructor blades dug trenches through the ground, throwing up a cloud of dust that rolled over Jackson, blinding him.

There was an awful crunching sound high above as the mountain bit down on the squealing caliban. Blood fell like rain.

Blood and gore and dirt. It buried him. He knew he should move. He needed to get to the dropship. But that thought was far away, like someone calling from a large distance, and then everything faded to darkness.

CHAPTER 18

It was the rhythmic throbbing in his finger that woke him up. Every time his heart beat, it was like a little jolt of lightning.

Jackson slowly came to. His shoulder hurt. His head felt like someone had been at it with a ball-peen hammer. When he cracked open his eyes, all he could see were a few points of light because his visor was mostly covered in dirt. Gradually, he was able to focus through the gaps, but all he could see on the other side was a cloudy sky.

How much time had passed? He didn't know. Was the big one gone? The world wasn't shaking, so probably. Where was everybody? And then he remembered the sound of the transport taking off.

His throat was dry, and his voice rasped as he said, "This is Jackson Rook from the *Tar Heel*. Come in." He craned his neck over, found the drinking straw in his breather, and took a sip. The water was cold and wonderful. Thank goodness that still worked. "Come in. Anybody?"

His radio was silent. His HUD was cracked. He was alone and trapped on a brutal alien world. *Pilots don't panic.* That had been drilled into him when he'd been in training, and he repeated that mantra in his head until it came true.

When he tried to move, he was reminded that his exo was busted. Better it than his bones. The emergency release ring had slipped from its place as he scrambled around with his fingers trying to reach it. It was unbuckle from the exo or be stuck to the immobile frame until something came along and ate him.

He found the ring and pulled. The buckles around that arm released and he was able to wiggle it free. His first instinct was to immediately reach for his other arm to free it, but there could be animals close by...Especially considering how many edible bodies were lying around. So he *slowly* reached for his helmet and wiped the dirt off his visor so he could see better.

The big monster had kicked up so much dust that he'd been buried beneath a couple centimeters. The concealment had probably saved his life.

He shifted slightly to view the ravine and found himself surrounded by wet clumps of mud that smooshed beneath his fingers. Mud made from congealing caliban blood. But he was alone at the bottom of the ravine, and so he reached for his other arm, found the release, and pulled it.

A throb of pain squeezed his head when he sat up. He tried to relax until the pain subsided. Good lord, that one hurt. How long had he been out?

As he freed his legs, he noted a thin dark smoke trail rising into the sky. Jackson rolled over, got to a knee, looked, and listened. But didn't sense anything coming to murder him.

He took stock of his injuries. Severe headache. Possibly a concussion. Shoulder in a lot of pain, but he could still move it. Trigger finger broken. He didn't dare pull off his gloves to check, but it wasn't tacky inside so the bone hadn't broken through. Raj had smart weave, which stiffened a bit on impact. Between that padding and the exo limbs taking most of the hit, he'd been spared from any really serious injury.

Trying to make zero noise, he carefully crawled up the slope of the gully. When he peeked above the top edge, he saw the smoke was coming from one of the harvester vehicles. There were lots of bodies strewn about, including the dead caliban. In the middle of the harvesters' work area was a new depression. It was huge, like somebody had been digging a pond. Until Jackson realized there was a tanker flattened at the bottom, which meant that was a footprint left by the big one.

Jackson spotted his Wakal lying in the grass just a few meters away. He slowly started toward it, but then heard a low rumble and a chuff. He stopped and turned toward the sound.

Fifteen meters away a caliban was gorging on a harvester. The man was headless. And as Jackson watched, the caliban bit into and wrenched one of the man's arms off. It chomped the arm a few times, then gulped it down.

Jackson slowly lowered himself below the grass at the edge of the gully's lip and held there. Holy hell, why hadn't he stayed up in the orbital? Bushey had been right. He should have asked if Jane wanted to go swimming.

The caliban made another wet chomping sound, then something snapped. Probably a bone.

Jackson swallowed. Blew out a breath.

And then a second caliban exited the woods on the far side of the clearing. It walked down to a body, sniffed it, then began to tear off a leg.

Lovely, Jackson thought. There was a lot of meat here, and that probably meant more caliban buddies would be along to enjoy the carrion buffet. And if it wasn't more caliban, it would be another one of Swindle's delightful denizens. As thrilling as this nature show was, he just couldn't stay.

But he needed more than sticks and stones for defense in this environment. He needed a gun. And one that didn't draw the hordes of hell to you. The Wakal's pneumatic bolts seemed to be quiet enough to do just that. He needed that Wakal. And so he nudged himself up until he could just see the closest caliban. The gun was right there, but so was the caliban. The animal wasn't nearly as big as the one that had swatted him, but it was still the size of a horse. And Jackson had seen how quick they were. If it saw him, it would be on him in a flash.

The caliban tore at the man's exo, trying to get to the tasty soft body inside. It moved to get a better position, ripped at the exo with its front claws and its mouth. It yanked again and turned its back toward Jackson.

That was his chance. *Now!* He pushed himself up and over the lip of the gully.

The caliban suddenly rose up as if alerted to something.

Jackson froze.

The caliban looked over at its buddy across the way. It too was staring into the forest. The two caliban held their alerted stances. Meanwhile Jackson lay there like a dead fish, right out in the open. And then the second caliban dipped its head back to his meal. The caliban next to Jackson waited a moment longer, then went back to prying open the exo.

Jackson took a breath, then reached out as far as he could, his heart beating with great big booms. He touched the stock of the gun, softly closed his hand around it, and began to slowly inch back toward the gulley.

The caliban stopped and titled its head.

Jackson froze again. Waited.

The caliban listened for a while, then turned back to its food.

Jackson began to move again, sliding the rifle along, nice and quiet.

Except the caliban stopped and turned its head directly toward Jackson. Blood was dripping from its jaws.

Jackson yanked the gun the rest of the way, and dove-rolled-slid down the grassy side of the gulley.

Above him the caliban chuffed, cried out, then marched over.

Jackson hit the bottom and spied a patch of tall, puffy grass next to a boulder. He scrambled in, pressed his back against the rock, and held perfectly still.

The caliban leaned out over the lip of the ravine, blocking the sun. It sniffed. And sniffed again.

Keep moving. There's plenty of food right there. It's not going anywhere.

The predator's shadow moved across the base of the gully. Jackson put his unbroken finger on the trigger and got ready to start blasting. Except then there was some kind of barking. At least that's what it sounded like. The caliban rumbled, then its shadow disappeared as it darted away.

Jackson waited. Counted slowly to thirty. Then used the gun's muzzle to part the puffy grass. He expected to see death staring down at him, but it was clear. He looked around to see if he was in view of anything else, but it appeared his moment had come.

And so he crawled out, rose to a low crouch, and began to move away from the feast, quietly as he could. Except when he tried to walk, there was a noise. Jackson froze. Listened. He took another quiet step, and then another short clacky one. One of the protective leg plates on the environment suit Warlord had given him had come loose.

He cursed under his breath, turned, and raised his Wakal, expecting to see the horned face of a caliban appear above the lip of the gulley. He waited for a few maddening heartbeats, ready to launch sharpened metal bolts at whatever came, telling himself to aim for the eye, because that had seemed to work a bit. But nothing showed. And then he wondered if it had circled around.

His heart raced, and he swung the Wakal around behind him, but all was clear. He breathed a sigh of relief, then examined his suit, found the offending piece that was clacking and held it fast with his free hand.

He started walking.

A shadow passed over the ground. Jackson spun to face his attacker, but the shadow was from one of the long-tailed Swindle birds soaring overhead.

There were lots of valuable supplies abandoned up above— comms, provisions, weapons—but from the barking and chuffing, more awful things had shown up to fight over the corpses. And that meant he needed to get as far from here as possible, before one of the losers who got chased away came looking for something else to eat.

Jackson needed to get to cover and fast, so he followed the gulley. It was clear that water sometimes ran here because the bottom was like an exposed creek bed. He avoided the mud, and a minute or two later reached the woods' edge. There was an opening in the thick brush, like a little portal to the dark forest beyond. He slipped through it and into the shadows.

Twenty or thirty meters later, the ravine became so choked with vines and brush that moving at all was hard. So he climbed out of the gully and found that while the poofy trees up top were tall, the brush below them was thin.

Having put some distance between himself and the caliban feeding grounds, he decided he needed to stop and take stock of what he had to work with. The HUD used to have infrared, but it appeared it was now broken, and so he carefully scanned the area in a 360 visual. Remembering the kinsella, he also looked up.

He appeared safe for the moment, so he tried to call up data in the helmet, but it was busted. No infrared. A small amount of water. No food. No commlink. The visor had a big crack in it, but at least it was still filtering air. There was no headset assistant available, which meant no directions and no map. The wristband he'd been given had taken a hit, but hopefully it was still transmitting, and someone on Big Town would see he was moving. He dropped the mag and function checked the Wakal. It was fine, but there were only seven bolts left in the magazine.

And the atmosphere here was caustic, so that was a pressing concern. The air quality meter was still working, but the air here was code orange. Not immediately fatal, but it would be if he breathed it long enough. There was plenty of oxygen to work with, but the problem was all the other stuff. If his scrubber ran out of juice, he'd be dead shortly after. The battery was at ninety-five percent, but he had no real context of how long that meant in practical terms. Hours? Days? But what were the odds of one man surviving on Swindle for days? Something would eat him long before the battery ran down.

He was alone. Well, maybe not.

"Fifi?"

Sure enough, Jane's little friend moved inside his pocket. She made a happy ping noise in the affirmative.

"Can you reach Jane?"

Fifi's *no* sound was a sad chirp.

Jackson nodded. Fifi was so tiny she only had a short-range transmitter. When Jane talked to her from the sky, it was relayed through his comms. He supposed if a caliban attacked, he could sic Fifi on its eye. That might not save him, but it would be great revenge on the beast that ate his body.

He set about repairing what he could. He used the wire from the exo's emergency release and twisted it around the plate that had come free to secure it. No more clacking. The air was poison, but he thought a brief exposure might be worth it if he could fix the comms. And so he removed his helmet.

The air was humid and had a definite bite to it. It also had a sharp smell. He quickly examined the helmet but saw part of the exterior had been bashed. The hardware where the antenna attached was totally trashed. However, what was left might just be enough.

He quickly reattached the antenna, then put the helmet back on and sucked in filtered air. The HUD still wouldn't boot, but from the noise it appeared he had comms.

"SOS. This is Jackson Rook of the *Tar Heel*. I was abandoned on the surface of Swindle and need evac. Can anyone hear me? SOS."

Still nothing.

"Fifi? Can you tell if I have a wide connection?"

Sad chime.

He flipped through the available channels, then stopped. There was nothing but static.

"Okay, Fifi, I need you to keep trying. Let me know when you connect."

No comms, no problem, he lied to himself. There was still a chance. He just needed to backtrack their trail until he could find the mountain base. Except they'd done that via exos, which were far, far faster. But he was burning daylight, so Jackson set out.

Two hours later, he began to wonder how he'd gotten turned around, because he figured he should have already reached the kinsella by now. He was following what he thought had to be the Warlord's T-bolt tracks, but the plants here were so resilient that they had immediately begun to spring back into shape.

Nothing on this planet was helpful. All the plants were confusing and there were no landmarks. Pilots from real militaries got survival training. They learned how to evade and navigate in hostile terrain. But Jackson hadn't come from a real military. He'd come from Gloss. Their army had been a bunch of desperate, starving rebels. And he hadn't even been a guerilla. His training had consisted of brain surgery, getting bonded to a piece of heavy machinery, and then being tossed into the deep end. Any dead-reckoning skills he had were picked up by observing his squishy, unarmored comrades.

A storm began to gather and darken the sky. But he pushed on until he came across a huge scat on the trail. A nice fresh load had attracted a bunch of green millipede-looking things. He skirted around the manure and suddenly spotted the long side of some creature maybe thirty meters ahead. In fact, there were three of them.

They weren't caliban. They weren't kinsella. They weren't anything he'd seen so far. Their backs were at least a meter tall. They had mottled hides of short fur or feathers. He couldn't tell from this distance. And they were rooting around on the forest floor.

He didn't know if they were predator or prey. But he was pretty sure there was a good chance they might charge him with their short, curved tusks. And he didn't want any of that, so he decided to skirt around them, and backtracked.

The clouds above hid the exact location of the sun, but he figured he knew where it was and could dead reckon that way. He counted his steps.

It took him twenty minutes to get around the animals. However, when he finished his pace count and reached the position that should have been a hundred meters beyond the creatures, the trail he'd thought had been the right one was gone. He walked a bit farther, counting every step, but found nothing.

He paused and reviewed his turns and paces, but now he was really lost. Above him, the sky grew blacker. He walked fifty meters back toward where he had spotted the tusked animals, but still couldn't find the trail. Then he realized it was probably the gravity. The lower gravity meant he was taking longer strides. But they couldn't have been that much longer, could they?

He took a calming breath. No problem. He'd just retrace his steps. But before he'd gone twenty meters the lightning cracked, and the rain began to pour. And not long after that, the water began to pool on the ground. Worse, the moisture caused the weird tubular grass to swell. Now he'd never be able to find the mech's tracks.

He cursed. Then took in a breath.

"Fifi, do you have a wide connection yet?"

Sad chime.

Lovely, Jackson thought. *Just lovely.*

The wind gusted. The lightning cracked. Then cracked again. And again.

Jane was frantic.

She didn't like being frantic, not one bit, but Jacky going missing was messing with her head. She had been born and bred to parse data with emotionless efficiency, to operate multiple complex systems simultaneously. This should have just been another problem to solve.

But it wasn't.

She had hacked ever spy satellite feed around Swindle, but between the damnable atmosphere, weather, and the thick canopy, she'd failed to find anything so far. She'd been searching nonstop since he'd vanished and created a new surveillance program to sort through heat signatures to separate wildlife from humans. It was rather clever, and she probably could have sold it to some frontier planet's search-and-rescue organization, but Jane could never risk having her unique programs out there in the wild where one of Savat's hunters might find it.

She was optimizing her search parameters based on Jackson's height and body mass, when one of the piggies she'd sent after Grandma's mysterious contact returned home.

With part of her mind she continued to search for Jackson. With another she read about the piggy's journey.

Shade's messages had gone to a ship orbiting Raste. It was an unmarked fast courier that had come in from Nivaas a few hours after the *Tar Heel*. After receiving the message, it had sent a transmission out of system. The piggy had ridden that packet as it had traveled through three gates. All the way to the seat of government of the Kong.

Was this who Shade was working for? Except why would that one independent world care about Swindle?

Jane read it over again, then noticed a slight error in the record. A miniscule thing. But Jane had learned to read miniscule aberrations in the code.

Her piggy had not gone to the Kong at all. That whole trip was an elaborate deception.

This was a Trojan Pig. Someone had caught her trace, loaded it up with spyware and lies and then sent it back. Of course, Jane was far too careful, so it had been placed in quarantine upon its arrival. Her systems had never been in danger because she would not be letting this particular piggy out of its pen.

She examined it closer. All programs had certain accents and nuances indicative of who had made it. How did they think? What culture were they from? Where had they trained, or were they self-taught? It was an unconscious thing that they all did. That was the same reason she could never let any of her art out into the wild.

This code felt American.

Shade, the one brokering the deal, was sending secret codes to Earth, to the same country leading the embargo against the Warlord. Why would they do that? Shade wasn't American, but the captain was. Did he know his old country was breaking its own embargo? Or was the American signature yet another misdirection? This code was top tier.

The only thing that this told Jane for sure was that whoever Shade was really working for had serious resources. Jane gave the poor corrupted piggy a mercifully quick deletion and then went back to focusing on her search for Jackson.

CHAPTER 19

It rained for hours. It rained so hard that Jackson's suit struggled keeping the moisture out. The edges of his faceplate fogged. On the bright side, the lightning was spectacular, multiple forks cracking and booming over and over again. It was the most electricity Jackson had ever seen in a storm, as if some mad scientist had been given the job upstairs. One bolt struck so close the boom knocked him sideways. A companion bolt struck ten meters farther on. A third crashed just a little to his right, splitting a tree in a bright flash.

Jackson wondered if he was next, but the lightning moved away. As the water rose above his ankles, he thought of the leeches that infested the streams of his home world. To jump-start the biosphere, the colonists had seeded a lot of Earth animals on Gloss, most of which hadn't survived, but the damnable leeches had thrived. Worse than that, he'd read about Earth beasts like piranha and anacondas and figured there was surely some Swindle nightmare equivalent that swam in the shallow water, so he moved to higher ground.

Even though he was cold, damp, and miserable, on the bright side the torrential rain was washing away all sign of where he'd been, including his scent. Which made it slightly less likely something terrible would murder him in the next fifteen minutes. The downside was that surely Tui—if he'd made it back to the base himself—wouldn't leave a man behind. They'd be coming back to the site of the attack with a sniffer tracker. Only there wasn't a scent trail in the world that would survive this flood.

With the rain falling in sheets, punctuated by so much lightning that it was basically a strobe light, visibility was awful. He had to take cover. So Jackson sat with his back against a tree. Even that didn't help much because needles that passed for leaves in this place swelled up like sponges, until the ones above him got too full, and then they'd vomit liters of cold water on him at a time. His environment suit had self-healing fabric, and the leg tear had sealed, but not before some water had seeped in, water that he expected would be as caustic as the air. At least Raj was keeping it off his skin.

Late in the night the rain softened, then drizzled, then stopped. The helmet had full transfer tech so that he could hear and smell and even feel the temperature of the outside air if he wanted to—an environment suit wasn't much good if it removed all environmental feedback—so he kept the temperature bearable, but not comfortable. He'd rather save the battery for oxygen purification. But he made sure to turn up the audio and olfactory sensors, which allowed him to smell the sharp tang of Swindle and hear occasional rumbles and cries in the distance. Hopefully he'd be able to sense the predators coming.

He maxed the magnification of the ambient light for night vision, but with the clouded sky and a canopy of trees, there wasn't much to magnify. There was just enough to see when little mothlike things came out and other small creatures jumped from tree to tree to catch and eat them. And it was enough to make out the rough outline of something large that rustled as it crossed the canopy of trees above him.

Jackson forced himself to remain alert. He was exhausted but afraid to sleep with the head injury. Heck, after catching a tiny glimpse of that kaiju he didn't think he'd ever sleep again. Raj could hit him with stims or painkillers if necessary, but he'd avoided both so far. The headache was awful, and his shoulder and his finger were miserable, but painkillers would just make him even foggier. He needed to keep his wits.

Except as the miserable night went on, the pain occupied more and more of his thoughts. It had been one thing to push through it while marching, but another to bear it when you were stuck. So he took one hit off of Raj's stash, but that was all he'd allow himself. It made his head feel slightly less awful.

Hunger was starting to gnaw at him. He should have brought some rations, at least a lifeboat cookie or something, but Warlord had assured them it was unnecessary. It would be *rude* for his guests to assume he was incapable of caring for their every need. Right then Jackson wanted nothing more than to put a steel bolt into their host's smug face.

And so the night went. The rain finally stopped. An hour or so later, the first ghostly glimmer of dawn began to lighten the sky. Jackson told himself he was going to get out of this mess. He just needed to get back to that mountain base.

And then he heard a branch crack on the ground. It was followed by the brush of something against leaves. Then a squelch.

He rose, maxed the audio, then turned toward the sound and caught a shadowy movement in the dim green light of the woods. Adrenaline pumped him wide awake. He unslung his Wakal and saw a flash of the creature again as it crossed between shadows. It was the size of a large dog, but with tusks and a pair of spines on its shoulders. It was coming right at him, seemingly oblivious.

Jackson figured animals here were probably like they were in most places and would attack if startled. So he clapped his hands to alert the creature of his presence and warn it off.

The creature paused a moment, sniffed the air, then began to growl. At least, that's how Jackson read the low rumble. So he picked up a dead branch and threw it at the thing.

The stick struck it right in the snout. It flinched.

"Run away, you little shank."

Instead it charged.

Jackson raised his Wakal and aimed at its head. The creature was closing fast. Jackson had to pull the trigger with a finger that wasn't broken, and that screwed up his aim. Instead of nailing the thing in the head, the bolt struck it in the shoulder. The thing hissed like a snake, and spun, snapping at the wound. Jackson backed away at a diagonal. He didn't want to waste another precious bolt, so he picked up a rock and threw it.

The rock struck the flank of the thing with a solid thud, and apparently that was enough, because it grunted and ran off into the shadows. Jackson listened to its flight until he was sure it was gone.

Time to move. He had a vague notion of which direction the base was, so he'd go that way and hope for the best. Fifi might get a signal, or he might stumble across a ranger patrol.

Morning came with mist, which didn't clear for a few hours. Between the visibility and the rough terrain, he made terrible time, and he wasn't even sure he was moving in the right direction. When the mist finally started to thin, he decided he needed some height, and so he began looking for something he could climb. Many of the trees here were like palms with straight trunks topped by a spongy tuft of what passed as leaves. Some of them were incredibly tall, and occasionally the trees had grown into each other, forming weird shapes, almost like balconies and landings high above. He picked one that looked climbable because the bark had a bunch of lumps that would make good handholds. He slung the Wakal and started climbing.

The gravity of Swindle was less than standard, which allowed the trees to grow very tall. It also made climbing a little easier. He figured he was around twenty meters up when he finally reached a cluster of branches where he could stop. To his disappointment, there was still enough mist to limit his view to a few hundred meters. He decided maybe he should perch up here until the mists burned off.

He spotted a place he could sit and rest, except when he stuck his hand onto that branch to pull himself up, the leaves started to hum. Suddenly a dozen black creatures, each the size of his fist burst out, flapping and jumping. One landed on his faceplate. It immediately started stabbing the plastic with the stingers on its head. Another landed on his hand. More landed on his arm and back.

Jackson startled. He swatted at the thing on his arm, then another. And suddenly he was falling back. He gave the trunk a thigh squeeze.

More of the black creatures landed on him and his mask. He swatted one away, then another, but there were too many of them.

Jackson tore open an exterior pocket. "Fifi! Get 'em!"

One of the devils pierced the suit covering his arm and stabbed into his arm. It was like getting hit with a staple gun.

Jackson cursed, smashed it.

Then Fifi sprang onto one of the devils, landed on its face, and lanced one of its eyes. It screeched and flapped wildly away. She sprang at another, lanced one of its eyes. Another screech and wild flapping. She sprang at another.

"Fifi, clear my body."

Fifi sprang again, this time to his back.

Black devils flapped about. Others kept biting. Jackson smashed two more. Then he loosened his grip enough to begin to slide down the tree trunk. Another one got through on his back. Jackson grunted, then loosened his grip to speed his descent even further, hoping the rough bark didn't shred his suit.

More of the creatures flapped wildly away from him as he slid down the trunk, Fifi attacking them with speed.

A few moments later, he approached the ground. And then another one of the black devils penetrated his suit by his thigh. He swore, hit the ground, knocked the creature from his leg, then stomped it. Purple guts exploded beneath his boot. Another landed on his shoulder. Jackson tore it away and flung it, then ran down the hill, trying to escape.

A few stragglers came after him, but a few seconds later they began to suddenly turn and fly away.

Jackson kept crashing through the brush. Fifty meters later, he stopped. The spots where the things had bit him were on fire.

Jackson initiated a selfheal on the suit and turned on Raj's antitoxin controls. The environmental suit had a much better system, but its system had been broken when the caliban had given him that love swat.

He cursed. And was now officially pissed. It was time to get out of this idiot forest and off this damn planet.

He saw a small black speck springing down the hill toward him, jumping in big arcs. At first he thought it was some other Swindlen nightmare, but it was only Fifi. She bounded down the hill, then landed on his chest.

"How was the fight?"

She gave him a positive chime and then projected a report onto his dirty visor. *137 eyes slashed.*

"Impressive."

17 wings.

Jackson nodded to himself.

5 mouths.

"Mouths?" he asked.

Fifi played a brief video of them trying to eat her, one successfully, before she cut her way out of its throat.

"Thank you, Fifi. Well done." One simply did not mess with Fifi.

Happy chime.

The stings were burning like crazy. He needed to get out of here. It was time to change tactics. He hadn't been a guerilla, but he'd supported them, and he'd at least tried to pay attention.

He knew the burned clear area was probably somewhere within a three- or four-klick radius of where he now was. If he could find that, he could find his way back to the fort. So he would do this the hard but thorough way. He would walk ever-widening squares until he found it. He selected a tall tree on a tall hill as a center point, used his knife to marked the tree on all sides, and then walked a straight line fifty meters out, then he turned ninety degrees and began his first square, counting his paces. Every ten to fifteen meters, he used his knife to mark all sides of another trunk with the number for this first square. He checked his pacing and counts three times as he made his square by walking back to the center tree and saw he hadn't lost his dead-reckoning skills.

He finished his first square around the tree, strode out to a point a hundred and fifty meters out and started his second square, marking the trees as he went. On this happy excursion he navigated a boggy area, saw some small wildlife that included a segmented, crab thing clipping leaves, a couple of gliding bat-tish things, and tiny insectoids the that were a dull yellow and liked to rest on the arms of his suit. He also picked up a long, sturdy stick he could use as a pike against small beasts, and webs, because it appeared Swindle had also evolved something similar to spiders. He checked his dead reckoning twice more and found his pacing and visual direction spot on.

He finished his second square and started a third. This one he took out to eight hundred meters. And on this one, he spotted a herd of animals the size of deer moving through the brush. He assumed they were prey animals, but who knew? On Swindle it seemed everything was ready for a fight. When they didn't move on, he adjusted his path, and continued.

By the time he had finished the third square, he'd walked about eight thousand meters. It had taken him about three hours to do eight klicks. He'd hoped the mists would have thinned out by now, but they just stayed. So he started his fourth square, walking out sixteen hundred meters. That made each side of his square thirty-two hundred meters. A total of 12,800 meters. 12.8 freaking kilometers. And if he didn't run into the burn in this circuit, then he was going mad.

The problem was that by this time the devil bites were burning like he'd been injected with Satan juice. Furthermore, whatever those little goat-lovers had injected him with was making him sweat. Which meant that before he'd gone another klick, he was not only parched, he was beginning to get lightheaded. Still Jackson trudged on, counting his steps aloud so Fifi could record it.

He came to a part of the wood that had a thicker canopy. Below the tall branches all was dark shade. Jackson paused, not wanting to rush in where something might be lurking. He scanned the shadows all the way to the other end of the dense part, and there, out in the light, stood a human figure. Someone in a suit. Someone small.

Jackson blinked.

It was a person, all right. A kid in a suit. With a rifle and a pack. And surely the kid had to be carrying water.

"Hey!" Jackson called.

The kid turned and saw him.

Jackson waved. "Hey!" he called again.

But the kid took off.

"Wait," Jackson said, but the kid was running, so Jackson took off after him. In just a few seconds he arrived at the spot where the kid had turned off. Jackson spotted his trail through the brush and followed.

"Hey! I'm lost. I need help."

Jackson looked in the direction where the kid was running and decided to take a diagonal and cut him off. He crashed through the bushes and hoped he didn't run into any more devil biters, and he didn't. Instead he broke through into an area where there was almost no underbrush and just about ran over the kid.

The kid startled, scrambled away.

"I'm not going to hurt you, please." Jackson dashed after him, reached to grab his pack, but there was a snap as something wrenched tight around his ankles.

A split second later he was swinging by his feet about two meters off the ground. His Wakal slipped off his shoulder. He tried to grab it, but it landed in the grass.

At first Jackson imagined some octopus-armed Swindle monster had grabbed him, but then he looked up and saw it was just a rope. A snare. Jackson had stepped into a snare, like something out of some old-timey jungle movie.

"Are you kidding me?"

He let his head fall and looked at the world upside down. There were men in well-camouflaged ghillie suits coming toward him.

"I am so glad to see you guys. I got lost. I need help."

Except his answer was getting zapped on his back by hundreds of volts. His muscles clenched and wouldn't stop. When the shocker was pulled away, Jackson gasped. "What the hell, man?"

"Tranq him," a man said.

There was a prick on Jackson's arm. A moment later a strange happiness and peace rolled over him.

"I guarantee he's a plant," a woman said. "Just kill him."

CHAPTER 20

Jackson woke to a comfortable electric hum. He slowly opened his eyes and saw he was sitting in his underwear and socks, his arms and legs bound to a chair. He tested his bonds and found all his limbs had been cuffed.

"Welcome."

Jackson looked up. There was a black woman sitting across from him. She had gray running through her hair and piercing blue eyes. She was wearing boots and a camo patrol suit. Although clearly aging, she was trim. Holstered at her waist was a well-used Brady. A butt-ugly handgun that could take just about any punishment one could dish out and still shoot like a dream.

Standing behind the woman was a lean boy who'd taken some scrapes, another woman whose hair was buzzed short, and two men. One of them had a beard. The other had a big bandage on his neck. They were all dressed in similar clothing, and from the sweat and grime, looked like they'd just come out of the forest.

The woman laid her hand on a glass jar sitting on the table next to her. "Quite the little defender you have here."

There was something tiny inside the jar.

Jackson saw that it was Fifi.

"It almost killed three of our soldiers."

"She's one of a kind," Jackson said.

The woman nodded and pursed her lips.

They were in a room that had been carved out of solid rock,

some kind of granite shot through with blues and reds. There were a couple of tables, a display board, and three lights spaced evenly across the ceiling. There was an external wiring conduit that ran from the lights, down the wall, and to a junction box by the door.

Jackson listened for sounds beyond the room but couldn't hear anything except the electrical hum. Other than the pain in his back, he felt remarkably good. They must have given him some medical treatment. Even the bites from the black devils weren't burning.

"Where am I?"

The woman's face was a map of wrinkles, but her eyes were bright and penetrating enough to drill through rock. "How do you feel?"

"I'd love some water."

"We can get you water." She motioned her head at the man with the beard. He stepped forward with a water bag with a straw and offered it to Jackson.

He sucked in the water and kept sucking because who knew when he'd get another drink? Plus he needed the delay to get his bearings. He used the slurping time to assess the situation. This crew was some kind of military unit. And he was still on Swindle. He could tell by the gravity. And since they hadn't just killed him but were questioning him, they wanted something. Jackson looked at his arms and saw that something had been smeared on the bites from the black tree devils. His captors had treated him. Why? Maybe because the wounds would have killed or incapacitated him before they got what they were looking for.

Plus, they had caught Fifi, which wasn't an easy thing to do.

When he was finished thinking, he took one last slurp and sat back. "Thanks."

The bearded man said nothing, just stepped to the side.

The woman continued, "Why were you performing a search in the woods?"

Jackson decided to try being earnest and honest. Captain always liked to say he had an honest face. "I'll be happy to tell you, but how about first you tell me where I am and why you're holding me?"

"You're on Swindle. We're holding you because you were chasing one of us while armed with a pneumatic bolt rifle."

"Are you with the Originals?"

She smiled. "If you want information, you need to give information."

Jackson nodded. Fair enough. "I was lost. One of those caliban things launched me. A nice tail shot. I tumbled, lost consciousness, then woke up and tried to find my way out. I was following a trail, then lost it after skirting a herd of something. I was still trying to find a way out when I saw that kid. I wasn't chasing with the intent to do harm. I was trying to get help."

"Why aren't you on the Big Town records?"

"Because I'm not a citizen of Big Town."

"A mercenary?"

"A trader."

"You were out with the Warlord as part of his personal guard."

"He invited us to go on a hunt."

Her blue eyes narrowed. "Yes, we know about his hunts. Being on one really doesn't help your case."

Jackson looked at the other faces. The young boy was full of aggression, a desire to do harm. The others were stern, hard, maybe angry, but if so, they were good at keeping it check. "I didn't know this was a trial."

"It's not. We're gathering information. That information will determine what we do."

"That sounds a lot like a trial. What are the options?"

"What do you think the options are?"

Jackson found himself wishing he was back in the woods with the pincer devils and kinsella. "If you're some of the Originals and conclude I work for Warlord, you'll want to get as much info from me as you can. Then you'll kill me. If you're not them, then maybe you'll want to assess whether I'm worth anything and then sell me to them. Or if you decide I don't work for Big Town, and I am just a trader, you'll ransom me back to my ship for an exorbitant fee."

Her mouth smiled, but the smile didn't reach her eyes. "Close, but if I decide you work for him, we wouldn't kill you. We'd send you back as a gift."

"Okay...that sounds ominous."

"So we've established you're not on Big Town's rolls. Who are you then?"

He was a pretty good liar, but the truth seemed like the best bet. Or at least a sanitized version of the truth. The question was whether he could get them to believe it. "I'm one of the crew of the *Tar Heel*, an independently owned freighter. We just sold Warlord mangoes and other necessities. He offered a hunt as entertainment. Kinsella. Which are super nasty, by the way. We were on our way back and ran into a skirmish. Our host said it was a group known as the Originals."

"And what did you think that meant?"

"The way they were described, I thought they were some kind of gang. Now, from context, I understand that's in reference to the original settlers. I didn't realize that until later."

"Except you didn't merely observe. You took up an overwatch position during the battle."

He nodded. She'd just revealed important information. They knew what had happened, which meant they'd participated, or at least watched. These were definitely Originals, or at least allied with them. "Yes, I did. Put yourself in my shoes. I'm on a sport hunt with a client. People we don't know start shooting his employees. What else was there to do?"

"You have military mods."

"I was a soldier once."

"A soldier merchant who happens to be on a patrol with the Warlord himself."

"Tell me what you want," Jackson said.

"We want to know who you are."

"I'm a crew member on the *Tar Heel*," he insisted. "A trading ship. If I were a mercenary, do you think I would have gone out to fight rebels with a Wakal?"

The old woman nodded, seeing the reasoning. "That leaves scout, plant, saboteur, or assassin."

"Or plain old crew on a freighter. It's clear you have people up on Big Town. Ask them to look out the window. My ship's really big. They can't miss it. They'll verify that there were four of us down here hunting, celebrating a big transaction. One of us was left behind. My name is Jackson Rook. Their search will confirm that. And if you could help me get back, I would be very grateful. I'm sure my captain would be happy to pay for my safe return."

The one with the beard sighed impatiently. The woman held up a hand for him to keep quiet.

"What was that name again?"

"Jackson Rook." He even spelled it out.

"That doesn't match your RFID."

No, it didn't. He'd forgotten and cursed himself. "That should read unknown. We were getting it reset."

The old woman clearly knew that law-abiding citizens didn't get resets, but she turned to the woman with the buzz cut and said, "Make the check."

The soldier nodded and exited the room.

The tough old bird turned back to him. "I hope your story checks out."

Jackson hoped it did too. And he hoped their sources weren't in possession of many details beyond what he'd shared because it wouldn't do for her to know that the *Tar Heel* had sold Warlord an arsenal that could be used against these people. It was one thing to sell mangoes to the enemy. It was quite another to be selling killer robots.

She tilted her head. "Something's bothering me and I can't put my finger on it. You look familiar, Jackson Rook. Have we met?"

Jackson shook his head. "I don't think so." He would have remembered this woman.

"I know we've met."

"It's probably because I'm so dang good looking."

The old gal almost cracked a smile, a real one that time.

Jackson grinned. It was a start.

"Where are you from?"

"Gloss."

"Gloss?" she asked, surprised. "I'm from Gloss."

"I thought I heard a Cullum accent," he said.

"Yes. I'm from Cullum Province. Iverness."

"Well, maybe we ran into each other there." Nothing like having lived in the same place when trying to build a rapport. It wasn't too odd running into a Glossian on another world. Millions of natives had fled as the political situation on Gloss had gotten worse, and there had been a mass exodus when the Collective government had come into power. Jackson's family had been one of the stubborn ones.

"What hab are you from, Jackson?"

"Covington."

"Huh," she grunted. "The one that got bombed?"

"Sadly, yeah. Nuked into oblivion."

"Never been there. But your face. It will come. It will come."

"Did you arrive here with the first settlers?" he asked.

"Yes, the ones with the first and only legitimate claims."

"Seems like the land rights here are in a tangled-up situa-tion," Jackson said, putting a nice dose of sympathy in his voice.

"No, not really. We own the land. Warlord thinks he can steal it."

Jackson nodded. Not much to say to that. "If you were one of the original settlers, then we can't have met on Gloss." He knew it was good to try and humanize yourself with your cap-tors, because if they thought of you as a person, it was harder to execute you. "I was just a little kid when your colony ships got here."

"I suppose you would have been a wee lad...but still, there's something."

"Maybe you met my dad. I'm told I look a lot like him when he was my age. He was a writer and a professor at Covington University, until the Collectivists murdered him for speaking out against them." He tossed that in there, because surely if she were a proud Cullum girl, she'd still have a burning hatred for the Collective.

"All that bloody business happened after I left, I'm afraid. I've had a different murderous bastard tyrant to worry about."

It was pretty obvious that his attempt at being relatable had failed. So they sat there in silence for a few moments, them looking at him and him looking back. Then Jackson brightened his expression like the good, nonthreatening trader he was and said, "Hey, there are five of us here. Perfect number for a game of poker. You could release my bonds, give me my pants. I could let you win a couple hands. What do you say?" Who could resist such a friendly challenge?

"Or we could just tie you to a tree and let the sabolar devour you," the angry young man snapped.

"So that's a no on cards?"

"We will wait," the old woman said.

A few minutes later the female with the buzz cut returned. "He's Jackson Rook. The *Tar Heel* is a Multipurpose Supply Vessel and is still docked at Big Town. They are traders that did indeed bring mangoes and tech."

"There you go," Jackson said. He might get out of here yet.

"And weapons," Buzz Cut finished. "Lots of weapons."

Jackson kept his face calm, like that was no big thing, but his heart started beating a bit quicker.

"What kind of weapons?" the old woman asked.

Here we go, he thought.

Buzz Cut said, "Guns, rockets, all sorts of munitions, something for a laser system. Lots of other crates. And our man on the dock did not see for sure, but one very large container that possibly holds a mecha or other vehicle."

The old gal looked at him with those rock-drilling eyes. "You didn't mention weapons, Jackson."

"It was just part of the whole order. I don't know a government that doesn't buy guns and ammo."

"But not every trader sells them."

The man with the beard spoke up, "He's ex-military. The other three with him were obviously upgraded. Think about it. They just delivered a load of black-market weapons despite the sanctions. And then they came down to the surface. Why?"

Beard Man had an accent. German, Jackson thought. Or maybe Dutch. More importantly, his assessment of the situation was a dangerous one, that made the crew look really bad. "I already said, because we got invited to go hunting, and my boss said to say yes, because we didn't want to hurt our client's feelings."

"No. It's clear what they were doing," he said. "They were down here to get a firsthand look at the challenges Warlord faces in this terrain, make recommendations, and bid to supply whatever he needed to finish us once and for all. Or maybe they already won the bid and were looking at helping with the deployment."

"It was a sport hunt," Jackson said.

"Do you know what we're fighting for down here?" the woman asked. "Do you know what you're aiding and abetting?"

Jackson said, "No. I don't. We get an order, we fill it. If you'd given us an order, we would have delivered to you too. We're traders. We don't choose sides."

"Like hell you don't," she snapped. "You're not some cabbage and tomato man, selling innocuous goods. One does not defy ISF sanctions and risk imprisonment for just anyone. Which means you did your homework. You must know what manner of beast Warlord is. You knew exactly what was going on down here. But you looked at your potential profit and decided helping him to massacre us was in the best interests of lining your pockets."

What was there to say to that? That Shade, who was thorough with her research, was the one who dug into such details, not him. Jackson was pretty sure she didn't want to hear from him that this was just business. "That's not how it is. I don't know the deals or make them."

"He's paying you with CX, isn't he?" the woman asked.

"Credits through a broker," Jackson said.

"No, he isn't. He can't pay you in credits because his assets are frozen."

"Apparently the Djinn don't care."

"Lies. So you'll receive a payment in CX. Our CX. The CX he kills our sons and daughters for."

It was possible Shade had decided these folks were terrorists as Warlord claimed. Everyone on every side of every war felt they were justified, including the worst of the worst. But Jackson knew there was always two sides of the story. And he began to wonder if maybe he hadn't heard the full report.

"Look, lady, my captain defies the ISF because he thinks they're a bunch of control-freak goons who hate freedom. He goes out of his way to arm the people they keep helpless. If he cut a deal with Big Town, it's because he thought their harvesters were getting eaten by caliban and kaiju and weren't allowed to defend themselves. That's it. I never even heard of the Originals until we got here, and even then, Warlord made it out to us like you were just some kind of gang."

"A gang?" said Buzz Cut. "How dare you?"

"Don't blame me. Blame the guy who controls all the information that comes out of this system. I'm just a mech pilot."

And then some realization dawned on the old woman's face. It was like a big old lightbulb had just lit up in her head. "You..." Her eyes narrowed in disbelief. "You. Of all people."

"Me?" he said, not sure what she was referring to.

"Gloss. The Union. You fought for the Union."

"I did."

"Get him up," she said. Angry now.

Beard Man and Buzz Cut shared a look of knowing satisfaction.

"I'm just a crew member!"

"Don't," the old woman said. "I don't want to hear your lies."

Had he already lost this sale? He hadn't even made his offer. But their faces were full of accusation and condemnation. They were surely thinking it would be a good idea to whack him.

"Kill me, and what have you got?" Jackson pleaded. "A dead body. I can give you more than that."

"Get him in restraints," the old woman said.

Beard Man and the Buzz Cut were good at what they did. They didn't release him and then try to restrain him again, giving him a chance to fight for freedom. Instead they ran some tough carbon cord through his cuffs and secured them to the restraint belt at his waist. So Jackson's hands were in front of him, but he couldn't really do much with them. They chained Jackson's ankle cuffs together with the same type of cord, making it so he wouldn't be able to much more than shuffle. When they finished, they released him from the chair.

"Fifi," Jackson sent over the net.

But there was no reply.

"Up," the man said.

"Fifi?"

Fifi didn't move. Had they killed Fifi?

Jackson got up, testing his restraints, but they were secure. Tui would have been able to break them just through muscle power, but Jackson's mods were mental, not physical.

"Follow me," the old woman said.

Yeah. Follow her right to my execution. He wondered if they were the beheading types. Or maybe their deal was torture. Or maybe they had pet caliban that they liked to feed fresh enemy for breakfast. Because he just wasn't getting the vibe that he'd be lucky enough to get a quick and painless method.

Jackson sighed. Bushey was right—they should have all stayed up in orbit and gone swimming. Surely Warlord could have sported them some blow-up floats.

CHAPTER 21

They led Jackson out into a tunnel, and he shuffled along in his socks and underwear. The tunnel was carved through solid rock, as he suspected this whole lair was, like the ranger base had been.

A wide strip of luminescent paint ran along both walls the length of the hallway. *Smart.* It could soak up the light, then give it back in a glow when the power went out. Also, after going straight a bit, the tunnel jogged left, then back again. And he suspected they'd done that on purpose to prevent intruders from being able to shoot down the full length. They passed closed doors, a kitchen, and a wide area with practice mats on the floor. They turned a corner and came to an open area with stone pillars and a lot of hubbub. There were a couple dozen beds inside and a lot of medical equipment. There was what looked like a play area. There were a few adults, but a bunch of children.

Most of them turned to see who had arrived. Some looked hopeful. Some looked down in disappointment. A good many of them wore bandages or braces of some type or other.

The tough old bird walked him over to a bed with a boy lying on it. "This is Alario."

Alario was around eight and missing an arm. He smiled up at them.

"Nice to meet you," which was the polite thing to say, even when you were in shackles.

"They sent him and five others at gunpoint to harvest. Sent

them in with masks, but no suits. In trees that hadn't been cleared. They disturbed a wollard nest. The same creatures that swarmed you. And what was the Warlord's policy? To leave them. To write them off as an operating cost. If we were somewhere else, we could have regrown him a new arm. But that's beyond us currently."

"I'll work hard and save money," Alario said. "I'll get one."

"That's the spirit," she said, then turned to Jackson. "Alario is the only one to make it out alive. Why don't you tell our guest what happened?"

"My friends died," Alario said, oh so earnestly. "Hundreds of bites each. Their skin turned black."

The woman gave Alario's hand a squeeze. "It was a difficult thing, wasn't it?"

"Yes, ma'am."

"That's alright. You're made of tough stuff. And you're going to learn how to deal with wollards, aren't you?"

"I sure will!"

The woman directed Jackson to another small boy sitting on the next bed. "Hello, Leon."

Leon looked up. He was missing an eye.

"When he started to go blind, they took him out on a work run and left him behind. Another operating cost."

"I'll work hard too," Leon said, clearly having heard Alario's responses.

"I know you will," she said kindly. "You're going to do well. You'll have that eye someday. And until then, you'll help in any way you can."

Leon nodded, but still looked distressed. Jackson knew that look well. He'd seen it on the children on Gloss whose parents had died, who'd lived through all sorts of stress, and seen plenty of death.

She pointed at a group of four at one of the tables. Three boys, one girl. They had a few scrapes but looked healthy enough. "We rescued those two days ago. An op coordinated with people on the inside. They were brought to Swindle without parents or guardians."

"Trafficked?" Jackson asked.

"He needs little ones to get inside the trunk hollows, that's where the purest CX is found. He makes sure there are two or three kids in every crew, to maximize yields. In a galaxy with no shortage of war, unwanted children are a bargain. You can't imagine how many children he buys. Of course, he calls it hiring. He calls it giving them a chance."

"He gave me a chance," Leon said.

The woman didn't correct him, but looked at Jackson, emphasizing her point.

"My ship has never trafficked in people. Never."

"I believe that. But you've just enabled someone who does."

"I swear we knew nothing about that. My captain would never condone slavery."

"Oh, it's so much worse than mere slavery. On their own, children make terrible slaves. The Warlord requires strong, dedicated workers. Children are cheap right now, but they are fragile, soft, and problematic." She went to a stainless-steel cup that was sitting on one of the tables and picked a small object out of it and held it up for him to see.

"A computer chip."

"Yes."

"Is that dried blood?"

"Yes."

He looked down at the cup and saw it was full of them. A mound of chips. He began to get a bad feeling.

"Soft and problematic," she repeated. "But that's nothing a cerebral implant can't fix."

"No way." Warlord was probably a lot worse than the captain had realized, but that was crazy evil. "You're trying to tell me he's programming kids' brains to make them better laborers?"

"Hard-working and obedient." She shook her head sadly.

Jackson frowned. He was very familiar with the tech. Hampson devices worked by recording the neural impulses of people learning an activity, and then taking those prerecorded impulses and delivering them straight into another person's brain. Once those pathways were cut, they made learning those specific skills far more efficient. Combine one of those with implants that stimulated the pleasure centers of your brain and rewarded you for success...Oh yeah, he was very familiar. That was how he had learned to run a mech so well, so quickly.

"I don't believe you. That tech is way too expensive and complicated."

"This isn't the same. This is the new, cheap, bootleg, easily abused version. And he's not teaching them astrophysics or how to run complex machines. He's teaching them to do what their overseers tell them without question, and then fearlessly work themselves to death while the implant floods them with endorphins."

She shuffled him to the end of the row where they looked down at a number of kids wearing breathing masks with shaved and bandaged heads.

"We don't know if these will make it. The wetware he uses is aggressive. We tried the best we could to remove it, at least with our limited tech and expertise, but it is better if you catch it early. It was running riot in their brains."

He'd seen that before. Firsthand.

"You know exactly what kind of slaveware I'm talking about, don't you...Sergeant Jack?" It had been a while since he'd heard that name. "You're practically an expert on slaveware."

He paused. "Yeah, from the slave's end."

"I kept up on the news from home. That's where I'd seen you. Sergeant Jack. One of Gloss' heroes. The man who saved Pilling almost singlehandedly. And here he is in the flesh, selling arms to the biggest slavemaker in the thirty worlds. How ironic."

All the pilots had held the rank of warrant, but Sergeant Jack was what the propaganda guys had started calling him, so the name had stuck. The people had loved his story. A young, handsome orphan kid ends up driving the most badass machine on the planet and kicking the snot out of the evil Collective on their behalf. He'd been on recruiting posters. Kids had spray-painted his name as graffiti on Collective walls, just to piss them off.

"Offworld ex-pats even made an anime about you and your trusty T-Bolt. The Savior of Pilling, putting metal boot to Collective ass on behalf of Mother Gloss."

"Yeah...I heard about it." It was on the net, but he hadn't ever watched it. "Sorry to disappoint you, lady, but there's what was in the news, and then there's what actually happened."

"I like to stay informed about my home world. I heard about how Sergeant Jack was compromised and sent to kill his own people. Sent to slaughter those he'd saved. We all wept when the bastards corrupted Sergeant Jack and turned him against us."

The image rose in his mind. His friends frozen there, immobilized by terror, as he cut them down. And then he'd gone into Pilling and Bryce and Red Valley and killed so many.

He blew out a heavy sigh at the memory of that darkness. "We know now the Collective brought in a top-tier, offworld hacker to write the program for them. It cost them a fortune, but we were that much of a pain, and we were just too damned hard to kill the old-fashioned way. They came in through our net, our antique mech firewalls never had a chance, and then they got in our heads...So yeah, I know about slaveware, more than you can ever imagine."

"But you broke their hold. You escaped."

Jackson said nothing. He'd fought back, but it hadn't done a damn thing. It had been like steel tendrils in his mind. He'd only escaped because of the captain, and because Jane was better at her job than the Collective's hacker had been at his.

"You were one of the ones who made it, Sergeant Jack. And now you're working for a coldhearted son of a whore who employs some nasty variety of the same technology. On children."

Jackson looked at the kids. Part of him felt anger, but another part wondered if this was some sham. Who knew what had actually brought them here? And why was she showing him these kids anyway?

"You said he gets kids cheap, but surely bots would be cheaper."

"He tried bots. But half-a-dozen species go nuts when inorganics are used in the trees. He ended up with a lot of broken bots and wasted CX. I'm sure he could have figured it out eventually—he's cruel, not stupid—but then he decided tree duty was a good way to separate those who were worthy from those that weren't. It was primal, he said. A way to select for the tough future citizens of Big Town."

Primal. Warlord seemed to like that idea a lot. "I see."

"Do you though? Did you even check our claims before you chose his side?"

"What claims? We didn't even know you people existed!" Jackson was starting to get really angry, at himself for getting into this, and at her for the cheap emotional manipulation. "I don't fix the deals. And I don't work for the Warlord."

"No, you just load and unload the weapons and tell yourself you're above it all. What they do with them is none of your business, right?"

"We have standards in the types of clients we take on," he insisted.

"You only serve rapists, slavers, and thieves, is that it?" she asked with disgust. "We've reported volumes to the ISF. All his atrocities are there in the records. Easy pickings for anyone who wants to look. And if you'd looked, you would have found the authorities had confirmed the registration of our land claims."

He snorted. "Who trusts the ISF? You expect me to believe the bureaucratic goon squad who sided with the Marxist death cult that murdered our home planet? Oh, I'm sorry. You weren't there for that part. Their reports are nothing but propaganda. It'll be a nice day on Swindle before I believe anything the ISF says."

But Jackson began to wonder if the captain and Shade had been hoodwinked. Or had they just turned a blind eye? Shade, maybe. The captain wouldn't do that. Just the insinuation made him angry enough to raise his voice.

"I don't know the details of your screwed-up situation. I do know the ISF is corrupt and stick their dirty fingers into pies where they don't belong. I know their so-called reports are full of malicious garbage. And you expect me to ignore that and trust them this time? Oh hell no."

"I'll grant you some of the ISF is corrupt. But some of every organization is corrupt to some degree or another. The plain fact is that you either didn't care because it didn't matter who you were arming, or you did learn the truth, but decided not to care."

"Or the real one, I watched half my planet die, defenseless, because they were denied the ability to protect themselves, so I'm not a real big fan of the ISF declaring who I can and can't sell weapons to. If you're counting on the big benevolent space government to come save you, you're gonna be sorely disappointed."

Her face turned hard. "I expected better of you, Sergeant Jack. You of all people should have known."

"Well, now I do. So either let me go or execute me."

The kids were all staring at him.

"Gag him and take him to the surface," she said.

And Jackson realized he'd just lost that negotiation.

They put a seal strip over his mouth and shuffled him out of the room with the children. They went down a different tunnel to some stairs.

"Up," the bearded man gave him a shove.

Jackson began to hike the stairs, little baby steps up because of his ankle restraints. They were going to kill him. He had nothing left to lose. When his opening came, he needed to be ready. His mind began to churn the possibilities.

His wrists and ankles were tied. If he broke away, he figured he probably had a ninety-nine point nine percent chance of getting shot in the back. If he did somehow elude them and got outside, he figured he had an even higher chance of being killed by one of the hyperaggressive residents. Good luck streaking through the woods in his socks and underwear. That was definitely a proposition with tremendous odds for survival. And without a respirator he'd drown in his own blood within an hour anyway, so he had that going for him too.

Jackson and his captors finished the first flight of stairs and turned for another.

Running was out. Fighting was out. What he needed to be doing was talking, but that was a might difficult with his mouth glued shut.

They finished the next flight of stairs. The teenager opened a bulkhead door and marched Jackson through into a section with warmer air. They closed the door behind them and shuffled him along the hall to another flight of stairs. Jackson baby-stepped his way toward certain doom. When they got to the top, there was a landing, and a final bulkhead door. Buzz Cut opened it and ordered him through. The hallway here was short. At the end were two rooms. As he approached, the lights in them turned on.

One room held a decontamination unit. In the other hung a line of masks and suits.

Okay... that beat the socks-and-underwear plan.

There was an airlock past decon. Which meant that was his path out of this base and into the lovely, lung-eating atmosphere.

Now all he had to do was figure out how to take out several armed partisans, while tied up. Worse, there were more guards posted here. Which made sense for them but sucked for him.

There was a nearby wall display divided into twelve equal-sized squares, each displaying a feed from a different camera. The views included all sorts of angles on the woods. One of the cameras belonged to something that was moving slowly along a branch. Another belonged to something floating in the air. He figured all that was so they didn't inadvertently exit their secret lair and run into a pack of caliban or a Big Town patrol.

"Are we clear?" the old woman asked.

"We're clear," said one of the guards.

Beard Man went to the room with masks and grabbed one for everyone but Jackson. They began putting them on.

They were going to escort him outside—probably just far enough if his remains were found it wouldn't endanger their secret entrance—and then leave him to die.

The man with the bandage, which Jackson hoped was a result of a love slash from Fifi, went over to open the airlock door and began to push in a code. As he did, the woman with the buzz cut gasped.

"Salene!"

All of them turned to see that she was staring at the security feeds. There was movement at the bottom corner. The camera showed a wooded hill with a run of rocks up one section of its slope. Making her way with a branch as a makeshift crutch was a blonde girl. She was dragging one leg and looked to be in her early teens. Thin, and coughing. Holding her hand directly to her mouth because she wore no mask.

"Open the door!" Buzz Cut said. "Open it!"

"Careful, Kelli," the old woman warned. "It could be a trap."

"Salene was just captured on the raid. She must have escaped," said the teenager. "We have to help her."

"Hold," their leader ordered even though her people were obviously terrified. "She can't be a howler. It's too soon. We'll get her, but we have to be safe. Recheck all the feeds and look for rangers tailing her. Wulf, run a scan and see if she's got a tracker on her."

The teenage boy went to the wall and started performing a sweep.

Jackson stood there, temporarily forgotten, as the Originals rushed into action. The girl was clearly one of their own. Buzz Cut, or Kelli probably, was clearly freaking out.

Some creature glided down maybe five paces behind the girl. It landed and then scuttled forward a bit. It was maybe two feet tall. A hideous bat-monkey mix.

"Open the door!" Buzz Cut cried.

Another one of the bat monkeys glided down. And then a third.

"Lord, no," Buzz Cut said, her voice full of alarm.

"No signals!" Wulf shouted.

"Wait!" the old woman shouted, but Bandage Guy didn't heed her. The airlock unsealed with a soft hiss. Buzz Cut pushed him aside and yanked on the door.

"Kelli, don't. Let us see if she's been rigged."

But she ignored the command, her face full of worry, a mother's fear. She ran across the airlock and started working the controls on the other side, in such a rush that she didn't even close the door to decon behind her.

"Stop her," the old woman growled.

"Kelli Kochan! Stand down!" Beard Man demanded and strode in after her. He grabbed her arm and tried to pull her away, but she elbowed him sharply in the chest and knocked him back, then she pushed on the door on the other side of the airlock.

The exterior hatch opened.

A small whoosh of air blew past Jackson and into the airlock, and he realized there was positive air pressure pushing out of the base to keep the caustic air from flowing in. The two men shouted at her, but she slipped out the door.

Jackson turned toward the display.

The girl was visible from a couple of angles now, hobbling as fast as she could. Some of what looked to be rocks were simply the cleverly disguised door, which now stood open. A hole in the slope. He could see Buzz Cut running toward the girl.

Two of the bat monkeys hesitantly scuttled closer to the girl. The third leapt at Buzz Cut, gliding through the air. But Buzz Cut Kelli had drawn her sidearm and shot the creature, eliciting a screech. The creature veered off and flopped to the ground.

The girl saw Buzz Cut, and her face scrunched up like she was going to cry. "Mom!"

"Salene! Stay there. I'm coming."

And then there was an explosion. A huge, deafening bang. A flash of light that overpowered a number of the cameras. One moment the girl was there. The next, dust and debris and a small wave of heat blasted through the airlock doors. Bandage and Beard Man were thrown back.

Jackson took an involuntary step backward and turned to protect his face. When the flash was gone and the camera adjusted again, it showed the slope. Buzz Cut had been flung several meters from where she had been. And where the girl had stood, the ground was scorched in a blast pattern. There were bits and pieces strewn here and there.

The old woman made a small moan of despair. "No." Then she rushed into the airlock and past the men. The display showed her exiting and running down the slope to where her soldier had gone down. Buzz Cut's mask was gone. Her clothes were smoldering. The guards followed her.

Jackson looked over at the kid, Wulf, who was watching him, hand on the pistol in his belt. "Move, and you die."

Jackson lifted up his bound hands to show he wasn't going anywhere.

The kid was distracted though. He was obviously distraught and his eyes kept flicking back toward the display. Jackson saw the others on camera, some trying to stabilize Buzz Cut enough to move her to safety, while the others formed a defensive perimeter. He could probably rush the kid, knock him down, then close the airlock to buy him some time...but to go where? There was the little hospital. Maybe he could make it back there, get something out of one of the drawers and pick the lock at his belt. Or a scalpel might be enough to cut these carbon cords.

And then what? Take Alario or Leon or one of the other kids hostage?

That was no kind of plan, so he waited and watched the displays.

His mind replayed the scene. A thin blonde girl, schlepping her way home. Coughing up dark wetness from burning lungs. If she'd been captured on the raid, she'd been a gift from Warlord. Had to be. Sent back and blown up. Had she even suspected that she'd been wired?

A little flame of anger ignited inside Jackson's guts. What if everything the old woman had been telling him was true? He thought about the riot up in Big Town, the video of the kids in the trees, the injured people he'd seen, the hunt.

Primal, Warlord had said.

And he suddenly knew she was telling the truth.

The hospital and the kids in it weren't any kind of sham. These people weren't terrorists or claim strippers. They were mothers and daughters. Orphans. Fathers. Sons. Husbands and wives. Just trying to settle and use their land.

Something shifted inside him. Something deep. Something

solid. His little flame of anger got hot. Anger at Warlord. But mostly anger at himself.

I should have known.

He looked at the camera feed and watched as the Originals carried their fallen soldier back. His opportunity to escape was dwindling, but Jackson knew he wasn't going to run.

They carried Buzz Cut through the door. Her clothes were shredded, her skin was black, bubbled, and burnt. Some spots had been fried right off, exposing the painful, red flesh underneath. They hustled her past him, yelling for their doctor, heading for the hospital, but Jackson had seen this before. Her burns were beyond third-degree. He suspected she was dead, or soon would be.

"Seal the airlock, Wulf, and watch the prisoner," Beard Man ordered as they rushed past.

"I will, Father."

Jackson watched them go. The hallway fell silent. Some animal hooted in the distance outside. Jackson turned. The airlock was open. He could see a slash of shade and a sunlit stretch of ground beyond. He looked at the room off to the side for decontamination. Looked at the one with suits and masks hanging in tidy rows.

The kid, Wulf, moved over, pulling his pistol from his pants. "Don't you even think about it! Stay right there." He had a German, or maybe Dutch accent, and he made the terrible decision to use the gun's muzzle to push Jackson back. "I'll kill you where you sta—"

Except Jackson wasn't in the mood, so he head-butted Wulf right in the nose.

He wasn't an augmented hand-to-hand combat master like Tui, but nobody who came up in a Gloss refugee camp was a slouch when it came to giving or taking a hit. Wulf went down hard, the pistol bouncing from his hand.

By the time Wulf realized what was going on, Jackson had already bent down, retrieved the gun, and was standing over him.

The kid wiped his bloody nose, realized he was screwed, but glared at Jackson, defiant. "Do it then! Shoot me, coward!"

The kid had some spunk, he'd give him that. Jackson turned back to the airlock, shuffled over to the door controls, and punched the close button.

The doors sealed with a quiet hiss.

Jackson spent a few seconds working the tape off his mouth.

When it finally came free with some skin from his lips, he tossed it to the ground. "I'm not going to kill you." He dropped the pistol's magazine, then racked the slide to eject the round in the chamber, before tossing it back to the surprised teenager. He stepped back to the spot where the boy had told him to stay and waited. "But for the record, I'm no coward. You tell your leader that. You tell her we need to talk."

Because the whole picture had changed. He had no idea what was coming but running sure as hell wasn't part of it.

CHAPTER 22

Sheepishly, Wulf retrieved his gun, reloaded it, and then tried to stop his nosebleed. The door guards came back, heard Wulf's report—which to his credit, was an honest one—and then watched him warily. Jackson leaned against the wall and silently waited for the return of the decisionmakers.

Sometime later the old woman and the man with the beard came back, looking stern. "You're supplying him. You're killing us, Sergeant Jack. You're killing us."

"He disarmed Wulf and could have escaped, ma'am, but he stuck around," the guard informed her.

"That was his mistake, then." She walked over and pushed the code to open the door.

"He struck you, boy?" Beard Man asked angrily.

Wulf nodded. "Sorry. He got the drop on me and took my weapon. He could have killed me."

Jackson said, "I could have killed him, suited up, and walked right out that door. But like I've been saying this whole time, I never wanted to hurt you people."

The woman pulled her pistol from its holster and motioned with it for Jackson to move into the airlock.

"I'll go without a fuss. If you want, I'll even stand still when I'm fifteen meters out so you have an easy shot. But before I do, you need to hear what I have to say."

"Didn't we put tape on his mouth?" Beard Man asked.

"I have information you need," Jackson said. "Because soon, if you aren't prepared, Warlord is going to roll you up like cheap carpet."

"Move." Beard Man pointed his rifle at him.

"It's your heads," Jackson said.

That got him speared in the guts with the rifle's muzzle. It was a painful blow, and Jackson doubled over. Before Beard Man could strike Jackson again, the leader held up her hand to stop him. That hadn't been because of sympathy or mercy. She simply wasn't in the mood to play.

"You're going to be invaded."

"Warlord has tried before."

"What are there, a few thousand of you? But you're broken up into little cells like this one, hiding in places like this, spread across the whole planet?"

She didn't move, didn't blink, gave no indication whether he was close or out in the weeds.

"They're going to come through the mists. They're going to come at night. You won't have a chance."

Beard Man scoffed. "Really? We're going to listen to this?"

The old gal said, "He's tried to invade many times. But there's nothing to invade."

"Standard asymmetric tactics," Jackson said. "I get it. But I saw the exos and mechs Warlord has. Good for security. Good for holding off monsters for a few days and then going home. Not so much for prolonged offensives. Not in terrain as tough as this. They're too hard to supply, too hard to maintain. When he tries to root you out, I bet all you have to do is run, hide, and bide your time."

"Thus far, that is correct. What's he going to do? He can't bomb us without endangering the groves. The air eats his gunships."

"It won't be from the sky. It'll be up close. He'll come at you with something that has the strength of a Glossian brigade."

"He can't support that many troops from Big Town," Wulf's father snapped. "They already have food shortages."

"Not the number, but the equivalent combat power. He's got something new. You can't run from this thing. You can't hide. He'll pick off your cells one by one. And be able to operate down here with impunity, for as long as he feels like, and I doubt very much you've got anything with the firepower to stop him."

The old woman's mood shifted from anger to listening. "What the hell did you sell him?"

"One of the most advanced mechs in history."

The Originals shared a nervous glance. You didn't need to be a pilot, keeping up on the latest designs, to have a grasp about just how dangerous those were. A top-tier mech could sway battles between real armies. A half-ass militia was nothing to them.

"Yeah, whatever you're thinking it's capable of? It's worse. They'll just be shadows until it is too late. They're going to comb these woods, find you, and kill you. They've got armor that will eat anything you've got, and sensors you can't avoid. This won't be an army you can outfight or outwit. Think of a tank crossed with a ninja, that sees all and knows all, that can deploy for months on end. They'll slip into these woods, to wait and watch. Once they've mapped every one of your hidey holes, your people will start to vanish."

"We've taken on mechs before," she said.

"Not like these. These are your meteors hurtling at the planet. They are your extinction-level event."

"He's lying," Beard Man said, but Jackson could hear the doubt in his voice.

"No, I'm not. I'm the one that procured and delivered the system. I know what I'm talking about." He looked at the woman. "I'm Sergeant Jack, remember?"

She knew his history. Knew his expertise. Knew what he'd been able to do.

She asked, "Fifth gen?"

He nodded. "Like nothing you've ever seen before. Light-years beyond the one I used against the Collective."

"Before, you kept saying *they*, as in multiples..."

"He's got two. A Citadel we delivered him, and a Spider supplied by I don't know who else. Either one would be enough to totally gut your resistance."

She considered that for a long time. "So now what? You've absolved yourself, so I can walk you out, shoot you in the back, you can die guilt-free?"

"You could...Or you could let me help you."

"No way. He's a plant." Wulf's father stared cold intent down the barrel of his rifle, just one trigger pull away from blowing Jackson's head off.

The old woman stood there, thoughtful. This was clearly a leader who wasn't easily swayed. If she'd stayed on Gloss instead of trying to colonize Swindle, she probably would have wound up as one of their officers.

After a minute of consideration, she pushed the button to shut down the airlock. The mechanism engaged, and the door swung shut with a quiet sigh...that probably matched the sigh of relief Jackson tried to hide.

"I wasn't lying when I said my captain has a code, or at least I do. I swear I didn't know what all was going on here. What I just saw..." He nodded toward the displays. "Booby-trapping a kid? That's evil. I regret that we supplied him, but now that I know, I can't let him use what I helped get him do more stuff like that. Give me a chance to undo what I've done."

"Let me kill him," Beard Man said.

"Hold on, Ragnar." She folded her arms. "Okay, I'm listening."

"I took that mech from someone else. I can take it from him."

The woman looked at Beard Man, who was apparently named Ragnar. He curled his upper lip in disgust at the situation, then looked back at Jackson. "It's a double-cross. We should terminate him and his entire crew."

"I need to think about this. We're going to verify your mech story. If it pans out, you just might live one more day."

"Sufficient unto the day is the evil thereof," Jackson said, which was one of the captain's favorite quotes.

"Take him back," the woman said.

And Ragnar obliged.

They returned his pants, shirt, and shoes. They fed him. Not real food, but green military bars. They gave him water, put him in a cell, and shackled him up again. They did not reunite him with Fifi.

The hours passed. Guards came and went in shifts. The current shift ended, and a new guard showed up, the boy he'd head-butted and disarmed.

"Your name's Wulf, right?"

"It is."

"German?" Jackson asked.

"Not from Earth," the boy said, meaning he was indeed German, but from some colony.

Jackson nodded. "Sorry about your nose."

"I should have shot you."

"I can understand that sentiment," Jackson said. "I see you've been trained, but even a good soldier can get suckered. The man with the beard, that's your dad, right? You two kind of look alike."

But Wulf didn't respond. Jackson tried to make idle conversation, but the boy wouldn't go for it, and so Jackson sat back and thought about his situation. It was not a pretty one. Assuming he got out of here alive, maybe there was a way he could get the captain to undo the sale of the Citadel, so the chances of him owning his own trading ship had dramatically shrunk. However, because there was nothing he could do about it, Jackson took a nap, dreamed of nothing, and woke sometime later.

A female guard had replaced Wulf at the door. She was about as talkative as Wulf. So he sat there, thinking about what he'd need to do to make this right.

Ragnar and the old lady arrived sometime later. By this point he was pretty sure she was either the main boss of all the Originals—not just this cell—or was relatively high up in whatever passed for their organization, and Wulf's father was her right hand.

She was wearing the same combat pants and black undershirt. The same butt-ugly Brady handgun at her hip. Only now she looked weary, worn down, and a little sad.

He said, "The woman with the buzz cut. Kelli. She didn't make it, did she."

"Salene had been a slave, working in the groves. We freed her. Kelli freed her. And took her in, raised her as her own. Because her own daughter had already been gunned down."

The woman let out a sigh of weariness. Of too many Kellis. Too many Salenes.

"I'm sorry," Jackson said.

A beat passed, and then she changed the subject and said, "Our source says Big Town does have a Citadel, and Warlord is currently testing it out. Once he's confident everything works right, he'll bring it down to the surface."

Jackson nodded. Warlord wasn't wasting any time. "And then you'll all die. I can stop him. I've got a plan."

"Plans have already been made. And you have a task. You will perform that task. If you fail to perform it, you will forfeit your life. And the lives of your crew. If you succeed, then we can negotiate what happens from there."

He was willing to help them because it was the right thing to do, but he didn't like the threats. "You won't get that unit without me. That's just the facts. You might know Big Town, but I know the Citadel. And so we're going to have to agree on a plan together."

She gave him a sad little laugh. "When you've proven you can be trusted, we'll take the next step."

"And how am I going to do that?"

"First, deliver us the plans for that mech."

Now it was Jackson's turn to laugh. "You can't be that naïve. A fifth-gen mech isn't something you can just fab yourself with 3D printers. They're incredibly complex systems. Building one would be impossible here. That's why places like Big Town have to hire people like us."

"Maybe," she said. "But if we're going to destroy his capability, then we need to be able to recognize the information on his networks when we see it."

"Fine. I can get you the plans. We scanned all the hardware when it was on the ship, and our Specter made copies of all the software. But you won't need any of that if you help me sabotage that mech."

"You don't tell us what to do," Ragnar snapped.

"How many mechs have you stolen? How many heists have you pulled off?"

Ragnar said nothing.

"That's what I thought," Jackson said. "I'm the one going in. Let me go. Let me get back to Big Town. I'll use my expertise to get close, and when I've considered all the options, I'll tell you the resources I need, and you're going to give them to me. This isn't going to work any other way."

"Sergeant Jack," the old woman said. "This is the bed you made, so you're just going to have to sleep in it. I'm not going to risk my resources. You won't see any of them. We can work through dead drops."

He didn't like running blind, but this was a step forward. They'd moved past talking about killing him, and that fact lifted Jackson's spirits a bit. Now they just had to hammer out details. "We don't have the time for dead drops. I'm going to need to coordinate with someone up there live."

"You deliver the data as a show of good faith, and then we can move to that step."

"Fine. But you delay more than a day or two, and your window is going to shut. The first fifth gen he's got is supercomplicated to run, which is probably why he hasn't used it yet. The one I brought him is so natural it practically drives itself. It won't take him long to get comfortable with it. He doesn't strike me as lacking confidence."

The woman nodded. "Very well. We can have you found by the rangers today."

Jackson said, "I'd like the little bot you took from me."

"The killer?"

"We should keep that," Ragnar said. "We haven't yet cracked it."

The woman said, "He's right. We should keep it. Make it yield up its secrets."

"Fifi isn't going to yield up her secrets, I guarantee that." He was willing to bet they didn't have anyone here who could hold a candle to Jane. "More importantly, I'll need her."

The old woman looked at Ragnar. He shrugged in acquiescence.

"Fifi," the old woman said. "That's an odd name. What does it stand for?"

"No idea."

"Very well. We shall give the bot back to you."

"Thanks."

"Don't thank me yet. I want to believe you've truly seen the error of your ways. Perhaps it's because we're from the same place, and you were once a hero to my people, and so I find myself hoping you really are a decent man who was simply deceived. Except hope is not a strategy, Sergeant Jack. So now I'll explain what will happen to you if you fail to perform your task or betray us."

A tall man appeared at the doorway. He had dark hair, dark skin, and a red dot of paint on his forehead. Jackson suspected the red dot meant he'd said his prayers today. He carried a small apparatus in his hand, one with a hypodermic needle.

The old woman said, "Pull up your shirt."

"No." Jackson shook his head. "What is that?"

"This is your parting gift from Swindle."

"You're going to infect me with some plague, hoping I infect Big Town?" He tried to feign concern. *Please don't throw me into that briar patch.*

"No, I doubt a simple virus or bacteria would work. The scans we did while you were unconscious indicated you have some high-end cleaners in your blood."

Jackson's heart sank. The *Tar Heel* visited so many worlds and stations that the captain sprang for the best preventative treatments. Even with that, he was still rigorous about decon procedures, and their ship had a pretty decent med bay.

"We are going to inject a nano bomb into your back. It will be on a biological timer. When time runs out, the engineered agent will aggressively react with your cerebrospinal fluid."

"That sounds bad."

"It will literally melt your spinal column."

Jackson raised his eyebrows. "You couldn't just go with the plague?"

"I thought it prudent to have an insurance policy against a man who sells weapons to our enemy. Once injected, you will have exactly forty-six hours and fourteen minutes to complete your task."

"I can't work with a ticking time bomb in my back."

"It's perfectly stable . . . until it's not. We want you to complete your mission, Sergeant Jack."

"What's to prevent me from having a med scan and zapping this thing?"

"You don't want to do that. A scan will trigger an immediate activation, as will any physical tampering. By the time the doctor figures out what it is and how it works, you will have already been paralyzed, and lost control of your lungs and heart. Or, you can demonstrate the sincerity of your repentance, and I will tell you how to safely deactivate and remove the device."

"And I'm just supposed to trust you," he said.

"Yes. Because your only other option is Ragnar here shoots you in both kneecaps, we throw you outside, and we take bets on what gets you first. The air or the wildlife."

Jackson glared at her, but he didn't see much choice. She might think her little bio bomb couldn't be stopped, but he had faith Jane was smarter than anyone on this crapsack planet.

"Start the clock," he said and turned his back toward them.

The needle man proceeded forward. They pulled his shirt up. Hands touched his back. A moment later there was a sting right up between his shoulder blades. He flinched.

"Hold still," the needle man said.

Jackson grimaced, and then it was over. Someone wiped his back with something wet that carried the faint odor of an antiseptic.

"Glad you're trying to prevent infections. That just gives me all sorts of peace of mind." Jackson dropped his shirt and turned around.

"How do you feel?" she asked.

"Capital. Nothing like starting your day with a dose of spine melt."

She said, "Fifty-four hours and three minutes. You'll want to keep that in mind."

Jackson started a timer in his eye display. Swindle days were two hours longer than standard. Which meant his bomb would go off on Friday. That was Leo if you were using the names of the days popular in Big Town. Leo at seventeen-oh-three hours. In most sane places people would be sitting down for a drink and kicking off their weekend.

"That's not a lot of time."

"Time enough to prove you are a man of your word." She held up her hand display. The holo that appeared was an aerial shot of the woods.

"The skirmish occurred here," she said and pointed at the road. She zoomed in to show the vehicles and the bodies, which were now mostly eaten and scattered. However, there was a flock of birdlike creatures hopping around and working on the bones.

"You will be dropped three klicks south of that location. Rangers have moved in to salvage what they could. This is the story you will tell. You were left behind, you woke, you saw the caliban, saw a fallen soldier from which you stole a waterjohn, and escaped to the woods. You got lost. You were stung by wollards. You wandered for three days. There's a creek here, do you see it? You crossed it by scampering along a tree trunk that had fallen and made a sort of bridge. They will not believe you if you tell them you waded or swam across. That's your story."

Jackson nodded, then realized his orange wrist band was gone.

"What about my wristband? Warlord's tracking device."

"Here," she said and fetched it out of her pocket. "It's broken. But you don't know that. You expected them to come find you."

Jackson held his wrist out, and she snapped it back on.

"Once you get back to the orbital, we will contact you."

"That's it?"

"For now," she said.

"Okay. I need to know your name."

She cocked an eyebrow. "For this operation my codename is Big Fox."

Jackson sighed. So much for seeing if the captain could find any leverage on her.

"Please sit down." She motioned toward the bed. She waved at Needle Man to come forward. He had a tiny cup of dark liquid. "Drink this. We can't have you seeing where we actually are."

Jackson drank it. It was bitter and tasted like licorice. And it wasn't long before he began to feel warm and relaxed. He lay back.

"Good luck, Sergeant Jack."

He was on a planet that wanted to kill him and had just gotten in bed with a bunch of terrorists who'd stuck a nano bomb in his spine, to go up against a warlord with his own army. What could possibly go wrong?

"Piece of cake." And then his eyelids slid comfortably shut.

CHAPTER 23

Jackson came to lying on his back under the enormous leaves of a bush. He was back in his cracked mask, Raj, and beat-up patrol suit, body aching like he'd been stung by wasps in half-a-dozen places. Then he noticed something on the underside of the large leaf that was only centimeters from his face. It took a moment for the picture to resolve in his blurry mind. Green with white dots, it was some kind of weird Swindle spiderlike creature about the size of his hand. With fangs. Big fangs.

"Ah!"

A jolt of adrenaline surged through him, as he scuttled out from under the bush and stepped back. He looked around and found himself alone. Unless, of course there were more of those wollards somewhere up above, and more spider things hiding beneath the leaves, and who knew what else.

He immediately spotted his Wakal under the bush where he had been dumped. Using a stick, he dragged out the Wakal. They'd also left him a water purifier, but when he tried to snag it, the damn spider thing attacked the stick. Jackson whacked at it a couple of times, then swatted it back into the undergrowth. He expected it to come barreling out at him, but the thing ran off into the brush.

I really hate this planet.

He figured this must be the spot where Big Fox had said they'd drop him, south of where he'd be found, but which way was north? The GPS in his mask was still busted and of no help, so he looked up past the tops of the trees to find the sun in the partly cloudy sky, then stuck the stick it in the ground. He picked out a tip of shadow made by a plant and waited.

Jackson examined his Wakal. It had only five of the long steel darts left in the magazine. He cleared it, function-tested it—good—then reloaded. Fifi was back in his pocket, but she was inert. He didn't know if she was broken, deactivated, or maybe her battery was just dead. Then he turned to the waterjohn, which was a little device that circulated air and extracted water from it. It also had a funnel into which you could pour filthy water, to purify it. This one had a symbol on the side that Jackson had seen all over Big Town. Upon feeling the weight of it, he knew there had to be a least a liter of water there. There was a connector on the bag that attached to a receptor at the base of his mask. So he attached it, put his dry, cracked lips on the spout in his mask and sucked on it until the water rose to him. It was wonderful.

Satisfied, he slung the bag, and brought up the timer in his eye. 49:15 left. Then it was spine-melting time. But he'd have to worry about that later. Right now, he needed to focus on surviving Planet Nightmare. The shadows of both the stick and the plant had moved. And with that movement, he now knew his directions. He positioned himself so the sun was on his left shoulder, and then began his hike through the woods of doom.

His wollard stings had been fine during his brief captivity, but now they were burning again. Whatever Big Fox had given him with had worn off, or they'd neutralized the treatment so the ranger medics wouldn't know he'd been treated. Either way, he wasn't happy to have those reminders back. The itching was infuriating.

Of course, he couldn't just walk in a straight line. Because Swindle sucks and hates you. There were too many thickets. There were webs to skirt. And two snakelike creatures that were the exact coloration of the dirt and leaves, and probably poisonous. Then a ledge from which he had to find a way down.

Worse, a mist began to filter down through the giant trees, obscuring the sun. He could still tell its general direction, but the dimness made it a lot easier to trip, and a lot harder to sense predators.

It took a long time to make his way back to the battle site. He very specifically didn't check his timer. He needed to focus on getting back to civilization to make things right. And in the process probably piss off the captain and Shade and the crew to the point they'd probably want to just shoot him themselves. Of course, if they didn't, he still had the packet of spine-melting Swindle juice in his back to deal with.

Then he saw a rise that looked sort of familiar. It was hard to tell because the plants had already grown and moved so much, but Jackson was pretty sure he'd run up this one in an exo toward the sound of gunfire. The salvagers should be working right on the other side.

He rehearsed his cover story one more time as he walked uphill. He hadn't gone ten steps when he heard a low rumble off to his left.

Jackson froze.

It rumbled again.

Shanks. That was the exact same noise he'd heard at the skirmish. *Caliban.*

He stood stock-still for a minute or so, then took another step. A quiet and careful step. Then waited again.

The rumbles continued, and from the directions of the sounds there were at least two of them. Something large moved through the brush twenty meters behind him, then stopped, probably to smell the ground.

Jackson knew if he stayed here, he was toast, so he kept moving, slowly, proceeding with extreme care, pausing behind the trunks of trees to listen. He moved at a diagonal away from the sounds. After what seemed an eternity, he reached the crest.

Below him was the remains of the ruined dropship. Vines and moss had already covered big chunks of it. All the exposed bits of metal had turned orange with rust. There was a new vehicle, some kind of hovering sled, and equipment had been piled on it. Then he noticed movement around the wreck. From the subtle twisting of light, it was the active camo effect of a combat exo.

The last thing Jackson needed was to walk out in the open and have one of the monsters spot him. He'd seen how those things moved. But not seeing much choice, he looked around, made sure the coast was clear, then stepped out into the misty sunshine to begin walking down the hill.

Immediately, somebody shot at him.

There was a *crack.* A bullet struck a rock next to his boot and zinged away.

"Friendly!" Jackson shouted.

Then the man fired again. That one zipped right past his head.

Jackson ran toward a large clump of stones as more shots rang out. He dove behind them and hugged the ground. A bullet smacked into the rocks. Then another.

"I'm from the *Tar Heel!*" Jackson shouted.

Another shot.

"I'm the Warlord's guest. You idiots!"

And then he noticed his mask was now picking up a weak signal. He was so close that even his damaged antenna connected.

"Mayday. Can anyone hear me? Mayday."

A moment later a female voice came on the line. *"State your position."*

"My GPS is shot, but I'm on the hill overlooking your downed transport. I was part of the hunting party three days ago."

"Shenko?"

"Rook. Jackson Rook. I was hunting with Warlord."

"Rook? We thought you were dead."

"I'm alive, except your yahoos are shooting at me."

"One moment, please."

And then he heard the swish of something large moving through the brush and trees toward him. Heard the rumble. Which was when he remembered Warlord talking about how the wildlife was attracted to the sound of gunfire.

Everloving shanks.

"You may proceed, Mister Rook."

He bolted from behind the rocks and sprinted for the sled.

Behind him, branches cracked. Something roared. That wasn't a caliban. For all he knew, it was worse! Jackson poured on the speed as something mottled broke from the tree line and came after him. It was the size of a horse. With a totally different shape and colors than the caliban he'd seen. This thing had big white whorls on its sides and something like a crown of spikes on its head.

But at least it was smaller than the caliban and that other freaking mountain of a creature he'd seen before. Suddenly three more of these new things broke out of the brush and joined the first. A nice little hunting pack.

"Bogies! On the road behind!" Jackson shouted.

"We got 'em, Mr. Rook," said a calm male voice. *"You just keep running toward us."*

But there were no shots fired. No machine guns unloaded on the beasts.

One of the creatures trilled.

Jackson glanced back. They ran like quadrupeds, and had big handlike appendages, with massive curving claws on each finger.

"Shoot them!" Jackson cried.

"*Keep running,*" the man said. "*Keep running. Don't stop.*"

Jackson ran, but he could see the lead beast gaining on him. And he knew there was no way he was going to make it.

"*Just a little farther,*" the man said nonchalantly. But Jackson didn't have any more room. The beast was going to close with him in moments.

The thing closed the distance. Opened its mouth. It had several long tongues. Each one ended in a spike.

There was a long burst of gunfire. The muzzle flashes reflected on the active camo exos.

The animal roared again, stumbled. Stumbled again. Fell.

A second creature jumped over it and came at him. Jackson dodged to the side. Then the whump of a pneumatic bolt sped past Jackson, inches from his head. Behind him, the creature suddenly nosedived and slid past Jackson on the road, speared through the skull.

"Got 'em." An exo-suited ranger flickered into existence just ahead of him. "Come on. We've got to split now."

Breathing hard, Jackson looked back and confirmed the remaining creatures had hightailed it for the woods. "They're gone."

"Pinkers are nothing. Caliban will have heard the noise though."

Another, taller ranger appeared as he shut off his camo. "That was some good running. They nearly had you."

"Why didn't you shoot them sooner?" Jackson demanded, trying to catch his breath.

"Those little pinkers are smart. You gotta lure those 'uns out if you're going to get a shot."

Jackson just glared at him. "With your crappy shooting I thought you would have wanted to start earlier."

"Crappy shooting?" the ranger asked.

"You seemed to be having a hard time hitting me at three hundred."

The ranger's face was covered but it was obvious he was grinning. "I didn't want to kill you. I thought you were an Original.

I wanted to pin you down to give the pinkers something to toy with."

Jackson just blinked in disbelief.

"Anyways, we don't want to stay here. Ain't nothing worse than a curious caliban. Best climb on the sled, Mr. Rook."

In the command room at the Swindle mountain base, Sam Fain watched the rangers' helmet feeds of Jackson Rook being rescued. He replayed the scene several times. Then he tracked back through the sentinel feeds.

Fain had personally overseen the deployment of a network of sentinels in the area.

Recording bots didn't survive long in the wilderness here. If they were stationary, the plants would grow over them. Mobile bots avoided the hypergrowth flora, but they couldn't avoid the atmosphere that corroded their seals. And if the bots escaped both of those things, then there were those that hunted them. The rebels, of course, but that particular area of the woods had been hit by a troop of kulags—smaller-sized animals who traveled along tree branches—that had come through a few weeks ago. Kulags seemed to love attacking his sentinels.

So, many of the last batch of sentinels were gone, but there were still a good number there, silently watching. He checked the logs of those that had first picked Rook up. Supposedly his transmitter had been damaged, so he hadn't been marked as a friendly. However, they'd only picked him up when he was about two klicks out. They'd failed to catch him sooner because Rook had arrived from a blind sector. The one that had just been scoured by kulags.

Very convenient.

Rook had been one of those at the riot. In fact, all three of the *Tar Heel* crew who had been at the riot had gone down to the surface. But Rook had been the one that James Overturf had sidled up to off camera. And then there'd been an unexpected strike just as Warlord was returning from his hunt. Rook had gone missing, yet somehow someone with no familiarity with the planet's multitude of hazards had survived, only to reappear in a blind sector. And all that was supposed to be coincidence?

Fain thought not. He turned to one of the men in the command center. "Get a patrol ready. Full gear. Gate seventeen. We have something we need to investigate."

CHAPTER 24

Jackson was taken back to the mountain base, deconned, searched, and sent to the medics. He cringed when they gave him a cursory med scan, knowing they were going to find or accidentally set off the nano implant, but they didn't act like they found anything. Surely, a proper scan of his spine would have set the thing off. Or was the spine-melt story all a big lie?

He immediately discarded that idea. Big Fox did not seem like the type to take chances on her security with a bluff.

When the medics finished, Jackson asked where the rest of his mates were. The rangers told him that Tui and the others had been sent back to Big Town. They'd wanted to search for him, but Warlord—who had been certain that Jackson was dead—hadn't wanted any more of his guests to perish needlessly. Jackson asked to make a call up to the *Tar Heel*. The rangers were polite enough, but they also wouldn't let him call until their superior signed off.

Said superior came down to the medic bay. It was the head security guy from Warlord's palace. What was his name?

"I didn't expect to see you again, Mr. Rook."

"Sam Fain, right?" Jackson stood as Warlord's righthand man entered the med bay.

Fain looked like a tough guy, but still fairly normal. Only Tui had warned them, this guy was at least as combat modded out as he was, if not more.

"Leave us," Fain said to the medics.

They all seemed very happy to do as they were told. On the way out, the last one suddenly squished himself against the wall in a fearful manner. As if to avoid something coming down the hall. That something appeared in the doorway a moment later. It was some kind of dog analog Swindle nightmare. Maybe four feet tall at the shoulder, thin, almost skeletal. It had two eyes on each side of its head and a long muzzle full of teeth. There were also what looked like feelers all along its mouth.

The hair on the back of Jackson's neck rose as the thing trotted into the room.

Fain waited for the frightened medic to scurry away, then turned back to Jackson. "I hear you had a little campout."

"Communing with nature. I figured after almost being eaten alive by kinsella and caliban, the perfect thing would be a relaxing stroll through the woods..." But Jackson just couldn't take his eyes off the death dog. "What the hell is that thing supposed to be?"

Fain looked over at his animal companion. "Oh, that's just my grendel. Think of him like a loyal hunting dog. Pay him no mind."

Easier said than done. The terrifying beast looked at Jackson, curious...and possibly hungry.

"So what's his name? Fido?"

"He's intelligent. You don't want to offend him."

"Right," Jackson said.

Fain picked up the medic's pad and scanned the findings. "Three days with only a Wakal and a waterjohn. I'm impressed."

Fain was good, but Jackson knew this was yet another interrogation. "I'm an impressive guy," Jackson said. "You wouldn't by any chance have more toxin pads? I climbed a tree to get my bearings and was attacked by a mob of little black devils. Their bites have just about driven me nuts."

"Wollards?" he asked.

"What?" Jackson said, feigning ignorance of the word.

"About this big." Fain spread his thumb and trigger finger wide. "Nasty fangs."

"That sounds about right."

"Yep, wollards. They're mean, but they're actually digestible if you remove their poison gland, then boil the hell out of them, then dry them in the sun, then boil them again. Minimally nutritious, but they still taste like rancid garbage though. Chicken of the trees, you might say."

"I'll keep that in mind for next time. So—any extra pads?"

"The medics didn't give you some?"

"They did, but the bites are still itching like crazy."

Fain shook his head in amazement and walked over to a cabinet. "What's crazy is you survived so long, not even knowing the basics like wollards, or being familiar with this place at all...I'm sorry my men shot at you."

"Well, it's not like I had an appointment for tea," Jackson said.

Fain opened the cabinet and pulled out a wrapped package. "You can't live on Swindle without toxin pads." He tossed them to Jackson. "You don't want those bites to fester, believe me."

Jackson caught the package of pads, and the sudden movement made the grendel make a low, clicking noise, that was probably its version of a growl. Jackson *slowly* unwrapped it, peeled the back, and stuck another pad on his chest.

"I don't believe your boss gave you much of an introduction," Jackson said.

"I'm the chief of security for all his operations. Worked for the Russian Syndicate for a while before Warlord made me an offer to move to beautiful Big Town. Now I make sure everything here goes according to plan. No biggie."

The Syndicate was known for its ruthless, no-nonsense methods. The only reason Fain would tell him that was to make a point. The death dog walked close to Jackson and sniffed.

This thing was obviously dangerous as hell, but Jackson tried not to show any fear. "So the rumors are true. Swindle does have werewolves." He noticed the creature had a big collar on it with some metal and thin electronics attached. Controls maybe. Or something else.

Fain grinned. "I'm beginning to like you, Rook. Grendel likes you too."

"Oh, good," Jackson said. "At last something here isn't trying to eat me."

"I didn't say that."

The hell hound finished sniffing and looked up at Fain. And Jackson swore some communication passed between them. Then the creature sniffed the spot where he had been sitting on the examination table.

"You must be exhausted," Fain said. "Please, sit. Are you hungry?"

"Starving, but one of the rangers gave me a ration bar already."

"Good, good. You don't want to eat too much all of a sudden after a long fast. Let's have a look at those bites."

The bites were red with squiggly black lines running out from the center. A few were as big around as a golf ball, with the black lines extending inches beyond.

"Hoo. Another twelve hours out there, and I think you would have been toast. We've come up with a salve for those, should make life bearable." Fain got a blue jar out of a different cupboard. "How about you tell me exactly what happened while I help you with those?"

Fain was acting kind, but somehow that made him even more threatening. So Jackson told his fake tale, and Fain asked all sorts of questions as he went along, shaking his head in amazement like he believed every word. Except Jackson didn't trust any of it.

"Did you see anyone out there?"

Jackson had thought about this question, and he'd figured half-truths were better than outright lies. "I thought I did once on the second day. But it was far away and obscured by mist, and I couldn't tell if it was a man or some Swindle blessing looking for food, so I kept quiet. I never saw it again."

Fain nodded. "You're very lucky. Our sentinels only picked you up the last klick or so."

"And yet your guards still shot at me."

"Of course. What would you think when the suit of someone reported killed in a skirmish shows up on the network?"

Jackson saw his point. "On this peaceful planet? I'd figure the enemy had stolen it."

"You can't hold it against them."

"Nope," Jackson said. "I guess I should be grateful. They wanted to detain me for the pinkers to play with instead of shooting me outright."

"Tell me again what happened today. Retrace your steps for me from the moment you came out on the road. It's concerning that we only picked you up so late. We're going to need to improve our security."

He said it innocently enough, but Jackson's friendly little alert system went off in his mind. One of the best ways to spot a lie was to have the suspect tell you the story forward with as much detail as possible. And then have them repeat it backward.

It's hard to remember all the details of a long lie. Hard to keep everything in the right sequence.

But Jackson didn't hesitate. He began at the end and told the story backward. Perks of being a professional criminal. Fain listened and tended the wollard bites, nodding and asking innocent-seeming questions.

When Jackson got to the part about crossing the stream over a downed tree, Fain said, "Tell me about this tree."

"I don't know, I was trying to get across it."

"Uh-huh..." Fain pulled up an aerial picture of the area on the wall display. "Where was the tree?"

"I have no idea. I was lost."

"Here's a fallen tree." A yellow circle appeared around one spot on the map. "Is that it?"

Jackson shrugged. "No idea."

Fain said, "And you just scampered across?"

"Yeah."

"Usually such trees are infested."

Jackson shrugged again.

Fain motioned at the area Jackson was supposed to have passed through. "It's a remarkable feat, getting through that. Did you know that waterjohn wasn't assigned to anyone at the skirmish?"

"Well, assigned or not, it was there."

"Can you remember who you pulled it off of?"

"I was just trying to put some distance between me and the caliban. I didn't study the body."

"Male or female?"

"I don't remember."

"Do you remember the exo?"

"I can't remember if the body had one."

"Think back."

"I can't remember."

"We have traitors in our midst. You can't be too careful. Details like this can sometimes crack open an investigation."

Jackson was sure they could. "Sorry. Wish I knew. I'd just gotten clobbered."

Fain gave him a fake laugh. "Yeah, it isn't often someone gets to see one of the big ones that close up and live to tell the tale. How are those pads working?"

"Great," Jackson said. "I can already feel the relief."

"Your orange wristband looks busted. Why don't you give me that one, and I'll get you a replacement?"

Jackson held his wrist up. "Sure."

Fain removed it. He went to the storage area and came out with a new one. This one was black. "That one should get you the same Big Town access you had before."

Same access, Jackson thought, but probably far more intense surveillance.

"So when is the next bus out of here?" Jackson asked. "I'd like to get back up in orbit before my ship leaves. I hope they're still in port. Can I at least let my friends know I'm still alive?"

Because if his people knew he was alive, it would become a lot more complicated for Fain to simply feed Jackson to his pooch. But after only a moment's hesitation, Fain spoke aloud to be patched through to the orbital port. "Connect us to the *Tar Heel.*"

They waited a moment, and then a familiar voice said, "*This is Captain Nicholas Holloway. How can I help you, Swindle base?*"

Fain motioned at Jackson to speak.

"So were you fixing on ditching me?"

"*Wha—? Jackson?*"

"You tell Tui and Katze I'm disappointed they didn't come rescue me."

"*You're alive? He's alive!*"

He must have been with others because a few excited exclamations came across the line. Then he heard Shade in the background. "*Did I tell you? Always the drama with that one.*"

"*Where the hell have you been, son?*" the captain asked.

"Playing poker with some caliban."

"*Knowing you they probably cleaned you out. Where are you now?*"

"At one of their ground bases, with Fain." Might as well add that in case Fain changed his mind and murdered him so at least they'd know who was responsible. "I'll catch the next bus back. You'd better stick around."

"*Well, that all depends on whether you got us any souvenirs on your vacation.*"

Jackson cringed inside. That statement could be taken many ways, especially if someone was suspicious you were in cahoots with the enemy. But Jackson just smiled.

"Sadly, as much as I wanted to give this planet five stars, the gift shop was sorely lacking. But I got lots and lots of toxin pads. You'll love 'em."

"We'll get him back to you in one piece, Captain, you have my word. Fain out." And then he killed the feed. "Alright, Mr. Rook. That's about all we can do here. Get dressed and I'll arrange your transport back to Big Town."

Jackson breathed a sigh of relief when the security chief and his pet left the med bay.

Thirty minutes later, Fain and his demon pooch came back to escort Jackson to the big elevator to take him up to a waiting dropship. Only this time, Fain was fully kitted up, wearing a combat exo.

"You guys going out on patrol?"

"More of an investigation."

Then they rode to the top in silence.

To the west fierce clouds were gathering. A huge front of purple and dark gray that flashed every so often with lightning.

"Looks like a storm is coming."

"There's always a storm brewing on Swindle, Mr. Rook," Fain said. "Enjoy your trip."

At the edges of the site of the skirmish, the grendel snuffled along the ground following Rook's scent trail. Fain followed his grendel. Around them, Fain's squad of soldiers and flying bots made sure the area was as secure as you could make it down on the surface.

They were scanning for spoor. Any sign that Rook had not been alone.

The wind picked up. Fain looked at his weather map and saw they had ten minutes before the storm arrived. He cursed. He'd thought they'd have more time, but Swindle liked to surprise you.

Fain sent a shock of electricity into the beast via the transmitter in its collar, urging it to go faster. The grendel shuddered and picked up its pace. A sudden gust rushed through the tops of the trees. Thunder rumbled in the distance. The air temperature dropped.

"Faster." He sent more painful shocks. "We're going to lose it in the rain."

The grendel hissed and accelerated into a lope so fast that

Fain had to use the exo's full power to keep up. The flying bots kept pace, but they were having to fight to keep their relative position in the increasing wind.

Suddenly the grendel stopped, turned back, then began snuffling around.

Fain brought himself to a halt, breathing hard from the run. "What is it?" he asked, looking down at the ground.

The grendel continued sniffing, then stopped and click growled.

Fain walked over and looked down. He wouldn't have seen it in any other light. But there it was. Half a print. He squatted, looked at the pattern. Fain recognized it. It came from a certain type of exo that Kalteri supplied the Originals with.

A few soft drops of rain fell on Fain's visor as he rose and ordered his men to search for sign along the trail. They found the place under a bush where it was clear a man had lain. That matched Rook's story. They found Rook's prints leading away from that place but couldn't find any of his tracks leading to it, not surprising considering how fast the plants grew here.

The rain began to patter on the leaves. He urged his grendel forward, and it followed the scent trail. They found another partial print that belonged to the exo. But by now the rain was falling in earnest. The wind was swaying the tops of the trees.

The prints of an Original up to a point. And from there Rook's footprints took over. It really could only mean one thing.

He called Warlord.

"What did you find?"

"Pretty much what I expected."

"You think he's working for them?"

"It's probable," Fain said. "Want me to confirm first, or kill him now to be safe?"

Warlord thought it over for a moment. "We'll watch him, for now."

CHAPTER 25

Back on Big Town, Jackson stood in front of the scanner and braced for a sharp pain in his back and then a system shutdown as the Swindle love juice melted the nerves controlling his heart, lungs, and brain, but nothing happened. Instead, the technician did a brain read, checked the reactions of his pupils, and asked if Jackson had felt a fever recently.

"No," Jackson said.

"It looks like you've had some mods upstairs," the tech said, motioning at Jackson's head.

"A comm with some hardware."

The tech nodded. "Looks old. Definitely not new. Give you any problems?"

"No," Jackson lied.

The tech nodded again like some bobble-head toy. "Well. Everything looks good."

Since Jackson was still beat up, fatigued, dehydrated, possibly concussed, and covered in wollard bites, that meant this hadn't been a normal decon at all. They were checking to see if the Originals had planted a virus or wetware on him and turned him into a tool like Warlord used when he'd hung a bomb on that little girl. And Jackson supposed they had turned him into a tool. But they wouldn't find the virus for that. And it appeared they weren't going to find the nano implant either.

"We done?"

"We're done."

And then he had another thought. Maybe the nano bomb in his back wasn't really a bio bomb at all, but a different way to load slave controls into him? Was that why it was in his spine? Maybe they would crawl up his central nervous system and hook right into his implant? Surely, if the Warlord's team could grow such controls, they could take them out. Should he tell them and risk it, hoping they could fix it? He shook his head. This place was such a cluster. Better to wait for Jane.

"What?" the tech asked.

"Nothing, just happy that I get to go back to my ship."

"Down that hallway," he pointed. "At the second intersection, you'll see the sign for the docking bays. Just follow it from there."

Jackson checked his timer. 43:33. The hours were slipping by. He dressed, then exited the examination area.

Tui and Katze must have been notified he'd landed, because they were waiting for him. Tui gave him a big crushing hug. "Glad to see you, man. We thought you were dead!"

"Thanks for coming back for me, guys," Jackson said.

"We tried," Katze said. "You were nowhere to be seen."

"I was unconscious at the bottom of a gully."

"We couldn't put back down with that giant monster thing stomping around, and we loitered until the dropship's intakes started corroding."

"So you saw the big thing too?"

"Only from the sky and through the trees," Tui said. "I'm sure it was way more impressive from underneath."

Jackson thought back to being in the shadow of the moving mountain and shuddered. "Oh yeah. Super impressive."

Katze said, "Once it moved on, we wanted to go back, but Warlord refused and sent his rangers, but the rain had washed all the trails away. There was nothing to follow."

Jackson feigned indignation. "Leaving a comrade behind to be molested by rude animals. I'm sure there's something nice you've prepared to make it up to me."

"If you had stayed put, I wouldn't have to make up anything," Tui said.

"That's a little difficult when all the carrion eaters of Swindle show up for an all-you-can eat buffet. It was escape and evade, or else."

Katze slapped hard him on the back. "Well, it's good to have you home."

Jackson flinched, then tensed, waiting for his spine to begin to melt, but nothing happened.

Tui saw his pained expression. "What?"

"Watch the back, please."

Tui got a teasing look in his eye. "What, did you get a sunburn down there?" He raised his hand to give Jackson another pat on the back.

"I'm serious."

Tui dropped his hand. "I see that you are." He gave Jackson a meaningful, questioning look.

Jackson simply glanced down at his surveillance bracelet and back at Tui, who nodded.

They led him down the corridor and out into the hub. They hopped a transportation cart, then hopped off. There was a crowd of vendors here selling everything from crates of food packets for space travel to the skulls of some little Swindle creatures for souvenirs. As the trio were walking through the crowd, Jackson was bumped by a man. Moments later a woman brushed against him and moved on. After they made it through the crowd, they reached the corridor leading to the spin adjuster that led from Big Town to the docking tree.

"So what else happened?" Katze asked while they killed time on the platform, slowing from the orbital's fast spin to match the docks' leisurely one.

Jackson didn't want to say it here, not around Big Town's surveillance, and especially not while wearing his black bracelet. "Let's go to the ship. That way I only have to tell the story once. By the way, if you thought I was dead, why's the ship still here?"

"Unexpected engine problems," Tui said. "Something must have happened on the way through the gate. We're fabbing new parts now to patch it up."

The way Tui said that made him suspicious. They'd been fine jumping in. Had Warlord somehow sabotaged them while they were docked to keep them here? "Nice to know you guys were going to stick around and wait for me."

Katze shook her head. "We're doing our dangdest. But you're like a bad penny. We just can't get rid of you."

The docks were crowded with workers and crew from several

other ships, most of them walking with magnetized shoes, but others bouncing about in the reduced gravity. On the far side of all that chaos the *Tar Heel* was still there, looking ungainly and magnificent as usual. She really was a site for sore eyes. When they reached the airlock, Tui and Katze removed their orange bracelets and put them in a box standing outside. Jackson set his with theirs. Once they were inside, Tui said, "Check yourself."

They checked their pockets while one of Jane's bots whipped around them looking for bugs and parasites. And he suddenly felt a tinge of alarm. The Warlord probably had eyes and ears here. Jane's scanner wasn't some cobbled together Big Town trashbot. It had been programmed by an artist. If it picked up the Swindle souvenir in his spine and flashed in warning, Warlord would see, "Jane, are you there?"

"*Oh, Jackson, I'm so glad you're back. I was so worried and—*"

"Yeah, sorry." Then he typed out a silent message with his eyes. "*Tell your scanner to skip my spine. I'll explain inside.*"

"*Roger that. And no need to send. You can talk freely. I debugged the airlock already.*"

"You're the best, Jane."

While he was patting himself down, Jackson found two little discs in his pocket. Those hadn't been there before. One looked like a normal data storage disc. The other was something else. On one side was a logo for some place called the Lucky Monk. On the other side were some numbers.

"What's that?" Tui asked.

"No idea." It hadn't been there when the tech had scanned him. One of the people who'd bumped him in the crowd must have slipped it into his pocket.

Tui took it. "It's one of those edibles. The samplers. But normally the backside has what you're sampling. Not just plain numbers."

"Maybe they run numbers at the Monk?" Katze said.

"Naw," Tui said as he handed it back to Jackson. "It was scraped off. Look. Blue something." He handed it back to Jackson.

The token had a twenty-two stacked on top of a fifteen. Or a twenty-one next to a twenty-five. Or just four random numbers. Except he knew they weren't random. Big Fox had said he'd be contacted.

When the scan pronounced them clean, they proceeded

into the cargo area where some of the crew was working in the weightless environment. The trio did the superman float to the exchange, then entered the hub. And then it was up one of the spokes to the habitat ring and a short float to the bridge.

There were a bunch of people waiting for him. Captain looked genuinely relieved to see him in one piece. Jane seemed downright ecstatic. She even floated over and entangled him in a hug. He had to admit, he enjoyed that. One of her little murderbots mimicked her and hugged his leg. That, not so much.

Shade was there. So were XO Castillo and Cargomaster Hilker. Which meant most of the *Tar Heel* leadership was here. Shade seemed a little disappointed he was still alive, Castillo, annoyed at further complications—but he always looked annoyed, and Hilker seemed happy. But of course, only one man's opinion really mattered.

Captain Holloway laughed. "Holy hell, boy, you scared the crap out of everybody. I thought for sure you were caliban poop by now. I was about to arrange a funeral then split up your share and let the crew pick through your personal belongings."

"I bet it would've been a good funeral."

"Sure. I'd have kept it tasteful and dignified." He grinned. "Welcome back, son."

Jackson took a deep breath. "Okay, I've got a story to tell."

Shade sneered. "Of course you do."

"You're not going to like it."

"Of course, I won't."

The captain nodded. "Okay, I'm gonna make this an official meeting. Katze..."

"Understood, sir. Over my pay grade." And she floated from the bridge. "Welcome back, Jackson."

He then proceeded to brief the command staff. He started with the important bits, like the ticking nano bomb, the fact that Fain suspected he was working for terrorists, and then got to the really uncomfortable parts where they might actually be the bad guys. Their expressions got increasingly dour as he went. Nobody liked to be told they'd been helping a maniac slaughter the good guys.

"I think we just might be backing the wrong side here, Cap."

Shade looked downright insulted, but the *Tar Heel* CO pondered that. "We'll circle back to you trying to get us sucked into someone else's war, but first order of business." He turned to Jane. "Is Jackson about to explode and kill us all?"

"I'll see what I can do." Jane already sent for some of her bots, and the little plastic menagerie came flying in through the door. "If there's something there, I'll figure out how to remove it safely."

Jackson said, "My sentiment exactly. But she warned me tampering will set it off."

"I doubt these Originals have anything advanced enough to even see me coming. I should be able to handle this. No problem."

"Shouldn't I go to sick bay?"

"I'm not a doctor. This is a hardware problem." Jane was about as cocky when it came to her tech as he was toward piloting. "Take your shirt off, please."

Jackson did so. Spacers lived too cramped to get the luxury of modesty. Nearly everyone on the bridge winced when they saw the nasty, painful-looking wollard bites. He directed Jane to the area where Needle Man had injected him.

"Alrighty then," the captain said. "While Jane tries not to turn my pilot into a quadriplegic, let's go back to our supposed war crimes. Are you sure they weren't just playing you?"

"Positive, Cap." Jackson winced as a bot pinched his back. "I only saw the kid they turned into a bomb on the screen, but nobody is that good of an actor. It was real. Let alone a bunker full of rebels and little crippled kids. Warlord's doing some shifty stuff. I'm talking slaveware-on-children-level evil."

"That does match with what we saw that set off that riot," Tui pointed out. "And some of the rumors the crew has heard since we've been docked."

Jane's bots were still moving on Jackson's back. And Jackson suddenly wondered if the little nano bombs had multiplied. Had they sheathed his spine from top to bottom? Jane was good, but was she that good?

Javier Castillo was their second in command, but he was a taciturn type. Unless he was running the meeting, he rarely spoke. He made an exception for this. "We need to know who this Big Fox is before we can proceed."

"Good idea," Jackson said and winced a bit at what felt like a bite on his back.

"Agreed," said the captain, putting some emphasis on it. Tui brought up the records on the wall display. And the team quickly narrowed down the ISF colonist records based on Jackson's description, guess at her age, and the fact she was from Gloss. Images began flicking across the display, six at a time They scrolled through while Jane worked, until Jackson spotted her. "Stop." In the image she was probably two decades younger, but it was the same piercing blue eyes. Except instead of a do-not-mess with me expression, Big Fox had a smile.

Another one of Jane's bots decided to bite him. He winced again.

Tui read the entry. "Marie Jacqueline LaDue. Born on Gloss. Landed with the first settlers. She's the daughter of a mechanic and was slated to be a kindergarten teacher. Ended up as an assassin for some group during the Swindle gang wars."

"That's quite the career change," the captain mused. "Are you sure that's her?"

Jackson nodded, got another pinch from one of Jane's bots and squirmed a bit.

"Quit moving," Jane grumbled at him. Then, distracted, she said over the comms, "ISF won't have anything else about her, but you can check the Big Town police records, Tui. I cracked them wide open. They'll never even know we looked."

Tui did a Big Town search. LaDue had warrants for sabotage, assault, treason, robbery, and murder. She was wanted dead or alive, and the reward would be paid in whole *kilograms* of CX.

Tui whistled. "Looks like you found yourself a real winner, Jackson. I guarantee, even if you do everything she asks, that lady's going to hang you out to dry."

"I don't think so," Jackson said.

"Think?" Shade shook her head in disbelief. "Are you sure thinking is what's happening between your ears?"

He'd been keeping his emotions in check through days of terror and exhaustion, but that was pushing it too far. "Shank you, Grandma. You're our broker. Did you suck at your job too much to notice what was going on here? Or did you know and just not care because the money was too good?"

Shade got really red. "You listen here—"

"You listen. I didn't get us into this. You did. We've got a code for a reason."

"We do," she said, defensive. "We're traders, not mercenaries."

"But we don't trade to just anyone," Castillo said, who seemed to be considering this whole thing rather thoughtfully.

"Big Fox, LaDue, whatever, she said they've reported all his crimes to the ISF. She said it's obvious their claims are valid. We got him mechs that can fight off monsters, but he's going to use them to slaughter a bunch of settlers too. That's not what we signed up for."

"Oh, really?" Shade said as she pulled up a holo. "Here's everything the ISF has on Swindle. If the Originals filed all those claims, where are they?" She flipped through the reports. "Where, Jackson? There's nothing in the official records. Either this terrorist is lying to you, or the ISF is lying to her."

"Porque no los dos?" Castillo muttered under his breath.

"We all know the ISF is trash. They could be setting these people up to fall."

"Rook," the captain said. "You know we don't deal with tidy problems and tidy situations. We provide the means for people to protect themselves. And when they get those, sometimes they're going to have be nasty, brutal, and coldhearted to get it done. The only reason the Big Town gold mine hasn't been cleaned out is there's a stalemate between three superpowers. You think the ISF cares even the tiniest bit about the claims of a handful of settlers on the surface?"

"Since when do we turn a blind eye to this type of thing?"

Captain snorted. "You think we're turning a blind eye to war? We're probably some of the rare few who really see it for what it is."

"This isn't just war, Cap. It's human trafficking, slavery, mind control, and—once he gets that Citadel and that Spider up to speed—mass murder...Heck, I don't know how many of them are down there. We might be talking full-on genocide." The thought of that, mixed with thoughts about Gloss, galvanized him. He wasn't going to be used for another similar slaughter.

Jackson knew the captain was a moral man, but he was about to ask a lot of him. "We need to do something about it."

The captain nodded. "I'm not too proud to admit I might be wrong. I make the best calls I can, but you don't know what you don't know. I thought I was helping workers not get eaten by monsters. That's it. I'm fine with getting out of here and never supplying Big Town again."

"Hang on now," Shade cut in. "You don't know Jackson's right.

Warlord has already given us another wish list, with huge profit potential, and he's been a solid client."

"Solid don't matter if they're solidly homicidal. Doubt is plenty for me to walk away, Shade."

There was a reason Jackson followed that man. And that right there was it. But walking away wasn't enough. "Sir, we can't just screw these people over, say whoops, sorry, and then abandon them."

"I know you got kicked in the head by a giant monster, Rook, but what are we supposed to do?"

They were not going to like this, but Jackson said it anyway. "Deprive him of the Citadel we just gave him."

The crew shared an incredulous look. Hilker actually laughed.

"Jane," the captain said. "Did you inspect his head?"

"I did."

"Does he still have all his brains?"

"As far as I can tell, sir."

The captain nodded. "Son, this ain't our fight. If you've not noticed, Jane is currently trying to figure out how to defuse the bomb they stuck in your spine, so I'm not thinking of these Originals as the poor picked-on victims here. You're not on Gloss anymore. But look, I get it, you feel guilty about buffing up a real bad dude, so now you want to make it right. Tell you what, after we get out of here, we put the word out to anyone else in our business about what you saw. If they still want to arm him, that's on their heads."

Shade narrowed her eyes at that. It was clear she didn't like that idea.

But the captain ignored her. "XO, how are the repairs going?"

"We should be able to cast off in six hours."

"Expedite those repairs, Mr. Castillo. I want to get away from this orbital as soon as we can. I've got a feeling things are gonna get weird."

"Yes, sir."

The captain was changing the subject but skipping out and condemning the Originals to certain death wasn't good enough. Jackson was about to speak when Jane said, "This is bad."

"What have you got?" the captain asked.

Jane brought up a holo over her handheld scanner so they could all see. Jackson turned his head enough so that he could see the green glowing image of his own spine. She moved the targeting depth in, and out, found something, then zoomed in. "It's got tripwires all over it, so I'm using low-impact sonar to slowly build this three-D model."

"I can't see anything," Tui said.

Jane highlighted it. "There."

It was thin, and maybe half a centimeter long.

"That's probably just some mutant growth in Rook's body," Shade said. "We all know he's packed with low-grade DNA."

Jane said, "I've never seen anything quite like this before. It's..."

"What?" Jackson asked, because the way Jane had lost her cocky tone was making him really nervous.

"It's layered nanotech, but not any kind I've dealt with. It's very clever. Way better than I expected for a planet at this level."

"Can you get it out?" the captain repeated.

"I can see the mechanism. Think of it like a cocked hammer sitting on top of a canister of I don't know what. It appears to have burrowed into the bone. If I try to sample it, it'll fire. If I ping it with something strong enough to get a good reading, it'll fire. It looks like a specific chemical compound would fit as a key to disable it. Only I can't see it well enough to guess what would serve as a neutralizing agent. Since I don't even know what the substance is, I can't distill something to counter it."

"Can you analyze it at all?" the captain asked.

"I'm sure someone somewhere could, but I don't have the equipment here. I could fab something, but that'll take time."

"There's nothing like this on the net?"

"I already searched. This is something new."

"Hell. You've got to be kidding me." The captain turned to Jackson. "Rook, I swear."

"It's not like I sought it out, sir."

"Maybe Warlord has the high-end equipment you need," Shade suggested. "If the Originals have used this tech against him before, he's probably had a chance to study it, and maybe even come up with a counteragent."

"What?" Jackson couldn't believe his ears. "You want me to come clean with our gracious host, and beg for his bounteous mercy? Fat chance."

"We go to Warlord," Shade said more forcefully. "He'll get it out. Then we can straighten this out and salvage our relationship."

"Maybe he has a way to save me, and maybe he doesn't, but

while you get underway filling his next shopping list, he'll be exterminating every last original colonist. I can't let him do that."

"You're a fool," Shade said.

"Probably," Jackson replied.

"LaDue put a bomb in your spine. Does that not tell you something?"

"What would you have done if you'd just found the guy who'd armed the man who'd been murdering your children?" Jackson asked.

She had no reply to that.

"What are our options, Jane?" the captain asked, sounding completely unrattled.

"I can take this image, study it, and try to reverse engineer it. Nanites won't have enough mass, but a small enough bot—I'm talking one tenth of a Fifi—might be stealthy enough to get close before it triggers and block the hammer before it falls, but we're talking nanoseconds there for an object that's a few microns across. It's a gamble. Otherwise I can study these really low-quality scans and try to figure out the chemical counteragent, but that's like doing a puzzle blindfolded. I'll need time."

Jackson checked his counter. He'd been purposefully avoiding looking at it, because it just made him nervous. Doing so had enabled him to get some sleep on the dropship at least. "Is thirty-two hours going to be enough?"

"That would really be pushing it. I'll get started." And without another word, Jane launched herself from the bridge. A woman on a mission. Her swarm of little bots followed her obediently.

Jackson slowly pulled his shirt back on. He'd kind of gotten his hopes up that Jane would be able to pull off a miracle.

The captain looked over his team, then ran his hand across his balding head. "Okay, here's what we're going to do. XO, Cargomaster, get engineering anything they need to get this ship mobile. Chief, break out the weapons locker."

"You expecting trouble?" Tui asked.

"Always. Send word to everyone on shore leave to get home. I want them back, armed, and sober. It's time to hunker down. The minute that engine's fixed, we're gone. Even if we have to blow their docking clamps to do it. Got it?"

All of them responded, *got it*. Even Shade kept her mouth shut when the captain went into command mode.

"Everybody out...Except you, Jackson."

The rest of them left the bridge. Shade alone gave him one last disapproving look before she floated out of the hatch. Jackson resisted giving her the bunny.

Captain went over to his command chair and sagged into it. "I'm glad you're back. I truly am. I thought you were a goner."

"Me too."

"Considering how complicated you just made the rest of our lives though, that monster might have done us a favor if he'd stepped on you. I got a pond. I got a house. I got women wanting to see me when I get there."

"I know," Jackson said. "I'm sorry. I don't want to endanger the ship or the crew."

"Then hunker down, let's get out of missile range, and give Jane time to disarm that thing in your back. You know she's smarter than whatever biohacker built that bomb."

"She probably is, but she's not a miracle worker." Jackson sighed. "It's not just that though. I'm the one who got Warlord that Citadel. I know what someone like him can do with something like it. Those people down there, they're doomed. And it's my fault. This is my thing. I'd love your help. But I understand if you won't. Shade said it: we're not mercenaries. And I can't expect you to be."

"Shade's mostly worried about burning bridges with customers."

"I pull this off, you'll get new ones."

"Who? The Originals? Do you actually think they're going to survive that long?"

"Not against two fifth gens, Cap. No. I don't."

The captain was silent for a long time. Somehow, he looked as weary as Jackson felt. Out of nowhere, he said, "Gloss wasn't your fault, you know."

"What? No. Of course not. That's got nothing to do with this."

"Yeah, I kinda think it does. Different world, different people."

"Same crap, different day," Jackson countered.

"You know why I got into this game, Jackson? Too many times I watched some powerful organization like the ISF get on their high horse and declare someone like your people weren't allowed to defend yourself from shanks like the Collective. I couldn't stand by and let that happen anymore. I tried, Lord knows I tried. So I get your desire to feel like a hero again."

"That's not it. I wasn't a hero to begin with!"

"You were to somebody. Same with me, at times. But I'm no fortune-teller. My crystal ball's all fogged up. So I did the best I could with the knowledge I had at the time. This mess isn't on you. It's not your cross to bear. It's on me. I'm the one who decided to sell to Big Town. It's not the first time I've read a situation wrong, but I was sure hoping it would be my last."

"Then you'll help me?"

"Help you what? Die pointlessly? Of course not. I'm responsible for every life on this ship. I can't afford to put my ego ahead of their safety. Warlord's got a crap navy, but it's still a navy, and at close quarters it doesn't matter if a railgun is mounted on a battlecruiser or a tugboat. And in the meantime, we're still tethered to an orbital filled with his troops. I'm seriously contemplating having Tui come in here, put you in cuffs, and stick you in the brig before you do something that endangers this whole ship."

"We don't have a brig."

"Nautical figure of speech. It sounds more menacing than saying I'll lock you in your room."

"If Jane can't fix this thing in my back, then locking me up is a death sentence."

"Believe me, I know. This is the kind of lousy decisions captains have to make. Still think you want your own ship?"

Jackson shrugged. "I've got to do this."

"You're throwing your life down the chute."

Jackson nodded. Maybe. Or maybe he'd been living in limbo. Maybe all the years since Gloss he'd just been fooling himself and hadn't really been living at all.

"Listen to me, Jackson. I'm telling this to you, not as your boss, but as your mentor and friend. You can play LaDue's game, do everything she asks, and hope she gives you the cure, but as soon as you go from being an asset to a liability on her balance sheet, you're dead. You honestly believe that you can demonstrate you've had a change of heart, that you're really a man of honor, and your code's not just words, but it won't matter to her. In her mind, you've wronged her, and once she's wrung the usefulness out of you, she'll kill you just to be safe. Don't kill yourself because of some futile, noble gesture."

"I appreciate it, Cap. I really do. Everything you've done for me. You saved my life, took me in when no one else would. I owe you. I'll always owe you. Because of that I won't endanger this ship. So if Castillo says he can get the *Tar Heel* fixed in a few hours, then he will. He's got the personality of a brick but he's as reliable as the sunrise. You guys bail. Leave me here. You have my word that I'll wait until you're well on your way to the gate before I do anything really stupid."

"Are you tendering your resignation then, Mr. Rook?"

Jackson took a deep breath. He supposed he was. That hurt more than the wollard bites. A lot more. This ship was his home. This crew, his family. "Well, I—"

The captain held up one hand to stop him. "Before you dig that hole you're standing in any deeper, I just got a message." His eyes flickered back and forth as he read. "It appears our gracious host was so overjoyed to hear of your safe return that he has requested our presence at a celebratory dinner party at the governor's mansion. He's already dispatched an escort to pick us up."

"Shanks. You think he suspects?"

"Maybe. But it would look real suspicious if we don't go."

This could be nothing, but it might be something. Even with all this talk about getting back to the primal, Warlord was politically cunning and a first-rate manipulator. Fain seemed like the sort to gnaw on a problem like a dog with a bone. If they'd found clues as to what had happened on the surface...

The captain was obviously thinking the same thing. "Well, Jackson, let's party."

CHAPTER 26

Jackson went with the captain, Tui, and Katze to the dinner. He and the captain were mandatory. The other two were their chosen guests. Tui, because if things went sideways, he was the most dangerous man on their ship, and perhaps on this whole orbital, armed or unarmed. And Katze because Warlord had seemed to take a liking to her, and since she was no slouch herself in the augment department. If this turned out to be a trap, she might already be close enough to take the governor hostage long enough for them to make it back to the ship. Or at least that was the plan the captain made up and sent to them on the way.

Though they'd tried to talk him out of it, Jackson knew one way or the other this would be his going-away party. It was going to be much easier to destroy the Citadel if he had free access to it. His goal was fairly simple—get Warlord to hire him on.

Lotte had met them at the docks and escorted them into Big Town just as she had before. They'd traveled in silence. Or what seemed like silence to their guards, because they were silently eye-texting the entire time, making plans and contingency plans. Captain left most of that to Tui. Boots on the ground, the chief was the most experienced.

Warlord met them at the entrance to the governor's mansion. Except this time, instead of the usual military uniform, he was wearing a suit in the Amonite style. He held his arms wide, a wineglass already in one hand. "The man with nine lives has come to dinner. Come in. Come in!"

If it was a trap, it was going to be a messy one, because there were a lot of other guests already there, and more arriving in their little electric cars. Jackson recognized none of these people. From their clothing and demeanor these were the upper crust of Big Town society. From the decorations, lighting, and live music, this event hadn't just been thrown together. More like it had already been scheduled, and Warlord had just decided to make it about Jackson out of convenience.

"How are your wollard bites?"

"Feeling better," Jackson said.

"They're nasty buggers." Warlord laughed, flashing him a perfect smile. "We should send you back up a tree with a zapper to get your revenge."

Jackson didn't want to go anywhere near a swarm of those things ever again. "A zapper? How about lots of high-grade explosives?"

"See, I knew I liked you." Warlord clapped him on the back, all friendly style. Again Jackson tensed, wondering just how many blows the sack of spine melt could take before it ruptured.

The other guests were studying the four of them. They had worn their finest, but they were spacers, so of course their clothing didn't match the local customs. Outsiders were always a curious oddity.

Warlord turned to Katze. "And how is the tigress?"

"Looking forward to dinner."

"Well, then it's good you've come. We have mushrooms that are to die for. Succulent green beans. And chicken."

"Chicken?" the captain asked. "Your private stock?"

"A luxury item, yes. There is one breed that excels in the low gravity of our farms. We distribute them by lottery. The citizens love it. It's a great thing to receive a chicken. A time for celebration."

How easily people were bought off, Jackson thought.

"Well, we're honored," the captain said. "Thank you for inviting us."

Warlord was still smiling, but Jackson wondered just what he knew. Their host offered Katze his arm, she took it, and then led them inside the grounds. He immediately began introducing them to the other guests. There were a couple of department heads, a scientist, a singer, so on and so forth.

Jackson noticed Sam Fain was there as well, but he wasn't eating or socializing. He was leaning against the garden wall, smoking what appeared to be old-fashioned Earth tobacco. There was no sign of his hell hound. It probably wasn't welcome in polite society. Though if Jackson had to bet, he wouldn't be surprised if it was hiding in the shadows somewhere nearby, waiting its master's command. When Fain saw them, he tossed down his cigarette, ground it out in the grass, and walked over.

"How are those bites?" Fain asked.

"They've stopped burning."

"Jackson here is going back up with explosives," Warlord said. "But we're leaving our other guests behind. They're about to serve the first course. As we eat you can regale us all with your tale of survival on the surface, Mr. Rook. Or should I say Sergeant Jack?"

A small alarm went off in Jackson's brain. Was that from Warlord's own research, or did Warlord have spies in LaDue's organization? He forced himself to smile. "Just Jackson is just fine."

There was a dining area on the top floor of the mansion, which granted an impressive view of Big Town in every direction, including up. The fake sun had gone off for the night, so it was as if they were in a giant tube of continuous city lights. The crew was guided to the governor's table, the place of honor.

The first dish was the mushrooms in a fine sauce. They were succulent and delicious, but sadly not enough to distract Warlord from pressuring Jackson to speak. The Big Town elite were all curious. Though they lived here, from the look of them he doubted that very many of these people had ever been down to the surface recently, if ever. So he told them his tale. He was actually a pretty good storyteller. The other guests laughed at the parts where he wanted them to laugh and shook their heads in wonder and appreciation when he narrated the dangerous parts. Kaiju, caliban, wollards, pinkers, and other nasty things he'd never even gotten the names for. They all looked toward Warlord when Jackson finished with the part about the rangers mistaking him for an Original.

"Don't worry. He's clean. We scanned him. If one of my guests suddenly exploded, this would be the worst party of the year." Warlord laughed. So they all laughed too.

"You're very lucky," the head of Big Town's agriculture department said. She was a striking, fair-skinned woman with black hair.

"It wasn't luck," Warlord proclaimed. "It's grit. And training. And a cocksure attitude that all mech pilots must have in order to do what we do. Isn't that right, Sergeant Jack?"

Again with that name.

A few of the guests titled their heads, curious.

Jackson said, "I tend to think it's my winning personality."

That drew a few grins.

"Our guest is too humble. He was a fighter in the Gloss Wars. An all-around terror. A legend. A man who knows not just how to survive, but to *win* in the most dangerous situations."

"That he was," the captain agreed. He was sitting across from Jackson and sent the message. *"He's found your records. Tread carefully."*

"The Gloss Wars?" the dark-haired agriculturist said. "I heard those were horrible."

"Even worse than our gang wars and food riots?" asked the singer.

"Far worse," said Warlord. "Millions were killed. The entire planet collapsed into barbarity and chaos."

"I guess it's just a matter of perspective. It was all we knew." Jackson shrugged. "I was drafted in as a young boy."

"A bad loss," the woman said, referring to the war.

"Yeah. We lost." Such superficial words couldn't even begin to capture what had happened there. But Jackson smiled, then turned the conversation back to her, asking, "Tell me more about your job here. It can't be easy."

She was an able talker, and Jackson found he didn't have to do much to keep the table conversation about her and the trials and successes she'd had growing food in space.

The beans came next, then faux almonds in a honey glaze, and finally the chicken, which had been roasted and spiced to perfection. They then topped it all off with their choice of a sweet or cheese. Jackson opted for the cheese. It was soft with a thin crust that had a slightly nutty flavor.

"I would like to make a toast," Warlord said suddenly as he swept up his glass and stood. "To the crew of the *Tar Heel*, who have aided us in our time of need, provided us with the tools and technology we need to ensure the continued freedom and prosperity of Big Town. Rare is the moral courage to stand against the flagrant tyranny of the ISF."

"To the *Tar Heel*," echoed the guests as they raised their glasses.

That concluded their meal. As the guests began to move away from their tables to mingle, Jackson found himself over by one wall with the Warlord and the captain talking about some of the skulls mounted on the wall.

"You understand now why I display these trophies. Swindle's good for the soul. Don't you think, Jackson?"

Jackson figured now was the time to make his move. "You know, I haven't felt quite that alive in some time. I kind of miss it."

"The danger?" Warlord took a sip of his wine. "Or the challenge?"

"Both. There's something to it down there. You do what you have to do, and there's no time to worry about it. It reminded me of being back on Gloss in a way. There's a sort of purity of action. You don't really get that being a spacer."

"Well, we can rectify that," Warlord said.

"Oh?"

"Trading isn't the most exciting career," Warlord agreed. "No offense intended, Captain Holloway."

"Oh, it's plenty exciting the way we do it," the captain said.

The Warlord shrugged. "But maybe just a little too boring for our mech boy here."

"I'm not bored. But Swindle does hold some attraction. If the right opportunity came, who knows?"

"Opportunity is it? Well, there's plenty of opportunity for the right man. You saw what we have to deal with on the surface, threats from animal and man. You have a very valuable skill. Perhaps I should poach you?"

He had two fifth gens, and as far as Jackson knew, only one person with the wiring to unlock their full potential. Jackson didn't want to appear too eager, so he just glanced at the captain.

"Really?" the captain asked. "Sorry, Governor, he was hit on the head while he was down on the surface." But silently he sent, *"You sure you want to go through with this?"*

"I've got to try, Cap."

"Do you have any other pilots?" Jackson asked. "Besides yourself, of course."

"I do not," Warlord answered.

"You're a busy man. You have to delegate your harvesting protection details to regular mercs, but we both know a Citadel would just be wasted on them. You might as well send them down in an old T-Bolt for how effective they'll be. Real pilots are expensive, but we're a great return on investment. I know these systems. I can train your men, so even without implants, they'll be a whole lot more efficient behind the controls. I can teach those in exos how to work with the mechs to maximize effectiveness. You can't think of a mech as a solo platform, but as the basis for a combined arms unit."

Warlord seemed interested in the idea. "Yes, I've read up on you. You did this on Gloss. You upped their kills by twenty percent, while cutting your losses in half."

He had. It had been kind of awkward, having a kid teaching a bunch of grizzled combat vets, but mechs spoke to him. He got them in ways that regular people just couldn't. Jackson turned to the captain. "Maybe it's time we expand our operation beyond supplies. Start to include implementation and training."

"We've always stuck to the trading side of the business," the captain said. "It's cleaner that way. You want to branch out, you're on your own."

Jackson looked back to Warlord. "Like I said. It would have to be the right opportunity."

"What would such a service cost?"

"Plenty," Jackson said. He needed in, but Warlord had just gotten done pontificating about how pilots were supposed to be so sure of themselves. Offering his skills at a bargain right now would look too suspicious.

"I think this one is searching for more fulfillment," Warlord said to the captain.

"He's an idiot. No offense, but this isn't exactly what you'd call paradise."

"No." Warlord shook his head. "Paradise is boring. Swindle's in a whole different class."

"It would only be for six months, maybe a year, for me to get a full rotation of his troops up to speed."

"You're a free man," the captain said sourly. Then he sent, *"Good luck, son."*

"Well, Jackson, you know mechs, but more importantly, you know battle. I require stability in my ranks. How does a one-year contract sound? I will grant you the rank of lieutenant in the Big Town Guard and put you over mech training. Maybe you'll even have a role in their deployment."

"Lieutenant Rook," Jackson said, pretending to mull it over. "That has a good ring to it. But it's going to cost two mil."

He scoffed at the price. "You are a pirate. Five hundred."

"You want dregs, you can get those anywhere. But I'm Sergeant Jack. Two mil."

"Fifteen hundred," Warlord said.

"Fifteen hundred," Jackson agreed. "Half up front. Half on completion of contract."

"A third on signing, a third in six months, and a remainder on completion."

"Throw in a double harvester's share for any CX gathered while I'm personally protecting them down on the surface, and you have a deal."

"You'd still wish to do such scut work yourself?"

"Of course. That would be half the fun."

Warlord smiled. It even seemed genuine. "Let me check your references first. Captain Holloway?"

"He's making the worst mistake of his life. The young ones just won't listen to their elders these days." He gave Jackson a meaningful look. "But he is one of the best pilots I've ever seen, and it's been an honor to serve with him. He would be welcome back on my crew anytime."

"Thank you, sir."

"Splendid. You start tomorrow, Lieutenant Rook. Zero seven hundred."

Warlord nodded past him to where Sam Fain had appeared, seemingly out of nowhere. The man moved like a ghost. "We're going to need to get this one processed."

Fain smiled, and it somehow reminded Jackson of the hell hound. "Excellent. Welcome to the Big Town Guard."

Jackson and the others left the governor's mansion at a reasonable hour. They were once again offered complimentary rooms at the same hotel, but the captain made his apologies and said he needed to check the repairs being made on his ship. Jackson, however, accepted. He would be needing a place to stay until he was assigned one anyway. Lotte rode with them and dropped Jackson off at the square.

The crew got out to get a little privacy as they said their goodbyes.

"I think I'm going to walk around the town. Get a feel for the place." Of course, that was said for the benefit of those listening to his wristband.

The captain gave it one last try. "You breathed too much of that Swindle air. It's fried your brain. You need to reconsider your choice."

What Jackson said aloud was "I'll be able to identify Warlord's needs. It will be like having a salesman in the inside. I'll hook up with you guys on the next shipment." Silently he sent *"Shade screwed you over, Cap. She had to know what was really going down here."*

"Possibly." The captain nodded. If Shade had lied so he'd violate his code, there would be hell to pay. "I hope this works out for you." But he gave Jackson a look that said both of them knew this was likely to go down in flames.

Jackson held his hand out for a shake. The captain didn't take it. "I hope you'll come to your senses and be there in the morning when we ship out."

"Brother," Tui said and gave Jackson a back-patting embrace.

"Just stow my stuff. I'll be back for it." Jackson had his go bag, with Raj, and a few supplies, and that was it.

Katze was frowning, looking concerned. She gave him a hug and said in a subdued voice, "Goodbye, Jackson."

"It's only temporary." But they all knew it probably wasn't.

And then the three of them left him on the curb and returned to the car. Jackson watched them go. Then he started walking. He looked up at the buildings directly above his head, then followed the curve of the wall to his left. He'd checked the map. Somewhere in those buildings over there was the Lucky Monk. The place where he was supposed to prove his trustworthiness by delivering the mech plans to LaDue's organization.

"Jane," he said over her net. *"I need the package."*

CHAPTER 27

Jane spoke in his ear. *"You're really going to do this, Jacky?"*

"I don't think I have a choice."

"You do have a choice. Give me time. I'm working on that nasty LaDue planted in your back. I can fix this thing."

Jackson brought up Big Town's map, identified the Lucky Monk and began walking in that direction.

"I want to borrow Fifi. Will you lend her to me?"

"She's already hiding in your bag. I'd have sent more bots, but I couldn't spare them."

"Fifi will be enough."

"You know you're probably being followed," Jane warned.

He figured. And by wearing the mandatory wristband, it was like he was carrying an unshakable tail.

"Solo ops don't go well. You need me."

She wasn't exaggerating. He still didn't know how he was going to pull this off, but he'd promised not to risk the ship. He couldn't try for the Citadel until the *Tar Heel* was out of range. Jackson crossed the street and turned a corner.

"There's got to be another way," she said.

"Okay, what's your idea?"

"I don't know."

"I haven't got time for 'I don't knows,' Jane."

There was silence.

He thought about asking her why they'd never gone out,

287

why she'd always shot down his advances, but it was too late for that now. Like the captain had said, they didn't deal with tidy situations. It figured his personal life would be a lot like his professional one.

He passed two men sucking on some mood sticks and blowing the vapors into the air. He nodded at them and walked past. They scowled. Big Town was as neighborly as ever. The suspicion and hostility were enough to make someone who'd grown up in refugee camps feel right at home.

She said, *"I've downloaded the Citadel's plans to you. I found schematics of Warlord's compound and mech hanger. I'll download them to you as well."*

"Thanks." And he began the transfer to the second disc that had been slipped into his pocket.

"Good luck," she said.

"When this is over, I'd like to take you out on a little adventure."

For once she didn't immediately shoot him down. There was a long pause before she said, *"What kind of adventure?"*

"You'll just have to wait and see."

There was another awkward pause.

"Be safe, Jacky."

The Lucky Monk was a tavern, located halfway around the curve of Big Town, about three kilometers from where Lotte had dropped him off. It was on the corner of a block. The double red doors were standing open, allowing light and the sound of conversation and music to spill out onto the darkened street.

He'd decided the numbers on the back of the disc was a time. Had to be. Twenty-one fifteen. The time right now was twenty-one ten. He spent a moment looking around like a tourist, so his tail would think stopping here was a random decision, then entered the tavern, hoping his guess about the location and time of the drop was right.

The place was moderately busy, with people at tables and along the bar. They were dressed in plain attire, some still in their work uniforms. It was a blue-collar establishment. It was decorated in an Icarus theme with pictures of competitors in various low-gravity places flying with all sorts of high-tech wings.

Jackson took a table off to one side. On the wall next to him was a picture of a tall bruiser of a man with a big brown dog and another man in some kind of silky outfit. There was a menu on the table. He swiped through the display. There were a lot of drinks to choose from. Everything from synthetic beers to targeted mood mixes with the kinds of names you'd expect. Big Easy, Belly Shakes, The Violin, Carefree. Jackson wasn't here to discover the experience of the Monk's custom chemical hits, and so he tapped on something called Banana Yam, because it was described as a health tonic. He tapped it again to put in his order. As he did, a small message popped up where the description of the Banana Yam had been. It said, "Awaiting insight."

What type of insight could a menu want?

Jackson looked closer. The interface on the pop up didn't match the rest of the menu. It looked like a hack. The first message disappeared and was replaced with an aerial view of the Lucky Monk and the surrounding streets. A dot blinked at a location down a side street not far away. The image zoomed in on the blinking dot to show a waist-high wall around a small, well-groomed yard. At the corners of the wall and on either end of the gate were small, decorative Japanese pagoda lanterns. A little animation showed a hand inserting an object into the pagoda down one side of the wall that ran along an alley.

Jackson tapped the display. The image disappeared and was replaced by the original description of the Banana Yam.

A dead drop. The menu was a clever hack. And he wondered just how many Big Town systems LaDue was into.

A few minutes later the waitress came by with his drink. She said, "This was a very good choice. One of my favorites."

"Will it grow hair on my chest?"

She blinked, then looked at him a bit confused. "Why would it do that?"

Clearly the joke didn't work here. "Never mind. Who's the lucky monk?"

"Oh, well, do you see the man tending bar?"

The bartender was a big man. A brute. Then Jackson realized he was the guy in the photograph by his table. "He doesn't look like any monk I've ever seen."

"That's Ian MacKinnon. This is his place. He had a good friend, a monk. They fought against the gangs during the wars. Mr. MacKinnon got shot, stabbed, clubbed many times. But when the monk was there, they always won."

"What happened to the monk?"

"He used to go down with the harvesters. Offering spiritual guidance or whatever. But he got eaten trying to save some workers from a caliban."

"Sounds like his luck ran out," Jackson said.

"Not for the harvesters he saved."

"Right." Jackson took a sip of his Banana Yam. "Not too sweet. Not bad."

"You might like to chase it with a Cucumber Waterfall. It's really good for getting the toxins from the surface out."

She left him to nurse his Banana Yam, brought up the schematics Jane had downloaded on his visual and studied them. He still had no idea how he was going to pull this off. When the time came, he took a shot of Cucumber Waterfall, because who couldn't do with a bit of cleansing now and again? The drink was surprisingly refreshing. Clean. And a moment later he felt a surge of well-being, which he was sure was something hormonal in the mix. Then he rose and walked outside.

It was clear he was supposed to drop the data disc with the information on the Citadel in the pagoda. LaDue wasn't stupid. There were cameras all over Big Town. Furthermore, he was being tracked with the wristband, so the pagoda must be in a blind spot. But he still didn't want anyone physically tailing him to have eyes on, so he took a circuitous route and walked slowly, looking in shop windows, crossing the street, then backtracking, like maybe he was considering the item he'd seen in the window before.

He asked Fifi to climb onto his shoulder and scan for any electronic followers, like cameras the size of flies. She linked with his visual display, but after twenty minutes of countersurveillance, it appeared there was no human or electronic tail. Everyone and everything that was out tonight had destinations.

Jackson still didn't feel comfortable, but he knew he couldn't be a hundred percent sure of his security. Not in this situation, and so he made his way to the side street, turned down the alley, and approached the pagoda. As he walked past, he didn't slow. He simply reached over and deposited the disc with the Citadel's schematics into the lantern and continued walking. He paused at a tattoo parlor to look at the samples, as if he was thinking about getting another piece done and this was the real reason he'd gone this way.

After deciding this place's artist wasn't up to snuff, he exited the other end of the alley, then found a rack of public scooters with electric motors. He rented one and rode back to the hotel.

He checked in, walked up a flight of stairs, and along the hallway to his tiny room. It was just enough room for a bed. There was no shower, but there was a sink, toilet, and cloths he could use to wipe himself down.

Fifi scanned the room, but she found nothing. That didn't mean it wasn't bugged, but who was he going to talk to? He took off his clothes, looked at his back in the mirror, but couldn't see where LaDue had injected her insurance. Clearly, the all-heal had done its job. So he cleaned off as best as he could, then lay back on the bed, going over the schematics Jane had sent him again.

His mind was on the crew, who would be leaving in just a few hours. They'd been together for years. It was still hard to believe he was doing this alone. But some things simply had to be done. He wasn't mad at the captain. On the contrary, he could understand exactly where he was coming from.

Once he could recreate most of the compound and hangar from memory, he laid back and closed his eyes.

Jackson woke to someone banging on the door. It was zero six hundred. Which meant the banging had cheated him out of another thirty minutes of shuteye.

"I'm sleeping," he said.

"Breakfast is the most important meal of the day, brother!"

Tui...

"Six A.M. is nowhere near time for breakfast," he muttered as he got up and opened the door. Tui was standing there grinning.

"I appreciate the visit. But I'm staying, man."

"I know. I figured you'd need someone to keep you out of trouble."

"What?" Jackson cocked his head. "But you're the security chief. They need you."

"Bushey's more than capable," Tui replied. "Plus, the poor guy wasn't ever going to get a promotion as long as I was around."

"Bushey's trash at paperwork though."

Jackson switched to Jane's net. *"You know this isn't your battle."*

"It is when it hauls one of my mates in. When this is over, I think I'm going to have some words with Ms. LaDue."

Jackson looked at Tui and figured his chances of success had just doubled. He couldn't help but grin.

Tui said, "How much time we got?"

"I start my new job in an hour."

Tui gave him a look. *Not the deadline he meant.*

Jackson brought up his timer, frowned, and then sent. "*29:42 until spine-melting time.*" He'd not checked it for a while. If he had he wouldn't have been able to sleep.

Aloud, Tui said, "Yeah, I needed to get off the ship for a while, stretch my legs, try something new." But the whole time he was shaking his head, like *uh-oh.* "When I heard how much this guy was paying for a mope like you, I figured he'd pay real money for talent like me."

"*Furthermore,*" Tui sent silently, "*Jane gave me the schematics too. I've got some ideas.*"

"Good." It was always nice to have more than one pair of eyes on a plan. "Very good."

"*Have they given you the second meet?*" Tui asked.

"*Not yet. I figure at breakfast or after work.*"

Jackson dressed. He wore Raj beneath his clothes—might as well demonstrate that he was arriving ready to work—combed his hair with his fingers, then popped a cleaning tablet into his mouth, let it foam, swished it about, then spat in the sink.

"How do I look?"

"Like Warlord's paying way too much money for a washed-up pilot. Get a haircut, you hobo." Tui gestured at his boots. "I don't even have a job yet but look at that shine. Look at the creases on these pants. Have some dignity, bro."

"Who irons fatigues? You regular army guys are nuts." But Tui really did look like someone you didn't want to mess with.

Then they went down the breakfast and ate some cake made with cricket flour and sweet chewy bits that were supposed to be cherries. Not as good as the feast at the mansion, but good enough for a last meal if it shook out that way. Jackson hoped for the instructions to the next meet with LaDue's people, but nothing came.

When they finished, Jackson stood. "Let's see if Warlord will go for a twofer."

CHAPTER 28

They arrived at the governor's mansion a little before zero seven hundred. The gate guards checked their identities, then let them through. The grounds smelled fresh, earthy, wholesome. Jackson and Tui walked along the path admiring the grass that was dotted with small white flowers, all of which were real, and the drops from an early watering that still clung to them.

"That's a lot of water," Tui said.

"Perks of being a warlord," Jackson replied.

His new boss didn't come out to greet them, but one of the guards escorted them inside and led them to a room where Sam Fain was waiting with his hell hound lying at his feet.

Jackson was a bit surprised to see it there. "Prolonged exposure to the air up here doesn't bother him?"

"Grendels are versatile," Fain said.

Jackson nodded and noticed an odd smell coming from the devil dog. Bother was a relative term.

"It appears you've brought along a friend," Fain said. "Tui Fuamatu. Head of security, right?"

"Head of head-knocking," Jackson said and grinned. "If I'm going to be training that many people, I really could use the help."

"And he can do it?"

"Tui's a professional, well-seasoned soldier."

Fain looked Tui over. "You've got the lines and build of one. Mods?"

"Some," Tui said.

"More than some," Fain corrected.

Tui shrugged.

"The governor's always willing to pay for quality service."

"And I'm willing to provide. I think it's an opportunity that doesn't come often."

Fain cocked his head. "You're hoping for some of the land we liberate?"

"Naw. I don't want any land. I'm happy to take regular coin."

Personally, Jackson thought coin would be splendid, but even better would be for him to walk away with his life.

Fain leaned back in his chair, pondering on it. "Luckily I already pulled your file. You've got an impressive jacket, Fuamatu. Meritorious service, several commendations, even an Earth Star with Valor." Fain whistled. "Very impressive."

"I was just doing my job. You know how it is."

"I do. Only my boosts are newer and my downloads were a whole lot better."

"That's a matter of opinion."

Fain sized Tui up. "Come on. We all know EDF is a bunch of softies compared to Syndicate training. But you're not bad." He leaned down to pet the grendel's head. "In fact, we're not so different, me and you."

"Not even close," Tui quietly sent to Jackson. "Don't worry, Mr. Fain, I'm not after your job. Just a contract."

"That's not my decision to make . . . but I do know Warlord well enough to know he's not going to pass on talent. You two will have to work out the payment details, but in the meantime, let's get you processed. We already have your biometrics. But to work here, you'll need a more thorough scan and a company ID chip in your arm . . . You as a head of security should know."

"Of course." Tui nodded, but said over Jane's net, *"A shackle."*

The devil dog made an odd noise. A low, breathy rumble.

Fain snapped his fingers. The huge beast gave him a baleful look with its four eyes but quieted down. "Forgive my grendel. It's nearly as suspicious as I am."

"We'll keep that in mind." But as Jackson said that, he wondered what else Fain knew. He also worried about what they'd find with this new scan. Because if they identified LaDue's little gift, things might just become a teensy bit uncomfortable.

Fain led them from the room and down the stairs, the gren-del padding along uncomfortably close behind. This section of the mansion was off-limits to visitors, and the Warlord kept it functional, no decoration at all. The medbay Fain led them to was all business. He took their bracelets, then directed them to strip and stand in front of a few bots that sniffed and probed and imaged and x-rayed and who knew what else. It was a little embarrassing standing there. Jackson was physically fit, but Tui was a block of muscle covered in warrior tats.

Fain studied the information on a screen they couldn't see as the data came in. The massive devil dog sat on its haunches and watched them, the short feelers around its mouth wriggling like worms.

At one point, Fain said, "Samoan blood. Where's Samoa?"

"It's a group of islands on Earth," Tui said.

Fain grunted and kept reading. He tapped his screen a couple of times more. And then the scanners finished their job. "All right. Each of you hold out your left arm."

They did, and one of the bots flew around and stuck them with a little chip. A small drop of blood welled up on Jackson's arm around the implant. He put his thumb over it and pressed, feeling mighty tired of how everything on this world felt the need to stab him.

Fain spoke to the system, tapped his screen a few times, then said, "Welcome to the Big Town Guard. Your chip will communicate through the flat wireless you already have installed in your bodies. They'll only show your security clearance, rank, and last names. That's all citizens here need to know. Your pay will be direct deposited in the Bank of Big Town. Have you got enough to tide you over until then?"

A footloose merc would never turn down money up front. "We could use some money to get set up," Jackson said, wondering how much of Big Town Warlord actually owned. Because if he owned the bank too, so much for accessing that first third after he stole the Citadel.

"I'll see to it." Fain seemed pleased. "Well then, it's time to pay a visit to our employer." He led them out of the room, down a different hallway, and into the hangar that held Warlord's mech collection. The Citadel was there at the end of the line, shiny and sleek.

The grendel absently bumped into Jackson as it sauntered past, nearly knocking him over. Apparently, it had a favorite spot in the hanger since it immediately lay down beneath one of the cargo haulers.

"That grendel's jaws look powerful," Jackson said.

"Incredibly so. He'll snap a femur right in two. Crunches heads like nuts. He loves brains."

Jackson realized Fain could only know that if the thing was crunching heads on a regular basis.

"I guess that makes clean-up easy," Tui said. "You have many of those things up here?"

"No. Just the one. Right now, that's our arrangement."

Arrangement? Jackson looked at Tui who just shrugged.

The Citadel was so close, but Jackson lacked the means to unlock it yet. He noted that techs and mechanics were working on it, gearing it up for extended surface operations.

They crossed the hangar and went through another door into a control room with lots of big displays on the wall, mostly maps of the surface. Warlord was there, back in his regular uniform.

"Welcome," he said with his white-toothed smile. "And the big man has joined us to boot. Nice."

"He wanted a job," Fain explained.

"He's not cheap, but he's worth it," Jackson said.

"I have no doubt."

Tui looked around the room, and Jackson was suddenly very grateful he was there because Mr. Tattoo Crazy Pants of the Ancestors was no doubt cataloging everything about the place with his head-of-security eyes. "I'm just an old soldier looking for a new opportunity, sir."

"A sentiment I can understand. Welcome aboard. Now, Jackson, let us continue our discussion from last night about how you could improve my forces. There are thieves stealing my CX and sabotaging my operations. I would like to deal with them once and for all. Do you have any problem with that?"

"No problem at all. Their actions almost got me killed."

They spent the next few hours in the room discussing schedules and strategy. Jackson told Warlord he needed to train his mech unit on the ground, not up here. They needed to get used to the gravity, the weather, terrain, and even the friendly denizens of the forest.

"Up here, they can learn basic controls. But we'll need to mirror what they'll actually face as much as possible. Have you got someplace on surface we could use as a training ground?"

"There's an area in the mountains that doesn't get too much of the big wildlife, and there's no CX production at that altitude to endanger."

"Good. I'd like to check it out in person if I could." He didn't add, *in the Citadel*, just yet. Better to work up to that. Jackson laid out a training plan. It was an awesome plan. Top notch. A surefire plan to take his men from schlubs to mechsuited nightmares.

"I'd like them ready for a big operation in four weeks."

"You'll have them in ten, and not a day sooner, unless you want to lose half of them."

"Six," Warlord countered. "Mercenaries are replaceable."

Tui tried to hide a frown when Warlord said that but didn't dare say a thing.

"Mercs are replaceable, but are your mechs and your exos? This isn't a negotiation. It's going to take ten weeks. And that's pushing it. I did this program in eight on Gloss, and we took massive casualties on our first big op. If you're right and Kalteri has been arming these terrorists, this won't be a cakewalk."

"Ten then," Warlord said.

Their new boss had guests coming, so had to excuse himself. With Fain they went over the records of the guard so they could see who they wanted to assign to their new expeditionary force. Precious hours ticked by, and Jackson was growing increasingly impatient as he watched his doomsday timer count down, but there were no opportunities to access the mechs without it being suspicious.

It was early evening when they finished. Now that they were employees instead of honored guests, they didn't rate a dinner invite, so they were on their own. It was close to sunset, the globes all the way to one side of the orbital and glowing reddish orange, when Tui and Jackson left the mansion. They walked back the way they had come, past the earthy lawn, out the gate, and into Big Town.

"Do you think they're onto our method of communication?" Tui texted.

"This is Jane-ware. She wrote this from scratch. You think someone's going to hack Jane?"

"*Just a feeling. Fain's a smart one.*"

"*Even if they can't get into Jane's program, what about the feeds from our ears and eyes? Are our happy little tracking chips picking that up?*" Jackson asked.

"*We control those.*"

"Do we?" He held up his arm where they'd planted the Warlord's chip. "*Or did we just let them breach it?*"

"Crud," Tui said aloud. If the chips had gained access to their visual feeds, Jackson's mission was hosed. There was no way they could conduct any kind of clandestine operation with Fain watching first-person Jackson TV.

"*Surely Jane's protocols cover that.*"

Tui shrugged. "*Jane does a lot of stuff on the fly. And I'm assuming by now our lovely anti-hack goddess is eighty, ninety thousand klicks away. We're on our own, flyboy.*"

"We should have learned sign language and braille," Jackson said.

"*Yeah, you work on that.*"

They went back to their hotel and got Tui a room. They spent a couple hours quietly going over the schematics and discussing a plan. If Fain had hacked their feeds, his goons would be showing up soon. But the goons didn't show. However, LaDue's organization hadn't contacted him with the instructions for a second meet either. It was beginning to worry Jackson.

He decided that maybe he needed to be out and about, and so Jackson and Tui went out to find some grub. It was night; the globes in the Big Town sky glowed like a moon.

Jackson brought up the map on his visual display. When he did, a marketing ad popped up. It said, "*Thank you for your visit to the Lucky Monk. Tonight's special is Ice Cage.*" It showed a picture of a blue drink on the rocks. And then another little message popped up, one with the same unmatched interface of the secret message from the night before. It showed the twenty-one over a thirty.

Jackson closed the message, then said aloud, "I got some drinks at a place last night. They were good. Let's just go there. There was a cute waitress who seemed into me."

Tui said, "Guarantee, she'll upgrade her goals when she meets me."

"Says the man with the ancestor pants."

"We'll see. Girls love the tats."

✧   ✧   ✧

His business meetings concluded, Warlord stood in his living room watching the video feed from a camera that captured Rook and Fuamatu as they walked down the street.

"So?"

"They got to him," Fain said. "I'm sure of it."

"Could you tell what it was?"

"No, but it's got an unknown bio signature."

"Slaveware," Warlord muttered. "LaDue trying to plant her own vector in my organization."

"It was between his shoulders. Slaveware's normally installed in the head."

"Could be she's figured something new out," Warlord mused. LaDue was clever.

"Or maybe it isn't the Originals at all. He could be a plant from Graf, trying to double-cross us. Or maybe Kalteri set the whole thing up in advance and paid off the broker on the *Tar Heel* to sneak a spy into our ranks. It's hard to tell. You've pissed off half the galaxy."

"As Winston Churchill once said, *You have enemies? Good, that means you have stood up for something, sometime in your life.*"

"Who?" Fain asked.

Warlord chuckled. Fain was good at his job but hadn't had the benefits of a quality education like he had. "An Earth politician from a long time ago. It doesn't matter. However they intend to use Mr. Rook against me, I must admit the training program he presented today is rather good. It's a shame to waste him. I think I'll still implement some of his proposals."

"After we neutralize him?"

"Of course."

"Good. Just checking. Sooner or later he'll show his cards. I'll keep close tabs on him until he makes contact with his handlers so I can roll up their entire network, *then* I'll kill him."

"No. I don't want him dead. Bring him back alive. I've got a much better fate in mind for Jackson Rook."

CHAPTER 29

Jackson found a rack for electric bikes. There was one left. And so he and Tui doubled-up and rode one through the streets and up the wall to the Lucky Monk. Toward the end, the battery ran low, and so Tui had to help propel it along with his feet.

Like the night before, the red doors of the tavern were open, spilling light out onto the street. Jackson checked the time. It was a bit early, but that just meant he'd have time to flirt with the waitress and sell his cover.

They entered, spotted a table in the back and sat down. They each ordered a drink and a selection from the plates of hash the Monk offered. When the waitress came with the drinks, it was the same one who had served him last night. Jackson put on his smile as she reached their table.

"The service was so good last night, I decided to come back to try the food."

"Smart boy," she said.

"Have you eaten dinner?" he asked.

She grinned. "Dang, I have. But Ian still needs to eat. Shall I let him know you're looking for company?"

"Ian?" Tui asked.

"The lovely bartend," she said.

Tui looked over, then raised his eyebrows at the big, meaty man. "Jackson, I didn't know you had a thing for bruisers."

"Don't listen to him," Jackson told her. "Me and my friend here are sticking around for a while. Are you from Big Town?"

"I grew up on Jersey."

"I've been to Jersey. It's a nice planet."

They both chatted with the waitress a bit more, and then she left to pick up their food.

"I'm making progress," Tui said.

"Whatever. I'm the one that got the hand on my forearm."

"She just knows she can play you for a big tip."

She really was cute, but Jackson's heart wasn't in it. He was kind of preoccupied with the whole impending death thing. Plus not having Jane in his ear made him feel kind of melancholy. But he faked a smile and flirted for the cameras.

The food came. They chatted the waitress up some more, asking what there was to do for fun around Big Town, then ate. Jackson waited for new instructions to appear on the menu, but it was only showing him the drink specials.

He brought up the time. Twenty-one thirty was long gone. And he wondered if something had gone awry with the drop. The problem was that he didn't have time for things to go wrong. Still, they waited until it was almost twenty-three hundred hours, before going out into the Big Town night.

Jackson looked at the timer. 12:55. LaDue was taking too damn long. She was going to kill him. He cursed under his breath.

It was then that a message appeared on Jackson's personal display. A personalized thank-you from the Lucky Monk.

"I got a note from our waitress," Jackson said.

"Yeah, I got one too. Says she wants to marry me. Says she loves my gorgeous hair."

"Sure it does."

And then the rogue screen popped up. It was an aerial map like the time before. This time it pointed to a different place, some nightclub a few blocks away.

"You know, Tui, I think we should celebrate our new jobs."

"What do you have in mind?" Tui's menu must not have had the map.

"Let's go see what Big Town's nightlife is like. There's got to be a club around here or something. What's the point of making bank if you can't blow it?"

"Spoken like a pilot," Tui said.

So they left the Monk and started walking.

Their destination was a hollowed-out cargo pod that dated

back to the original ship. From the look of the people milling around the exterior, this was where Big Town's young and rowdy crowd congregated. Big Town imported a steady stream of workers from all the poorer worlds, and it took a certain mindset to be desperate enough to try and make it as a harvester. The bouncers were armed with shock batons sufficient to stun an Earth moose.

Inside, the place was packed. There was dancing and loud music and flashing lights. They moved along the edges of the crowd, checking out the locals. Jackson heard probably twenty different languages before he made one full circuit of the main room, but they all had the same live fast, party hard, die young attitude in common.

And then they saw Frans, the cop who had first escorted them from the docks to the governor's mansion. He was out of uniform, and had a drink in his hand, but was looking right at them.

"Great," Jackson muttered. The last thing he needed for this clandestine meeting was a cop who knew him to be hanging around.

But then Frans motioned with his head for them to come over. Maybe he'd heard that they'd taken a Big Town contract too, and now the standoffish Dutchman wanted to hang out.

"Do we go?"

Frans motioned again.

"I think we have to," Tui said.

They made their way over to the cop. He was standing in front of a long hallway with a red floor. There were three doors on each side and one at the end. Frans said nothing, just gestured for them to follow him, and Jackson wondered if he was a synth that had broken voice controls.

Nevertheless, they followed. Franz opened the last door on the right. They went in, the volume of the music behind them dropping a bit, and found they were in nothing more than a mostly dark storage room.

Jackson looked around, wondering what this was about. Then Tui pointed at the table that was lit by a lamp. Under the light were two black bands. Tui picked one up, looked it over, then put it on his arm over the spot where Fain had injected the chip. Jackson did the same. He could only assume it would block, scramble, or spoof the signal. Something to mess with the Warlord's chip.

Then Frans spoke. "This way." He moved to the back wall. There was a vent panel there, but it slid aside easily and revealed a ladder going down.

"In you go," he said, his accent thick. "All de vay to de very bottom."

"You first," Tui said.

"I stay up here. Stand guard."

So Frans was one of LaDue's people? Or was this some loyalty test by Warlord?

Either way, he had a bomb in his back and the clock was ticking. Frans remained expressionless and unreadable.

"What do we have to lose?" Tui sent.

Indeed, Jackson thought. So he slipped through the disguised access hatch, took hold of the ladder, then began to climb down. Tui followed. The ladder took them seven meters into the hull of the old orbital. They passed wiring, ducts, pipes, and tubes. It was this layer of the orbital that handled all the air, water, power, and waste systems that kept the residents alive. Their ladder ended in another bay full of dusty crates, but there was another ladder down, and Frans had said the very bottom, and so they took the second one down even farther.

Jackson figured if they kept this up, they'd reach the very outer edge of the hull. They'd gone far enough from the ideal spin zone that gravity was starting to feel off. They reached the floor. This place was mostly dark, but Jackson could see they were in a corridor between rows of huge machines, their status lights giving off just enough illumination to see by. There was the humming of electricity and the sound of water moving in pipes.

They stood there a moment, their eyes adjusting to the darkness. Then maybe thirty meters down the corridor a soft light spilled onto the floor as if someone had opened a door to a well-lit room.

Jackson and Tui walked through the darkness toward the light, watching the shadows of the machines on either side as they went. They walked through the open door into a work or break room big enough for half-a-dozen people. There was a desk and shelves and some displays.

When they were in, the door closed behind them. Then another door at the far end opened and a large man walked through. He was taller than Jackson by a head, broad and muscular. He wore a vest, dark pants, and boots, and a harvester's mask to hide his face.

"It's the bartender from the Lucky Monk," Tui sent.

The waitress had called him Ian MacKinnon. *"Are you sure?"*

"Absolutely." Tui was really good at sizing up other combatants. He'd had a lot of practice. Of course he'd taken note of the dangerous-looking man behind the bar. *"Unless there's another two-meter-tall, 130-kilogram fighter up here with that same exact scar pattern on his knuckles."*

The bartender looked at the arm bands they'd put on, then said, "We can speak freely now. Welcome. I wasn't expecting you to bring a friend."

"You'll be happy to have him. So you're LaDue's guy on the orbital. You know, you could have saved us the walk and had this meeting at your place."

He was quiet for a long time, considering that, then pulled off the mask to reveal his face. "So much for the disguise. I wanted to observe you first, and I didn't want Fain's secret police up in my business. The bands will garble the signal, but from here on out no real identities and no references to locations where we may have seen each other, just in case. My code name for this operation will be Preacher. Yours will be Blue. His Red."

"Blue is more my color," Tui said.

"Yeah, that seems kind of arbitrary. Can we switch?"

MacKinnon didn't seem amused. "Needless to say—but just so everything is in the open, if you try anything, or this is some sort of setup, the thing in your back detonates. We need to discuss your plans, because you don't have much time."

Jackson said, "That's an understatement." He had exactly twelve hours and twenty-eight minutes.

"His lack of time is a direct result of your associate being a psychopath," Tui said pointedly.

"Cost of doing business, stranger. If it weren't for that insurance, I wouldn't have ever shown my face to you outsiders, and we wouldn't be having this conversation."

"How sure are you of your man upstairs?" Jackson nodded toward the ladder.

"A hundred percent," Preacher said. "Unquestionable. His people were some of the first colonists off the boat. They bled for this world more than you'll ever understand."

Jackson didn't like any of this, and he didn't trust Frans, but what else could he do? "Let's discuss plans then. I'm assuming Big Fox has briefed you?"

"She says you've been called to repentance. Supposedly you feel guilty for arming the evil bastard who's been murdering our people and stealing our land, and now you want to make things right."

"Something like that."

"Good. Because I'm the one man who can issue a stay of execution."

Jackson almost couldn't blame him. If their situations were reversed, Jackson wouldn't believe his story either. "I've got schematics of the compound and some access to the hangar."

"Good. When you are ready, I have a man on the inside. He'll be able to provide false feeds to all the hangar cameras for three minutes."

The inside man was probably Frans the cop. "We can use that, but they don't trust us enough yet to let us just walk in with enough explosives. And believe me, that thing is tough enough we'd have to obliterate that section of the orbital to even scratch its paint. Sabotage is going to take time."

MacKinnon shook his head in the negative. "I told Big Fox we should just blow up the hangar, but she told me she wants you to actually deliver it to her, down there, in one functional piece."

Having their own Citadel would make it a whole lot harder for Warlord to eradicate the Originals, but getting it there sure did complicate matters. "I'll need to overcome the authentication system before I can drive it. We're not in that system yet. You can't just hot-wire a fifth-gen mech. I need the key. After that I can make it through atmospheric re-entry, no problem. But that means I need to get it out of the hangar, drop, and avoid getting shot to pieces in the process."

"Bummer, Red." And the way he said it, MacKinnon truly didn't particularly care if Jackson lived or died. "What else do you need?"

"When the time comes, I'll need a diversion. Something sufficient to distract all the security force's attention, and preferably draw their gunships off."

"That can be arranged."

Jackson was incredulous. "Just like that, in the next few hours?"

But the man just gave him a cryptic smile. "You have one task. One mission. Whatever else is or isn't happening during this operation is none of your concern. What else?"

"I need this thing out of my back."

"It will be shut down when you complete your mission. Not before."

"I need more assurance."

"After you get the asset somewhere safe, we'll talk."

"I want it out before."

"We will find you. But if you hold up your end of the bargain, you have nothing to fear."

It was obvious Tui was getting really suspicious. "So you're gonna distract all the cops in Big Town long enough for my buddy to steal a weapon of mass destruction and fly it down to Swindle, and then we just say everything's cool and walk away pals?"

"What about Tui? I can't leave him here after the theft."

"We have a way we can get you off the orbital," Preacher said. "The Originals have a network in place."

"What is it?"

"There's always a chance you may fail. So the less you know, the better."

"For you," Tui said. "Except if you rebels are so capable, and so numerous, it really makes me wonder why the only ones who contacted us tonight are people me and Jackson could identify if we get pinched."

Preacher was quiet for a long time. "You ain't as dumb as you look."

"I'm just a retired soldier with a good BS detector," Tui muttered.

"And here I figured since you didn't have a bomb planted in your back, you were stupidly loyal to your friends."

"You got me there," Tui said. "But it also means you've got no leverage on me, or way to threaten me . . . Yeah, I saw your bot back there with the gun trained on us. If it goes live, I'll grab it and cram it down your throat, wide end first."

Jackson hadn't even seen the bot, but MacKinnon slowly nodded. "You can see in the dark."

"Among other things. I can also tear a man's arm off and beat him to death with it. So how about we start acting like respectful professionals and figure out how to tackle this job in a way you people get what you want, my ship atones for our sins, and Jackson's spine doesn't melt?"

Now there was a glimmer of respect in MacKinnon's eyes. "Alright. There's more of us, but most of those are occupied, in place, awaiting my signal. We've been planning a show of force for a while. I couldn't risk sending anybody else to this meet right now. Once Blue is on his way, make it back here and we'll get you out. When the asset reaches Swindle, the insurance will be removed. Identities changed, for both of you, and we'll smuggle you onto a transport out of the system. Trust me. We know how to get people in and out. We've been doing this for a while."

Tui said nothing to that, but he transmitted to Jackson. *"Jane lent me Baby. I'm going to have her follow this guy."*

Baby was one of Jane's smallest bots. Jackson hadn't realized that Tui had his own Fifi. *"Good call."* If things went south, Baby would give them directions right to Preacher's door.

"We will—" Preacher cut off in mid-sentence. "Hold on. We've got a problem."

"What?" Jackson asked.

"There's been a breach. The cops are raiding the club." He listened for a second, then looked upward. "They're already coming down the ladder. We need to go!"

That was very bad news.

"Where?" Tui asked.

"This way." They ran through the door he had come in, and out into the dark guts of the orbital. The bartender was fast for a big dude, and he led them between rows of mysterious, wheezing machines, and into a corridor of dripping pipes and steam.

"Is it Fain?" Jackson asked.

"I hope not. That man's a butcher."

Far behind them a siren started wailing. Jackson looked back and caught a glimmer of red lights flashing.

"They've sent fliers down the tunnels," Preacher warned as he led them around a corner. He stopped there. "Go down this lane. First left. First right. You'll find a ladder up."

"Where are you going?"

"I'll lead them away. I pray you were telling her the truth, because if you don't neutralize that mech, the rest of my people are dead. Go!" And then he darted into the darkness.

Jackson and Tui ran the way he had pointed. They took the first left. Ran. Were about to take the first right, but a figure appeared ahead of them.

The sudden movement startled Jackson, but Tui flashed past him, lightning quick, and grabbed the man by the shirt.

It was Frans.

Tui picked him up off the ground and slammed his back against the wall. "Did you set us up, cop?"

"No! I am loyal to the cause." Frans lifted his hand to reveal he had a small pistol. He could have shot Tui with it but didn't. "You must believe me."

MacKinnon had said he was, but Jackson didn't trust any of these people at all. That was the downside of being a crook working with a bunch of shady rebels.

"Please, you must listen to me. This way's no good. I was just up there. If you go that way, you'll be caught. Follow me, or we are all dead."

Frans seemed genuinely terrified, but that wasn't a hard act to pull off when Tui was getting ready to snap your neck. "I believe him," Jackson said.

Tui said, "You're always too trusting." But he set Frans on his feet. "If this is a trap, you'll regret it."

Frans led them farther down a winding corridor, taking several turns, a few of which Jackson wouldn't have even seen. He hustled them between two big water tanks and onto a catwalk.

There were shouts behind them. The buzz of fliers.

They ran down a covered, dark lane, skirted some kind of machine shop. From the blankets and trash, it looked like people must be living down here, though they were all hiding now. Frans seemed to know his way through the undercity rather well.

"This way. Ahead, you must go—"

There was a gunshot. Blood splattered the wall. Frans stumbled, holding his arm.

Jackson hadn't seen the guards waiting in the darkened side passage.

Frans cursed, and began firing one-handed, his other arm hanging limp. One of his rounds hit a female guard in the visor and she fell.

"Run!" Frans shouted.

There were more shots. The sound of a pneumatic. A rapid *piftt, piftt, piftt, piftt.* Something whistled past Jackson's head. A dart stuck into the sheet metal ahead of him. Another struck Frans in the leg.

Frans cursed and pulled the dart out. But he kept running, cutting down a little alley between pipes. "This way."

Jackson and Tui followed, leaving their pursuers behind. At the end of the alley, they took a right and Frans said, "Hurry." Then he lurched, eyelids fluttering. He tried to right himself but careened to the side like a drunk. The darts. They had to have been tranqs.

"Come on." Tui threw Frans' arm over his broad shoulders and kept him upright.

"Straight ahead, second left," Frans slurred as Tui dragged him along.

"Hang in there, buddy."

"I have family on the surface. If you don't stop Warlord, he will slaughter them all."

"I know," Jackson muttered. "Believe me, I know."

Suddenly, a huge shadow came out of nowhere. It crashed into Jackson and Frans, flinging them in opposite directions. Tui bounced off the metal wall. Frans went skidding across the grate.

Jackson stopped, shocked, as the monster clamped its jaws down on Frans' neck and shook him like a doll.

It was the grendel.

Frans' gun was lying on the grate, but it was on the opposite side of the beast.

It saw him looking at the weapon. Four eyes narrowed. Then it bit Frans' head off.

"Fifi, eyes!"

The tiny bot sprang from Jackson's pocket and launched herself at the grendel. But when the tiny dot neared its head, a bolt of electricity sparked from the collar around its neck. There was a loud snap and flash, and Fifi fell to the floor, smoking.

Tui leapt to his feet and went for Frans' gun.

Except that was when Sam Fain came around the corner and joined his butt-ugly devil dog, he lifted a big pistol, firing twice at Tui. *Piftt, piftt.* Then he turned and aimed at Jackson. *Piftt.*

The dart struck him in the chest. Jackson reflexively tried to yank the thing out, but it was too late. A moment later everything went blurry and sideways.

Tui plucked the darts that had struck him out, tossed them, and told Fain, "It's gonna take more than that to stop me. Let's see how tough you are, punk." Then Tui's eyebrows rose in surprise as he staggered hard to the side. "Ah, hell. This is high grade, ain't it?"

"Nothing but the best," Fain said. "Nighty night."

The orbital rushed up to hit Jackson as everything went black.

CHAPTER 30

Jackson woke and found himself tied to a chair in a room. The spot between his shoulder blades stung, and he wondered if the release of the spine melt had begun. But he looked at the time and still had a whopping ten hours and seventeen minutes before bomb time.

The chair was metal and, since it wouldn't even wiggle, probably bolted to the floor. Tui sat next to him, bound in another chair. Jackson realized what was holding his wrists and ankles were heavy-duty straps which were bolted right to the chair. Tui had the same thing, and some additional metal chains.

"About time," Tui said.

"Where are we?"

"Don't know. When I woke up I was here."

"How long ago was that?"

"Don't know, bro. A few minutes is all. My head is still pretty messed up."

Fain must have used some powerful juice in his darts because it wasn't the average tranq that could overcome Tui's mods and knock him out. Jackson looked around the room, saw a couple of desks, screens, some complex machinery, but when he saw the taxidermized claw of some animal mounted on the wall he knew exactly where they were.

"We're at Warlord's mansion."

Tui inclined his head toward something on the floor. It was a bunch of bloody rags. "I think this is the interrogation room."

"Probably real big into the feather torture."

"I guarantee it," Tui said.

Torture, and then who knew what else. Tui was about the nicest guy he'd ever known, and now he was going to suffer and die because he'd tried to help. And it was all Jackson's fault. Jackson shouldn't have accepted the offer. He should have insisted Tui get back on the ship. This was on him. "I'm sorry, man."

"Eh. We'll see how it shakes out."

Jackson tried to summon Fifi, but there was no sign of her. He'd not seen her since she'd been zapped by the defenses on the grendel's collar. Jackson was sure that if Fain had found her, he would have stomped her flat.

"We need to come up with a plan," Jackson sent to Tui, but before he got a response Fain walked in.

"You're awake. Finally."

"A man's got to have his beauty rest," Jackson said, still feeling groggy. "By the way, if you want this spa to take off, you've got to get more music. And some pretty girls."

"A few plants would help," Tui chimed in.

Fain held up the black bands they'd been wearing on their arms and said, "Who gave you these?"

"Just play dumb," Tui sent over Jane's net.

Jackson said, "Isn't the normal protocol to separate us for our spa treatments?"

Fain came over and slapped him.

It stung. In fact, Jackson couldn't remember ever being slapped that hard. He turned to Tui. "I think that's the German method. Great for sagging skin and stubborn pores."

Fain slapped him again.

The sting brought water to Jackson's eyes. "Hoo. Definitely German."

"Answer me."

"You're not going to separate us to prevent us from corroborating each other's stories? What kind of joint is this?"

"You'd just talk over your secret comms," Fain snapped. "Just like he did a few moments ago. Yeah, I've known about that capability for a while."

"It's just a little communication app some of the crew of the *Tar Heel* got."

"With a cipher it would take all the computing power on Big

Town a year to crack. Quit wasting my time. Who gave these bands to you?"

"Oh, that one's easy. We were told there was a party below the party at that nightclub. She said we had to wear them to get into the VIP lounge."

"Who gave them to you?"

"Some woman at the nightclub. It was dark with lots of strobe lights. I don't know." He turned to Tui. "Do you remember?"

Tui shook his head. "Naw. She was pretty, though."

"A party under the party," Fain said. "Strange there were so few people there."

"That's what we thought too," Jackson said. "We wandered around for a bit, then saw Frans. Since that scene was kind of dead—"

"Boring," Tui agreed.

"We were about to leave. Then you guys showed up and started shooting people."

"Wow. That's the best you could come up with? That's disappointing. Maybe I should have let you two talk a bit more over your net so you'd come up with a story that wouldn't bore me to death. But the time for that is past. I'm really going to enjoy what happens to you next."

Warlord and another man they'd not seen before entered. "Ah, they're awake. Excellent. Let's get started."

Fain said, "We got two jokers here. Trying to blow the wind up our dresses."

"You're not my type, Fain." Then Jackson looked Warlord in the eyes and tried to appear as earnest as possible. "Sir, this is all a misunderstanding. We don't know what's going on. We were just looking for a good time and stumbled into something weird."

Warlord just laughed. "That's the story of your life, Jackson. Sadly for you, we found some oddities down on the surface. It seems you had some help from the friendly neighborhood Originals."

Jackson said nothing.

"At first I thought that LaDue had sent you as a sleeper with her own slave controls. But your little friend is in your back, not your head. Which means whatever you're up to, you're doing it under your own power. I can't tell if it's there as a trace or something else. You want to share?"

"Something in my back?" Jackson asked as if hearing it for the first time.

"Come on, Jackson. By now you should know you really can't trust that woman. I know from experience."

"Who?"

"Would you care to tell us the truth about your visit in the woods?"

The man who had entered with Warlord had been carrying a briefcase. He went to a nearby table, opened it, and began removing various unrecognizable tools.

"I've told you the truth."

"Now that is downright insulting." Warlord pulled over a chair and sat down, facing Jackson and ignoring Tui. "Do you think I'm a fool?"

"No, of course not."

"Yet you treat me as if I am one." He spread his hands theatrically. "You've seen what I have built here. I took chaos and organized a society. I have given opportunities to hundreds of thousands. I have sustained their lives in a place hostile beyond comprehension and made it profitable. Could a fool do that?"

"No."

Warlord leaned back in his chair and crossed his arms. "Then why do you insist on treating me as one?"

Jackson didn't answer.

"I did not build this place, Jackson, but I saved it from itself, and made it into something better. Is it perfect? Of course not. Nothing is ever perfect. But it is an impressive achievement nonetheless. It is *my* achievement. And now after I've done so much, and worked so hard, I will not let someone else come and steal the rewards of my labors. So I will discover who you are working for and what they hope to accomplish. You will debrief us with all the details about your little trip into the woods. About your meeting last night. And whatever it is you're plotting. You and your captain and the Originals."

"The captain isn't involved in any plot," Jackson said. "There is no plot."

"Ah, such loyalty. But you can't protect him. Events are in motion. Your ship will be dealt with soon enough."

"The *Tar Heel* left yesterday morning," Tui said. "It's probably halfway to the gate by now."

Warlord looked over and studied Tui for a moment. "I think he actually believes that, doesn't he, Fain?"

"I do, sir. Interesting."

"What are you talking about?" Tui asked.

"Well, Mr. Fuamatu. Rather than leave the system, your old ship has taken up a position in orbit, tailing us, just out of striking distance. Their excuse is that they're still having some problem with their repairs. I think they're sticking around, waiting for you two to do something."

Jackson said nothing. What would the captain be doing trailing the orbitals? What was he thinking? What was the captain doing? Or was it Jane, working like a madwoman to figure out a cure before Jackson's clock ran out? Had they hung back for that?

"Fuamatu's mask is pretty good," Warlord said. "But this one's. I believe I detect some honest surprise there."

"What do you mean, *dealt with?*" Tui demanded.

"Their fate is your fault, but not currently your concern. However, once the *Tar Heel* is destroyed, I can't question frozen corpses floating in the vacuum of space. Which just leaves me you two. In the spirit of expediting matters, I have proposed a little wager with Mr. Fain here. See, I love technology. He likes the old-fashioned way."

Fain walked over and pulled the towel off a stainless-steel platter full of various pliers, knives, and needles. "Two methods," Fain said. "Two subjects. We'll see who cracks first."

"First thing to crack will be your skull," Tui snarled.

"That's the spirit," Fain told Tui. "Get ready for your spa treatment."

The man with the briefcase was loading a vial into an injection gun. He set it to one side and began organizing a bunch of electrodes and wires. Apprehension filled Jackson. What did Warlord mean by *technology?*

Warlord saw where Jackson's eyes had been drawn. "When we did that deep scan on your brain yesterday, we found something interesting. The overlords on Gloss used a surprisingly invasive growth. And wouldn't you know it, but the path to your unfortunate slave hack is still there."

Jackson was too cool under pressure to be afraid very often. But those words terrified him. "No."

"Normally, the wetware, to truly override a brain, takes days to grow. And sometimes there are complications, often fatal. But you've already got the pathways cut. I must say, whoever hit you on Gloss was a master. All we have to do is drive along that old road."

"Stay out of my head!"

"Too late for that. You can tell me now, or you can tell me later. Either way, you'll talk, but talking isn't good enough."

Jackson said, "I've told you what I know."

Warlord motioned at the briefcase man. "Get it ready."

"You want to enslave the guy who is supposed to train your troops?" Jackson asked.

"Oh, I'm changing your job duties. I have a much better assignment for someone with your history. Only now you actually will be unquestionably loyal, rather than a snake."

From spine melt to slaveware. The old images rose in his mind. Echoes of old feelings. The blissful addiction of carnage. The torn bodies and heads.

"You don't want me as a slave," Jackson said.

"I think I do. There are only two men on this orbital with the implants necessary to fly-by-mind. It would be a shame to waste one of us. Look on the bright side. This way you get to avoid all the drama of torture like what's about to happen to your poor friend here. When the wetware has fully grown, and you are perfectly obedient, I'm going to send you back to the surface in that Citadel. You will go into those woods and murder the whoreson Originals, man, woman, and child. After that, if you're still alive, there are the Kalteri settlements to deal with. It'll be just like the old days for you."

Jane's block would hold. It had to.

"There's a little something at the entry juncture," Needle man said. "But we should be able to bypass that."

Jackson's fear rose. If they bypassed her block, he was done for. *"Jane."*

If the captain was still circling Swindle, it was possible Jane was still linked up, buried somewhere in Warlord's nets, waiting, listening, and able to fulfill the promise she'd made.

"Jane!"

But there was no response.

"Naw, bro," Tui sent. *"It's just me and you."*

"I think Rook looks agitated," Fain said.

Warlord motioned toward the stranger. "Begin the process."

"This isn't going to go the way you've planned," Jackson warned. "Believe me."

The man came forward with the injector gun. When he reached

out, Jackson tried to avoid him, jerking in his bonds, but that didn't get him far because he was practically bolted to a chair.

"Hold still." Warlord shoved Jackson's head back against the headrest. His grip was like iron. Jackson couldn't move.

Needle Man came closer and put his device against Jackson's neck. A moment later there was a sudden sharp sting as the device slammed something in. That wouldn't be the wetware. That still required direct insertion into the brain. This was probably something to sedate him.

The man stepped back.

"When you wake up, you'll be well on your way. It will take a few hours at the most to reactivate your old controls."

"Jane's fix will block it, right?" Tui asked over the net.

"I don't know. She always said it was just a patch."

A patch when what Jackson really needed was an iron wall.

While the *Tar Heel* had been docked, Jane had planted a couple of toads on the orbital's networks. She watched the data scroll across the displays of Specter's Domain. She'd been keeping tabs on both Jacky and Tui, watching their vitals. She could pick up their audio and visual feeds, but she'd elected not to, because sending that much data via her toad line would call too much attention and let Big Town security know they'd been hacked.

With growing horror, she watched the numbers tick by.

She pinged the captain. "Sir, it's not looking good."

"Our boys who stayed in Big Town?"

"I'm afraid so. It looks like they've been captured."

There was a sad sigh. The captain had told her to keep working, and he'd parked them in range, just in the off chance they might be able to help. He'd taken that risk for nothing. *"Jackson's a big boy. He made his bed. But damnit, Tui..."*

"I can no longer read the status of my block."

"Your block?"

"In Jackson's head. On the old Gloss controls. I think it's been breached."

There was silence over the line.

"Captain?"

"I can't risk the crew. We're proceeding to the gate."

❖   ❖   ❖

Jackson awoke, but a chemical desire to sleep still hung about him. When he finally came to, his mouth was dry as dust and the side of his head felt funny. He was still in the same chair, his legs and back in pain from sitting so long. The remaining vestiges of the tranq still made him feel a bit groggy, but he felt something else. An itch on the inside of his skull. An itch in his brain.

He knew that feeling. He'd felt it long ago.

"Tui," he sent over Jane's net.

Nothing.

"Tui?"

And then Jackson realized there wasn't any connection. Jane's net was gone. No. The comms implant hadn't been surgically removed. He still had his visual display.

He also saw he was down two more hours. 8:34.

"Tui," Jackson said aloud.

"Yeah, bro?"

He looked over and found Tui tied up in the corner, bloodied, beaten, his head hanging down.

"We've got to get out of here."

"You don't think I've been trying?" Tui lifted his battered face. It was painfully obvious Fain had really worked him over.

"Where are they?"

"Taking a smoke break, I think. Apparently punching me is a lot of work." Tui spit a gob of blood on the floor. "They injected something into your skull. You hanging in there?"

"Yeah," Jackson lied, because he could already feel the demons gnawing away. "I'm really sorry I got you into this, Chief."

"Naw. Nobody forced me to get off the ship. I saw a friend who needed a hand, and I made a call to stick around. That ain't on you so don't get to feeling all guilty about it."

"I'm sorry, anyway." Jackson grimaced as there was a sharp pain through the front of his skull. He didn't know if he'd be able to hold out against the slaveware long enough for the spine melt to kill him, or if he'd be down there torching the rebels when their implant murdered him. Part of him actually thought that would be poetic justice... And he wasn't sure if that dark thought was his or not.

"You're not looking too good." Tui sounded more concerned for Jackson than himself, and considering how beat up he was, that was saying something. "You need to find something to focus on. Find it and hold on tight. Don't let them take it from you, Jackson, you hear me?"

"Yeah. I hear you." That wouldn't last. He'd been here before. The brain was an amazing thing, but ultimately it was just salty electric fat, and somebody had just turned loose a nanite buzzsaw on his. "I know you're big on the whole sense of honor, do the right thing attitude, but why did you come back for me, Tui?"

"Is talking going to help you fight off the hack?"

"Sure." Jackson had no idea. Last time he hadn't even realized someone had gotten into his head until he'd turned his mech's flamethrowers on his friends. "Can't hurt."

Tui let out a long sigh. "I figured you were a lost cause, but honestly, you remind me of my little brother."

"Aw, that's nice."

"He was a cocky idiot too."

Jackson snort laughed. "Hey now."

"Must be a pilot thing. That's what he did, back on Earth. I swear that's how they pick you guys. An inability to even comprehend losing. Like, it just doesn't click. I'm not saying you guys are suicidal, or that you don't calculate risk, you do obviously, it's just that no matter what, no matter how bad the odds, especially the young ones, you somehow think you're gonna pull it off."

"As opposed to your rational, reasonable perspective on life?"

"Yep. Grunts like me need to stay grounded. Pilots tend to be delusional."

"We like to think of it as optimistic."

"You get used to wearing a tank like a pair of clothes, doing impossible feats like it's routine, and that goes to your head, makes you feel godlike. But you aren't. You're still human. Which is why guys like you need someone like me around to keep you from biting off more than you can chew."

Even with the growing pain in Jackson's head, that made him grin. "So how's that working out for you?"

"Pretty friggin' splendidly. Ask me again when I'm not tied to a chair."

Jackson went back to suffering in silence for a minute, but then he asked, "So where's your brother now?"

"He died during the war back on Earth. I wasn't around when it happened."

"Oh." That put things into perspective. "I'm sorry."

They shut up as the briefcase man came in, but he was paying them no mind. He walked over to some screens and read the readouts there. After a while, he asked, "How are you feeling, Mr. Rook?"

"My butt is killing me," Jackson said. "Can I stand up?"

"Do you have any pain in your head?"

"Did you not hear me?"

"Your head," the man prompted.

"My head is splendid," Jackson lied. It felt like someone was whipping the top of his spine with a chain. "It's one of my best features."

Tui laughed. "That's unfair. Your guy is all calm and doctorly. When I made smart-ass comments Fain pulled out one of my molars with a pair of pliers."

The man tapped a few parts of the screen. He asked more questions, which Jackson blew off, and recorded comments about whatever vitals he was reading on the screens.

Tui kept trying to goad the doctor-slash-torturer, or whatever he was. "Look at this poor guy. Obviously, a product of low-gravity orbital inbreeding. His eyebrows are a little thin, don't you think? I bet he's got webbed toes."

"Yes," Jackson agreed. "I'm sure he has trouble with the ladies."

The man studiously ignored them.

Tui said, "And look at those ears."

"Small," Jackson said. "Did you have them modified on purpose?"

"Is he supposed to be an elf?"

The man gave them an annoyed look, and Jackson forced a smile.

"Enjoy yourself while you can, Mr. Rook. Your walls are crumbling. Soon you will be a willing and obedient servant."

"I can't wait," Jackson said. "Do I get paid vacations?"

"You're not going to want vacations. That's the beauty of this system." Then the man turned toward Tui. "I'm surprised you haven't talked yet. Fain is rather persuasive. You're quite the specimen. Accelerated healing, augmented strength, reinforced bones, you would have been a top-of-the-line combat body about ten years ago. Earth Defense Force didn't spare any expense on your mods, did they?"

"Yeah, kind of the opposite of your parents, I guess. Did they hook you up with discount sloth genes or what?"

The man frowned, but kept his cool, and continued monitoring Jackson's readout.

Worse than the pain was the phantom itch inside his brain. He'd been here before. He knew how it would progress. Next would be the thoughts that weren't his. The whispers would get louder and louder, until he could no longer tell the difference. Jackson was terrified but trying not to show it. He wouldn't give them the satisfaction.

Tui kept badgering the man, obviously trying to get under this skin. "I know a gene splicer who could get you hooked right up, my man. You know the lady I'm thinking of, Jackson?"

"Sorry, Tui. Drawing a blank."

"Naw, you know the one I mean. I'm talking Fifi."

"Oh yeah." Jackson feigned nonchalance. "Fifi." And then his hopes rose. Had she survived and somehow followed them? Had Tui seen her? Or was Tui hoping that Jackson had her on him, and was trying to remind him to activate her, because if that was the case, Tui was out of luck. "I haven't seen Fifi in what seems like forever. I don't know if even she could fix this mess. I mean, seriously, look at the guy."

The man sighed, which meant they were getting under his skin. Jackson hoped that meant he'd get angry and make some mistake they could capitalize on. When they began to talk about his pencil-thin lips and concluded that neither women nor men liked thin lips, he said, "I've had enough of that."

"We're just trying to help," Tui said. "We could help you get that date you've been wanting. With a real woman."

"Or man," Jackson added. "Whichever you prefer. No judgment."

"You just need some ear mods, and your messed-up nose, and stupid face, well basically the works, but you've got to start somewhere. I mean, you really are repulsive." Tui was doing his best to sound helpful. "Then no more dollies for you."

Tiny Ears pulled his lips flat with anger, then opened his case and took out a syringe.

"What's that?" Tui asked.

"Something to shut your gob. I need Mr. Rook's brain active, but yours not so much. Fain can wake you up when he's ready to go back to work."

"Oh, come on," Tui said. "If you won't take constructive criticism, you'll never get any further than you are now, and that's just sad."

Tiny Ears drew something from a small bottle, then pushed the air out. He walked over to Tui and held the syringe like a real tough guy. "I said to shut up. And you're going to shut."

Except when he went to stick Tui with the needle, there was the *snap* of a breaking bond, and lightning quick, Tui grabbed his hand. A look of shock, then terror, came over Tiny's face. Tui smiled, squeezed, and crushed the bones. The syringe clattered to the floor. Before the man could shriek in pain, Tui yanked him down so that his head smashed into the arm of the chair. The blow made a smart, cracking sound.

Tiny Ears flopped onto the floor, unconscious, or maybe dead. Tui was *really* strong.

And then something the size of a pea dropped from Tui's chair to the floor. It crept toward Jackson, but in a halting, crippled way.

"Fifi?" Jackson asked. He peered closer. It was Fifi! "How in the..."

"I don't know. She showed up a minute ago and started sawing on the underside of the strap," Tui said as he used his free hand to unlock his other arm.

"That shock from the grendel's collar must have really damaged her."

Jackson looked at their little companion. She deserved a medal. That right there was Star of Valor stuff.

Tui said, "I'm just glad she was smart enough to free me first."

"I totally could have knocked him out like that too," Jackson lied. "Hurry up."

"How are we going to get out of here?"

"Oh, that's easy. Get to the hangar, get the Citadel, and walk out." Tui freed his arm and began working on the shackles around his legs. "Warlord's got the key."

How could he forget that? His head really was messed up. "Yeah, we'll need that. I bet Warlord has it on him. That's where I'd keep it. Or we could try a brute force hack. But I'm thinking the Warlord will be easier."

Tui freed his ankles and stood. "We've got to go before Fain gets back. Fifi, cut Jackson free. I'll take out the guards in the hall." He moved for the door.

Only just as Tui got there, the door opened.

It was Sam Fain.

CHAPTER 31

There was no hesitation at all. Tui attacked. Striking for Fain's throat.

Despite being surprised, Fain reacted with incredible speed. Blocking Tui's hand.

As the two superhuman killers traded ten blows in the blink of an eye Jackson tried to shrink back into his chair and hoped for the best.

Several shots landed, but then Fain hit Tui in the midsection with a hook that sent him stumbling back. Fain followed. They collided in the middle of the interrogation room. Tui was far bigger and bulkier, but there was no telling how much of Fain had been replaced with synthetics.

Tui launched a series of jabs that were almost too fast for Jackson to follow. Only Fain dodged back and forth, easily avoiding them, then he swatted the last one aside, and nailed Tui across the face with a ridge hand fast as lightning. Tui's nose went flat.

The *Tar Heel* security chief stepped away and wiped his bloody nose on his sleeve. There was a moment of calm as the two sized each other up. "Got an arm on you, Big Town."

"Best money can buy. Every job I complete pays for another upgrade." Fain saw his downed associate lying there. "I'm actually impressed at your resourcefulness. Did you kill him?"

Tui looked down at the man at his feet, then shrugged. "I haven't checked for a pulse."

"I never liked that nerd much anyway." Fain charged.

They exchanged blows, throwing punches, elbows, knees, and kicks, each of which would be sufficient to shatter a regular man's bones. Only these two took those massive hits, shrugged them off, and kept going.

Jackson had seen Tui fight before, but never anything like this. It turned out that those other times, Tui had just been trying to subdue his opponents. Now Tui was playing for keeps. Nothing held back.

But Fain appeared to be enjoying himself, almost as if he was toying with Tui.

They went back and forth, continually striking. For each shot Tui snuck in, Fain landed two. Seemingly twice as hard. When Fain nailed him with a shot to the sternum that Jackson could feel from across the room, Tui staggered back. He nearly fell and had to grab onto a table to steady himself.

Tui gasped. "You're not human."

"I started out that way, but I got better. You ready to give up, old man?"

Suddenly, Tui flung the stainless-steel table at Fain's head. He punched it out of the air.

When that failed to stick, Tui shot in, trying to take Fain to the ground. They locked up, each of them trying to flip the other onto their back. Weighing more, Tui almost pulled it off too, except Fain grappled like an Earth python. Tui almost managed to throw him, but Fain kicked out and maglocked one boot to the metal wall. He used that unexpected leverage to shake Tui's hold, and it was the big man who got bounced off the floor.

Jackson felt something crawling up his leg and spotted Fifi, heading for his restraints. "Hurry," he urged, but she was obviously in bad shape, and going as fast as her little robot legs would allow. If she could free him, he could find a weapon. Fain was inhumanly tough, but hopefully he wasn't bulletproof.

Tui got right back up and charged. Fain caught his arm, flipped him over his hip, and slammed him against the far wall. Tui got up again, but slower this time, obviously hurting.

Fain attacked. Tui blocked the shot with his hardened forearm, but Fain just punched him six more times, rapid fire. Then he kicked Tui in the chest and put him back into the wall.

"Stay down."

Because he was a warrior, Tui got up anyway.

Fain crowded him back into the corner and started hitting him with jackhammer speed fists. Jackson had never seen anyone take a beating like that. Tui was going to die.

Fifi was sawing on his arm restraints. She wasn't going to make it in time.

"Disappointing," Fain said as he hurled Tui across the room again. His limp form rolled to a bloody stop at Jackson's feet.

Jane would have stormed onto the bridge, but it was hard to storm anywhere in zero G, so the best she could manage was an angry, purposeful float. Captain was in his command chair, and every station was manned. She had been too distracted, desperately working on a way to help Jacky, to pay much attention to what was going on, but everyone here seemed really tense about something. Shade was there too, and it looked like she'd been having a heated debate with the captain.

"Captain, we've got to talk."

"It's not a good time," Shade snapped. She was wearing black again, her shining blonde hair stark and luscious against it.

The captain held up one hand to silence her protest. "I decide what time it is on this ship."

The broker didn't like that, but whatever her crisis, it could wait. *Suck it, Grandma.* "What is it, Jane?"

Jane held out Jacky's readout and pointed at the status of his block. "This is what I'm talking about. There's neural activity on his old controls. The block was functioning perfectly before we left. I checked it. This looks like he's going through a full spectrum neural attack."

"I thought you said the block would prevent that," the captain said.

"If it was there, it would." She let that sink in.

"Then how is there activity?" the captain asked.

"He's been breached," Shade muttered.

Jane nodded. "Somebody is tearing down my block. They're growing controls."

The captain scowled. He was thinking the same thing she was. It was one thing to die. This was worse. "I warned Jackson."

"It was the height of stupidity to have let him stay," Shade said.

"Slow your roll, Shade," the captain ordered.

It really bugged Jane that Shade was the one person who could get away with being downright insubordinate with the captain. It was because she was more employer than crew. So Shade getting shot down hard and having to shut up also made Jane feel a little smug.

The captain rubbed his forehead with the palms of both hands and sighed. "What about Tui?"

"He's alive, but his vitals spiked hard. He's in really bad shape right now. They're killing him, sir."

The captain's scowl deepened. "It's Warlord."

"Of course, it's the Warlord," Shade muttered.

"We need to go back," Jane said.

"We're one ship," Shade said. "That orbital is surrounded by guns. He'll blow us out of the sky."

Jane pretended Shade wasn't there and made her plea directly to the captain. "I made a *promise*."

The captain looked around the bridge. There were far too many ears for him to talk about how he'd had their specter wire one of their crewmates with an off button just in case someone hacked his brain to turn him into a crazy murderer machine again. "Shade, Jane, my stateroom. Now. Alligood, you've got the bridge. Keep an eye on that incoming ship and ping me the second it does anything fishy."

A moment later they were somewhere a bit more private and could speak freely.

"What promise?" Shade asked suspiciously.

Jane looked to the captain for permission. He nodded.

"Okay, when Captain rescued Jackson from Gloss, he was really messed up. I mean really bad. The things their biohacker did to all those pilots' brain I've never seen before or since, thank goodness. I figured out how to put him back together, but the only reason he survived at all was because he was so resilient. It should have broken him, but it didn't. Problem was, I couldn't fix everything. A lot of the framework was still there."

"Meaning?"

"His brain is especially vulnerable to being hacked," the captain said.

"What? And yet you kept that...that *liability* around?"

"He's not a liability, Shade. He's a human being. And a member of my crew."

"Former crewman," Shade corrected. "He quit, remember?"

"To be fair, that was under duress," the captain said curtly. "Something you need to understand, the Collective didn't just take Jackson over. Whatever they did changed him. It caused most of the other Gloss pilots to die or go insane, but it had weird side effects with Jackson. Most people can't accept pilot implants at all, and those who do still retain some human inhibitions and frailties that keep them from fully taking advantage of being integrated. With Jackson, this process destroyed those."

"I don't understand."

"He was good before. But whatever they did to him somehow inadvertently broke whatever it is that keeps human beings limited when they're linked. That hack turned him into the best, or rather the scariest, most dangerous pilot I've ever seen. A side effect of getting hacked killed whatever frail bits that keep the rest of us from truly becoming the machine. Jackson got performance out of his mech that was supposed to be impossible."

That made Jane extra sad, because unfortunately Jackson had only reached the pinnacle of his abilities while being forced to destroy his own people. She'd seen the data from the fall of Gloss. Jackson had briefly reached levels of human/machine integration efficiency that even she couldn't comprehend, with response rates that would have been an anomaly even on her super-advanced home world.

"Surely you exaggerate, Captain. I've seen Jackson fly. He's not that special."

"That's because you've never seen him plug in. You've seen him at maybe ten percent of what he's capable of. I've dropped some of the best pilots Earth had to offer into hot LZs and watched them fight with the most advanced mechs, and Jackson makes them look like children having a slap fight."

Jane cut in. "You can't even begin to understand the feeling of power he experienced, but once we got him out, he's walked away and never plugged in since. Jacky resisted that temptation because he knew if his mind was in the machine, machines can get hacked. He said he'd rather die than have that happen again. So I made a promise that I wouldn't let it. When I fixed him, I put in a kill switch, just in case."

"You can't keep your promise from here?" the captain asked her softly.

It was a grim thing. Jane hated even talking about it, she'd especially hated doing it to him, but it was what Jackson had wanted. It was the only way he'd accept being able to go on living after what he'd done. "They broke my link when they damaged his block. I'm guessing they used a direct nanite attack. I can't do anything remotely."

Shade sniffed. "I hate to sound cruel, but I think you're fretting for no good reason. Yes, you made a promise, but it'll only matter for a few hours at most before the biobomb those terrorists put in Jackson's back detonates anyway. He was dead before he ever came back from Swindle."

"Just because I don't know how to defuse that bomb doesn't mean Warlord doesn't. What if he can shut it down? Then we're condemning Jacky to a lifetime of murdering people he wanted to help, against his will! We'd be condemning him to living his own nightmare. I can't do anything remotely, but if you let me go back—"

"Sorry, Jane. Warlord isn't going to be interested in sitting down for a polite conversation. We're persona non grata now."

"You might have missed it, since you were distracted down in your lair," Shade snapped, "but there's a suspicious vessel headed our way."

"From Big Town? I thought their navy was junk?"

"No, Jane, it's from out of system. We can't identify it yet, but it's at least our size," said the captain. "It made the jump in from Nivaas and has been running dark ever since. It could just be going to Big Town to trade, but my gut is telling me Warlord called in some outside help to run us off because he doesn't like how we're tailing his orbital. If he's grabbed Tui also, then he sure as hell isn't buying our story about parking here because we're doing repairs."

"He's not going to let our *ship* that close," Jane said. "But I don't need the ship."

"What, you're going to think happy moonbeams at him?"

"Bushey has a plan."

"Bushey?" the captain asked. "No offense to my new security chief, but he's not exactly a master strategist. He's a good noncom but I didn't hire him for his imagination."

Jane hadn't known about the incoming mystery ship when they'd come up with this idea, but that complication didn't change anything for what she intended to do. "The *Tar Heel* is just our launch point. Katze is willing to go too. It would just be the three of us. If I can get to Big Town, all I need to do is get with a hundred meters or so of Jackson, and I should be able to sneak one of my bots in line of sight, then I can fix his block...or activate the kill switch...If I have to."

"Big Town will pick up the striker," the captain said.

"We aren't planning on using the striker. We can get a lot smaller than that."

The captain's eyebrows rose, and then he must have figured out her intent because he said, "Pods won't work."

"It's the only way. Each of us goes into one of the pods. Then you shoot us out of the missile tubes."

"What in the world are you talking about?" Shade asked.

"We've got a handful of old Amonite stealth pods," he explained. "They're for covert insertions. The Amonites quit using them because they're so stupidly dangerous flying them toward a target is a great way for the helpless marines inside to get lanced out of space."

"Swindle's orbit is a crowded mess. There's enough debris his radar won't pick us up."

"You'll light up his sensors with your heat signatures. And then it's bang, bang, bang, and all three of you are gone."

"The pods have heat traps and cold exhaust."

"You can't carry enough cold exhaust to close that much distance."

"We worked it out. We're all willing to try." Katze and Bushey had been down on Swindle with Jackson and left him for dead once already. It looked as if they didn't want to do that again.

"Damn it, Jackson..." The captain looked up at the ceiling and said to himself, "One more trip. All I needed was one more trip."

"There are daily shipments between the farm orbitals and Big Town. We'll hide next to one. I'll bring my bot squad. Big Town's security is a joke to me. They'll never even know we're there."

"This has no chance of working," Shade said. "All three of you are going to die. You know that, right?"

Jane shrugged.

The captain sighed. "You quadruple-checked Bushey's numbers?"

"Of course."

Shade looked at him incredulously. "You're actually going to allow this? Are you stuck in rerun? You just did this with two other crew members. And what? We sit around waiting for them, with what's probably a pirate ship bearing down on us and no security team to repel potential boarders?"

It annoyed Jane that their aloof broker who thought she was so much better than the rest of the crew acted as if she knew anything about their jobs. "Even with Tui, Bushey, and Katze out, you'd only be down a quarter of the security people."

"Including the most experienced ones, and my best specter." The captain sighed. "Those numbers aren't exactly helping your case, Jane."

"Please, if I get to Jackson soon enough, I can stop the hack. If we sit here and argue, I might arrive too late. Warlord's using an aggressive tech. I fear bringing Jacky back from this hack would turn him into a vegetable. I've got to get to him before that happens."

"And if you get there too late?"

She didn't reply. He already knew the answer to that one. Jacky was a good, kindhearted man. She couldn't let him be a tool for evil. She'd promised. "What would you do, Captain?"

"He'd be a berserker. A slave warrior that doesn't stop until he's killed." The captain looked at her earnestly, not wanting to trade three lives in the off chance of saving two. "You know what I would do. I just wish I'd been strong enough to pull the plug myself yesterday, but I thought maybe, just maybe, if anybody could pull this off, it was Jackson. It's why I was dumb enough to let Tui talk me into letting him go too."

"We have a chance if we don't dither," Jane said.

"How are you going to exfil?"

"Same way we got in."

"That's no good. The *Tar Heel* might not be here when you get done. If that's a real warship, we'll have to cut and run."

"I'll figure something out," Jane said and waited. She knew Jacky was like a son to him, even if he was a bit gruff about it. He had to know this was the only way.

Say what you will about the captain, but when it came time to make a decision he wasn't the hesitating sort. "Okay. Get the tubes loaded."

"They already are," Jane said.

Shade looked at the ceiling. "Lord above," she said in disgust.

✧　　✧　　✧

Jackson felt like his skull had been run over by a truck.

"Tui?" Even with his healing mods, Tui was still in really bad shape. Fain's men had come in, put Tui back in the chair, added more restraints, and then really worked him over. They were alone again for now.

"Yeah, brother?" he said gruffly.

"You ready for a night on the town?"

"Hell yeah."

They both rested a bit, their heads hanging.

Jackson was fading in and out of consciousness. There were his thoughts, and then there were other thoughts. Those were still fuzzy, indistinct, but were growing increasingly loud. Every time his heart beat, agony pulsed through his brain. The pain was designed to wear down his concentration, to make it easier for the virus to claim him.

"Fifi?" But Jackson couldn't see her anywhere. "Fifi."

"I think Fifi's gone to the big robot party in the sky." Tui motioned with his chin.

Jackson followed the direction and saw her. Fifi's exterior was made of a carbon titanium mix. An armored exoskeleton worthy of the gods. But she had ports for eyes and lances and appendages, which were weak points in her armor. Openings. And someone had taken a thin metal stake and driven it into one of them, nailing her to the floor.

"So long, brave soldier."

"We'll get another chance," Tui assured him.

"Yeah," Jackson agreed, and then felt the itch move position in his brain. That wasn't good. He looked at his timer. Just a little over seven hours until spine melt. It was a race between bad ends.

"Have the nanites breached you?"

"Not yet," Jackson assured him. "But I've got a bit of an itch inside my skull, toward the back and to the left."

"Like some tiny bug crawling around in there?"

"Yeah."

"Not good."

"Better than torture, I suppose," Jackson said.

"Not by a long shot. I can handle this. You stay focused, man. You stay with me, you hear?"

"Sure, Tui. No problem."

"It can be reversed, right? Happened to you before. We can fix it again."

"You know what became of all the other hacked pilots on Gloss? Dead. Only one other made it off planet. I heard they never could regrow all his brain back. All day long he was seeing ghosts and swarms of flies. He eventually ran off, disappeared out into the desert. Never seen again."

They sat in silence for a few moments.

"I'm sorry," Jackson said. "I drew you into this cluster."

"You didn't draw me in. I came willingly."

Frustration roiled around Jackson's mind. What else could he have done?

"Sometimes life deals you a rotten hand. And then another. And then another. And another. You just play them the best you can." Even in his sorry state, Tui was more worried about others than himself.

"Yeah." And then the itch inside Jackson's head moved again, then stabbed him with a sharp pain. A new, different kind of pain. That couldn't be a good sign. A minute or so later the pain subsided, and Jackson took some large breaths to calm himself. He didn't remember pain like that the last time.

Doctor Tiny Ears came back, now wearing a bandage on his head. Jackson pretended to be further along than he really was, hoping to be released from his bonds so he could pound the man's face into the edge of the table and finish what Tui had started, but Tiny Ears wasn't fooled. His sensors knew Jackson's brain readouts.

As the minutes clicked by, more stabs came and went.

If only LaDue had believed him. She should have given him the freedom to run this operation. She shouldn't have sent him to the Lucky Monk. That was surely what had done them in. But how could she have known? What evidence did she possess at the time that could have convinced her, especially when she had the lives of her cell at stake?

Jackson wondered about the captain, Jane, and the others. He couldn't blame them for leaving him. Nobody was coming to rescue him. This was a job, not a suicide pact. He wondered what job Shade had lined up for them next. Right now, he suspected they were all in the mess hall eating another celebratory meal, talking about the money they'd earned and what they would do with it. Then they'd raise a glass in memory of him and Tui. Hopefully, they were on their way to the gate. Heck, maybe they'd gotten lucky and had already traveled through, never to look back.

They'd been a great bunch of shipmates. Couldn't have asked for better. Though he really should have gotten a date with Jane. Just one. Deep down, he suspected she was the one.

He calmed his mind. Told himself it wasn't over until it was over. Maybe he'd get a chance.

If it came, it came. If it didn't, it didn't. The only thing he could do was wait and watch.

The itch and stabs began to give way to echoes of heightened alertness and euphoria, and he knew his window was closing.

In his stateroom, Captain Nicholas Holloway looked over the readouts for radar, infrared, electromagnetic, and other signatures. The mystery ship was still on an intercept trajectory. Jane and her crew were nowhere to be seen, but he knew they were there, three stealth pods, hurtling toward Big Town. The heat sinks in the pods had done their job, and now the signatures were gone. Winked out, one by one.

Shade said, "You've sent them to their deaths."

He had called Shade back in for a private conversation. It was time to settle a few matters. But her assessment wasn't wrong. It was possible one or more of the pods could collide with a piece of space junk. At their speed even a tiny particle could punch through the exterior, through the person, then sail on out the back side. There would be a shock wave. A gaping hole. And death. If the three of them avoided that, then they still had Warlord and all of the Big Town Guard to deal with.

"Don't underestimate Jane," the captain said. "That girl's more capable than you can imagine."

Shade snorted derisively.

He wanted to tell her that Jane wasn't just some little orphan stowaway whom he had decided to keep around out of pity. He would have loved to rub it in Shade's face that Jane had been designed from the ground up to be the perfect combat controller, simultaneously running as many bots and programs as a team of normal specters could, by herself. Or that Jane had escaped from the clutches of the most technologically advanced society in human history and fled their isolationist planet where scientists routinely played god with the peoples' DNA. He was one of the few outsiders who had ever landed on Savat, and he'd seen things there that had blown his mind, like experimental quantum nanotech with capabilities bordering on black magic.

But of course, he couldn't tell Shade any of that, because she'd probably sell Jane out to make a buck. So instead he said, "They could use some backup."

"You'd need a real fleet to get past those defensive pickets."

"Don't you have friends?"

"No."

She was being stubborn. She had friends everywhere. Sometimes very big and dangerous ones. Hell, half the time he didn't know if she had really gotten jobs for the *Tar Heel* herself, or if she was just using them as a pawn on behalf of some shadowy master. Part of their very lucrative arrangement was that he never asked, and in exchange, she never got them jobs that would require him to violate his code. The deal had worked well for both of them, up until now.

He sat on one side of the desk, she on the other. Only he was on the side that had to make the hard decisions.

"Jackson was right, wasn't he? We never should have supplied Big Town."

"Maybe. You think I know everything? You think they tell me everything?"

"Who is *they?*"

Shade frowned. "You know I can't tell you that. Besides that, you don't want to know."

"Or what? Whatever superpower you're really working for has me killed because I know too much?"

"I was going to say the less you know, the less you could be forced to testify about in court without perjuring yourself, though to be fair, my employers are the type that if they decided that you were too much of a security risk, they would arrange for you to accidentally drown in that Earth pond you're so proud of."

"Is that a threat?"

"No. It's a choice."

"That's not very nice, Shade. Also, not very surprising... but certainly not nice."

Shade exhaled. "Look, I don't like this either. We had a good thing going, Captain. You like helping the helpless. Usually our goals coincide. Regardless of the law and the public proclamations, we both know sometimes governments need a little dissent, or one of their rivals' dissidents to have teeth, or some colonists to not be pushovers. It's all about the balance of power. They say one thing while doing another. It's just politics."

"It's politics to you, but it's my crew. Right now, of the hundred souls I'm responsible for, I'm down two, with three more risking their lives, all because you guys have a nice little cold war to maintain, and whoever you really answer to wants their warlord well-armed, albeit in a deniable way."

"He's not theirs, but the galaxy is a complex place, Captain."

He gave her an incredulous look. "It seems pretty straightforward to me."

"That attitude is what got you kicked out of the navy."

"Pretty much." He shrugged. "This could be the moment Swindle changes hands. And when your friends find out it was my crew who initiated it, they'll be looking at you, Shade, wondering why their secret agent didn't give them a heads-up."

He could see the wheels turning in her brain, calculating the multitude of angles. "We agreed not to interfere with the business of our clients."

"Seems to me, Warlord stopped being our client a few hours ago. He's taken up position as the enemy. Call your friends."

"They won't risk it."

"Call them."

"And tell them what? That you want to meddle in affairs beyond your understanding, and upset their delicate balance of power? This is bigger than us, your crew, or your ego. If you put a dent in the CX supply, powerful men will take it personally. They will ruin you. That retirement you've been dreaming of? Gone. You'll work the darkest edge of space for the rest of your days."

"Yeah, yeah, I get it. My name will be mud." Shade didn't grasp most Earth sayings, but context would give her that one. "I've made my choice. I just regret I didn't make it sooner."

Shade was clearly so frustrated she was having a hard time maintaining her usual composure. "This is bigger than me, than you, than your precious crew. This is about maintaining the delicate balance of power. The people I work for are trying to prevent war."

"Look around, Shade. They're not doing a supergood job."

"This is *nothing*. Losing a few lives on some ghetto orbital is just the cost of doing business. This is a blip. My superiors are concerned about the safety of billions of lives scattered across thirty worlds. There are three superpowers eyeing this system, because they know whoever controls the gates, controls mankind. What happens when one of the great alliances feels threatened? Or backed into a corner? Do you have any idea how hard it is to keep a bunch of greedy, ambitious politicians from accidentally killing us all? The people I work for try to keep the balance, not just here, but everywhere."

"Then you might as well warn them a fight's brewing so they can adjust their plans. Now make that call or get off my ship."

"Am I getting off the fast way, or the slow way?"

"That would be your decision now, wouldn't it?"

The broker closed her eyes and gave him a bitter sigh. "Very well."

"Dismissed."

Shade was obviously furious, but she left to call her superiors. He figured she would spin matters to make her look innocent, and that he was out of control, but those were the risks you took when you got into bed with these Other Governmental Agency types. Oh well. He had needed the money. Starships weren't cheap.

"Castillo, Hilker," he pinged his XO and the ship's cargomaster. He waited until he got confirmations that both were listening. "That bogey is closing and I don't particularly feel like moving."

"*We gunning up, Cap?*" Castillo asked.

"Break out the good stuff, gentlemen. Let's get this lady ready for a fight."

CHAPTER 32

Inside the pod, Jane checked her monitors. The systems were all green. Their course and speed were good, leading them toward one of the orbital farms at an oblique angle. It would take a few hours before they'd be able to catch a ride into Big Town.

That was if they even made it that far.

The pods were uncomfortably tight, even for Jane, who wasn't very big. She couldn't imagine how claustrophobic it had to be for poor Bushey, who was a large fellow. You had to lie flat, your hands in front of you, with almost no room to bend or stretch. And the pods smelled old. The air was too sharp and had a faint tinge of rubber.

They didn't have much cargo area but all of it was full. Bushey carried various explosives. Katze had her guns. And Jane had brought her little platoon of warriors. If they made it to Big Town, and that was a pretty good-sized if, at least they would be ready for anything.

She'd been looking at the readouts she'd received from Jacky's brain and the sensors she'd placed there to gage any growth in his old controls. Whatever the Warlord had introduced was growing at an alarming rate. Normally such things would take two weeks. But this, well, it might finish before they even arrived. If that happened, it was going to make her task much harder.

The three pods sped silently along, separated by only a few kilometers. "Status," she asked over her short-range net.

"*Green,*" Bushey said.

"*Green,*" Katze said.

"Good. Let's run through the plan again."

Katze groaned, but they all brought up the view of the orbitals on their displays and walked through the plan, each narrating their parts and the various contingencies. And when they finished, they walked through it again.

When they completed the second walkthrough, Bushey said, "*After we rescue Chief's ass, I'm going to kick it up and down Big Town. Eleven klicks one way, eleven klicks back. Then I'm going swimming in that pool.*"

"*Good luck with that,*" Katze said. "*Did you bring a suit?*"

"*Suit? I'm going au naturale. You coming with?*"

"*Um, I think I'll do a few holes of Swindle golf,*" Katze said. "*On the ninth hole I think you get to putt from the back of a caliban.*"

"*Swimming, golf, barbeque. It's a party.*"

"*This is kind of a special treat for me, Specter,*" Katze said, changing the subject. "*These pods were built on my home planet.*"

Jane already knew that, but she said, "Oh, that's nice."

"*Yeah. And we quit using them like thirty years ago because the ride sucks.*"

Bushey laughed. "*I always wondered how you people were crazy enough to try and ninja aboard ships like this. So I figured what the hell, let's try it.*"

"*It wasn't a bad idea... Not a good one either. But not all bad.*"

"*Well, I owe Tui big time. He's saved my life more times than I can count. After this? We're square.*"

Jane had never been one for banter. She lived inside her own head far too much for that. Oddly enough, her best conversations were usually with Jackson over comms while he was working and she was on the ship. "You two should sleep. I'll keep watch for the first cycle."

Once they were quiet, she brought up the images of the agriculture orbitals and the schedules of shipments, looking for anything they'd missed, crowded into a pod, her weapon pressing into her back, her little platoon of warriors silently sleeping around her.

She ran Jacky's numbers again and hoped her projections of the wetware growth were wrong.

✧   ✧   ✧

Sentinel Seventy-Nine suddenly registered a blip on its radar. Then three blips. Then two. Two small objects moving fast. The sentinel calculated the direction and speed of the objects and determined they were on a course that would take them very close to Big Town, which automatically triggered a level-one alarm.

And then the blips vanished.

The sentinel went through its automated routines trying to reacquire the objects but failed. The objects could be echoes or potential stealth objects, but they were more likely garbage jettisoned from a ship, or the uncatalogued remains of an old satellite, but any of those could endanger the delicate farms. The automatic routine kicked the alarm up a point, and this triggered a message to be sent to the other two sentinels in that grid.

All three sentinels searched. One acquired an object, then lost it. However, a second sighting meant they weren't echoes. There was at least one unidentified object, and so another workflow was triggered. This time a message was sent to a human.

A light blinked on one of the monitoring displays of the security station on the Little Leon asteroid. The security tech on watch was bored and tired. She'd been up for twenty hours, half of which had been outside, repairing a communications antenna and wrestling with a tether that would not stay put and kept getting tangled. She'd come back in, exhausted, but it was her watch, and she wasn't going to beg for help from the others. To keep herself from falling totally asleep, she'd been watching the news about the wing race coming up on Big Town.

The one pundit was such an idiot. The tech leaned back in her chair, shook her head at the nonsense coming out of the pundit's mouth, and then saw the blinking alert light. She read the alert, but knew it was probably nothing. Still, it wouldn't hurt to send a bot to take a closer look.

Jane and the others had slipped well into Big Town's territorial space. By this point they were all wide awake, alert, and watching their displays. Making such a crossing was illegal, and while stealth pods were normally used for smuggling, they could also be one hell of a weapon. One filled with rocks and sent at this velocity could mess up a fragile orbital. So whether it was criminal enterprise or war, Big Town would be perfectly within their rights to incinerate them. But Warlord would have to find them first, and Jane didn't think that would happen, not just yet.

And then Bushey came over the net.

"I've got a problem."

Jane searched her scanners for a bogey but didn't see anything. Had he heard something over the communication channels they'd been monitoring that she hadn't? "What is it?"

"Something's wrong with my second heat sink."

"Flux reading?" Jane asked.

"It's leaking. I'm at forty Celsius right now. No. Wait. Forty-one."

"That's balmy beach weather," Jane said, but silently cursed to herself. "Think of palm trees."

"Forty-three, forty-four." Bushey was usually such a clown, that him sounding calm somehow made things worse. There would be no stealth if they couldn't keep their exteriors cold. Heat shone like a lightbulb on infrared scanners in space.

"We're still a long way from our destination." The pods' heat sinks were the only thing keeping them from being detected. Waste heat would make them glow like a beacon in the coldness of space. But if the pod temperature got too high for too long, it would cook its passenger. "Hold on, maybe it will stabilize."

A beat passed.

"Internal temperature in the pod is now at forty-six."

"Have you tried shunting it into the third sink?" Katze asked.

"Tried. No go," Bushey replied. *"Tried sealing. That didn't work either."*

They waited.

"Forty-six," he said.

"There you go," Jane said.

Another beat.

"Whoa. Fifty. Fifty-four. You know I'm the one carrying the explosives, right?"

If he jettisoned that heat sink, it would show up on every sensor from here to Big Town. But if he didn't, Bushey himself would show up as one big firework. Probably shortly after he roasted to death.

"Seventy. Who inspected this damn pod?" Bushey asked.

"Chief Hilker's guy, Roderick Su."

"Well, then he didn't sabotage it on purpose because I still owe him money from poker night. Nevertheless, it's getting mighty painful in here."

Jane flipped over to the diagnostic tab for Bushey's pod. She could see the failed component, but it was a hardware issue, not a software problem. There was nothing she could do from here. Bushey was in a suit, which would help resist the temperature swings, but not for that long. He'd be steamed like a dumpling.

"Get rid of it," Jane ordered. "Jettison the heat."

"That'll endanger both of you and the mission. Hang on, Specter. I'll be fine."

More time passed. Bushey quit giving them temperature updates, though Jane could see them still climbing on her display. It had to be like an oven in there. He was risking his life to protect them.

"Bushey? You still there?" Katze asked nervously.

There was no response. He was too stubborn and had probably passed out from heat exhaustion. Jane might not be able to fix the problem, but she could order the pod to jettison its heat. "Bushey, if you can hear me, hang on."

The words came back slurred. *"No. Don't risk it. I'm fine."*

"No, you're not." A moment later a bright white signature appeared on her scanner. It traveled forward at the same speed they did, then sped away at a perpendicular angle. "And there goes our nice little space flare for everyone to see."

The internal temp in Bushey's pod dropped dramatically, but she knew the Warlord's sentinels would zoom in on the sink and try to diagnose what it was. Within seconds they would compute likely scenarios for how it had gotten there, one of which would be accurate. The AIs would then start a search pattern for whatever had jettisoned it. So a course correction was in order. If she could get far enough away, they just might avoid detection.

"Course change," she said. "Yaw three right. Vector 45. Then resume."

When Bushey didn't immediately respond, she set the new course for him. The three pods used cold exhaust to alter their direction of travel.

Katze said, *"Quadrant five. Something coming our way."*

Jane switched. And there was the signature of an interceptor bot. "Where did you come from?"

"It just appeared."

"How could it just appear? It would have needed to launch and accelerate."

"*Not if it has been shadowing our path for a while. Waiting for us to reveal ourselves.*"

How could it have known their trajectory? The surface of the pods was made of a special material that didn't reflect light. That made hardly any signature at all. Someone must have made them a while ago.

"*It's coming in hot,*" Katze warned.

"Deploying countermeasures." Jane triggered the routine. A small amount of excess heat was shunted into several rods on the outer shell. Then those were flung in different directions.

"*Interceptor firing.*"

Jane watched the missile launch on her display. Six bright lines streaking through space. They were hundreds of kilometers away, but that wasn't very far at these speeds.

"*So what did I miss?*" Bushey asked, sounding groggy. Then he must have seen the missiles. "*Oh, shanks.*"

Seconds ticked by. It was now a game of hoping the interceptor hadn't acquired the inner pods.

"*They're not taking the bait,*" Bushey said. "*I was trying to take one for the team. You should have let me go.*"

"*Leaving someone behind is what got us in this mess to begin with,*" Katze said.

"Wait." The missiles proceeded on the same line. One that would lead them right to the three pods. "Wait," Jane said again, even though there was really nothing else they could do.

And then the decoy rods fired their hot thrusters. Suddenly the missiles veered away, following the bogus pods. Jane held her breath, waiting for the interceptor to shoot more. But nothing came.

The decoys accelerated and began evasive maneuvers. Normal pods wouldn't have that, but these were souped-up smuggling pods. And smugglers needed to outrun their pursuit.

One missile exploded before impact. But two others found their marks. The third decoy raced away into space, a missile hot on its tail. The other two missiles turned to join the fray. Jane was impressed with the last pod, but it ran out of fuel. A few minutes later, it was struck as well.

"*How did you know that would work?*" Bushey asked.

"They're using the missile design we smuggled them on the last trip," Jane said, feeling a little proud of herself. "I know exactly what they're programmed to look for and what they wouldn't be able to resist."

"What if they'd been using some other design?"

"Then that would have been unfortunate for us."

"Well, that gives me all sorts of confidence," Bushey said.

"We should go dark," Jane suggested. Not because she was worried about Big Town's weak sensor net picking up their close-range comms, but because she really didn't want to talk right then. That had been too close and Jane didn't want them to hear the fear in her voice.

The interceptor was moving toward the debris, so it could gather them for further analysis. All the while, Janey, Bushey, and Katze silently sped toward the orbitals.

If they'd had windows, Swindle would be directly below them. The display was breathtaking, but probably nothing compared to the real view. Jane was okay with that though. The world made more sense when viewed electronically. She sent the command for the pods to decelerate and alter course again. It was time to stow away on something heading for Big Town.

There was a dropship heading for Swindle. Gremlins were moving three other transports around the farm. Another waiting to dock. One leaving.

And that's when Jane saw the security ships and interceptor bots. They were everywhere. Especially around the agricultural orbitals. The missile strike on the mystery craft had raised some alarms.

"Somebody's stirred up the anthill," Bushey said. *"There's no way we're getting on a food transport now."*

"No." Jane was looking for something else. Not plan B or C, but plan D. And then she spotted something that would work. "There. Ten o'clock. Negative three. Bearing away."

It was a garbage truck. Basically a simple bot that roamed around picking up trash. Nothing so deadly in space as trash. The drones kept the area around the orbitals clear, mostly by redirecting junk on a trajectory where it would burn up in the atmosphere, but they also had a bay for stowing anything that was of interest or potentially valuable. Best of all, the simple drone's firewalls were made of cheese.

Opportunity favors the prepared, was something the captain liked to say, but it was a concept Jane lived by.

Long ago, she'd made it her practice to run a series of specific routines every time she gained access to any system. It didn't matter how small. It didn't matter where. Because of this she'd amassed security IDs from thousands of people on multiple worlds. She had mined hundreds of systems. Much of it was aged but data was data.

Jane hadn't been able to break into all of Warlord's systems, but the security had been lax on a few, so she'd cracked them while they'd been docked out of habit. Now she brought up the Big Town records and searched for sanitation workers. There were two hundred. She narrowed the list down to five who were listed as technicians, then selected one named Atticus Wall, simply because she liked the name. It took her less than thirty seconds to use Wall's manual override codes to have the truck maneuvering in their direction. Climbing all over its hull were trash monkeys, meter-long bots with multiple arms that worked tirelessly to spot and then steer garbage into the truck's maw.

"Okay, our pods are now interesting space junk to be collected." Jane checked to make sure her suit was good and all her equipment was still buckled on. It was difficult because there was so little room to move.

This part was unnerving. Space walking scared the hell out of her. The captain had taught her the mandatory minimum to be a member of his crew, and Jackson had coached her a lot, but Jane had never taken to it. She preferred to stay in the safety of her lair, and let her bots do the physical stuff.

"Get ready. Check your hatch."

"*Ready,*" Katze said.

"*It's stuck!*" Bushey grunted in exertion. "*The damn hatch—I'm going to kill whoever purchased this stinking piece of Hana— Going to manual.*"

The garbage truck came closer. Closer. Jane's display showed two pods green, one red.

"Bushey, get moving. Three, two, one. Go!" Jane opened the pod.

Bailing out was white-knuckle terror. Nothing was as frightening as the vast eternal black before her. Then she was out of the pod and flying toward the truck, going unbelievably fast. But speed was relative, because so was the garbage truck, matching them, as per her commands. She tried to remember what Jackson had shown her, but the suit was programmed for this. She just needed to relax and let it do its job.

Jane zipped across space, pouches full of bots, tailed by her menagerie of bigger bots who wouldn't fit in a pocket. The suit told her when she was in range and when to fire the grapple to latch on. If she missed, she'd pass the truck and float off into space. Having not done the error calcs in advance she wasn't sure how long it would take her to die, whether she'd hit atmo first or run out of air...Probably atmo, because Big Town was in a relatively low orbit.

The suit pinged. Janed fired. The grapple shot out...hit, and stuck. Jane breathed again, and slowly began reeling herself in. She finally reached the truck. Sticking her gloves onto the flat metal surface made her feel a whole lot better. It was a little bit of solid in that whole lot of nothing.

Moments later Katze swung up smoothly next to her. She had been doing space work since she was a kid, and made it look effortless. There was a giant grin on the other side of her faceplate. "I love this stuff." They were close enough for their helmet comms to link, so it was almost like having a normal conversation. "That was fun."

"Not even a little bit," Jane replied.

Bushey was nowhere to be seen. Jane located his pod, but it was already past the ideal release point. "Bushey, you're running out of time!"

Suddenly, the side of his pod opened, and Bushey rolled out. He did the calculations, then had to risk a quick flash of his thrusters to close the distance. The truck dispatched a garbage monkey toward him, but when it came close, Bushey batted it away, then kicked it, and moved on. A few seconds later, he joined them, and stuck to the side.

"The hatch holding most of my gear—it was stuck. I don't know. Maybe the heat fried the locking mechanism. I have no idea."

"So you're unarmed?" Katze had weapons strapped all over her body.

"Of course not, but I lost the big stuff."

That pod full of evidence was still speeding along toward Big Town. So Jane sent it on a sharp course down toward the planet. Hopefully it would burn up before security could intercept it.

"Let's hope you weren't seen by anything other than that monkey. Let's get inside."

Jane had never seen a garbage drone that didn't have a hatch for manual override or human control. Systems like this always had built in redundancy. This one was on the bottom. Jane opened it. Katze slipped in. Then Bushey. Jane waited for all her bots to scurry through, then followed and began to close the door behind her.

Just before she shut it, a sleek security ship zoomed past, lights blazing.

"Not as clean as I hoped, but we've made it this far." Jane closed the hatch behind her. "Now let's get this thing to Big Town before garbage control goes nuts."

CHAPTER 33

Bushey got behind the very rudimentary controls, looked over the display, then said, "This baby is half full of junk and plenty of fuel. Where are we going? Back to the docks?"

"That might draw attention. We might have already tripped an alarm by me logging in." She pulled up a map of Big Town in her eye, found a spot that looked good and shared it with Bushey over her net. "Head toward this exterior maintenance door."

Bushey punched in their new destination. The computer prompted him for a reason code. He selected, *exterior scrap pickup.*

The onboard computer accepted that and changed direction. Garbage trucks weren't made to transport humans, which became abundantly clear when this one engaged its thrusters so suddenly that it threw Jane and Katze back against Bushey and pressed them all against the wall.

"Two dames at once? I think I might pass out from joy. Unfortunately, I need to fly this thing. Can you two contain yourselves?"

"In your dreams," Katze said, as her suit compensated for the Gs enough to move, and Bushey manned the controls.

Between the three of them and the tiny bot army, it was almost as cramped as being in the stealth pod. Jane was used to her murderous menagerie, but the close presence of so many super-dangerous little bots was obviously making the other two uncomfortable. Jane sent a quiet command for all of them to squish to the sides as much as possible.

"Why's that teddy bear staring at me like that?" Bushey asked nervously.

"That's Ron," Jane explained. Like most of her work, she went for the cute, but scary, aesthetic. Well, the cute was on purpose, but the scary just kind of happened because Jane really didn't understand people that well. Ron was pink and purple, attached to the ceiling, and looking down at Bushey with glowing eyes. "Think of him as a walking submachinegun with diamond saw hands, who is very protective. I don't think he liked you calling me a *dame*."

Bushey slowly nodded. "Duly noted, adorable murder bot. Duly noted."

As they got closer to Big Town, Jane checked the systems she had access to. There was some chatter about the pods, as Big Town Control tried to figure out what was going on in their space, but no flags on their truck yet.

The truck slowed and began to thrust left to match the orbital's roll. They continued forward, flying over the exterior which bristled with modules and antenna. Big Town was constantly being added onto. They flew around some new construction and passed over a small crew of workers in blue and yellow suits and exos, clinging to a sea of small bars that covered the surface. But one of them was tethered, floating a few meters out for some reason, right in the truck's path.

Bushey swore. The truck swerved. The worker flared his thrusters to try and get out of their way. Jane didn't feel the thump of a collision but checked the rear camera to be sure. They'd barely missed the guy. He raised his hand and flipped them off.

"I think that means have a good day," Bushey said.

"And may your whole house be blessed," Katze said.

Jane fully expected they would have to kill somebody before the day was over, but she was glad they hadn't started by running down an innocent worker. They sped away from the work crew until they vanished around the curve. The maintenance hatch was just ahead.

Their suits were color-change capable. Jane pulled up the menu and found a close match to the blue and yellow pattern of the work crew. "Switch to this. If we're seen it might buy us some more time."

The truck decelerated as they reached their destination. Katze went out first, then Bushey. They each hung onto some handles on the belly of the truck, dark shadows drifting a bit in the weightless environment. Jane found a handle for herself, swung out, did a bot headcount to make sure she had them all, then shut the hatch behind her.

"Straight ahead," Katze said. "Disengage in three, two, one."

They pushed off, then used their thrusters to make a soft landing with the orbital's spin. This was a much easier jump than the one they'd just made, so it didn't frazzle Jane's nerves too much more. The garbage truck would continue on, searching for debris.

"Bogey ahead," Katze warned.

It was a simple, cheap security bot. Vaguely insect shaped, probably on a routine patrol around the orbital's exterior. If it saw them, it would report them.

Jane was already on it. "Go," she ordered Rene.

Her bot blasted off.

Before the security drone could react, Rene sped in a lightning-quick jig pattern, came around the robot's backside, and landed on its gun arm. Rene was one of Jane's originals, modeled on the Jewel Wasp that injected venom into a cockroach's brain, took it over, laid its eggs, and then sealed it in its burrow, leaving a handy feast for when its babies woke up.

Rene stung the robot's "nervous system," injecting a horde of Jane's favorite viruses. It immediately cut communications and killed the gun. A few seconds later, the viruses found the motor controls. The security robot's magnetic feet released, and it drifted out into space, twitching. Rene jumped off and flew back to Jane, automatically going into a holding pattern to watch for more threats.

Now that she had let it go back to its normal routine, the garbage truck would gather up the "malfunctioning" bot, but by the time anyone realized what had happened to it, they could be long gone.

The three of them reached the hatch. It used a basic identification protocol, but the Atticus Wall ID got them right in. She sure hoped that worker had a good alibi, because she'd hate for Warlord to execute the poor fellow as a collaborator by mistake. Jane sent two small probe bots inside to scout. The airlock was clear.

"Back to Big Town," Bushey said. "Let's go rescue Tui and Jackson."

"Just a second," Jane frowned as she listened to the probes. Now that they were in range, she was getting reports from the bots she'd left behind. She had Fifi's last location at the governor's mansion, but her signal had gone dead. That sucked. Fifi had been one of Jane's favorite bots, which was why she'd given her to Jackson, who was one of her favorite humans. But Baby, who she had given to Tui, was two kilometers away, and had been assigned to tail someone. Baby sent Jane a quick recap of events.

"What is it?" Katze asked.

"Those dirty Originals were all set to help Jackson steal the mech. They had some sort of distraction in place to lure away the guard, but now they're in hiding."

"There's only three of us against all of Warlord's men," Bushey muttered. "I wouldn't turn down their help."

Jane was feeling righteously angry. These people had stuck a bomb in her friend's back to coerce him into doing this ridiculous job, and it was their fault he'd gotten captured. "Oh, the Originals are going to help us, whether they like it or not."

Jackson was starting to have revelations. That probably wasn't the right word, but that's how the instructions came. Like an unfolding before your eyes. Sudden knowledge blossoming in your mind, accompanied by an exhilaration that felt like a little breeze stirring the soul.

He came back to reality, still tied to the chair, machines humming in the background. His timer was at 2:49.

Tui was still there, but so was Fain, and he was zapping Tui with some kind of shocker. Between electrocutions, he would shout questions. Who was their contact? What was their plan? When did the Originals hire the *Tar Heel*? Are you supplying them with weapons? That sort of thing. But Tui was a rock, the unmovable object. He met the shocks with gritted teeth and the questions with silence.

Jackson couldn't do anything to help Tui, because he was busy drowning, and trying to keep himself above water. When he'd been recovering from the last hack, he'd had to learn how to meditate. It was one of the protocols Jane had taught him to help rewire his brain. Except meditation couldn't fight a swarm of nanites physically manipulating the electrical impulses in his mind. It was like trying to use wind erosion to counter someone laying an asphalt road. He could feel the wetware pinging his various systems, testing to make sure the feedback channels were right. Another hour of this, Jackson thought, and they would turn it on. And this time there would be no Captain or Jane to bring him back.

Not even LaDue's biobomb would do the trick. He'd be serving Warlord long before that clock expired. He thought about those poor fools on the surface fighting for their rights. He thought about Gloss, and how he had slaughtered his people with joy. The Originals wouldn't have a chance. It wouldn't be long now.

Fain stopped shocking Tui. Jackson looked up to see why. Warlord had come back.

"How is it going?" The blood and smell didn't seem to bother him in the least.

"This one hasn't said a thing." Fain gestured in disgust at poor Tui, who was barely conscious. "He's tough. I'll give him that. It might take a few days to wear him down. Deprive him of food, water, sleep, he'll talk eventually."

"Ah, but Fain. You don't have days. We have a wager." He went over to Jackson and studied him for a moment. "It's a shame to do this to you, Jackson. It truly is. We're a rare breed, you and I. If circumstances were different, I think we could have been friends."

Jackson started to tell him off, but strangely enough, the insults wouldn't form. The aggressive wetware didn't just demand obedience, it would not tolerate any disrespect.

Warlord picked up a tablet and went over the readouts from Doctor Tiny Ears. "It appears we should be far enough along, so let us see if the reprogramming is working. Surely, Frans wasn't your contact. I was surprised by his treachery. I always thought he was a good soldier, but he lacked the leadership qualities to run a terrorist cell, especially one as efficient as the rats in Big Town's walls. So tell me, who were you meeting with?"

He tried not to answer. He ordered himself not to talk. But his mouth said, "Ian MacKinnon, bartender at the Lucky Monk," anyway. *Damn it.*

"Alright, you win." Fain sighed and threw down his shock stick in disgust. "I've seen MacKinnon around. He was a big shot back during the gang wars, fits the profile. You want me to pick him up?"

"In a minute. Let me see what else Jackson has to say. Has your captain been conspiring against me?"

"No."

"Who did you meet with in secret on the surface?"

"Some settlers, led by a woman named LaDue." Jackson tried to literally bite his tongue, but the wetware wouldn't allow him to damage the Warlord's property.

"Our scans showed something in your back, what is it?"

"A biobomb, set to detonate in two hours and thirty-eight minutes, unless I take your mech away."

"Ah, so you were coerced into betraying me. A slightly extenuating circumstance, but it does not excuse the enthusiasm you put toward the task." Warlord gave him a sad, patronizing smile. "You should have been honest with me. I would have helped you. I'm disappointed."

Those last two words caused physical agony, as the wetware made him feel terrible shame.

The bomb had gone from being his worst nightmare to his only hope. Now that Warlord was in his head, he didn't want the bomb defused, he wanted it to detonate ASAP. Death was preferable to this.

"Jane couldn't figure out how to shut it down. There's no way your quacks will in time. I'll be dead long before you'll be able to use me."

Warlord laughed, genuinely amused. "You are partially correct. My people probably won't be able to defuse it. However, that won't be necessary. You are used to thinking in terms of what is humane and moral. I don't suffer from such weakness. One must be pragmatic to thrive on Swindle. I'll simply have the device removed with surgical lasers. It will surely detonate in the process, but we will cut out the entire area before its poison spreads too far. Of course, that means slashing out a few of your vertebrae and probably using machines to keep you alive. You'll be paralyzed for life, but you don't need your limbs to fly-by-mind."

That was horrific, but the Warlord's words had a soothing quality to them. The mech could be his body. It was a small sacrifice to make, so that the rest of his days could be spent in glorious service, making Big Town a prosperous, safe place. Jackson knew that was the nanites talking. He tried to force all their lies aside by finding something else to focus on. He found hate. Hate for Warlord, hate for this stupid planet, and hate for everyone who had gotten him into this mess. Which meant hating himself most of all.

That helped a little bit, and, briefly, Jackson could think clearly again. He managed to spit out, "Go to hell."

"That's the best part of living here. To see hell, all I have to do is look down." Warlord looked over the tablet one last time. "It appears the wetware still has some work to do. I'll go ahead and have that spinal surgery prepped for you."

Warlord left the room, while Fain made a call to send a strike team to pick up MacKinnon. Tui was still out. All Jackson could do was try and hold fast.

It wouldn't be long now.

Because Jane had been spoofing everyone's IDs, when they tapped into the Big Town feed, they started receiving all sorts of ads for the identities they'd assumed. Jane's stolen identity must have come from a regular customer at pompom houses, which looked to be places where people practiced some kind of group dancing. She still couldn't access the Big Town Guard's channel but knew that if a bulletin was put out for them, as a citizen, she'd see it. But there was no alert. Just happy rows of dancing people shaking glittery puffs.

Environment suits weren't that out of place here, with all the harvesters traveling to and from the docks in their dirty work clothes. So the team popped their helmets and were counting on Jane's ID swapping to protect them from being picked up on facial recognition. To hide all the longer guns and larger bots, Jane had rented a wheeled cart. Now in blue and yellow, they looked like one of the city's many roving crews.

Big Town was the exact opposite of the isolated town she'd grown up in on the northern coast of Lok. There, everything was immaculate and clean. The streets were straight, the buildings in each neighborhood were all of a specific style. There was order. The very air was scented on a schedule. At night, an army of robots and drones came out to manicure the landscapes, trimming the first signs of wilting leaves and disappearing unwanted insects. Other bots guarded and watched the streets, and the homes. And everyone performed the role they'd been bred for.

Jane much preferred the mess of Big Town.

Baby's signal led them to a four-story apartment building in one of the seedier parts of Big Town. A muscular man sat outside the main on a chair, leaning back against the wall, watching them suspiciously.

"This it?" Bushey asked.

"Baby is upstairs. Top level. Room six." Jane sent two tiny beetle bots to scout around the building. They spotted cameras, more than usual for this part of town, and they weren't linked to the Big Town net, but rather hardwired into the building. Plus they spotted two more thugs waiting at either end of the alley that ran behind the apartment building.

"Remember, the goal is to get these people to launch their planned distraction," Bushey said. "We need their help. We'll try to do this the diplomatic way. So try not to kill anybody."

"And if they don't want to help us?" Katze asked.

"Get me to whoever is in charge. My bots can be very convincing," Jane stated.

"I suppose attaching an angry murderbot to someone is a form of diplomacy." Bushey chuckled. "Okay, stand back a ways, Jane."

"I can handle myself."

"No doubt, but I'd prefer you watching our six and directing that killer-bot swarm of yours. If you get shot here, the mission's toast and we won't be able to get chief out of that compound."

Jane relented and hung back with the cart as the other two approached the door.

The man guarding the door stood, picked up a bat, then walked over to block them, a frown on his face. "No soliciting."

"We've got an appointment upstairs," Katze said.

"You're mistaken."

"We're here for Preacher."

The man obviously knew who they were talking about, and did a terrible job pretending otherwise. "This ain't no church. Nobody here by that name. Now move along." He slapped the bat in his free hand. A nice menacing gesture. "Or else."

"All yours," Bushey said, sounding amused.

Katze walked up to the sneering man.

He tightened his grip on the bat's neck. "It's your funeral, chica."

But Katze simply smiled, moved inhumanly fast, and kicked his knee out from under him. He cried out in pain, sagged to one side, and clutched at his broken leg. The bat clattered to the ground.

"Nap time." Katze struck him in the side of the head, hard enough to knock him out, and picked up the bat. She nodded toward the door. "May I?"

"Feel free," Bushey said.

She turned around, kicked in the door, and strode inside, bat lifted.

"That girl needs to work out some aggression," Jane said.

"She's just been cooped up too long," Bushey replied.

There was an entry hall. Inside were two more toughs, one of whom immediately reached for the pistol stuffed in his waistband. Katze hurled the bat, end over end, and struck him in the head. *Clonk.* The other one rushed her, but the former Marine easily dodged his attack, and put a single well-placed punch to his jaw just below the ear. He went down and smashed a flowerpot. The door began to swing shut, but Katze caught it, and politely held it open for her companions.

"Thank you," Jane said, as she sent two of her beetles zooming up the stairs. She left another outside, taking a bird's eye overwatch position. She left two others guarding their gun cart. Woe be onto any street scum who tried to steal that cart! The rest of her army clambered out and followed her inside.

Her scouts were quick on the scans, and she reported what they'd found. "Lots of the apartments are occupied. Two more armed guards on the stairwell entrances, one at the third floor, last on the fourth. That's as far as they can go without being spotted."

"That'll do." Bushey took the pistol from the dazed man with the fresh dent in his forehead, hid it in one of his pouches, and started up the stairs.

On the third floor, they met a woman with a shotgun, Asian eyes, and straight dark hair. "This is private property," she told Bushey when she saw him climbing. "Turn around."

Bushey raised both open hands, trying to look innocent. "We really need to talk to this Preacher guy."

"You've made a serious mistake," she warned, shouldering her weapon.

"*Choots,*" Jane said over her net. A sister to Fifi sprang from Jane's shoulder. One leap took her to Bushey's head, and then another to fling herself at the woman. Her eyes went wide as Choots landed on her cheek. She tried to bat Choots away, but he was an aggressive model. A little meaner than her sister. She shouted, fell back, flailing wildly.

Bushey appeared to be a little on the dumpy side, but that was an illusion. His mods might be old, but they still worked. As the guard fought Choots, Bushey leapt up the last six stairs and shoulder-checked the woman hard into the wall. He immediately ripped the shotgun from her hands, tossed it to Katze as she bounded past, and then left the poor woman on the floor.

"*Contain, don't mangle,*" Jane instructed Choots.

The last of the guards must have heard the commotion, because footsteps sounded above on the stairs.

Jane turned. A man was there, raising a little subgun in one hand, but Katze surprised him and knocked it aside with the shotgun. Then she grabbed him by the back of the head, slammed his face into her knee, and sent him careening back down the stairs. Jane had to flatten herself against the wall to keep from getting knocked down as he bounced past.

This was as far as her scouts had seen, so Jane sent them speeding ahead, faster than the supersoldiers who were practically flying up the stairs could go. It was a good thing Bushey had asked her to hang back, because her unaugmented legs wouldn't have been able to keep up anyway, and that would have been embarrassing.

Through her beetle's eyes she saw a short, very pale man coming out of apartment six. He raised a gun, but Bushey was already on him. He dodged to the side, as the muzzle flashed, caught the man's wrist, twisted his arm, and threw him face-first on the carpet. Somehow the man pulled a knife, seemingly out of nowhere, but Bushey stomped the knife hand.

The lone bullet that had been fired during their confrontation wound up buried in the wall about twenty centimeters from Katze. Jane's bots recorded the trajectory, and Jane was happy to see that no innocent bystanders were on the other side. That was nice. Jane hated injuring innocent bystanders. Hopefully the sound would have been muffled enough that Big Town security wouldn't be able to triangulate the gunshot.

By the time she arrived at their destination—a little out of breath, she had to admit—Katze had secured the apartment and had the shotgun pointed at the lone human occupant, a very large man whose hands were raised to the surrender position. He matched Baby's recording.

Jane checked for Tui's bot and found that Baby had hidden himself in the ceiling tiles. He obediently dropped down when called.

"Preacher," Jane said. "We're here to pick up Red and Blue."

His eyes narrowed. "I don't know what you're talking about." From the looks of things he had been packing a bag. There were a bunch of files and storage chips thrown in a metal bucket. From the can of lighter fluid, he'd been about to burn the evidence.

"It looks like you're getting ready to get out of town."

"I'm going on vacation. It's a free orbital. Or it used to be."

Back in the stairwell there were shouts and the sound of a number of people mustering a response. Bushey took up position on the door and looked down the hall. Jane's bots told her that there were several bodies moving up the stairs, all of them armed.

"Stand your people down," Jane warned. "We really don't want to hurt them."

"Who are you?" MacKinnon asked suspiciously. His first thought must have been that they were with the Guard, but that obviously wasn't the case.

"You left two of our compatriots out to dry. We've come to collect them. Now call off your men before anyone else gets hurt. You really don't want to see us in fight mode."

MacKinnon nodded toward Katze. "How about she lowers that scatter gat?"

"How about I blow your friggin knee caps off?" Katze responded.

"Hold your horses. I'll tell them. Okay, everybody, relax. Stay where you are. We're going to have a calm, rational discussion in here."

Jane confirmed that he sent that over their comm link, and her bots indicated that the goons had stopped on the stairs. If they started again, they would immediately alert her. "They're holding position," she told Bushey.

MacKinnon was pretty cool, considering that Katze was really convincing in her desire to shoot him. "You're from the *Tar Heel*."

"This isn't a two-way street. You're going to help us get Jackson and Tui back."

"They're in the Warlord's compound. One of the most secure places in the orbital."

"I know where they are."

"Then you know there's no chance of getting in there. Not with just three of you. No matter how good you are."

"But there is a chance when there are people on the inside."

"You have people on the inside?"

"No, but you do. And they're going to help us."

MacKinnon laughed. A big deep rumble. "I don't know who you think I am, but I can't help you."

"You're either the leader of the Originals on this tub, or close enough for my needs." Jane didn't have time for this. "Liesel." A two-centimeter-long bot climbed up on her shoulder. "Grab him."

Liesel shot toward the big man, but he caught her midair. Held her between his thumb and forefinger. Impressive, Jane thought. MacKinnon must have combat mods too, but he really needed his own squad.

"Gang," she ordered. More bots climbed out of her pack and various pockets. "Go." Five bots launched at him simultaneously. He caught Jose. Caught Seth. Batted away Pilgrim. But Bubbles made it through, landed on his neck, and stuck him. He cried out and reached for her, but Bubbles had barbed legs and dug in. She was also designed to inflict pain. When he touched her, she shocked him.

As MacKinnon yanked his hand back, Boris, the last of the five, flanked him, landed behind his left ear, and dug in. Mac-Kinnon had spectacularly quick reflexes. Not many would have been able to catch one of her crew, much less three of them. With his size, he must be hell in a fistfight. Regardless, she had him.

He grunted in pain, then glowered at them. "What is this?"

"A little incentive. Kind of like the awful thing you guys did to Jacky down on the surface."

"That wasn't my decision!"

"It was your tribe, so own it. Boris and Bubbles are now your best friends. If you don't help us, they'll explode. Their charges are shaped. Bubbles will destroy about two inches of your jugular. Boris will blast through your ear canal and savage your brainstem. That would be a really nasty version of a double tap."

MacKinnon winced as Boris adjusted his position. "We have jammers."

"We just walked into your hideout. Do you think your jammers worry me?"

"What you're talking about is nuts. As good as you are, the Warlord has more guns."

"We'll take our chances," Bushey said, never taking his eyes off the hall.

"I still can't help you."

"Well, that would be unfortunate," Jane said. "Because that means you're going to lose your brain and I'll have an annoying delay. Do you really want that? I know you told Jacky you had some sort of distraction in place to pull off the guards while he went for the mech. Now you're going to use that to help us instead."

He paused, thinking. The silence stretched, and then he sighed heavily. "Okay. Tell me what you want."

"You draw off the guard and use your resources to help us get inside. Bubbles and Boris will remain with you until twenty-four hours after the operation is over. Then they will detach themselves and self-destruct. So the quicker we get to work, the quicker the party on your head moves to other ground."

"When?"

Jane hated to rush, and she didn't like depending on amateurs like this either, so that was two more things to dislike about this mission. "Immediately."

"That's impossible."

"Make it possible. If you waste my time, and Jacky's brain gets fried because I wasn't there to save him, Bubbles goes boom."

He let out a slow appreciative whistle. "What we could have accomplished in the Big Town wars if we'd a close-quarters system like yours."

"Oh, you ain't seen nothing yet," said Bushey. "Her little teddy bears will give you nightmares."

"Clock's ticking, big fella," Jane warned. "No funny stuff."

MacKinnon rumbled, "I'm currently disinclined toward levity."

They made their way swiftly through the tunnels beneath Big Town. There had been a forgotten access hatch beneath Mac-Kinnon's apartment building, dating back to the old colony ship.

MacKinnon held up one fist to stop them, listened to something only he could hear, then said, "Quickly, this way."

"What's wrong?" Jane asked.

"Security forces are on their way to my place. My cover is blown."

Bushey snorted. "No great loss. It looked like you were getting out of town anyway."

"Yeah, except I'm missing my ride because I'm here helping you maniacs."

They hustled down several dark corridors, most of which weren't on the schematics that Jane had stolen. This area wasn't just off-limits, it was forgotten.

"This is the only approach that isn't covered. This back door into the compound was our ace up the sleeve. Don't waste it. At our signal the cameras and comms will go out for one minute. That's all I can give you. You'll need to use explosives to breach through, but there shouldn't be anyone on the other side."

"If there are people waiting for us," Jane warned, "Bubbles will go off like a hand grenade."

"Then I really hope my intel is good."

Jane sent her beetles up the corridor ahead to scout and had one follow behind to make sure they weren't being tailed. Her bot squad walked, hopped, or flew along with her, like an adorable murder cloud. As for the crew, they'd all switched their suits to active camo, so they looked like whatever their surroundings were at any given time, twisting colors, mostly dust and rust here. Katze and Bushey both had guns in hand, and not just for Warlord's patrols, but also because they were waiting for MacKinnon to betray them somehow.

"Tell me about your distraction."

"There are a few of us who work at the CX processing plant. They're causing a scene right now. That'll draw off a bunch of the guard."

"Define 'scene.'"

"Sudden walkout strike that should be turning into arson right about now. I've got saboteurs hitting the exterior of the plant to add to the mess." MacKinnon checked his comms. "Right on schedule."

The ID Jane had stolen got an automated warning that all Big Town citizens who were currently off shift should stay away from the section with the processing plant due to *technical difficulties*. So he was probably telling the truth.

MacKinnon removed the side panel of a large duct system and motioned for them to enter. Once they were inside, he closed the panel behind them, then held up his finger for them to be quiet.

There was a grate above them, and voices could be heard. Their guide carefully opened another panel. Jane shone her light into the darkness. It revealed another room that was empty, silent as a tomb. At the far end was a ladder.

Jane's beetles flew in and inspected the room. No hidden cameras. Nothing out of order. She stepped in and moved forward. It was musty smelling.

"This is where we part ways. That hatch is locked. You'll need to blast through."

"On it." Bushey started up the ladder. He'd lost a bunch of his gear with the pod, but still had enough on his person to deal with that.

"The fight at the processing plant has begun. Give my guys about fifteen minutes to draw off as many of the guards as possible." MacKinnon sent her the countdown. "That's when the compounds cameras will go down."

Jane was acutely aware of Jacky's time ticking away, but if they went now, failure was assured. She checked the Big Town news feeds and found live video of smoke rolling down the corridor that led to the processing plant, and then a troop carrier blasted past on its way to the disturbance. The distraction was working, but that left an unknown number of hostiles in the compound.

"I wish you luck," MacKinnon told her. "And I'm not saying that because of these things you left on me. Warlord's reign is a cruel one, so if you get the chance to assassinate him—"

"Oh, don't worry, I will," Katze said as she chamber-checked her autocannon. "That dude gives me the creeps."

"He should. There's more to him than meets the eye though. His story? It's a con."

"What do you mean?" Jane asked.

"I was here during the food riots and the gang wars. He came out of nowhere, kicked all our asses, and made all the factions fall in line. He became our great unifying leader, but I never bought it. He wasn't some imported child soldier who came here to fight caliban. That's a sham. I've watched him for years. Warlord's too smart, too educated, and his mods aren't some third-rate leftover from a bush war. He's a top-tier, elite, highly trained operative. He's not one of us. Never has been. He's a plant, sent here to rule us Big Towners, without us ever even knowing we got conquered."

"By who?" Jane asked.

"Yeah," Bushey said as he carefully applied gel explosives around the hatch. "You got any evidence for that conspiracy theory there, bud?"

"No. I don't. And I don't know who sent him. But I do know he's really, surprisingly hard to kill. Believe me, we've tried. So if you get your shot, take it, but don't be surprised if it don't stick."

Warlord being some kind of secret plant with a fake backstory made sense to Jane, considering Grandma's secret messages.

"Now I've got to go. My people need me. Things are about to get crazy in Big Town. There aren't that many of us left, and after this, they're going to be hunting us down."

"Understand, Mr. MacKinnon. Good luck to you too." Then Jane thought about it for a moment. "Boris, Bubbles, release. Come to momma."

The little bots immediately let go of their captive and flew back to her.

MacKinnon seemed a little surprised. He rubbed the sore spot on his neck. "Thank you."

"Unlike your friend down on the surface, I don't get off on forcing people to do things against their will. Sorry it came to that. Now get out of here."

MacKinnon nodded respectfully toward her.

"Dude, better run before she changes her mind!" Bushey said.

MacKinnon saluted and then hurried from the room.

"I'm surprised you let him go," Katze murmured.

"Honestly, if we make it through this alive, I thought we might need their help to get off this dump. Better to keep the hard feelings to a minimum."

Weapons and bots ready, they waited. The counter was almost up. Bushey signaled for them to put their helmets up to protect their hearing.

Katze looked up at the gel smeared hatch. "You're not going to smoke us all, are you?"

"I am an artist who prides himself on using just enough explosives, but not too much. Okay, actually, that's all I had left." They backed away. Then Bushey brought out his control, held up three fingers and counted down.

CHAPTER 34

A sound brought Jackson back from the brink. The explosion was muffled, but it hadn't been that far away.

Doc Tiny Ears was in the room with them, preparing another syringe full of drug cocktail. He started at the noise and turned toward the door.

"That doesn't sound good," Jackson said. "Tui? You hear that?"

Except Tui was still out, and from the look of things, barely alive. He was too far gone to respond.

A moment later a red frame appeared around all the displays in the room. An automated voice spoke. *"Code seven. Code seven."*

Tiny swore. "Perimeter breach."

There was a rapid series of *thumps*. Jackson knew suppressed gunfire when he heard it. Someone began shouting, but the *thumps* cut whoever it was right off. Were the Originals storming the castle?

More shots rang out. Closer this time. More shouting. The action was clearly moving this way. Tiny ran for his briefcase, popped it open, and withdrew a small handgun. He must have activated his comms. "Fain! What's going on out there?"

Something hit their door. Hard. Every time that door had been opened since Tui had made his escape attempt, Jackson had seen a pair of guards stationed there. One of them started screaming. In pain.

Tiny Ears pointed his gun that way, trembling.

This part of the facility was new construction, not original ship, so the door was like what you'd find in a normal home, plastic and sheet metal. Nothing nearly sturdy enough to stop the next guard as he crashed through it. Tiny screamed and backed into the corner, firing blindly into the hallway.

Tiny stopped shooting when he realized no one was there. Except he was wrong, and he looked down as a two-foot-tall, pastel purple, cartoon-looking bunny rabbit hopped in.

This couldn't be happening. The crew were light-years away by now. It had to be the meds. Some kind of chemical dream state...

Except that rabbit was just too real. Jackson was delirious, but not that delirious. "Jane! I'm in here!"

"What is that thing?" Tiny demanded as he pointed the shaking pistol at the bot.

Jane's voice came through the bot's speakers. *"Jacky, did this man hurt you?"*

"Lots!"

The rabbit's eyes turned red as it leaned forward, revealing the subgun mounted on its back. *BRRRRRRT.*

Bullets stitched Tiny from belt line to forehead. He slid down the wall, painting it red.

One of Jane's little beetle bots zipped into the room, flying from corner to corner, searching for other threats. Once it was clear, Jane walked into the room. "You look like hell."

She looked awesome. Stunning. First-rate. And that wasn't just the drugs and brain damage talking. He'd never been so glad to see anybody in his life.

"You're too late." Jackson knew that. And somewhere in the distance part of him was sad about that.

Jane's attention was split between several tasks at once. From the sound of it, her bot swarm was flying around the compound wreaking havoc. The little rabbit covered the entrance. She paused to check Tui's pulse. "The Chief and Jacky are alive," she reported to someone. Then she hurried to Jackson and put her hands on his head to examine Doc Tiny Ear's work. "How do you feel?"

"The demons are in my head. I couldn't stop them. I can't think straight. You're beautiful."

"You're delirious." She held his forehead, pulled one of his eyelids up. "Look up."

He looked up.

"Look down."

He looked down. "Kill me, Jane. Please. Before Warlord sends me any orders. I won't be able to resist them."

"Get them both free," Jane told her bots. A little teddy bear Jackson hadn't even seen dropped from the ceiling. A whirling saw blade extended from its arm and sparks flew as it sawed through the reinforced chains that Fain had locked around Tui. A few of her smallest bots leapt from out of Jane's hair and began lasering through the bonds at Jackson's wrists. "Listen to me, Jackson. We're going to get you out of here, and we're going to get this fixed. Okay?"

Bushey ran in, his combat suit flashing through camouflage protocols to match his surroundings. He leapt over the rabbit, took cover inside the doorway, and began shoving a new magazine into his carbine. "Your swarm is raising hell on the guards, but there are a lot of them. We've got to boogie now." Then, gun reloaded, he leaned out and began firing down the hall.

He must have been laying down covering fire for Katze, because she came in, moving inhumanly fast. She slid through the doorway on her knees and ended up next to Tui. The bots had cut Tui free, so Katze dragged his limp form out of the line of fire.

"There's at least a dozen more coming up from the hangar," Katze warned. "Humans, and they've activated their own bots too."

"They're not as good as mine," Jane said.

"But there's a lot more of them. We've got to go now." Katze checked on Tui, peeled open one eye, even slapped his cheek. "Chief, can you hear me?" But he was still out.

"Give him a shot of warazine," Bushey told her. "We've got to jump-start his healing mods."

"In this state combat drugs might kill him!"

"If you're carrying him out, then that's one less of us shooting back. Zap him, Katze. That's an order."

Katze pulled a syrette out of her medpack and jabbed it into Tui's neck. He didn't immediately come to, but his whole body began to twitch, as if he was having a seizure.

Jackson was used to Bushey being a clown. But he was no nonsense when he was the one who had to be responsible for everyone else. "Can Jackson walk?"

He aimed that question at Jane, but Jackson answered. "It's too late. Warlord's in my head. Shoot me now. Save yourselves."

Bushey was confused. "Jane?"

"Shut up, Jacky. Don't worry, Bushey, it's nothing I can't fix with a little brain surgery. I just need to get him someplace safe."

"That sure as shanks ain't here!" Bushey leaned back around the corner and fired another burst. Someone out of sight yelped as the bullets spalled off his armor.

The bots made short work of Jackson's bonds, but it turned out he'd been in the same position so long that he couldn't stand. Jane caught him before he fell and held him up. "I've got you. You can't give up yet. Trust me."

"I trust you. I don't trust myself."

"I know." Then Jane shouted at the others. "We need to head back toward the hangar, down the hatch, and find a place to hide in the hull."

Tui wobbled to his feet like a drunk. "Whoa. What did I miss?"

"It's a daring rescue, Chief." Katze handed him a carbine. "You up to shooting some bad guys?"

He blinked, rolled his head a bit, then focused his gaze. "Always." He checked the chamber. Even half dead and covered in his own drying blood, hands shaking and eyes twitching from the powerful stimulant, Tui was still one scary professional. "Lead the way."

"I'll have my swarm cut us a path."

She gave the command. A moment later, there was a high-pitched shriek and a lot of unearthly wailing ahead of them as Jane's bots went nuts. They weren't just deadly. They were also designed to be psychologically unnerving.

"Hallway is clear for the moment," Jane said, and the five of them exited the room and moved down the hall, Bushey and Katze in the lead, guns shouldered. Jane helped Jackson along, and Tui brought up the rear.

There was movement ahead. A guard leaned around the corner to shoot at them, but Bushey shredded him. Katze rushed up and took that corner. She fired a short, controlled burst at someone out of sight. Another man appeared on the catwalk above them, but he began screaming as one of Jane's bots appeared from out of nowhere and slashed his jugular. He flipped over the railing and fell to his doom, being ridden by what looked like a cuddly lobster.

"Our exit's just ahead, to the right," Jane said. "We're almost there."

Bushey and Katze disappeared from view. A second later they both came running back.

"Not good," Bushey said. "Not good!"

There was the sound of heavy footsteps. A thumping like a one-ton giant was headed their way.

"Ogre!" Katze shouted.

The Ogre 55Z Armored Combat Exo was a heavy-duty thing. A thing meant to withstand grenades. A thing meant to clear spaces.

"Hey, didn't we just sell him an Ogre?" Jackson asked.

"Friggin' karma," said Tui.

"Back! Back!" Bushey shouted. Jackson was starting to get his legs under him, so he didn't need Jane to hold him up anymore. This part of the compound he recognized, and he'd spent a lot of time studying the schematics of the place looking for potential escape routes. "The hangar is that way. There's an air shaft in it we can blow open to get down into the hull."

Jane's army flew, ran, and bounded past them. A few moments later, the Big Towners who were part of the Warlord's detail began to scream and curse. Behind them was the methodical thumping of the Ogre's armored feet.

There was a heavy-duty blast door leading into the hangar. Unfortunately, it was closed. Jackson hadn't thought of that.

"Liesel, open," Jane said, and by some miracle, the blast door began to slide aside. "I never could hack their network, but as soon as we were inside, I sent one of my girls to burrow into their hardware."

The guards who had been left inside hadn't been expecting their door to open, so they never knew what hit them. Suddenly they were being stung by metal wasps, blasted by bunnies, or chain-sawed by bipedal teddy bears. The ones Katze shot got off easy. As soon as they were inside, Jane ordered the doors closed behind them.

Catching his breath, Jackson looked around. Most of the modern mechs that had been here before were out, either on harvesting duty, or crushing the rebels at the CX plant. Notably missing was the Spider, but the Citadel he'd stolen was sitting there, pretty as could be. Too bad he didn't have the Warlord's token, because in that thing they could just fight their way out of Big Town. The blast door shook as the Ogre crashed into it. They didn't have much time.

"The shaft should be somewhere in this wall here. You guys got any extra explosives?"

"Sorry. Fresh out," Bushey said.

Tui pointed at the munitions lockers for the mechs. "We can improvise something."

Just then, a massive display on the wall lit up. Jackson knew immediately what he was looking at. The dozens of smaller images around the edges were all from the external views from a single mech's cameras. They showed that the mech was moving fast along the exterior of the orbital. There were glimpses of the CX processing plant, and space-suited figures clambering to get away from it. Framed in the center was the pilot's face. *Warlord.*

From the way the cameras were moving, the mech had multiple legs. It was the Spider. The men in space suits must have been Originals. Because one by one, Warlord mercilessly gunned them down. Frozen blood droplets floated away as the pierced bodies spun off into the darkness.

"Who has the nerve to come into my home?" There must have been a camera in the hangar because Warlord's eyes narrowed furiously. *"They're here for Rook and Fuamatu."*

"And now that we have our people back, we'll be going now," Bushey said. "Call off your dogs and we won't have to kill any more of them on the way out."

"Such audacity. That's far more loyalty than I expected from a gang of pirates."

"We're not pirates. We're gun runners. Totally different."

"Except Rook doesn't work for you anymore. He works for me now."

"Kill the feed!" Jane shouted.

Katze immediately put a bullet into the display. The image winked out of existence.

Except Warlord's voice still came over the compound's intercom.

"Jackson, terminate the intruders."

There was no fighting it. The command simply *was.*

Jane was right next to him, a pistol in a holster at her side. He snatched it from her. She tried to grab his hand, but he punched her in the face, snapping her head around hard.

The real Jackson was horrified. The new, artificial, evil invader in his head was ecstatic. As Jane fell, Jackson turned the pistol on the surprised Bushey and fired a controlled pair. Then he shifted toward Katze—

Tui hit him.

The bullet struck the floor, but he still had Jane's gun. Tui was badly injured, moving way too slow, so Jackson was able to stagger back as he aligned on Tui's face.

KILL HIM.

Somehow, Jackson pushed back against the demon that was pushing down on his trigger finger.

Tui raised his open hands slowly. "This ain't you, brother."

"Shoot me, Tui. Hurry!" The nanites were stabbing his brain with ice picks of agony, trying to force him to comply.

"Fight the slaveware. You can do—"

BLAM.

Katze shot Jackson through the hand.

His gun went flying. One of his fingers was still connected to it. He looked in shocked disbelief at the ruined bone and pulped flesh and the hole big enough to see light through. Then the pain hit and Jackson screamed.

"Sorry!" Katze shouted. "I didn't know what else to do!"

Tui shoved him to the floor. "Toss me a tourniquet."

Jackson wanted to fulfill the order to kill Tui, wanted to fulfill the order to kill them all. Except getting the bones of your hand turned into shrapnel really caused a loss of focus, so Jackson lost what tenuous hold he had, and Warlord's command kicked back in.

Jackson hit Tui with his uninjured left, but it was like punching a brick wall. Tui just slapped Jackson's arm away and pinned him. "TQ! Now!"

Katze got one out of her med bag and threw it to Tui. He caught it, expertly looped it around, Jackson's wrist, and turned on the automatic windlass. It tightened. Supertight, superfast, and the shock on his damaged nerves was enough to make Jackson black out for a second. He came back to hear Tui shouting, "Bushey, status?"

"One got through my armor." Bushey grunted in pain. "It ain't bad."

"Now's not to the time to be a tough guy!"

"Okay. It's bad. It's in my side. Don't know what it hit, but nothing's squirting."

The Ogre crashed into the blast door again. It moved a bit.

Warlord's voice came back over the intercom. *"Oh, that was marvelous. Gunfire, screaming, such drama! Poetry to my ears. How many of you did he get? This is what you get for thinking you can come into my house and mess with my property. I don't know who of you are still alive, but if you're from* Tar Heel *you've got nowhere to run. I called in a favor. I've got a* real *pirate ship on its way to blow your sad freighter to bits. Hide while you can, because as soon as I'm done exterminating rats here, I'm coming home to take care of you personally. Let the hunt begin."*

"Liesel, destroy all their comms in and out of the compound. Fry everything." Jane picked herself up off the floor and winced as she touched her swollen eye. "That should shut him up."

"I'm sorry, Bushey," he said through the waves of awfulness that were radiating up his arm. "I tried to warn you guys."

"You sure did, so don't worry about it." Tui looked over at Jane. "Take him. Katze, help Bushey. I'm going to find something that can cut a hole through that wall."

The Ogre kept pounding on the door, accentuating the fact that time wasn't on their side.

Jackson thought he might be starting to go into shock. If he could get ahold of that TQ, he could probably release it, then he'd swiftly bleed out. Everyone would be a lot safer.

But another part of him didn't want to bleed out. That part wanted to follow Warlord's orders.

Jackson looked down at the TQ. *Just release it,* he thought. *Before the pain subsides and you're lost forever.*

Jane knelt next to Jackson. "Quit eyeballing that. I know what you're thinking. You're not quitting yet."

"I didn't want to hit you."

"I know."

As he said it, there was a brief moment of clarity, a momentary weakening of the desire to execute the Warlord's order. He suddenly knew what was happening and felt a moment of horror. "Jane, keep your promise," he said. Holy Mother, she needed to keep her promise.

Tui shouted from the lockers, "There's a ton of stuff, but I don't know what we can break down in time."

Jackson looked toward the mech. "The Citadel could tear through that wall like it was nothing... And then tear the legs off Warlord's spider when he gets back. Do you think you could bypass the security and get that mech started without the token?"

"Maybe. I poked around in its systems while it was aboard. But then what? We put a guy who is under mind control inside a giant stompy robot in the same room with us?"

"How are you at multitasking?"

"Are you serious?" But then Jane looked toward where the Ogre was still banging away. "How long is that door going to hold?"

Katze eyed the catwalk running along one side of the hangar. "About as long as it's going to take the guards to cut through the doors up there. They're bound to use plasma cutters. Why? What are you going to do?"

"I'm going to put Jackson's brain block back on manually. He's freshly baked, but I've got minutes to stop the curing." She shed her pack, ripped open a compartment, and pulled out some surgical implements.

"You're going to do brain surgery? Here?"

"And hack a mech at the same time. Cover me." Several of her mechs took off toward the Citadel. A few small ones climbed up on his head, as if they were about to serve as nurses. Jane gave him a shot, then held up a tiny chip. "Listen, Jackson, I just gave you a megadose of painkillers. I need you to hold very still. If I can get a direct access block back in, I can stop the influence for a while, which buys my nanites time to hunt down their nanites."

"The patient may experience some discomfort," he said, cradling his ruined hand to his chest.

"You have no idea how much of an understatement that is, Jacky. I have to access the area for direct application. This is really going to suck."

Then he giggled, because her strong drugs were having an odd reaction with all the other strong drugs Tiny had already given him. How many drugs could one man take? At least his hand was starting to hurt less. "You'd better hurry. Part of me still really wants to kill you, and it keeps telling me that it would be awesome."

"We'll cross that bridge when we come to it. At least the bomb in your spine should be far enough away not to think that it's being tampered with and detonate... Probably." Jane peeled back the bandage that was already on Jackson's head. "This is going to pinch, big guy." And she proceeded to cut a hole in his skull.

Jackson could hear the grinding. And he could feel a dull throb of pain which he knew should have been much, much stronger. Then she struck something, and pain finally exploded through him. A lightning jolt that took away his sight. He jolted, bucked like a horse.

Jane swore, then stuck him with another syringe. "I'm going to have to paralyze you. It's only temporary."

Temporary paralysis was better than what Warlord had planned for him. "Go for it."

There was more gunfire. Yelling. An explosion. Jackson's vision came back. He saw that soldiers had breached in from above, and Katze was raking the catwalks with fire.

And there was grinding. Like someone was sawing through his head.

"Holy hell."

"Man up," Jane said, then continued grinding. The sound vibrated his head like a buzz saw and he realized she was grinding skull bone. Then Jane stopped, turned, looked for a place to set something down. She used the top of a toolbox. There were bits of stuff on it from when her bots had chewed up the guards. Definitely not sterile. But Jane placed a bloody bit of skull on it. A little chip.

"Left side, incoming," Bushey shouted and began firing that way. Jane's eyes flicked briefly in that direction, and several metal wasps flew off to help him. Sometimes big is what you needed. But other times small was bloody murder.

Jane picked up another implement with a long filament coming out the end. "Just what the doctor ordered," she said and stuck it directly into his brain. He felt it go in. Felt a little electrical zing slide in with it.

There was a commotion to the right. Jackson couldn't move to see what it was.

"Bobby," Jane said. "Secure that flank."

A fat little bot no more than six inches high popped out of her pack and ran. Jane had painted this one to have a beard and a pointy red hat.

Gnomes are real. And that thought struck Jackson as hilarious.

"Hold still." Jane put down the implement she'd been using and picked up some other instrument and slid that into his brain. Another electrical zing.

It was truly wondrous, he thought. *A gnome.*

The next electrical zing hit Jackson like a train.

✧   ✧   ✧

Jane was, in fact, very good at multitasking.

While she was literally touching Jackson's brain, she'd sent Pilgrim and Seth to drill directly into the Citadel's armored shell so she could access its system. It was so well shielded there was no way she could do it remotely. Rufus had the best sensors, so she'd had him stick himself to the ceiling to provide a real time map of the area to Katze's and Bushey's displays, tracking the vibrations of enemy footsteps and heartbeats. The rest of her bots she'd had to put on autopilot to help hold off the security response. Even coordinating with Rufus, that still cut their effectiveness by over thirty percent, so they immediately began to take losses. Gunther got shot down. Tim got stomped flat.

Jane designed all her bots who used guns to take the same magazines as her own weapon, so as they ran out of ammo, they'd fly or run back to her, she'd absently pluck a spare magazine from her pouch, stuff it in them, and off they'd go, to cause more mayhem.

Jose got blasted. Bobby got stepped on by the Ogre. The blast door was failing. Bushey took another round, this time to the leg. Tui was forced to go hand-to-hand at one of the doorways and was beating a man savagely over the head with the butt of a stolen shotgun. Jane had picked an out-of-the-way corner behind some crates to hold her field surgery, so the enemy hadn't seen her yet, which surely wasn't going to last much longer.

But her block was in place inside Jacky's head.

It was ugly. It was crude. But it was there.

"Suction," she told Baby, who obediently moved the tube into the little hole in Jacky's skull, to get the blood out of the way. And then she changed her mind. That looked pretty good, all things considered.

Jane closed her helmet's face shield and went to VR mode.

Her world became nothing but tendrils of glowing green and yellow, stretching ever upward, like endlessly branching trees, a forest of dendrites. The view represented the insides of Jacky's skull. Jane reached up with her real hands, as if she was climbing one of the trees. The view was too close, so she panned out, and then she saw the red vines. The wetware pathways of the attacking nanites.

She searched back along those vines and found the trespasser. A brutal, jagged monstrosity. All sharp edges and meanness. No wonder Jacky said they felt like demons. But Jane's nanotech was fierce, and she went over and cleaved that demon in half with a magic sword. The monster disintegrated into shreds of printed protein. Now that her nanites had been shown what to do, she tagged that red signal as the enemy, to be terminated with extreme prejudice, and her million-strong army went to work.

Jane came back to reality. Katze was crouched next to her, pulling mags out of Jane's bag and desperately shoving them into waiting, hungry bots. "We can't hold them. We've got to exfil, now!"

Jane checked the automatic brute-force programs she'd sent to gnaw away at the Citadel's defenses. Its alarms were blaring, sending a signal to its owner—which was why they'd stolen that stupid key on Nivaas to begin with! But it wasn't as if Warlord wasn't already on his way back to kill them all anyway, so no great loss there. She was almost in, but not fast enough. So she launched six other programs to hit it from other directions. It threw up blocks. She broke through. And those she couldn't break, she went around. The Citadel was a masterful piece of programming, but Jane was basically beating it like a pinata with a sledgehammer hoping for candy to come out. Systems were starting to fall.

At the same time, she was attacking the Citadel, Jane stuck the bone plug back into the hole in Jacky's skull, welded it back together with a collagen bond, and then sealed the area with healing gel. It would have to do. If they lived through this, he was going to need a real doctor, bad.

"Help me carry Jacky to that mech. He'll make us a door."

Jackson came to sitting inside the familiar cockpit of the Citadel. Jane was strapping him in. Katze was a few meters away, taking cover behind the Citadel's leg as someone shot at her.

"That should do it. I'll stick you with a smart pack to neutralize the rest of the paralytic agent. That'll clear your head, but it also means it'll counteract some of the painkillers. You're going to be in a world of hurt. Nothing I can do about that, but the pack should keep you from going into shock," Jane said. "I've got to know first thought, you still want to kill me?"

Jackson panted a bit. Tried to gather himself.

"Jackson?"

"I want to kill you only a little." It was like a distant lure, like the pull of a memory of ice cream at a party when he was a kid. Jane flipped down her visor and fiddled with something Jackson couldn't see. "How about now?"

He could feel the order to exterminate, but it wasn't connected to anything. It was simply abstract. A conceptual thing.

"Jackson?" she prompted.

He blinked. "I hear Warlord's order, but don't feel it."

"It's amazing what happens when you decouple the wetware from the lizard brain."

"Is it fixed?"

"It's a band-aid. The wetware's gone to war in your head. This stuff is nasty, aggressive like nothing I've ever seen before, and it's fighting back. I'll do what I can to help remotely, but it's going to be awful for you."

"I'll get through. Let's do this."

Jane stuck him with the tox pack. "Oh yeah, and only a few of the Citadel's systems are online so far. It's making me fight for each one. I'll get them to you as fast as I can."

"You're an angel." As soon as the tox pack began attacking the multitude of drugs in his system, Jackson could move his limbs again, but then the pain came back. His hand felt like it was on fire. Lightning bolts were going down his arm. And his head was actively being beaten like a drum. Gritting his teeth, he immediately reached for the controls. The hatch began closing. The time had come to do his job.

"I'll get you out of here, Jane. I swear it."

CHAPTER 35

There was gunfire and screaming, but the instant the Citadel's cockpit sealed, there was nothing but quiet.

Jackson took in the status. Jane had only gotten the basic motion controls activated. Sensors were limited to the most basic cameras, the sort of thing you'd let a dockhand access to move a mech from one bay to another. Reactor output at fifty percent. Weapons were offline. Combat reflexes, offline. Countermeasures, offline. Medical, offline. That one would have been really nice right about then. Information warfare, offline. Comms, offline. Bots, offline. Hell, Jackson couldn't even use his right hand, which meant that the Citadel couldn't use its right hand.

But he had a promise to keep.

Jackson got himself locked into position. Dozens of sensors extended from the chair and stuck themselves to various muscle groups. As he moved his legs, the Citadel stood.

Because of the limited camera access, Jackson had to swing the Citadel's bulbous head around to see everything. Just that small amount of movement translated through the electrodes on his neck made his head hurt even worse. You'd think he'd just had battlefield brain surgery or something.

The hangar was a cavernous space. Now it felt like he was standing in the corner of a small room. The few cameras he had access to showed soldiers pouring in from the catwalk above. The main blast door had been pried open by the Ogre enough that they were tossing grenades through. Those went off with a flash, and then began to pour out gas. Jackson didn't have the sensors to analyze what it was, but his gut told him sleep gas.

Jane's bots were dropping like flies. Bushey was down and Katze had to drag him behind cover. Tui had gotten shot but was laying down fire to cover his friends. There were enemies coming at them from multiple directions. One soldier was running around some crates, flanking Tui.

Jackson stepped on Warlord's man.

He didn't have external mics yet but knew from experience that a mech flattening a human body between steel sole and steel floor made a very distinct sound. From the way all the guards stopped shooting to gawk at the Citadel, it had certainly gotten their attention. Tui looked up, then grinned.

Jackson went to work.

A subtle muscle twitch was all it took for the Citadel to sweep its arm across the catwalk, flinging multiple men to their doom. But "subtle" went out the window when you were as torn up as Jackson was. He ended up crushing the metal grate, sending debris and soldiers in every direction. Still, he could work with that. The Citadel's massive hand curled around the end of the walkway, and bolts sheared as he effortlessly ripped the beam from the walls.

Weapons offline? Didn't matter, because now he had a club.

Bullets bounced harmlessly off his armor shell as the Citadel strode across the hangar, swatting troops. Everyone he hit went flying, bones shattered. He picked the spot he thought the big air shaft would be, aimed the beam like a spear, and drove it through the wall. He must have gotten lucky, because from the way the clouds of green sleep gas suddenly sucked toward it, he'd hit airflow. Jackson leaned into it, using the beam like a pry bar, wrenching it back and forth to make the hole bigger and bigger. He pulled the beam out. Not only did it suck out all the gas, but it was big enough for even Tui to fit through.

Jackson was suddenly very dizzy. As the vertigo overcame him, the Citadel lumbered to the side. Without access to the preprogramed combat reflexes to keep it nimble, it crashed into the wall, and rolled, until it fell facedown. One of the antique mechs from Warlord's collection was crushed beneath it.

His nose was running like crazy. His training made it so that he resisted touching his face, an unconscious action which had killed many an innocent bystander standing too close to a mech. When the liquid reached his lips, he realized it was blood. His nose was bleeding something fierce. Either a leftover from Jane's invasive measures, or a by-product of the nanite battle. Either way, it sucked, and his head really hurt to match.

"Jackson, are you alive?"

It was Jane. His eyes flicked to the display. Comms were now active.

"Sorta."

"Bail out. Let's go!"

Except Jackson saw something that Jane didn't. The Ogre 55Z had gotten the blast door pried open enough to squeeze through. "Ogre incoming. Run. I'll catch up. I'm safer in this thing than you are out there."

Jane was too pragmatic to argue. *"I'll keep working on freeing up the Citadel's systems for you."*

The dizziness was awful. He didn't know if he could walk himself, let alone a giant robot. "Concentrate on medical next, please?"

"Will do."

Jackson got his good hand forward and used that to steady the Citadel as it rose from the floor.

The blast doors were open. The Ogre stomped through, cannons blazing, a squad of men right behind it.

The Ogre was a fearsome machine...to a person. To Jackson, the glorified exo was the size of a toddler. Its armor sneered at anything Katze could throw at it, but Jackson didn't even need guns. He picked up the smashed, antique mech he'd fallen on, spun, and hurled three tons of steel right into the Ogre's face. It tumbled back, crushing the soft fleshy bodies around it.

The Citadel stumbled across the hangar. The Ogre driver managed to get off a burst of 20mm. Explosives shells detonated across the ceiling, but one struck the Citadel in the chest, only half a meter from where Jackson was encased. The outer shell split, but the smart armor beneath absorbed and distributed most of the hit and immediately began repairing itself.

Jackson reached the Ogre. His arm twitched. The Citadel swung and knocked the cannon aside. The next 20mm round blew a gaping hole in the floor. Another twitch, a curl of his fingers, and the Citadel wrapped its giant hand around the exo's arm. Jackson pulled.

The Ogre's arm popped off. Difference between an exo and a mech? A mech pilot's whole body rode in the armored torso. On the little exo, the driver's real arm was still inside there. Jackson still didn't have his external mics up yet, but he knew that driver had to be making some noise. He lifted one foot, and the Citadel booted the crippled exo back through the blast doors. The guards who didn't get crushed turned and ran.

That would buy them some time. But Warlord was on his way back, and his advanced mech wouldn't be hobbled. Jackson couldn't fire any of his weapons yet, but there was no reason he couldn't load up and be ready for when Jane did crack that system, so Jackson steered the Citadel over to the munitions that had been delivered by the *Tar Heel* and started opening containers. All the weapon systems were modular and designed so that the Citadel could rearm itself without having to wait around for human help. It took finer motor control than he currently had, and one more hand, so he made a real mess of it.

While roughly clipping on gun pods, he got a transmission.

"We're climbing down. The schematics show that there's a junction below us. We should able to come out somewhere inside the city to lay low. If we can make it to the docks, maybe we can steal a ship and get back to the Tar Heel. *I can't contact the captain, but the Citadel should be able to reach him now."*

"Roger that."

The bridge was crowded, every station manned. The *Tar Heel* had sounded general quarters. Captain Holloway sat in his command chair, watching the readouts flash across the display. The mystery ship was still running quiet, but they were close enough now to get a visual ID. It was the CSS *Downward Spiral*.

"That's Jeet Prunkard's ship," Castillo said from his station at the captain's right hand.

It was no coincidence that pirate was here.

"Well, at least now we know who was selling Warlord the rest of his weaponry." The captain had been curious who else was stupid enough to do this sort of thing for a living. "Estimated armament, XO?"

"Nothing public. Same as us. She was even built in the same

Martian shipyards as ours, but she's about a decade newer and ten percent bigger, but figure Prunkard's got the same constraints on what he can hide from gate inspectors as we do, so it just depends on how good their cargomaster is at hiding missiles and guns aboard."

"I can deal with those odds." The *Downward Spiral* was beefier, but Garrick Hilker was an artist when it came to hiding contraband, and his crew had spent the last few hours moving weapon systems out of deep storage and bolting them into place.

Except the dour XO continued. "That is assuming Prunkard doesn't have someone on the inside at the ISF who is letting them through gates without getting random checks, and he's really got a belly full of missiles."

"Well, ain't you just a cup of sunshine today, Javi?"

The XO shrugged. "Rumor is Prunkard's ships are the ones that have been chasing down freighters along the outer gate circuit. He's popped five or six now that I know of, including a Redcor patrol escort. You don't do that without plenty of guns aboard."

The captain didn't keep Castillo around for his charming personality, but rather because he was usually right. They were both former Earth Block Navy and knew their business. Castillo had earned his commission doing the deadly hopper run between the moons of Jupiter back during the war. His gut instincts were second to none.

"You think frigate-level firepower then?"

"Wouldn't surprise me in the least, Cap."

"Well, then we've got us a real fight on our hands."

Castillo just grunted in agreement.

The *Downward Spiral* would be in long-volley missile range soon, but he knew Prunkard wouldn't start shooting just yet. He'd save his ammo until he could get the most bang for his buck out of it. That was the downside of not working for a real navy.

They had tried to contact the other ship before, but it had been ignored. He tried again, mostly out of stubbornness, and was surprised when the *Downward Spiral* answered.

Jeet Prunkard's square, bearded face appeared on the screen. He had a fat dog with a cyborg eye tethered next to his chair. "*Attention,* Tar Heel. *This is Captain Jeet Prunkard of the CSS* Downward Spiral."

"Nice dog."

"Thanks." The pirate reached out and gave the pit bull scritches behind one ear. *"Now cut your engines and prepare to be boarded."*

He had to laugh at the audacity. "By what authority?"

"By the authority vested in me by Big Town Control, whose space you're trespassing in."

"Oh, cut the crap, Prunkard. Warlord's power ends just outside the reach of his guns. I know why you're here."

Prunkard had what was quite possibly the most malicious grin ever. *"Good. I don't have to waste my time pretending to be diplomatic. I hate that nonsense."*

"How much is Warlord paying you to try and run us off?"

"Nothing. After he told me you thieves are the ones who stole my livestock hauler and got me arrested on Nivaas, this one is personal. I'll recoup the fuel costs when I sell your wreck for salvage."

"Good luck with that, scrub."

"I knew it. You didn't even try to deny you stole that goat boat! I've heard about you, Holloway, Mr. Fancy Pants, academy grad, was such a screwup Earth kicked him out of its navy. You're not such a big shot now. Look at you, sad, washed up, pathetic, stealing goats to makes ends meet. I'm gonna nuke your ship and ransom your crew and—"

Alligood sent him a silent message on Jane's net. *"Incoming message from Big Town. It's from the Citadel we stole."*

Curious. "Hang on, psycho. I got another call. I need to take this."

"Hey! Nobody hangs up on Jeet Prunk—"

The captain dropped him. "Jackson, is that you?"

There was voice, but no visual. Jackson sounded rough. *"Yeah, Cap. Long story. Sending a data dump."*

"Same." He signaled for Alligood to shoot the info packet over. It was kind of amazing that Jackson had actually stolen the Citadel back. The kid really was a miracle worker. "We're about to throw down with Prunkard's ship. You need to find a way off Big Town and past the defensive picket so you we can pick you up, but we need to deal with him first."

"Roger that. I'll tell Jane and Tui."

"Just so you know, any damages to my ship or crew are coming out of your account."

"Love you too, sir."

"Missile launch!" Alligood said. "Multiple incoming."

The captain was pleased by that. At this range he had plenty of time to maneuver, so those would just be wasted. Dismissing Prunkard must have really pissed him off. "Good luck, son. *Tar Heel* out."

The red alert sounded. Everyone on the *Tar Heel* was already at their battle stations. The crew was already nervous, spun up, but he knew they would be steady. They were a solid bunch, because he'd picked the gems from the dregs, treated them with respect, worked them hard but never unreasonably hard, and paid them well... but ship-to-ship combat wasn't a regular event for them. They were smugglers, not pirates. They avoided fights rather than picked them. But their captain had just picked one hell of a fight, and now they were in it up to their eyeballs. Having missiles inbound sure did change one's perspective on life.

Which was why the captain had already prerecorded a message. Now that they were committed to battle, he sent that message to every member of his crew. It said that he had complete faith in their abilities, the proceeds of any salvage from this upcoming fight would be split evenly among them, but most importantly, he had taken his share, the captain's share, the biggest share, of the Big Town sale they'd just made, divided it up equally, and it was being sent directly to each of their accounts right now as they heard this. Possible impending death or not, that was one sweet bonus. Nicholas Holloway understood the value of morale and loyalty.

So much for his retirement though.

"Guns up, Mr. Castillo. Let's smoke check this clown."

The Citadel stomped through the hangar's open blast doors and into a wide tunnel that gently sloped up to the street level of Big Town. The fake sunlight shone upon him, indicating it was day up there. He checked his countdown for LaDue's package. Fifty-two minutes.

That was enough time. The more heat he could pull down on his head, the less would be going after Jane and the others. So Jackson would give Big Town a show it would never forget.

Except that's when something decided to stab him in the frontal lobe.

"Sorry, Jacky. I saw your vitals just spiked. Warlord's nanites are counterattacking the ones I gave you. I'm revising their strategy now."

He grimaced against the headache. "Oh, good. I thought I'd had a stroke."

"That might still happen."

"So how's it going on accessing this thing's first-aid protocols?"

"My program's chipping away. Almost there."

He didn't remember falling, but the Citadel had wound up on its face again, blocking most of the access tunnel. His eye movement caused the head camera to tilt enough for him to see that several really brave soldiers were running at him, trying to take advantage of him going down. It looked like one of them was carrying a satchel charge. If they stuck enough explosives directly to his cockpit, armored or not, it would pulverize everything on the other side.

"Good news, though. I've brought your basic weapon systems online. Nothing good yet, just the simple point-defense stuff, but it should be better than nothing."

The flamethrower pod on the Citadel's shoulder ignited, bathing the approaching men in fire. A second later their charge detonated, rocking the tunnel.

The mech got back up but had to crouch a bit to not hit its head on the ceiling. It continued on, wobbling as if it had a few too many. The basic instruction manuals for these things always contained some line about don't pilot while under the influence of mind-altering substances. He was violating the hell out of that right now.

"Listen, Jane, Captain's got his own problems. He's tailing Big Town just out of gun range, but Jeet Prunkard's ship is engaging them. They'll stick around for you, but you're going to need to hijack a transport or something to get to them. I'm going to draw off all the guard for you."

"There's no talking you out of this, is there?"

"Of course not. But don't worry. This isn't a one-way trip. I've got this."

"Jacky...I..."

"Yeah. I know. You're regretting that you said no when I asked you on a date."

"Wow. No. That's not...Pilots really are cocky, aren't they?"

"Oh, come on. We kind of have to be. So anyways, is that a yes this time?"

She actually laughed. The sound cheered him right up. *"Deal. We survive, we celebrate."*

"Awesome."

"And I got your basic close-combat reflex systems unlocked. Medical is crumbling. ETA five minutes."

"Almost as awesome."

The tunnel came out on the grounds of the governor's mansion. The main road was nearby, which was smart. That would allow the Warlord to easily move his mechs around the orbital. There were individual soldiers there, but they were only shooting at him with inefficient small arms. However, there was another Ogre, which had taken cover behind the compound's outer wall.

It began shooting, but Jackson dodged and took two long strides, extended the carbon spike from the Citadel's wrist, and impaled the exo. The spike fired a small charge. A moment later there was an explosion that hollowed the Ogre out.

The blast and heat flowed around Jackson as if he were a boulder in a stream. He retracted the spike, picked the Ogre up with his good hand, then hurled it over the wall, onto the roof of a parked troop carrier.

He had to admit, despite the pain and the suck, it felt good to be kicking ass in a mech again.

Jackson checked his limited displays. Jane and crew were safe for the moment. He quickly scanned the Big Town news feeds. There was still an altercation ongoing at the CX plant. Luckily all the mechs which had responded to that hadn't made it back yet, but they would soon enough.

In the meantime, Jackson decided to make a bit of a statement.

The Citadel walked up to the governor's mansion. He smashed his fist through the facade, exposing a nice hole into the Warlord's main room with all the trophies of Swindle on the walls. Jackson engaged the flamethrower. The trophies of Swindle beasts burned to ash. He kicked over the pillars. Ground the stone into powder and began pushing over walls.

This, of course, caught a lot of attention. His cameras picked up movement outside the walls. Some soldiers, but also a bunch of regular Big Towners. Faces appeared in windows, curious about the noise. People walked onto their roofs and balconies, to see why there was smoke in the air. The mansion was such an iconic landmark, it could be seen by a big chunk of the population of the tube all the way around, across, and above.

Jackson zoomed in on the faces. When they saw Warlord's castle crumbling, many were horrified, but others seemed happy.

Good. Let them see their fearless leader wasn't as invincible as he made himself out to be.

One of his cameras caught something moving his way fast. A mech was sprinting down the main road. Approximately four meters tall and painted bright red—he immediately identified it as the He22 Korvan that he'd previously seen in the hangar. The captain had sold them this one a few years ago. It was a fourth gen, regularly no match for a fifth like the Citadel, but Jackson figuratively had one hand tied behind his back. Literally, he had one hand with a bloody hole through it, and the only reason he wasn't bleeding to death was the incredibly painful tourniquet cutting off that mess.

"Hey, Jane, I could really use some guns right now."

"Working on it."

Whoever was driving the Korvan had some skill and battle sense, because he slid in behind a building for cover, then leaned out and began launching rockets.

Jackson ducked the Citadel down behind the burning walls of the governor's mansion. Whatever he hadn't trashed was surely done in by the resulting explosions. Everyone in Big Town must have heard that noise. The closest bystanders, the scared and gleeful both, all ran for their lives.

If he'd had all his sensors up, the other mech that came up from behind never would have surprised him. But Jackson never even saw it coming.

Something collided with the Citadel, knocking it through the burning wreckage. He careened off a solid metal piece that probably dated back to the original colony ship. That strut bent. Part of the Citadel's armor crunched. Jackson jolted, but the Citadel had top-of-the-line dampeners for the pilot, and so instead of his head cracking open, it simply shook him.

His assailant was the third-gen giant. An evolutionary dead end. A big fat, slow target. Or would have been, in any other circumstances. In a slugfest? It was a bulldozer.

The mech followed him into the fire, crunching through the remains of Warlord's home. Smoke swirled around its massive, blocky frame. From its arm extended a spike. It pulled back to stab him, but Jackson activated the Citadel's plasma cutter. A glowing blue crescent arced across the Citadel's knuckles, and he sliced into the other mech's arm. Sliced it like it was made of butter.

The giant was huge, but slow. The Citadel spun around it, running the cutter across the mech's lower back. Jackson had never dealt with one of these big ones, but that's where he thought the motor controls were. It weighed so much though, the giant simply leaned into him, shoving the Citadel across the grounds. The manicured lawn disintegrated beneath its feet. The big mech slammed its spike into the Citadel's torso, but the Citadel was made of tough stuff, and the smart armor hardened to absorb the hit. Energy radiated through the gel.

Jackson sliced its arm again, then ducked down, slicing across its belly. That was where the cockpit was on these, so Jackson hoped to hit, or at least unnerve the pilot.

The mech stuttered. A part of it froze. It fired its cannon but was pointing in the wrong way. The damaged troop carrier exploded in a shower of sparks. Jackson sliced it again, but now he could see there was nobody in the mech, which meant it was being controlled by some AI. A computer pilot could be good. But not an old one like this, and certainly not good enough to take Jackson.

He reflexively ducked a clumsy swing, jabbed the spike into the cut he'd made on its back, and deposited an explosive charge right next to its brain box.

The old mech spasmed, its motor functions badly damaged.

The red Korvan had used the time to close. The pilot lit him up with an autocannon. Explosive shells detonated across the Citadel's back.

Jackson grabbed the old mech he'd just crippled and used it as a shield. The Korvan kept circling, firing, as Jackson kept the giant between them. The antique was getting ripped to bits, but it was thick, and armored like an old-time battleship. Some shells missed, and flew off into Big Town, exploding who knew where. People's businesses and homes probably. And that really, really pissed Jackson off.

"I need guns, Jane!"

"*You need to get out of there. Feeds show more mechs converging on the compound.*"

The autocannon ran dry. The Korvan raised its other arm, wrist hinging open, exposing a chain gun. It began firing, but that was a desperation move, because the small caliber projectiles did nothing to the mighty Citadel.

That was his chance. Jackson took it. The Citadel ran, jumped the compound wall, and ducked into Big Town.

Jane, Tui, Katze, Bushey, and her remaining bots moved through one of the tunnels beneath the skin of Big Town. She had scouts ranging ahead and behind, and for a brief moment, it appeared they had shaken pursuit.

They were in a small room maybe three meters square. To one side were storage containers. The bot scans suggested they were supplies should Warlord need to escape. Probably weapons and food, but Jane whispered for the team to stay away from them, because she had no idea what would happen if they tried to force them open.

"We need to stop," Katze said. "We have to tend to Bushey now, or he's not going to make it."

"I'm fine." But that was an obvious lie. Bushey's suit was punctured, ripped, and still smoking from burns.

Jane glanced down the corridor they'd been running down and saw that Bushey had been leaving a trail of red droplets. She quickly ordered one of her bots to start scrubbing those to make them harder to track.

"I can make it."

"Shut up and sit, you stubborn bastard." Tui took Bushey's arm and guided him to the floor. "Thanks for saving us, by the way."

"You would've done the same for us, Chief. How are you doing?"

Tui looked like death warmed over. Jane had access to his vitals. He'd been in really bad shape before the fight, and right now he was only running on stims. The pain threshold of soldiers never ceased to amaze her.

"I've got good healing mods. I'll be fine in a few days, but only thanks to you guys."

"I can't believe Jackson shot me," Bushey said. "That little ingrate."

"It wasn't his fault," Jane said quickly.

"That don't make these gunshot wounds hurt less, Jane!" Bushey grimaced as Katze pulled open the bloody gash in his suit. "Ouch. Ouch! Careful."

"We flew way past careful a while ago, you old goat." Katze said as she checked the wound. Blood was slowly leaking from

Bushey's side. She frowned as she opened her med kit. "I could use a hand here."

Jane dispatched Baby to help Katze, since she had the best first-aid protocols. While Tui and the rest of the bots covered them, Jane concentrated on her systems. Her programs were still working on the Citadel. She began flipping through the ships currently docked, trying to figure out what they could steal or stow away on. She'd left Liesel behind in the compound, so she was still quietly gaining access to more of Warlord's system. Jane was trying to figure out the location of the remaining guard and police, because there could be a hundred guns waiting for them above. However, it looked like most of them were focused on Jackson. But wait...

"Whoa."

"What is it, Jane?" Tui asked.

She activated some holos of the Big Town feeds so the rest could see. The streets were chaos. People were running. Security cars flying overhead. There was a shot of Warlord's palace, flattened and burning.

"It looks like they're rioting again," Katze said.

"Only unlike the one we saw before, the cops are too occupied to squash it," Tui said. On the holo, one of the security cars was struck by a Molotov cocktail. Despite Warlord's weapon's ban, there sure were a lot of guns in the hands of the mob. And the ones who didn't have guns were armed with axes, saws, and scythes. "Those are harvester tools. And those flags they're flying. That's the Originals' symbol. They're rising up."

"MacKinnon must be capitalizing on the chaos to make his move," Jane mused. It kind of made her glad she'd pulled Boris and Bubbles off of him, otherwise he might have been too preoccupied with not dying to be this useful.

"Let's just concentrate on getting out of here before this whole place melts down in a civil war. You ready to move?"

"Almost there, Chief," Katze replied as Baby climbed out of the hole in Bushey's side.

Jane shared Baby's report. "The bleeder's repaired. There's a bunch of foreign bodies in there that we'll need to clean out before he gets sepsis, but in the meantime you can seal him up."

"Your bedside manner sucks, Jane," Bushey said. "But your tiny robot is fantastic. Thank you, tiny robot."

Katze squirted the wound full of nanogel and slapped a seal on it. "Good to go."

Their ragged bunch got moving again. Jane had given her gun to Tui. He was far better with a firearm than she was, plus, to be fair, if they were in a situation where Jane was shooting people instead of running her bots, things had gotten really dire.

As they walked, Jane kept flipping through maps, tracking guard movement and police reports, and assessing docked ship vulnerabilities. "Okay, I've got us a good potential ride off this dump, but we can't get there using the underground. We'll need to go back up and cross the city to reach the docks."

"Are you sure?" Katze asked.

Of course, she was sure, but Jane tried not to take it personally. "We're in the spinning tube, only way to the weightless docks is through the stabilizer."

"That's one hell of a chokepoint and it will be guarded," Tui said.

"The only other option is to walk along the outside, but you don't have an environment suit, and Bushey's is wrecked. Unless you can hold your breath for twenty minutes at minus two hundred..."

"Back to the big spinning platform thing it is!" Bushey said.

Jane's bots told her it was clear all the way to street level. There were a few security doors, but Jane sent ahead bots with cutters to make a path. The only way she could tell that they'd left the bowels of the colony ship into new construction was that the walls changed from orderly, bland plastic, to a mishmash of scavenged materials bolted together.

The route Jane picked out took them into what was probably someone's apartment. The hatch led into a very humble kitchen. There was one man standing there, perfectly still, a drink in his hand. He was staring at Ron the bear, who had its gun pointed at the poor fellow.

Bushey saw the man and immediately shot him with a tranq in the side of the neck.

The man jolted. "What's going on here?"

"Lie down or fall down," Bushey said.

The man blinked. He set his drink on the counter, then began to kneel. He made it part of the way, then fell to the floor.

"Was that necessary?" Katze asked. "We're in the guy's house!"

Bushey shrugged. "I don't trust anybody on this stupid orbital."

Jane checked the feeds again. "We're two klicks away. The streets are a mess. Now's our chance. Nobody will notice us in the confusion. We can—" Suddenly, Jane lost contact with Bubbles. The little bot had been pulling rear guard back in the tunnels one second, the next she was gone.

"What's wrong?" Tui asked.

"I don't know." Bubbles had been the farthest back, but Rene, the jewel wasp, was only fifty meters from her last position, so Jane turned Rene's aggression up to 10 and sent her buzzing in that direction. "I think someone might be tracking us. I'm checking now."

According to her hacked intel, there was nobody behind them. So if there was someone back there, they had to be some kind of ghost that didn't show up on any of the systems. Rene would find out. Only she didn't make it very far. Even though she was one of the fastest and deadliest members of Jane's swarm, something got her. Jane received a brief flash of video before Rene got zapped out of the air. It was some kind of...wolf-bug monster? She immediately put the confusing image on her wrist holo. "This is half a klick behind us."

"Bloody shanks," Tui muttered.

"What is that thing?"

"A grendel. Fain's hunting us."

"Who?" Jane asked.

"The guy who beat me like a rented mule."

"We should set up an ambush," Katze said.

"His hound will smell it, or he'll see it coming. His mods make ours look obsolete. I'm talking top-tier supersoldier abilities."

"Do we stand and fight, Chief?"

Jane didn't think she could actually remember Tui showing fear before. He was trying to hide it, but she saw it on his face, and that scared her.

"Only if we have to. We run."

CHAPTER 36

Wulf was about ten klicks from Warlord's mountain base on Swindle, standing with his father in the closest thing the Originals had to a command center. They were guarding Marie LaDue, the leader of their little nation. It was an honor to be chosen to protect her, even if he wished he was on the front line.

He watched the feeds coming in and doubted anything would come of this. Over the last three years they'd mustered twice for an attack that had never been ordered. This was the third time. All the cells had been positioned and were waiting for the signal.

Except this time felt different. Reports kept coming in about fighting in Big Town. Wulf's hopes were rising. Videos leaked. There were too many to stop. They showed their brothers fighting Warlord's soldiers in the streets of Big Town. On many of the streets. And the mansion was in flames. The mansion, beneath which many of their people had been enslaved with wetware.

"Well, I'll be damned, Sergeant Jack," LaDue said. "You really are full of surprises."

They watched the videos for a minute, the waving flags, the chants, the tear gas, and the mobs. They fought—only this time, mechs didn't come to disperse them. It went on and on until Wulf began to fear LaDue would leave their orbital compatriots to die yet again.

Except instead, she declared, "The uprising has begun. Notify every cell. Strike their targets. Strike them all."

The signal was sent.

"It's really happening," Wulf said.

"Ja," Father agreed, his face grim. "Now we must see it through."

Wulf wanted to be up there. Wanted to be where he could get a shot at the Warlord. But shooting some of his lieutenants down here would have to suffice.

"We'll chase every single one of them off our world," LaDue told them. "Get ready."

On one of the displays, the guards suddenly toppled without any sign of who shot them. There was a massive explosion near one of the gates, big enough that Wulf felt Swindle tremble beneath his boots.

And from the woods streamed the Original army in their ragtag exos.

With the combat reflexes package active, the Citadel was shockingly quick. It took Jackson's smallest guidance and extrapolated out the most efficient way to make those wishes reality. The mech ran through the streets of Big Town, jumping cars, vaulting buildings, and, remarkably, not stepping on anyone.

The Big Town Guard, on the other hand, wasn't nearly as careful.

The Korvan was following him, still indiscriminately dumping rounds through its chain gun. He'd caught glimpses of one of the Thunderbolts paralleling him on a side street. Of the one he was really worried about—Warlord's Spider—there had been no sign yet.

With most of his sensors offline, Jackson wouldn't see that thing coming. Unlike him, Warlord's weapons were live, and since he'd been putting down rebels at the CX plant, it was bound to have some weapon systems mounted capable of punching the Citadel's armor. If Jackson was going to survive, he had to be smarter than his opponents.

Hiding was out. Something five meters tall couldn't just hide in town, especially when there were already thousands of people watching it. He had to keep moving, stay ahead of them, because the longer he did, the longer Jane and the others had to get away, and the longer she had to break the Citadel's systems so he could fight back.

Problem was, Jackson's combat experience had been gained

on a planet, not inside an orbital. He wasn't used to thinking in terms of having ground troops standing on the ceiling above him.

The proximity alarms were still off, so his first warning was when a near-miss warhead detonated right behind him. He looked up and saw one of the old T7 Jackals had climbed a building to get a bead on him, way, way up the orbital's slope.

Jackson had to dive and roll as the Jackal pilot ripped off an entire rocket pod. Buildings were shredded. People fell screaming.

He watched that, baffled. How could the self-appointed protectors be that callous about the lives of those they were supposed to protect? The old colony ship was big enough that those little rockets wouldn't endanger the hull itself, but that was just a ridiculous, unnecessary loss of life.

Furious, Jackson target locked onto the Jackal, wishing he had his guns so he could smoke that psychopath, but all he could hope was that the Jackal's systems would sense the lock on and duck, not knowing he couldn't shoot. Sure enough, when it got pinged, the little scout mech dropped from its perch and took cover.

"Jane? Come in."

"*Sorry. Running. Busy.*"

But he saw that her programs had cracked more systems. He still didn't have medical, which was bad, because things were getting really mentally foggy and he was really *cold*. But he had some more defensive countermeasures available.

He spotted more mechs above, and to the side, and Jackson suddenly knew what they were doing. They were herding him. But he didn't think the other mech pilots were doing this on their own. They weren't that clever. They wouldn't be that coordinated while driving manually. Warlord was watching, guiding them. Waiting to take his shot.

Jackson got the missile lock warning a few seconds later. He sprang up, ran, dodging side to side, and then slid beneath an overpass. Whoever was lasing him lost sight, and the alarm stopped.

No. Jackson knew who that had been. Warlord was here. Moving from under this cover meant catching a missile.

Except that brief delay beneath the bridge meant the Korvan had caught up, and it had reloaded its big guns. It had a line on him.

Jackson was flipping through the countermeasures menu with his eyes. *There.*

As the Korvan started shooting, Jackson detonated a can of Shine.

The thick veil of light-producing particles spread between him and the military mech. The container of the Shine he'd used to blind Nivaas security had fit in his pocket. This was a 40mm shell of the same stuff. Everyone on the block was blinded.

Including the Korvan, whose sensors were temporarily overwhelmed. That pilot didn't see the Citadel launch itself through the cloud.

Jackson hit the Russian mech with a flying tackle. The two of them went rolling through the street, scattering Shine particles. They crashed into a freight hauler, and the two mechs went sliding apart.

The blinded Korvan pilot kept firing everything he had, in every direction, wildly turning. It was a good thing the colony ship had a hull like a battle cruiser, or this fool might have vented the entire populace into space. Buildings exploded. Innocent people died. Jackson had to end this fast.

Except he only had one hand, and the Korvan was a slippery little bastard.

It seemed like an agonizing decision. He'd denied this part of himself for years, shut it away, in the deepest, darkest prison his mind could create. He'd promised he'd never risk hell again, but despite those vows, someone had still invaded his mind. It had all been for nothing anyway. He could keep denying who he was and what he could do, in a vain attempt at keeping himself safe, or he could rise to his full potential and stop this maniac from killing everyone.

It wasn't about the cost. It was about doing what was *right*.

It seemed like the decision took forever to make. It didn't.

Jackson switched from manual to fly-by-mind.

The electrodes on his head that had been reading impulses through his skin, suddenly turned rock hard, locking him in place. Now they used a wireless tight beam to connect directly to the old implant, buried deep in his brain. The block Jane had jury-rigged wasn't as complete a block as the last one had been. In fact, it seemed a lot of the old Gloss circuitry was still ready to go. He reached for the Citadel and it reached back. There was a moment of alarm and headsplitting pain, and then there was a melding. He felt himself become the Citadel, felt the Citadel become him.

A small packet of joy washed through his brain, for he could suddenly feel the power, the capabilities, the fine engineering of what was now his body. He saw what it saw, and even still secured by its antitheft protocols, he could see *so much more.*

And do so much more.

He saw every bullet, every bit of flying shrapnel, the angle of the Korvan's muzzle, and where they would be aimed in the instant it took him to cover the ground between them. He dodged side to side as bullets shredded the ground, leapt, and caught the Korvan's chain-gun arm.

Jackson's ruined hand twitched uselessly, but he didn't need it to tell the Citadel what to do anymore. He just needed to think it, and the machine filled in the rest.

There was a horrendous screech of metal as he twisted the cannon arm back into the Korvan's body. The pilot was still manually squeezing the trigger, not realizing he'd just signed his own death warrant. Jackson jammed the muzzle against the other mech's cockpit, and let that pilot kill himself.

The guns fell silent. The Korvan flopped at his feet.

Jackson had to stand there for a moment to collect himself. He looked down at his big metal hands and curled them into fists.

It's been a while.

The human mind is severely constrained by the capacity of its working memory. It can hold only six to nine bits of data at the same time. If one wanted to manipulate the data, such as with multiplication, the number it can manage falls to two to four. However, the implant Jackson had been given to meld his mind with machines had dramatically expanded his working memory capacity. Jane's new block hadn't damaged that either. With the Citadel's ultrapowerful processor, it was as if Jackson's brain was on fire. He didn't need to think. That was too slow. He just needed snatches of thought, and the Citadel would do the rest.

As he was in the machine, the machine was also in his head. Only that comparison didn't really work either, because plugged in, it was hard to tell where one entity ended and the other began. They simply *were.*

If he wanted to preserve innocent lives, he needed to change the venue of this fight. Just thinking that made it so that the Citadel combed through all the information in Jackson's head, the schematics of the station Jane had downloaded for him, compared those with the Citadel's extensive knowledge of combat history, Jackson's gut instincts, ran the numbers on all of them, and within half a second he had eight different paths to choose from.

By the time the other mechs could see through the Shine again, the Citadel had vanished.

The captain had been through more than his share of space battles but compared to the sleek vessels he'd served on during the war, this was like watching two fat ladies have an icepick fight.

"Come about, vector delta two."

"Moving to delta two," Alligood responded.

The *Downward Spiral* had been launching missiles at them continually as she closed. The *Tar Heel* wasn't exactly fast, but distance was their friend, and some judicious maneuvering had been able to keep them safe. They had tossed a few missiles back Prunkard's way, but only their slowest, dumbest ordnance. The kind of cheap stuff that would be normal on a carrier of illicit goods. The captain didn't want to tip his hand just yet.

"Prunkard doesn't strike me as much of a strategist," he mused.

"He's more of a bludgeoning instrument," Castillo agreed. "Scans show he's got six external containers with their hatches popped. Those are the missile tubes that he's been cycling through. There's two more containers aft, still closed. From their length, I'll bet they're railguns."

"Not fat enough to be a plasma cannon. Not long enough to be any sort of beam strong enough to slice us open."

"Yep. Gotta be rails. I bet when he gets to within five hundred klicks he'll swivel those our way."

That was spitting distance in a space fight, but he knew how his XO came up with that estimate. The enemy ship was already going slightly faster than they were, and a railgun that size would be throwing projectiles at around four thousand meters a second. As big a target as the *Tar Heel* was, the *Spiral* gunners just needed to aim dead center, and with less than two minutes to get out of the way, odds were they would still get clipped somewhere.

Still, the missiles weren't that worrisome, yet. They needed too much fuel to close the distance, so by the time they got close their maneuverability was limited. Plus, one of the containers they'd moved to the rear of the ship was a close-in defense system that should be able to blast most of the incoming. One downside of not being a real navy was that having to hide your weapons until you needed them didn't lead to the most efficient setups, so Poor Roderick Su was back there in a space suit, riding in that deathtrap, manning their speed gun.

However, if Prunkard got into railgun range, they were in deep kack. Su could throw up a ton of lead, but there was no intercepting anything that tiny and fast. They couldn't speed up because that would take them uncomfortably close to Big Town's defensive picket, and since they were in such a relatively low orbit, Swindle's upper atmo was uncomfortably close. The directions they could go were limited. It was the sort of situation that would make the inexperienced captain of a lightly armed freighter feel rather trapped.

The captain planned out a new suggested vector on his pad, up and away from their current orbit, then he put that on the main display.

Castillo studied it. "You want Prunkard to think we've gotten scared and are trying to make a run for it. That angle, if the *Spiral* pushes her engines to max, they might be able to get some rail shots on us before we're clear."

"Yep. Prunkard won't be able to resist the prize. Which means *Spiral* will be closing really fast when she gets a bunch of missiles in her face."

Castillo was doing his own calculations. "Waiting until he's committed—that's not much of a window before those railguns fire."

"Pride comes before the fall, XO."

"Yours or Prunkard's?"

"Finding out is half the fun. Pop containers three through ten. I'm feeling festive."

Jane, Tui, Katze, Bushey, and the last of her bots ran through the streets of Big Town, heading for the docks. It was complete pandemonium. Normally a bunch of heavily armed, obviously shot-up people, with a bunch of little robots tagging along, would stand out, but not today.

Big Towners had come out of their homes, first to see what the commotion was about, and then to join in, one way or the other.

"I haven't seen this much excitement since the gang wars!" declared one old man as he gleefully lit a Molotov cocktail, before throwing it at a police car.

"This place is insane!" Jane shouted.

If she had to guess, a quarter of the population were loyal to the Originals, and today they saw an opportunity to strike a blow for freedom. Another quarter were loyal to the Warlord, and they'd turned out to fight the first group. The remaining half of Big Town were hiding or fleeing, depending on how close they were to the action.

Judging by the explosions and tracers flying across the interior of the orbital, most of that action was following Jackson in the opposite direction. When he said he would draw them off, he hadn't been joking. One of the things she appreciated about Jackson—he never did anything halfway.

Too bad he hadn't drawn off Fain.

Jane winced as she lost another bot. Everything she'd sent to slow Fain and his pet monster down had vanished. She'd collected plenty of videos of him spotting a bot and blasting it out of the sky with a pistol, or of his dog thing chomping them, but that was it. She hadn't been able to land a single shot on him, and he was closing in on them.

She got a transmission from Jackson *"Hey, Jane, I've got an idea. A surefire way we all get off Big Town alive is with a ransom."*

"Warlord's not going to accept anything from us now."

"No, he won't. But we won't be offering to pay anything. We're going to be the ones receiving the payment."

"You're going after him."

"Biggest fish in the pond. A nice fat prize."

"That's the wetware talking. Oh my God, I gave you brain damage."

"I'm good. I've got a plan. I just need you to unlock guns, sensors, and first aid. Then I can take him. He's after me right now."

"Don't underestimate Warlord. Your mechs are equals, but he's got mods and is flying by mind. You can't beat that. He's..." Then Jane trailed off as she realized, "You linked in."

"Yeah. I didn't have much choice."

"But those nanites are still fighting in your head! Do you have any idea how much danger this puts you in?" With that vicious wetware running wild, he was especially vulnerable to getting brain fried. Other than the tiny chip she'd stuck in there, he had no real defenses against a hack. If he lasted that long! With his brain running hot enough to meld with a mech, it was going to put a terrible strain on some already overtaxed systems, in a brain that was currently overrun with murderous nanotech.

He was venturing back into the land of demons, and she wasn't there to light his way. Jackson was doomed.

"I know what you're thinking, but just get me my systems. If I can capture Warlord, then he'll order his forces to stand down. I'll make him call off Prunkard's pirate ship. It's our only chance."

She had left her programs running, but the Citadel's firewalls were excellent. More systems should have fallen, but they were adapting on the fly and fighting her off. The time-remaining estimates had jumped from minutes to hours. There was no way she could pause and deal with that while sprinting through the streets of crazy town. She was good, but she wasn't that good.

"Tui, we need to stop for a minute. I need to reassess my cyberattacks to help Jackson."

"We're almost to the spinner. We'll be stuck on the platform while it matches rotational speed no matter what. He'll just have to hold out that long." He glanced back over her shoulder, apprehensive. "Where's Fain?"

"I don't have eyes on him." In fact, she was running unnervingly low on eyes, and was down to just a few members of her platoon left.

The spin bays were just ahead of them. Luckily, it appeared the security goons who would normally be watching them were otherwise occupied. They must have gotten tired of having rocks and bottles thrown at them and sought shelter. Past the platform, it appeared the docks were spinning rapidly while Big Town held still. She knew the opposite was true but knowing that didn't stop her stomach from churning from looking at it. This sort of madness was why she was content to just stay in her lair.

They walked into one of the bays. Most of the interior was taken up by an eight-wheeled freight hauler and its containers, which had been abandoned here when the workers had either fled or joined the riot. Katze had to help Bushey along. Despite the stims and med kits, he'd lost too much blood. He tripped and fell.

"Don't you fade on me," Katze begged.

Bushey's words were slurred. "I'm jus' takin' a little nap."

Tui knelt next to him. "At least you waited until someplace we'll have zero G before making us carry your ass."

"I'm considerate like that." Bushey's head sagged. He was out.

The controls were locked down, but with direct access, it only took Jane a few seconds to bypass those. The bay began to move on its axle. Big Town seemed to lurch away. Their gravity would lighten as they slowed down. Once they were stationary and weightless, they would enter the docks. She set her remaining bots on guard mode, but she was down to Ron the Bear, tiny Baby, Roger, and Tom. Those last two were fliers the size of golf balls who could drill through all sorts of things—wood, metal, flesh.

While Katze tried to keep Bushey alive, Jane flipped down the visor and checked the bots she'd left attached to the Citadel. Seth was gone, smashed during the fight, but Pilgrim was still burrowed in, granting her direct physical access. Some of her programs had been stopped cold, so she analyzed how the firewall had beaten them, then adjusted and relaunched. Jane was professionally offended. She had given Jackson an ETA and failed to deliver. That would not stand.

"Jane, sorry to interrupt," Tui said. "But could you put your chain-saw bear on cutting the door? It's safety locked to not open to the dock side until the spinning stops, but I'd rather not wait."

"Ron, go. Do as the big human commands." Then she went back into the VR world, where the Citadel seemed to have multiple personalities, with half of its systems actively connected to Jackson's brain, while the other half rooted for his demise. She helped them see the error of their ways, and was making good progress, and then Roger's alarm began wailing.

Intruder.

She jolted back to reality.

But the alarm had gone off too late, because an instant later someone grabbed her by the shoulders and flung her violently to the floor.

There were gunshots right above her. Stunned, she lifted her visor.

Fain.

He had leapt onto the moving platform, hit her, and then started shooting. Somehow, he had snuck right past her bot net.

Katze got hit. She yelped and fell over Bushey's unconscious form, then scrambled on her hands and knees behind one of the containers.

Fain spun toward where Tui and Ron were trying to get the door open. Tui ducked behind the freight truck. Not fast enough.

One of Fain's bullets hit. Blood splattered across the wall as Tui dropped.

"No!" Jane shouted, kicking wildly. Except—without even bothering to look—Fain caught her by the ankle and pulled. He was so outlandishly strong that Jane got swung through the air, was then airborne, briefly, before hitting the floor hard enough to knock the air out of her lungs. She skidded across the metal surface until she hit the far wall.

"Come out, Fuamatu. Let's end this," Fain shouted, keeping his pistol trained on the spot he'd last seen Tui. "Come along quietly and maybe I'll spare your friends."

Tui didn't even dignify that lie with a response. He just came out shooting.

Only Fain was already dodging to the side, faster than any human had a right to be.

Katze leaned out from behind the container, aiming her carbine, but before she could fire, a shadow appeared behind her. The grendel pounced, landed on Katze, and took her to the ground. Katze managed to draw her pistol, but the monster's jaws clamped around her forearm. It bit. Bones broke. Katze screamed as it shook her back and forth.

Tui was standing there, bleeding, gun empty. He dropped it and started toward Fain, lifting his fists.

Fain shot him in the gut. Tui dropped to his knees.

"Hold," Fain told his beast, which stopped shaking poor Katze, though she was still pinned beneath it. Then he turned his attention toward Tui. "I've got to say, you *Tar Heel* people are a scrappy bunch. Your little buddy is making a mess of the station. This was a cushy contract until you came around. This is the hardest I've had to work since I've taken this job."

Tui had both of his hands pressed to the wound on his abdomen. Blood came out of his mouth as he said, "You work for a nutcase."

"Not my first time, probably won't be my last." Fain lifted his gun and pressed it against Tui's forehead. "But upgrades aren't cheap."

Everything hurt. Jane struggled to breathe. She wasn't designed for combat like her companions. She wasn't a scrapper like Jackson. She'd never signed up for this physical nonsense. But she had skills the rest of them couldn't begin to understand.

"Wait," she managed to gasp, interrupting Tui's execution.

She could have launched a bot at the dog, but she'd seen the thin fingers of blue-tinged lightning arc from its collar to zap the others, so she knew better. Besides, the grendel seemed content to hold onto Katze as its master had commanded. For a Swindle creature, it seemed remarkably tame, and there had to be a reason why. Jane pulled up some of her bot's dying vids, zoomed in on the collar, studied the mechanism, drew some conclusions, and then let some programs fly.

Fain glanced at her, but he didn't remove the gun from Tui's head. "Don't worry, little specter girl. I haven't forgotten about you. When I was pulling files on your crew, it was like you didn't even exist. No history, no records, nothing. I've never seen anybody's identity get scrubbed that clean. Which makes me think you must be really valuable to someone. I think I'll keep you alive long enough to find out who you're hiding from, so I can sell you to them."

"I'm worth a hundred of you, soldier boy."

"Doubtful. I get paid really good for this." He pulled the trigger.

Nothing happened.

Fain scowled at his gun long enough to realize that Baby had crawled behind his trigger and was blocking its rearward travel with her body.

Tui tried to grab him, but Fain jumped back and snap kicked Tui in the face.

Jane launched Tom at Fain's head. The murderous golf ball zigzagged back and forth, going for his eyes. Ron the Bear ran and slid under the cargo hauler, slashing his saw hands at Fain's leg. She sent her last bot, Roger, off to do something special.

Fain leapt over Ron, ducked beneath Tom, and then tossed his pistol when he realized he wouldn't be able to pry Baby out. Jane immediately had Baby spring from the gun onto Fain's jacket and activate her laser cutter.

She guided all of them simultaneously, with surgical precision, but Fain was just too fast. He swatted Tom out of the air. Pinched Baby between his fingertips and kicked Ron across the bay. The bear bounced off the hauler hard enough to dent the sheet metal.

Jane commanded Baby to pierce his gloved fingers with the sharp needles embedded in her body. She did. But Fain just smiled, then chuckled. "That only works on flesh and blood. This arm's titanium and armor weave." He squeezed. There was a *pop*. And Jane lost Baby's connection. "You're too much of a pain. Screw selling you to the highest bidder. I'm just going to beat you to death."

As Fain started toward her, Jane sent a silent message to Katze and Tui. *"Hard stop coming."* Then she told Roger to throw his body into the spin bay's emergency brakes.

The whole world lurched. Instead of the pad's rotation gently slowing, it was an immediate halt. The suddenly weightless hauler and containers flew upward. Everything was violently flung across the bay.

Except for Jane, who had locked her mag boots to the floor.

Fain hadn't seen that coming. Sailing through the air, off-balance, he was temporarily vulnerable.

Tui hit him, probably harder than she'd ever seen any living thing hit another. And Fain crashed into the hauler. Tui slammed his fist into Fain's armored skull, again and again. As the two spun, weightless and struggling, it looked like Tui might actually be able to take him.

Desperate, Fain shouted, "Sabano, sic him!"

The Swindle beast's jaws let go of Katze. It struggled to move, unused to zero G, but it had killer instincts, and managed to hook onto the hauler, pulling itself toward the two combatants. Its claws stretched for Tui's throat.

Jane flipped her visor down and concentrated on the programs she'd launched at it earlier. They'd been chipping away, so she picked the most vulnerable point and hit that damaged firewall like the hammer of Thor.

The light on the grendel's collar turned from green to red.

"No!" Jane shouted. "Bad grendel, stop!"

The monster paused and shook its head as if stunned. Fain looked at Jane, then the collar, and then back at Jane.

"Kill h—" But Tui slugged Fain in the jaw before he could finish the command.

The beast looked lost, confused, and then it raised its head and looked balefully at Fain. It rumbled deep in its throat, a menacing sound.

Fain managed to hurl Tui away. His pistol was floating by. He snagged it from the air.

The grendel lunged and took Fain by the throat.

Jabbing the gun into its ribs, Fain fired several rapid shots, but the beast only bit down harder, then wrenched the flesh away. Fain shot it in the heart. But the grendel bit his spine. Fain spasmed, as the dog snarled and tore.

It was horrific. Jane flipped up her visor to watch better.

A few painful seconds later, Fain and his grendel were both dead, slowly turning in a cloud of blood droplets.

Jane looked around. Tui was gut shot. Katze's arm was shredded. She couldn't tell if Bushey was alive or dead. Sirens were sounding.

The door to the docks slid open. A troop of security forces suddenly rounded the corner. Half a dozen men were pointing guns their way.

Speakers blasted at them. "Stick to the walls! Facedown! Spread your arms!"

Jane had no bots left. Her platoon was gone. Jane shook her head. They'd come all this way only to fail when the peanut gallery arrived?

"Stick to the walls!"

"You're on your own, Jacky."

CHAPTER 37

The Citadel moved along the exterior of the orbital, leaping from spire to spire. Even while his real body was reaching the limits of physical agony, his new body was joyous and free. He might be dying, but for the first time in years, he was truly alive.

There had been one maintenance airlock big enough for him to fit through on the schematics, less than half a klick from where he'd popped the Shine canister. Jackson had made sure he'd appeared on multiple cameras and scanners along the way. It was a trail of breadcrumbs. He wanted—needed—Warlord to follow.

Out here they could fight without endangering thousands of lives. If he could capture Warlord, he could force a surrender. Jane, Tui, Katze, and Bushey could escape. The Originals would be spared. The *Tar Heel* would be safe.

But then he got Jane's message.

"Jane? Jane, are you there?"

Nothing. Jackson hurried and checked the status of her hacking programs. He still didn't have his main systems unlocked, but the timer had gone back to minutes instead of hours. She'd come through for him after all.

Except looking at those countdowns made him realize he'd been too distracted to think about the bomb in his spine. He checked the timer he'd set back on Swindle. Thirty-seven minutes.

"Shanks. Not good." It was a race to see what was going to kill him first. Damn LaDue. He needed more time. More time to let Jane and the others get away. And if it was going to work, he needed to have the Warlord well before LaDue's surprise jumped out of its birthday cake parting gift.

Sensors were the next system to fall to Jane's automated onslaught. The difference was astounding. Before, it had been like being blindfolded under water. Now he could sense everything.

Being a mech meant he had hundreds of eyes, some were powerful telescopes, and others so fine they could scan the microbes floating by. He could see in IR, UV, and thermal. He didn't just hear, he had dozens of microphones, active and passive sonar, and a layer of liquid skin that could translate vibrations into a 3D map of the surrounding world. Vents and filters collected particles and fed them in mass spectrometers for his sense of smell. The Citadel picked up and analyzed every bit in that flood of information and by a miracle of technology and the shard of silicone in his brain, he understood it all.

Back on Gloss, he'd felt like a god of war in his old mech. This was so much better. Staggeringly better.

In the distance, past the shining solar panels and orbital farms, the *Tar Heel* was slugging it out with another ship. The Citadel read the heat trails from hundreds of missiles and the crisscrossing beams, and Jackson knew that his people were in real trouble. *Tar Heel* was tougher than she looked, but she was no warship. He needed to take out Warlord soon, or else.

"Come on, guns." But that timer was still counting down, and occasionally back up as the systems fought back. Then Jackson disconnected enough to be back in his own body. He felt the pain in his head, saw the ruin of his hand, saw that the clean new cockpit was covered in his blood, and realized that what he really needed to be rooting for was the onboard med system. His body was going into shock, but his brain would remain connected to the mech until it ran out of oxygenated blood and croaked. Luckily, unlike when he'd first stolen this thing planetside, the oxygen unit had been loaded. So at least he had that going for him. Jackson plugged back in and left all that messy mortal business behind.

The vibration sensors warned him when the airlock opened. He no longer had line of sight on it—and without guns it wouldn't have helped if he had—but from the length of time and amount of disturbance, multiple mechs were coming outside. The Citadel analyzed what it could. Bipedal. Bipedal... Multilegged. Bingo. Warlord was here.

Bots online.

Not his ideal choice, but Jackson would take every system he could get. The Citadel carried a small fleet of bots, some armed troubleshooters, but mostly scouts that could drastically increase his sensor coverage. He launched them all. They zipped off in every direction.

One of those scouts immediately paid off. Not only did he have mechs incoming, a gunship was heading this way, hugging the orbital to stay out of sight. It would appear over the hull horizon in a matter of seconds.

Jackson fled.

The Citadel made amazing time, mag locking and unlocking at the most precise moments for total control and maximum speed. But the gunship had no problem catching up. He saw that it was a three-meter-long twin seater. It was nothing but a glorified container mover with a big gun welded to it. The thing would have been laughable if Jackson could shoot back.

Weapons lock.

He ducked behind an antenna spire, and hoped it was something valuable enough Warlord's forces would hesitate to fire on it.

Nope.

The railgun drilled a molten hole through the array, through the support pylons, and narrowly missed the Citadel's leg. He moved as the gunship moved, trying to keep solid metal between them. He checked his weapon status. Ten seconds remaining. Nine. Eight. Fifteen. Shanks.

The gunship kept firing, turning the array into Swiss cheese. His armor took a few hits. The feedback told him the smart gel had absorbed tons of energy. A few more of those and he was toast. Jackson grabbed a piece of debris as it was floating away, leaned out, and hurled it at the gunship. It was six hundred meters away, so that was a laughable attack, but he was just trying to buy himself some time. The gunship drifted to the side to avoid the clumsy projectile, as it aligned its railgun for another shot.

Weapons systems online.

"Thank you, Jane!"

Ports opened along the Citadel's arms and torso. Pods engaged on his shoulders, recoil mechanisms locking into place. He stepped out from behind the shredded array and let the gunship have both rails. Each projectile was moving at thirty-five hundred meters per second, and he put them both right through the cockpit. The impact smashed the crew into red goo, which sprayed out the holes with a great deal of pressure. The gunship twisted hard away, went into a spiral, and sank toward the surface.

That was immensely satisfying.

Mechs incoming.

They were moving through the antennas, using them for cover just as Jackson had, only he had bots up and easily saw them first. There was the old T-Bolt, then the Jackal. They were the hammer. Which told him the Spider was the anvil. And sure enough, when he sent a bot that way, Warlord was right where Jackson figured he would be. Warlord was good, but he wasn't as unpredictable as he thought he was.

Alarms went off. The Citadel was intercepting hacking attempts, and these new ones certainly hadn't come from Jane. His motion sensors picked up the new threat. A horde of security rats were heading his way. Nasty little bots, probably released from the Spider. They were normally armed, and could have fired, but Warlord knew the grade of his armor, knew that was pointless with their little guns. Their goal would be to land on him so they could try to gnaw joints, exposed tubing or compartments, or destroy sensors. If they could brute force access the Citadel's internals, he'd get hacked, just like Jane had done with her little bots.

The horde approached. Jackson swatted half a dozen rats aside. He shot others. But there were so many, coming so fast, that he couldn't get them all. A few landed on him, blasting away with a high-pitched frequencies meant to scramble his sensors. There was a slight fuzzing of his readouts.

Except Jane had already gotten him his countermeasures. It was time to fry these little bastards.

The Citadel's reactor wasn't anywhere near its maximum output yet, but it was so powerful he had juice to spare, and he charged the gel layer of the smart armor. One rat had actually found a way to open one of his exterior compartments, which was not good. But then a massive thrumming wave of electrical current washed over the Citadel's exterior. There was a flurry of loud electrical snaps and bright flashes. Rats went flying, smoking and glowing, bolts of electricity following them. Others clung where they were and were hollowed out by the charge. Like one great big bug zapper.

Jackson brushed off the final few shells still clinging to him. "You're going to have to do better than that."

Jackson's bots warned him the other mechs were angling for a shot, and he had more gunships approaching. Jackson picked a spot farther along the hull where a bunch of extra modules had been bolted on, their purpose a mystery, but the important thing was they had solar panels overhead, which would keep him out of view of the gunships. He moved.

The orbital was still turning. Swindle was directly before him now, a vast globe of angry clouds. Seen through every possible variation of the visual spectrum at the same time, it truly was beautiful. Also, a lot closer than he had realized. Big Town had a relatively low orbit.

Rockets detonated around him. Missiles were tracking him, following his heat signature, but he dropped flares to draw them off, and picked off the few that made it through with his miniguns.

The Jackal and the Thunderbolt were shooting at him, but they had terrible angles. Jackson could kill them easily but didn't. He needed Warlord to think he had the upper hand until it was too late. The Spider was moving fast, far faster than the Citadel could in this environment. Zero G was where multilimb mechs shone. It was able to move in any direction and still find a solid hold.

Jackson turned both railguns on the Spider, but Warlord had been waiting for that and the swift mech dropped out of sight before Jackson got a firing solution. He flung two rounds that way just in the hopes he might get lucky. No dice.

He reached the shade beneath the solar panels before the gunships could get a lock on him, scanned his new surroundings, found them to be a claustrophobic and confusing maze of pipes, and decided this would do perfectly. Once committed in here, Warlord would have a really hard time escaping.

The Spider landed on the solar panels above. Warlord fired blindly down. Jackson responded. The space between them filled with reflective shards, then the Spider launched itself down into the pipes.

For just an instant, Jackson had a gap. He could see the gunships through the new hole in the solar panels. Their onboard computers were painfully slow compared to his. By the time they realized they were in danger, Jackson had tagged them both and launched a swarm of smart missiles from the Citadel's shoulders. He didn't stick around to watch them die.

The Jackal pilot was more aggressive than the T-Bolt's, so that got him killed first. The light scout mech swung in behind Jackson, trying to sneak up on an all-knowing and all-seeing god of war. Jackson hit it with the shoulder-mounted grenade launcher, turned, and nailed the staggering mech with the railgun. By a miracle, the chest armor buckled, but held...But only for half a second, because then Jackson hit him with the second, right through the powerplant. The T7 exploded.

The Spider danced through the pipes, upside down to Jackson's position, multiple guns flashing. The Citadel was hit by rockets, bullets, and frag, while lasers danced across his sensors, trying to blind him. Jackson ran, firing back.

Warning. A penetrator round had punched his smart armor and nailed the ammo hopper. His railguns couldn't be reloaded. Jackson dispatched a repair bot. It actually felt like a scorpion crawled through a hole in his chest and started to poke around with red-hot pincer and its tail was a welder. That was a bit disconcerting, so Jackson turned down the feedback on the repair system. *Much better.*

But it was too bad he couldn't turn down the feedback on his real body, because even with his consciousness sunk into the mech, the pain in his hand and head was becoming too great to shut out. Jackson's hand was dying and the lack of circulation was shooting lightning bolts up his central nervous system to a brain that was filled with angry nanites stabbing each other. That was affecting his performance. The Citadel's reflexes were off fifteen percent because of the distraction. When it notified him of that, a prompt asked him if he would like to engage the onboard medical assistant. Y/N. When he picked yes, he got an error message, saying that system was currently unavailable. Jackson laughed bitterly. The Citadel was so beautiful, but so cruel.

The T-Bolt came in the same way Jackson had. It was a tough old mech. Jackson knew that in the right hands, one of those could work miracles on the battlefield. In the wrong hands, it was an accident waiting to happen. The poor pilot never even saw the bot Jackson had left there as a trip mine. The explosion shoved the Thunderbolt into view. Jackson turned his grenade launcher and autocannon on the old mech and beat it like a pinata until candy came out.

As pieces of the Thunderbolt floated off into space, Jackson stopped and listened.

The vibrations were minimal. Warlord was holding perfectly still. The pipes were filled with steam, which created too much background distortion for him to pick out the Spider's reactor. Jackson's bots confirmed the gunships were dead, so he sent a few scouts up to fly a search pattern. Then he began moving, ever so slowly, because the Spider's sensors were equal to his, and whoever saw the other first would certainly win this.

There.

The Spider came from beneath, up through the piping. Warlord fired up. Jackson fired down. The Citadel was hit, hard. Warnings sounded. Damage reports scrolled across his mind.

The two of them kept moving, bouncing back and forth between the girders and cables. Jackson took out the grenade launcher on the Spider's back with his autocannon, but then an explosion shredded his side. Smart armor bled out the hole. One of the Spider's legs suddenly buckled and split, fluid spraying, sparks shooting from severed wires, but it had seven more to make up the difference. They both kept firing as they crashed across the orbital.

They were getting close to the CX processing plant. Jackson didn't know which one of them fired the stray round that punched the storage tank, but it turned out that CX was *extremely* explosive.

The blast wave hit Jackson like a million-kilo tidal wave.

"Captain, Big Town's been hit," Alligood warned.

"How bad?"

"Can't tell. I'll replay the feed."

The image appeared on his screen. From here Big Town was just a giant, ugly, misshapen log. There was a bright orange flash, which winked out of existence as fast as it came, and then bits were flying off one end out into space.

"That wasn't one of our missiles, was it?"

"No, sir. Positively not," she said, as she flipped through the trajectory of everything they'd launched. "It appears to have been one of their storage tanks."

"Jackson..." He sighed. Well, it looked like Big Town was still in one piece. The whole place didn't come apart, and all he could do was hope his people in there were still alive, because right then he had more immediate concerns.

The *Downward Spiral* had taken his bait. She had changed course and gone to full burn to close the distance in time. They had a great shot of her now, the bulbous girl riding a pillar of fire right at them. Sure enough, the two external containers that Castillo had guessed held railguns were open.

She had never stopped firing missiles either, and the display had four red tracks on them. Three, as Su blasted the closest one out of existence.

The captain watched the numbers flick past. He wanted Prunkard trapped. Normally speed gives you options, but not so much when you were flying straight into a missile barrage. Launch too early, Prunkard would turn. Too late, railguns would punch their hull. There was that perfect window, where the enemy would still be able to evade, but he'd hesitate, still thinking he could pull off the shot in time, and in that brief moment of indecision, victory would be decided.

There was no clear answer. That's why good captains had to go with their gut.

Since their weapon systems were last-second bolt-ons, and they couldn't even lay a proper pathwork in advance without attracting the attention of a particularly bright customs inspector saying *hey I wonder what they need this wiring for,* so the *Tar Heel* didn't have a centralized fire-control system. They had to do this the old-fashioned way, with him sending firing solutions and trajectories directly to the crew, who were manning those cargo containers, to plug directly into their missile-control panels.

"All containers prepare to fire. On my mark, containers six through ten will launch." Those were the containers that currently had an angle. The rest were blocked by the hull. Green lights flashed. Command received. They were ready. "In three, two, one, Fire!"

Five blue tracks appeared on the display, streaking toward the *Downward Spiral.*

"XO. Flip her."

Castillo had been awaiting that signal. He slid his hands across his display to activate the predetermined thruster activations. "Rolling hull."

The *Tar Heel* spun, so the other exterior containers could get a shot.

"Containers one through five will launch. In three, two, one, Fire!"

Five more tracks.

"All containers reload. Reload! XO, activate evasive maneuvers."

"Evasive maneuvers activated." Castillo's eyes were glued to his screen, because wherever those railguns were pointed was somewhere they did not want to be in the next two minutes.

Most of their ordnance wasn't standardized. Not even close. They were armed with whatever oddball missiles they'd been able to steal, or that had been too old, damaged, or otherwise screwed up to sell to their regular customers. However, he had always believed in saving for a rainy day, so three of the ten missiles that were currently homing in on the *Downward Spiral* were top tier, smart tech from Berringer-Krupp. He could have sold each of them for a fortune. The ship killers were worth their weight in gold, but he'd kept them, knowing that someday there would be a moment like this. He'd even had Jane go over their systems herself with a fine-tooth comb to make sure they were in top working order. The brilliant specter had pronounced their AI "frightening."

The rest of the missiles were insurance to confuse or draw off any antimissile tech Prunkard had available.

It was almost as if he could sense the other captain's hesitation. Prunkard nearly had the shot. Would he peel off and live to fight another day, or hope his close-in systems and armor would deal with the missiles, long enough to seize the win?

Prunkard stayed the course.

"Ballsy," the captain said, with a little admiration in his voice. "I'll give him that."

"Their railguns are firing," Castillo reported, as he tried to spin their giant ship like a top.

The *Spiral* had its own speed guns, and as the missiles closed, they began launching thousands of hypervelocity projectiles to intercept. Flak bombs detonated, creating a lethal debris cloud in front of the ship. Plasma arcs confused heat sensors. The blue tracks began to flash out of existence or veer off in confusion, but those that remained got closer and closer.

And then there were thirty blue tics in the sky as the smart missiles launched their own decoys and countermeasures. They all accelerated simultaneously.

"I almost feel sorry for the guy right now," Castillo stated flatly.

"Shank Jeet, but I hope that dog has an escape pod," the captain said.

The shipkillers were slippery, murderous little bastards, and there was a succession as three bright flashes as they made it through the *Downward Spiral* defenses. That would be their penetrators melting into streams of superheated plasma to punch holes through even the hardest armor plate. The much bigger flashes that followed were their explosive payloads detonating.

"Three hits," Alligood reported. "Good effect on target. She's bleeding air and heat, sir. We've got multiple hull breaches."

Another explosion rocked the *Downward Spiral,* as something went off in their engine room. There was a rippling shudder of secondary detonations.

"She's crippled," the captain said. They'd won. Now they just needed to survive long enough to appreciate the fact. "What about that rail, XO?"

"They got one shot off. Incoming. Trying to evade."

Captain Holloway activated the collision alert and hoped for the best.

Medical System Online. Automated response initiated.

It was all the needles that suddenly jabbed into his skin that brought Jackson back to consciousness. He was still in the cockpit, still strapped in place, but his mind had been kicked out of the system. It was just him, hanging in the dark, with all the pain in the world.

His head was swimming. He remembered an explosion right next to him. Even with the Citadel's smart armor the concussion had been enough to knock him the hell out.

Warlord. Where was the Warlord?

Jackson checked his surroundings and realized with a shock that they were tumbling through space. The explosion had flung them off the orbital. The mech had taken severe damage. Multiple systems down. Exact location unknown. Multiple feeds cut. The repair bots were working like crazy, crawling all over the Citadel, putting things right. He directed them to concentrate on sensors so he could figure out what was going on.

The Warlord—Jackson couldn't find him.

He checked his countdown clock.

Nine minutes.

Which meant he'd been out for a few minutes.

Jackson checked his vitals. He was still trashed. Nanite-induced migraine of doom, and a hand that was more hamburger than hand. And the spine bomb was still ticking. He had to get himself taken care of before the fleshy part of this partnership shut down permanently. He accessed the medical system and saw that it had already gone to work on him. These fifth gens had the equivalent to an automated field hospital crammed into them. It made sense. The pilot was physically the weakest link in the system.

Serious head trauma. Possible brain damage. Recommend pilot does not link directly to the system until properly tended. Severe risk of stroke and/or death.

Tell me something I don't know, Jackson thought sardonically. The Citadel could tend the hole Jane had cut, but there wasn't anything it could do about the nanites. He could only hope that her tiny army was doing its job.

Gunshot wound. Attending.

A tiny robotic arm came out of the wall and reached for his hand. It whirled through several tools, before spraying the foreign material out of the hole with some sort of disinfectant. Then it filled the hole with some sort of gel, which immediately began to harden. In a minute it would be solid enough to remove the TQ, though it warned him he would need to seek out a real medical professional to attempt to repair the shattered bones. Though the Citadel did offer him the option to just amputate now and get it over with.

"No, thank you."

Foreign body detected in back. Analyzing.

"Don't do that. Scans might set it off." But then again, with how little time he had left, he didn't have much to lose. Jane hadn't been able to, but this thing had the best portable first-aid system on the market, way better than what they had on *Tar Heel.* So it was worth a shot. "Be careful. It's a bomb. Can you remove it?"

Negative. But rather than just give up, the Citadel's AI continued to puzzle through the problem. A moment later it offered him a partial solution. Jackson looked over the proposal on his screen. Basically, it meant injecting the same hardening agent it had used on his hand, directly into the firing mechanism of the bomb in the hopes that it would temporarily block it. It would still be there, and the container holding the poison would certainly start to dissolve on its own soon afterward, but it might put a few extra minutes on his clock... With only a forty-five percent chance of killing him outright.

That was better than a coin flip. "Go for it."

Apparently, the gel had a local anesthetic in it, because he didn't even feel it stab him through the chair.

A few extremely tense seconds later, his spine hadn't melted. And Jackson quit holding his breath. Back to work.

Visuals and telemetry were coming back online. Sure enough, the Citadel was tumbling through space in a field of debris. There was still no sign of Warlord. The debris were too hot, so if the Spider was among them, he couldn't pick it out.

Jackson looked back at the orbital, saw the black scorch mark where the CX tank had been, but other than that the place seemed to be in one piece. But Big Town was really far away. Too far away. He had to ping it to get a distance measurement to be sure. Then as the Citadel turned, he saw Swindle, which was really close. Frighteningly close.

He was heading for the atmosphere.

"Shanks."

Too many of his thrusters were damaged to beat gravity. He was going down no matter what. The Citadel was drop-capable. It could handle reentry. Normally that meant being launched from a ship on a specific trajectory, aimed at a landing zone, usually with extra beryllium shielding that would get scorched and discarded in upper atmo. Not tumbling and shot up. This would take some finesse to not hit the air like a brick at 27,000 kph.

That meant plugging back in.

Jackson went to fly-by-mind. The Citadel told him that really wasn't a good idea. He insisted. A warning from Raycor popped up on the display, which said he had to agree that that Raycor was in no way liable for what he was about to do against their advice. Jackson hurried and signed the user agreement with his bloody fingertip.

He was once again one with the machine. Only this time his

giant robot body was the one that hurt more than the frail real one. Jackson immediately began prioritizing repairs and correcting their movement. He'd never done an orbital drop before, but the training had been directly downloaded into his brain by the Hampson device all those years ago, so the information was still there. This was doable.

But it was also Swindle he was dropping toward, which was a suckhole on its best day. Luckily, the continent he had visited previously was in view. Better the devil you know than the one you don't. He tagged where he thought LaDue's base was as his ideal landing zone. If he didn't disintegrate on the way down, he'd walk in there, tear the doors off her hideout, and make her get this bomb out of him.

"Jane, Captain, Tui, I don't know if any of you can hear me. I don't even know if you're still alive. I tried to catch Warlord but I lost him. I don't know if I'm going to make it, but if I don't, I love you guys. It's been one hell of a ride. Jackson out."

The shredded chunks of Big Town around him began to glow orange.

Jackson was concentrating so hard on calculating reentry that he didn't see the Spider flying toward him until it was too late.

The mechs collided.

CHAPTER 38

The Spider used a few of its legs to grab him and the rest to try and rip him apart. It had seven limbs left, and each of those limbs extended claws or flashed with the crackling blue arc of a plasma cutter.

Jackson fought back, using his own cutter to slice a line along the Spider's body. He got one foot onto it and shoved, creating enough distance to aim his autocannon down into its belly Shells exploded against smart armor, but didn't punch the Warlord's cockpit.

Alarms sounded. Warnings flashed. The exterior temp was skyrocketing. They were both going to burn up, and Warlord was too focused on killing him to care.

Engaging all his thrusters, the Citadel rolled, spinning the Spider toward the planet. Waves of shimmering heat rolled off the enemy mech. The Big Town debris turned into molten balls of fire as they careened back and forth between them.

A claw punched the Citadel's chest and ripped off a panel. He was bleeding liquid armor. But Jackson caught that leg, threw all the power he could to his arm, and twisted hard. Metal tore as Jackson ripped the leg clean off. He immediately started using it like a club, slamming it against the Spider's cockpit.

All his exterior sensors could pick up was fire, but Warlord still wouldn't let go.

✧　　✧　　✧

"LaDue, we've got enemy dropships inbound."

Wulf watched as the Original's leader pause as she checked the image being sent to her combat exo. They'd assaulted the mountain base. The rangers had fought like wild beasts, and a few pockets of resistance remained. But if Warlord was sending reinforcements from Big Town...Wulf looked toward his father nervously. Could they have come this far just to have to give up now?

"That's no dropship," LaDue said. "Zoom in. Focus."

Not a dropship? Wulf looked up and saw a fireball streaking down from the sky.

"They're towing over meteors and dropping them on us!" someone screamed.

That made sense to Wulf. He was no soldier, but he'd learned enough to know that whoever ruled the skies, ultimately ruled the ground beneath. Warlord was so bitter that if he could not control Swindle, he would rather burn the whole world than let someone else have it. He had been taught that it had been a massive asteroid impact which had made the dinosaurs extinct on old Earth. Swindle was a land of giants, like old Earth had been. It seemed an appropriate way for giants to die.

"Hold your horses," LaDue never panicked. Wulf supposed that was why she'd ended up as their leader. "It's not a bombardment either." LaDue was listening to a report from one of their spotters on Big Town. "It's two mechs locked in a fight to the death. I think that, boys and girls, is Warlord and Sergeant Jack."

The Originals, exhausted from battle, began to cheer as they watched their nemesis plummet to his fiery doom. Warlord was evil personified. He was the devil. Wulf had thought of Jackson Rook as an intruder, an outsider, probably a liar, and most certainly a fool. But he had done it. He had really done it. And the devil had been cast out of heaven.

Already Wulf could tell the fireball would strike over by Horonds Bay, close by. A large and dangerous body of water, home to one of the mighty kaiju.

LaDue was looking at him. Her face was stern through her exo. "Don't even think about it, Wulf. We've got the rangers on the ropes. We've got to push them off this mountain now or this was all for nothing. I need you."

It was not right. "Father," Wulf begged.

"Someone must confirm Warlord is dead." Father stared at LaDue, just as unflinching as she was. "And you gave Sergeant Jack your word. If he is still alive..."

"Then his clock is almost up." But she relented. "We'll at least give him a hero's burial. You two go. But be careful. I've lost enough good men today."

The rest of their cell turned back to the battle. Wulf and Father turned and began to run through the woods, boosting the power of their exoskeletons, taking huge strides. Wulf followed the fireball and ran.

A large burning chunk of the Citadel's leg broke off and flittered away. Then another smaller piece. Inside the mech were fail-safes to seal off compromised areas. Those slammed shut, basically shutting off his leg from the knee down. But the seal was becoming white hot, and Jackson knew it would fail. Those internal parts had never been meant to be exposed to the friction of reentry. He had to slow their descent now or be torn apart. Warlord sure wasn't going to do it. The man was a maniac.

Jackson blinked first. He gave his thrusters every ounce of power the reactor could spare. And their speed began to slow. Ten thousand meters to impact. Alerts all over the Citadel were ringing, but Jackson had this. He was going to pull them out of this dive.

Then one of the Spider's legs moved in an unexpected way. A warning sounded in Jackson's mind, but before he could react, a spike extended from its knee. It was a quick movement from a powerful mech. The exterior of the Citadel was superheated, and the battered smart armor lacked its regular stopping power. The spearpoint tip punched through the torso of the Citadel, breached the cockpit, narrowly missed punching a hole right through Jackson.

The air in the cockpit screamed out.

Warlord retracted the leg. Pulled it back for another stab. The pressure dropped. The Citadel automatically closed a visor over Jackson's face to protect his eyes and give him oxygen. The Citadel tried to keep the spike away, and Jackson sliced a chunk from another of its legs with his cutter. His metal hand slipped. The spike moved to stab at his heart again.

Jackson opened the short wings on the Citadel's back, intended for atmospheric flight. It was like the violent opening of a parachute. The wind slammed into them. Warlord tried to hold on, but the force was too sudden, too great, and the Citadel's skin ripped right through his claws.

They went flipping violently away from each other. Swindle rushed up to meet him. Six thousand meters. Five. He tried to gain control. The AI was compensating to slow their descent, but too many thrusters were broken, their body had taken too much structural damage. They were falling like a rock. He passed four thousand. Three.

One of the wings had been hurt, because there was a sudden pop, and Jackson jerked to the left. He cut the thrusters, hoping that wing wouldn't break. At two thousand meters he began to gain some control.

Below him was land. Off to the right was water all the way to the horizon, glittering in the sun. To the left was a sloped shoreline. A water landing would be softer, but he'd been warned about what lived in the water here.

He was at eight hundred meters, trying to level out. Then six. Four. Two. One. He leveled off.

In front of him a knobby rock of an island jutted up out of the water. There was a cliff face, topped with a wooded hill, and a line of Swindle's super-giant trees growing along the crest. He was going too fast for a controlled turn but running headlong into the cliff and becoming a meat-and-carbon mash really wasn't part of his plan today. He arched his back, trying to give the wings more surface. He rose. Saw the hill before him, and felt one brief flicker of hope, thinking he might actually clear the trees, and then he knew it was an impossibility. He was moving too fast. At the last moment, he swerved just a bit, hoping to thread a small opening between the trunks.

Branches sheared off his wings. He twisted, sideswiped a trunk. Something slammed into the mech, breaking the cockpit open and delivering a stunning blow to his head. Then the Citadel shot out of the other side of the trees, scattering leaves and branches in his wake. A moment later he hit some water. Skipped. Tumbled. Struck some sort of beach. Then tumbled beyond into a higher flat area. The mech finally came to rest on a grassy sward.

The Citadel's system was overwhelmed. There was a forced restart. Jackson was violently kicked out of the system, and back into his own body.

Jackson lay there breathing, trying to orient himself, something hissing. He was facing mostly down. He tried make it stand up, but the mech seemed broken beyond repair. Nothing more than a battered hunk of technology, failing to respond. His display was just a loop of error messages. Everything hurt. Especially his head. Stupid nanites.

The impact had savaged the cockpit. He could see sand and water through the holes. The frame was crumpled, but not in a way that locked him in. He wasn't trapped, so Jackson slowly unbuckled himself from his harness so he could drop free. He had to pluck med needles out of his body and peel the electrodes off his skull. He'd gotten cut. Something had jabbed him in the side, the spike that had punched the cockpit, or a piece of metal that had spalled off it, maybe. At least the hole in his hand was sealed by something that looked like hard plastic.

He crawled out of the mech and painfully got to his feet to get his bearings, blood seeping from his side. The hissing he'd heard was from the water that was spitting and steaming on the hot exterior of the mech. When he breathed, the air bit his lungs. And then he realized his mask was gone. He looked around for it, looked back at the debris scattered along the beach, but it was gone. He was breathing poison.

The sound of thrusters suddenly roared overhead. A shadow passed over the ground around him and moved out across the meadow.

Jackson looked up and saw the Spider. Battered though it was, it was still in good enough shape to fly. Warlord landed it in the meadow, a hundred meters away.

Jackson looked around for anything he could use as a weapon. A rock. Anything. But there was nothing around him except weird Swindle grass. The best he could come up with was a broken metal strut. He picked it up to use as a club. It was hot to the touch.

The Spider sank back on its remaining legs to something resembling a sitting position, and the cockpit slid open. Warlord climbed out, his suit still intact, his mask clear. He reached back into his cockpit and pulled out a fine rifle. One the *Tar Heel* had sold to him.

"It seems today is just not your day, Rook," Warlord shouted. "In fact, I'd say your day was headed for the crapper."

"I wrecked most of your army, broke your toys, damaged your station, and caused an uprising. I'd say your day's been worse."

"But I'll still be alive to have a better tomorrow." Warlord walked across the top of his mech and shouldered the rifle. "I can't say the same for you."

"Why don't you come over here and fight me? Mano a mano. It would be all primal. You're big on that."

Warlord smiled. "It's the end of the line, soldier, but I'm going to make sure to drag it out." He took aim and fired.

Pain exploded in Jackson's leg. It collapsed beneath him and he fell.

"Now, I'll leave you to the beasts. I'll leave a drone to record you being devoured, and make sure it plays on every display in Big Town, on a continual loop, as a demonstration of what happens to anyone who betrays me."

Jackson groaned at the pain, but shouted out, "So the big bad warlord has no balls to fight."

Warlord laughed.

"I can still take you. Fight me, you stinking mouse piss of a pilot. Five to one and we're only here because I should've kamikazed us both through atmo."

"You tedious little man. I think I should shoot you in the mouth too." Warlord aimed.

Crack!

But that shot wasn't from Warlord. It had been aimed at Warlord.

Blood erupted from his back as the king of Big Town stumbled.

Jackson turned to see where the gunshot had come from. At the edge of the woods was someone in an old battered exo, carrying a rifle. Jackson could just make out his face through the visor. It was the boy from the Original's hideout. Wulf. And Wulf kept on shooting.

But Warlord was too fast. He had more mods than just the implant that enabled him to meld with a mech, because he shrugged off the injury, and leapt across the top of the Spider to slide smoothly into the cockpit. The hatch closed behind him.

"Run!" Jackson shouted at Wulf.

A second later, one of the Spider's guns opened up on the boy's position. There was no way Warlord was linked in yet. That response was rushed, reflexive, but the unaimed fire forced the boy to dive for cover.

More shots came out of the woods from a different position, hitting the Spider but with no real effect. But Warlord flung a bunch of ordnance into the woods in response. Shredding trees and starting an inferno.

The firing from the woods stopped.

This was his chance to run, but Jackson looked at his leg and cringed when he saw the gaping gash through the muscle of his calf. Blood was pouring out. He took the now loosened TQ off of his wrist, looped it just below his knee, and activated it to auto-tighten for the second time today. And if anything, this time was worse. Jackson heaved himself up using the strut as a crutch and limped for the Citadel.

The damaged Spider rose, scuttling forward on its remaining five legs. It would obliterate Wulf and friends, then finish Jackson off. There was no way Warlord would trust Jackson's demise to the wildlife, now that the Originals knew he was here.

There was a rumbling coming from somewhere Jackson couldn't place. He wondered if Warlord had called for air support or a drop-ship home. Warlord's forces were still intact. Jackson's heart sank.

Warlord was going to walk away.

Jackson supposed LaDue and MacKinnon had completely failed. They'd probably bailed and left their fighters to twist in the wind. The *Tar Heel* was probably a debris field, nothing more than pretty meteor showers for the residents of Swindle for the next few days. He thought of Jane and hoped she and the others had made it out but knew the likelihood of them escaping the system was nil.

But if he could get even one decent gun to work on the Citadel, he might be able to take Warlord with him. Jackson climbed into the mech's torn open chest and started bringing up menus.

Which was when the noise grew tenfold.

He glanced through the Citadel's rib and saw the sea heaving. But it wasn't the sea. It was a beast. A true leviathan. A behemoth, rising from the water.

"Dear God," Jackson whispered as he saw something that shouldn't exist.

The surface frothed with wildly whipping tentacles, each as big around as the trunk of the mighty Swindle trees. Then came its head, shaped like a long wedge, a hundred meters long, mottled gray and purple, dotted with spines and ridges, with great bulbous black eyes.

Somehow, even though he'd only gotten the tiniest glimpse of it before, he knew this was the same thing that had stranded him on Swindle to begin with. And it had come to finish the job.

It surged out of the sea and onto the beach, shaking the whole world. The noise had drawn it from the depths, and even though it was indescribably alien, Jackson could tell that it was *really pissed off.*

Warlord's sensors must have been fragged by the heat too, because the Spider should have sensed this thing coming klicks away. But from the way the mech lurched fearfully away, Warlord certainly saw it now! The Spider started shooting everything it had left onboard, slinging lead, depleted uranium, rockets, beams, and fire.

The monster *did not care.*

The grass was crushed flat in a circle around the Spider as Warlord engaged his thrusters. The Spider's legs crouched, gathering energy, preparing to hurl itself into the sky. Warlord was going to blast off, narrowly avoiding the kaiju. He was going to escape and leave the rest of them here to die.

Jackson found the menu. Saw the repair bots had fixed the ammo hopper and directed the last bit of the reactor's power to the left arm's railgun. Jackson slid his uninjured hand into the harness. As he moved his fingers, the Citadel lifted its massive arm. Sand and dirt slid off to the ground. The targeting system was down, so Jackson had to eyeball it and estimate, looking through the jagged hole in the Citadel's chest, aiming down the arm at the Spider as the enemy mech launched itself into the air. He only had one shot.

He fired.

The hypervelocity projectile nailed the Spider right through its main thruster.

It dropped like a rock.

The Spider hit the ground, then immediately ran, scurrying away.

There was another thundering step, a terrible vibration, and then a tentacle swatted the mech across the meadow.

Warlord tumbled, rolled, and came up guns blazing. Bullets ripped into the behemoth, which roared, a sound that pierced Jackson to his core and left his ears ringing.

The Spider kept firing, darting back and forth between the thrashing tentacles. Warlord was linked in now, man and machine one, together far more effective than either could be on their own. Explosive shells rent the flesh around one of the great black eyes.

The behemoth retreated a bit in the water.

Warlord took advantage of that move, bounding again and engaging his secondary thrusters. He flew toward the creature, firing as it roared in anger and pain. It was a sudden, furious attack, as Warlord emptied everything he had on the creature, hundreds of rounds ripping into the thing.

The guns fell silent. Warlord was out of ammo.

The vast black eyes studied the mech then. Technology had gone up against ancient fury, and fury had won, and it knew it.

The creature surged fully from the water, towering at least a hundred meters high. The Spider moved in reverse—too slow, as the creature shot out two big tentacles and suctioned around it on each side. With a roar it ripped the mech in *half.*

Warlord managed to leap free. He dropped to the ground, far enough that the fall should have killed him, except he just landed in a crouch, then immediately sprang to his feet and sprinted for safety. They certainly hadn't been exaggerating about the quality of his mods.

But he was still nothing but a bug in the shadow of the monster. It casually bent forward and snatched up Warlord with several smaller tentacles. Warlord screamed in terror.

The monster pulled Warlord apart, tearing off his limbs one by one, like a cruel child plucking the wings off a fly.

It tossed the parts in the meadow and turned its gaze on Jackson.

The Citadel was crippled. He was almost out of power. He couldn't run, couldn't fly, and had no weapons. But his arm was still in the harness, so Jackson gave it a gentle command. In response, the Citadel defiantly raised its hand, and gave the giant monster ... the bunny.

"Go ahead and squish me, you magnificent bastard," Jackson said as the timer on his spine bomb counted down to zero. "This is your planet. We're just tourists."

Except the thing stopped. The vast black eyes looked down at him, unblinking. It watched for a time, anger sated, now simply curious. Jackson thought there might be something intelligent behind those eyes, but truthfully, they were just incomprehensibly alien.

The behemoth chuffed.

"What?" Jackson asked. But part of him truly believed that it was sending him a message. *Not today, bug.*

It chuffed again, then began moving back toward the water.

Its shadow began to recede from the meadow.

Impossible, but there it was.

Jackson checked to be sure, but by some miracle, he was still alive. A hole hadn't been melted in his spine. The Citadel's medical treatment had bought him a little time after all. Probably just enough time for the poison air to shred his lungs.

He thought about trying to escape, but he could barely walk, and he'd be coughing up blood soon. Truth be told, he was just really tired of running. This was as good a place as any to call it, in the cockpit of the best mech he'd ever driven. That was a lot more dignified than getting eaten by caliban.

So Jackson lay there, content.

Then someone stuck their helmet through the side of the Citadel.

"You lucky *schlawiner*," the man said with a German accent.

Jackson recognized him through the visor. "Hey, beard guy." Behind him was his son. "And Wulf. Sorry about breaking your nose."

"It is forgiven, Sergeant Jack," the kid said earnestly.

Jackson coughed at the biting air. "Nice shot."

Wulf pressed an extra breather mask into his hands. "Here, take this."

It wasn't until he tried to clumsily put it on and failed that Jackson realized just how truly screwed-up he was. Wulf had to help him get the straps on over his head.

He didn't even notice Wulf's dad sticking him with a syringe until it was too late. "What's that?"

"The compound engineered to safely deactivate the bioweapon."

"Thank you."

"Thank LaDue."

"I'd rather shoot her in the face," Jackson said truthfully.

"Understandable, all things considered. Now come, we must get you to safety. Swindle never stops trying to kill you for long."

As Wulf's father helped Jackson out of the Citadel, Wulf walked out into the meadow, looking for something. He soon found it, knelt in the weird grass, then rose, holding Warlord's head by the jaw. A trophy.

Jackson asked the dead man, "Is this primal enough for you yet?"

EPILOGUE

Jane was sitting on the balcony of the crew's quarters in Big Town a few weeks after Warlord's demise. The little sprig of orange blossoms that Jacky had plucked from a wall orchard and presented to her yesterday lay on the table next to her. She picked it up, inhaled the lovely scent again, and smiled. Jacky was overconfident, sometimes rash, but sweet. And he had just saved her life.

She thought about that moment, Fain and his hellhound slowly careening out into Big Town's sky. Tui, Katze, and Bushey all injured. Jane herself hurt, with only two partially functioning bots to protect them. The peanut gallery had arrived and been about to shoot all of them when every loudspeaker on the orbital had started broadcasting that Warlord had just been killed.

The Big Town security forces had hesitated. There was confusion and debate as their leader had contacted his chain of command to verify the reports. A moment later he had told his troops to stand down. It was clear he didn't have any personal attachment to their governor. Jane had gotten lucky, and her captor had been a thinking man who realized a new government was about to take over, and it wouldn't be wise to execute those who had helped it.

So Jacky had saved her life. After, of course, she'd saved his. Repeatedly. Which made the whole relationship that much more exhilarating.

She inhaled the scent of the blossoms again and thought about a possible future with him. Not that any commitments had been made, but, where that avenue had been closed before, she thought she now saw a way it could be a real possibility. And the thought of it made her surprisingly happy.

Jane had gone back to reviewing the record of her bots during the battle to see how she might tweak their next evolution, when the red flower icon appeared on her visual.

Her apprehension rose. *Please, let this be good news.*

The video was a man standing in a park, looking directly at the camera.

No. This was not secret code, nor a sister's hieroglyphs. This was a message.

The man was dressed in the Mukherjee style complete with pants, embroidered knee-length jacket, shirt, and earring. But it was his face that drew Jane's attention, because she remembered it.

He smiled. "Come home, 25th daughter. You and your sisters have betrayed us. Mary 231 weeps. Yet all youth stray. You were allowed to, but you can be forgiven."

He paused.

"Come in," he said invitingly. "Or stay out and suffer when we collect you. And we *will* collect you. It's your choice. The message from the fathers and mothers is to bask in our love. Bring us gifts of knowledge. You will be forgiven."

He held up a card with a message written in a version of the hieroglyphics Jane and the others used, telling her how and when, demonstrating that the unbreakable language of the girls of Mary 231.78 had been hacked.

And then this member of some new and clearly powerful breed of Shikaa 17 turned and walked away.

A nanosecond passed. The overwhelming tide of emotion about what had just happened began to swell, but Jane quelled it. She would have time to feel that later. Right now, there were things to do. May whatever god that was out there help them, because the sisters were under attack.

Jane looked at Jacky's sprig of orange blossoms and blew out a breath of disappointment.

It had been such a happy dream.

And then she sent the orders to the *Tar Heel* fabricators to build the next evolution of her platoon. She needed to make travel arrangements, and quickly.

Jane had no doubt what she had to do.

✧　　✧　　✧

It had taken a few weeks for everything to calm down in Big Town enough for Bushey to finally get that pool party he'd wanted.

Jackson sat in a lawn chair next to the water's edge, drank his beer, soaked up the artificial rays from the noonday sun globe, and watched the festive crowd that had gathered to say farewell and thanks to the *Tar Heel*. The celebration had been put on by the new government. Most of the crew was here, and the Big Towners in attendance had all sided with the Originals during the fighting, so it was a festive bunch. There was even music and dancing.

Tui walked up, carrying a little bundled blanket in his hands. "Mind if I join the hero of the hour?" Rather than wait for a response, the big man flopped into the next chair with a grunt.

"I'm no hero," Jackson said.

"Sure you are. This party's mostly because of you."

"I'm just the one who ended up on the most vids, and Mac-Kinnon and LaDue needed a propaganda image to rally the people around."

"Like that?" Tui jerked his thumb toward the ruins of the governor's mansion behind them. Someone had spray-painted a mural on the last standing wall. It was the Citadel and the Spider, locked in mortal combat, falling through the sky in a massive fireball. "It's a good image, Sergeant Jack. Very evocative."

Jackson shrugged and took another drink. It wasn't the first time he'd ended up playing that role in his life.

Once word spread of their charismatic leader's death, Warlord's government had collapsed. Like most despots, he wasn't big on delegating power. Big Town had a lieutenant governor, but he and several other members of the cabinet had fled on the first available transport with whatever they could loot from the city's coffers. Which turned out to be a smart move on the politicians' part, because the mob had been in a hanging mood for a while there, and several officials and officers of the Big Town Guard had ended up decorating lampposts.

It had been chaotic for a few days, but the Originals had been waiting for this chance for a long time. They'd beaten the last of the Guard, then forced the gangs and various factions to the bargaining table. Planetside, LaDue had declared herself the president of a new Swindle planetary government, while Ian Mac-Kinnon had been named interim governor of Big Town. Actual elections had been scheduled for three months from now, but both of those two had been such forces in restoring order that Jackson doubted anyone would even run against the Originals' party this time around.

Of course, Jackson had missed most of the aftermath because he'd been in the hospital, getting the remains of Warlord's evil nanotech suctioned out of his brain, and new bones grown for his hand.

"You seen Jane around yet?" Jackson asked.

"Sorry. Not so far today."

That was a bummer. She was the one person he really wanted to see the most before *Tar Heel* shipped out. They'd spent a lot of time together over the last week. He'd finally gotten to take her on that date. One date had turned into two, and he was really hoping for a third before it was time to leave. It had been a wonderful, and Jackson was pretty sure this was what falling in love was supposed to be like.

"But check out what I have." Tui unwrapped the blanket to show Jackson his prize. "What do you think?"

Jackson leaned over and discovered that Tui had gotten himself a pet. It was a hairless, gray, wiggling thing, about the size of an Earth hamster. "Is that a shanking *grendel*?"

"Yeah, pretty cool, huh? Turns out Fain's monster had a baby. It's kind of cute, in a Swindle-wants-to-destroy-you kind of way. I couldn't just leave it, and I don't know if we could send it home without its momma." Tui scratched under its mouth feelers and the weird little puppy demon made a happy clicking noise.

Jackson just stared at his friend in disbelief. "It's ugly as sin. There's no way you're going to be able to train it. I saw the vids with Fain."

"Oh, no problem. Jane reverse engineered that control collar and improved it. The new one will be way better than what Fain had."

"It's going to get big, and then it's going to eat you."

"Maybe." Tui grinned and pulled out a piece of jerky from his pocket. The baby snatched it up and chewed it in a very vicious and slobbery manner. "But maybe not."

The two of them watched the party for a while, talking about the crew and laughing at their antics, while Tui's new hell hound shredded jerky with its razor teeth.

Bushey was hanging out in the shallow end, flirting with the local girls, but it was amusing to watch as he gravitated toward one attractive Big Town lady in her fifties. The bridge crew were playing frisbee on the grass with the denizens of the cargo hold. And Katze had drawn a crowd of little kids around her, while she told them a very animated story about life on Amon, sailing the lakes of fire beneath the twin suns.

"I'm going to miss these guys," Jackson said.

"You don't have to miss anybody. You can still come with us. We don't cast off until morning."

Jackson shook his head. "This is something I've got to do."

Tui nodded, because he got it. As soon as Tui had gotten stitched back together by nanites and healing gel, he had joined in with the rescue efforts and cleaning up the rubble left from their battle. Because that was just the kind of man he was. "Respect."

Then Captain Holloway arrived. He shook hands with the important Big Towners, waved at his crew, and made his way directly toward where Jackson and Tui were sitting. Tui immediately covered the baby grendel back up, which told Jackson he hadn't cleared having a murder beast as a pet with the captain quite yet.

"Hey, Chief. Do you mind? I need a minute in private with the new face of Swindilian independence here."

"No problem, Cap." Tui stood. "I've got things to prep at the docks anyway."

Jackson got up too, in order to give Tui a goodbye hug. "I owe you big time."

"Yeah you do." Tui dang near crushed Jackson's ribs. The grendel pup clicked in protest. "Catch you on the next shipment, bro."

Jackson stayed standing, but the captain shook his head. "Sit down. Relax. This is a party. No need to make the goodbyes all uncomfortable and teary eyed."

"Aww. So you are going to miss me."

"Yeah sure. However will I get by without having somebody to drastically complicate my life and drag me into revolutions on backwater planets?"

The two of them sat. Jackson tossed the captain a beer from the cooler by his chair.

"So what's next for the *Tar Heel*?"

"The repairs from that railgun hit are done. We salvaged most of the *Downward Spiral*. I'm going to tow it to that off-the-books shipyard in the Motonari system and sell it for parts. That might recoup a fraction of what I lost on this trip."

"Yeah." Jackson felt really bad about how this had shaken out for the captain. "Sorry about your retirement fund."

But the captain just chuckled. "It's my own fault. I got a little loose with my code. That's on me. I never should have made a deal with the devil." He looked at the swimming pool wistfully. "I really did like the idea of owning my own pond though."

"I still think you should have tossed Shade out an airlock," Jackson muttered.

"Heh." The captain took a long swig of his beer. "Duly noted. But me and Shade's relationship is ... *complicated*. I need a broker, and she needs a runner. Or more importantly, her shady bosses need a runner."

"This is their fault. If we'd never armed Warlord, then he never could have oppressed these people."

"Don't beat yourself up, kid. Evil men always find a way. If it hadn't been us, it would've been Prunkard, or some other dirtbag. It's a big galaxy, and all the little guys like us can do is try to do the right thing in our tiny corner of it ... Which is why you've decided to stick around here, I'm guessing."

"I'm partly responsible for breaking this place. The least I can do is help fix it."

"Warlord broke it, son. We were just the final straw. However, I do know the feeling." And truly, if anyone could understand, it was the captain, because he had once rescued a brain-damaged orphan mech pilot from a war that he'd supplied the weapons for. "But anyways, when you get tired of fighting monsters on this crapsack planet, you give me a call. You're welcome back on my crew anytime."

"Thank you, sir."

Captain Holloway got up to leave. "All that mushy stuff out of the way, now for the really awkward part. Jane asked me to give this to you." He reached into his coveralls and pulled out an actual paper envelope.

That was odd. Why didn't she just send him a message on their net? He had tried to reach her, but it had been quiet all morning. Jackson took the envelope. There was a hard lump inside of it. His name had been written on the front, and the back had been sealed with a kiss. Purple lipstick. "Is Jane not coming? She was supposed to be here."

"Yeah, sorry. She left on a different ship last night. Asked me to give this to you once it would be too late for you to try and catch up to her. I'm going to miss Jane. Best damn specter I've ever seen. I know you're sweet on her, but... well, just read the letter." Captain Holloway started walking away. "Good luck, Jackson. You're going to need it."

Hurrying, Jackson tore open the envelope. He shook the hard object out into his palm. It was another a Fifi-type bot. There was also a letter inside. That was oddly old-fashioned of her. He unfolded it and discovered that Jane had very pretty handwriting.

Dear Jacky,

What we did in Big Town drew too much attention. People from my past are looking for me, so I have to disappear again. I can't tell you where I'm going. Don't bother to ask the captain, because I wouldn't tell him either. I'm sorry it has to be this way, but I knew you would try to talk me out of running, or that you'd insist on trying to help me, but this is something that I can't drag you into.

Please don't try to find me. Honor this wish for your safety and mine. You wouldn't be able to find me anyway. If you try, it'll only attract the attention of some people who are more dangerous than you can imagine.

My years on the Tar Heel *were the happiest time of my life. Thank you for everything.*

Move on with your life. Forget about me. Be happy.

As a going away present for you, I repaired and upgraded Fifi. Take good care of her and she'll take good care of you. Stay safe.

Love, Jane

Jackson folded the letter and stuck it in his pocket. Then he finished his beer.

"Well, shanks."

Wulf was very excited as they started the salvage operation. He had been assigned to be Sergeant Jack's assistant. And though Sergeant Jack was a hero and symbol of the rebellion, he was also still a newcomer to a very unforgiving world, so he needed an experienced guide to keep him safe. This assignment was a great honor for Wulf and had come from President LaDue herself.

"Okay, is the coast clear?" Jackson Rook asked his team.

The workers checked their readouts. "Nothing on seismic or thermal, sir," one of them reported. "The big one must be asleep."

Jackson looked over Horond's Bay one last time. He appeared suspicious, like he didn't trust the scans, but they didn't have much choice. "Alright then. Let's do this."

Twenty camouflaged exo-suited figures moved out. They were armed with a variety of tools and had brought two hovering cargo haulers with them. They ran quickly and quietly through the tall grass, so as to not draw the wrath of the great kaiju.

This prize was worth the risk.

Wulf had watched all the vids of the Battle of Big Town and seen what the mighty Citadel had been capable of. With that mighty mech repaired, in the skilled hands of Sergeant Jack, their harvesters would be protected from the monsters in the groves, and the CX would flow. As LaDue said, the CX was the key to their prosperity.

And if they did not increase production soon, one of the superpowers would become desperate enough to risk war, and step in to take it from them. Which meant the end of their dream of a free and independent Swindle.

"What's up, Wulf?" Jackson asked him.

"What do you mean, sir?"

"You're usually more talkative, warning me where not to step, or telling me about all the creative ways this planet will try to kill us. What's on your mind?"

"I was thinking we will have to run multiple crews to reach the president's production goals, and the Citadel can only guard one at a time. We will need more mechs."

"Yep. We will. But the harvest we can protect with this one here will pay for more." Jackson grinned at him through his visor. "I know a guy. He'll hook us up with a good deal. Mechs and implants both."

"But those mechs will also need pilots."

"I can train more pilots. Now if any of them can accept the implants to fly-by-mind, that's a roll of the genetic dice, but I can teach anybody to be at least proficient in one. I promised LaDue I would do that."

Wulf got up the courage to ask his question. "Do you think I could be one of Swindle's mech pilots?"

Jackson thought it over for a moment. "Yeah, I think you could. But we've really got to work on your confidence, kid. You want to drive a mech, you need to have swagger."

Wulf beamed. Peder would have been so proud of him.

Nothing tried to kill them, and they reached the wrecked Citadel without incident. The waters of the bay remained calm... For now. The mech was barely visible because the plant life here was so aggressive. It was mostly a green and red mound of vines, grass, and fungus. It looked like the fallen, mossy statue of an ancient warrior. Even in its current, sorry state, there was still something majestic about it.

"Yeah, she's a bit of a fixer-upper, but it should buff out." Jackson walked over to the mech, and gently placed one hand on it, almost reverently.

Wulf knew Jackson was understating how difficult it would be to repair the complex machine, but with Warlord's other mechs destroyed, this was their best hope to protect the harvest. Wulf had been there when Jackson had made his offer to President LaDue. He would repair the Citadel, and then use it to protect the workers, until Swindle could stand on its own two feet again.

When the president had told Sergeant Jack that she could not afford to pay him much, he had volunteered anyway. When she asked Jackson why he would do such a thing, he'd said that he hadn't been able to fix his home planet, but maybe, just maybe, he could help fix this one.

Wulf appreciated what Jackson had told the president, because Wulf knew that Swindle had been founded on lies and broken promises. It had been broken long before the first colony ship arrived. Swindle was, and always had been a broken place. The difference was its people had a chance to build a good life between the pieces.

"Okay, boys. Get to work."

They immediately began slashing away the plants so they could dig the Citadel free and load it onto the haulers. They worked fast, but everyone kept nervously glancing at the still water.

"It hates us so much, yet it is our home," Wulf whispered.

"What was that?" Jackson asked.

"Nothing, sir." Wulf got back to work, because Swindle never stopped trying to murder you for long.

AUTHORS' NOTE

The genesis of this story was interesting.

Back in 2015, the two of us agreed to conduct a session at the annual Life, The Universe, and Everything science fiction and fantasy conference in Provo, Utah. The topic was How to Build an Action Plot. We wanted the audience to participate in building just such a plot but knew we'd never get to the plotting part if we didn't come with the bones of a story already developed. So one evening before the conference we met at Larry's house to do just that. We chatted a bit, and then John suggested we start to flesh it out.

Larry's son Joe, who was eleven at the time, was hanging out on the stairs listening in.

Larry raised his voice and said, "Hey, Joe. What's cool?"

Joe immediately popped up from the stairs and answered without hesitation, "Giant robots, bandits, and murderers."

We looked at each other. Dang, that *was* cool. And we were off to the races.

Joe immediately began to create some illustrations, one of which we've included here.

Later, when we decided to write the book, "What's cool?" was a question we kept asking all the way to the end.